APOCALYPSE
RISE OF THE ANTICHRIST

M C I Hinchliffe

APOCALYPSE
RISE OF THE ANTICHRIST

First published in Australia by M C I Hinchliffe 2021

Copyright © M C I Hinchliffe 2021
All Rights Reserved

 A catalogue record for this book is available from the National Library of Australia

ISBN: 978-0-6450992-1-8 (ebk)
ISBN: 978-0-6450992-0-1 (pbk)

Cover artwork by M C I Hinchliffe © 2021

Typesetting and design by Publicious Book Publishing
Published in collaboration with Publicious Book Publishing
www.publicious.com.au

All characters and events in this publication are fictitious, any resemblance to real persons, living or dead, or any events past or present are purely coincidental.

No part of this book may be reproduced in any form, by photocopying or by any electronic or mechanical means, including information storage or retrieval systems, without permission in writing from both the copyright owner and the publisher of this book.

Contents

Prologue: Genesis of the Antichrist 1
Discovery 17
Pope's Plight 35
The Brethren Unite 45
The Oldest Bank Account 60
The Secret Book of Saint John 67
The Crusade Begins 79
A Fool's Hope 106
Assassin's Plight 131
Rise of the Antichrist 159
Britain's Recourse 175
Brethren's Flight 239
Checkmate 270
Dawn of the Apocalypse 287
Epilogue: From the Ashes of Hell 307

Prologue:

Genesis of the Antichrist

Jerusalem, Israel

The cramps from Mary's pelvis were verging on climactic. This one caused her to halt her clumsy but rapid gait as she pressed both hands on the large bulge that protruded from her abdomen. Mary was nine months pregnant. As the contraction eased, Mary resumed her urgent flight. A few hundred metres ahead lay the foundations of the local hospital—all she had to do was get there.

Nine months ago, her ex-boyfriend Mustafe had forced himself upon her. It was in her own bed while her parents, totally unaware, slept ten metres away. Mustafe was supposed to leave an hour and a half before but he stayed. 'I don't want to go yet. Please can I stay a little longer?' he said while looking into her eyes and stroking her long, dark head of hair. They sat on the lounge in almost complete darkness—only a small lamp in the hallway providing a source of light.

Her full lips met his and her heart skipped a beat. His words touched her singleness, but fear of retribution was ingrained. 'You must go. If you don't leave soon, my father will surely throw you out.'

'I can't leave you yet, I love you.'

LIE!

****

Another cramp pushed the baby a bit further towards life. She had to stop again.

****

'All I want to do is fall asleep next to you.'

ANOTHER LIE!

He gazed into her eyes. 'Please let me stay a while longer?'

Mary formulated a plan. They stood up from the lounge, walked over to the front door, opened it, and shut it again. They walked up the stairs side by side, matching their footsteps. As best as they could tell, the creaking from the staircase portrayed only one set of footsteps. Mary walked along the hall with slightly exaggerated steps to conceal the tiptoeing of Mustafe's feet behind her. She led him into her bedroom and told him to crouch down behind the bed and not move. Mary went about her usual bedtime rituals of cleaning her teeth and changing into her nightie, before getting into bed. Mustafe joined her. He had already stripped down to his underwear. After turning off the bedside light, they snuggled together under the sheets. Her plan had worked.

Mustafe closed his eyes but Mary dared not—if her father caught them like this ...!

Mustafe's hands began to explore her young, supple body. At first, she did nothing as his touch both excited her and terrified her. His hand grabbed for her underwear, but this time she pulled his hand away. 'Stop it, they will hear us,' Mary whispered.

'Please, I love you,' he whispered in reply, and then continued.

LIE!

Mary tried to push his hand away again, but he put his full weight upon hers, pinning her down. 'Stop!' she said as loud as she dared.

'Please, I love you, I love you, I love you ...'

LIE, LIE, LIE, ALL LIES!!!

He proceeded to penetrate her.

'Stop!' she said again. But he didn't hear her. His mind was focused on only one thing. Her efforts to push him off were pointless as his muscular young body was too strong. The faint ambient light barely reflected the terror in the whites of her eyes. In minutes, it was all over. She could finally push him off. 'Get out!' Mary said as sternly as a whisper would allow. Mustafe pulled his trousers on and headed for the door. Mary grabbed him and turned him towards the open window.

'Out that way you idiot!' He looked at her in dismay.

'Out the window or I will throw you out!' She pushed him towards it. Mustafe stuck his head out and saw a means to clamber down. Mary pushed at his back and he submissively went out the window. He turned round briefly and said, 'I'm sorry' and continued his flight down the outside of the house. Soon he was gone.

Mary went back to her bed, bruised and shaken. She huddled under the sheets like a fetus and her hands would not stop shaking. Her eyes stared relentlessly into nothingness, void of all but distance.

Four weeks later, the local doctor confirmed her worst fears—she was pregnant.

The first betrayal came from Mustafe. 'You're what?!'
'You heard me,' Mary replied.
Mustafe stood up from the seat bench in the school quadrangle and ran both hands through his thick, black head of hair. 'Shit! What are we going to do? I'm seventeen years old for God's sake.' He looked at her. 'I don't have enough money for an abortion.'
'I don't want an abortion,' she said softly.
Mustafe's jaw dropped. 'You want to keep it? Are you totally insane?!' He suddenly realised he was shouting and stopped before he caught the attention of other students.
Tears began to flow down Mary's cheeks. 'I thought we could keep it and get married. No one needs to know. And after we are married, my pregnancy won't matter. We can have our baby. You said you loved me!'
Mustafe was pacing back and forth like a caged animal. Suddenly, he stopped and bent down close to her. The extensive whites of his eyes highlighted the rage and fear within him, and it terrified her. 'You're mad! You planned this from the start, didn't you?! This is just a big game to you, isn't it? Isn't it?!' The disdain in his lowered voice became stronger, his teeth showing behind the sneer. 'We get married, we have a baby, you suck my life away—just to satisfy your mad fantasies. You're probably not even pregnant!' He stood up and pointed at her. 'Keep away from me, you hear?! You're mad. Don't ever speak to me again you hear?! Or I'll kill you! Just keep away.' Mustafe stormed off.
Mary sat on the seat alone, tears flowing down her cheeks. She sobbed.

The next betrayal came from where she least expected it.

'Dad? Please say something? Anything? Mary's stomach felt like it was going to erupt from her mouth. She turned to her mother for support, but Sophia just sat there on the lounge, her head in her hands as if to hide from the harsh reality. 'Mum?'

Joseph's steely stare cut right through Mary as she stood before him, her soul bare. The juggernaut of severe emotions bludgeoned through his mind, pushing logic and sense aside. Finally, he spoke. 'What did you expect? I told you from the start he was no good. He wasn't even Jewish! We gave you a good home and this is the way you repay us? You have disgraced your mother and I, as well as the family name. Get out of my house!' He stood up from the lounge and turned his back to her. 'You are never to contact us again. As far as we are concerned, you are dead, and will remain so.'

Mary's head throbbed. This could not be happening. 'Dad, please?' She looked down at her mother. 'Mum, please say something?' Sophia didn't look up. Mary knew her father ruled supreme. He laid down the law and the rest of the family obeyed. Mary grabbed her mother's hands to reveal her face—tears were streaming from her eyes. Slowly, she turned her face away from Mary, still silent.

Mary reached for her father, but before she could turn him towards her, his arm shot out and he backhanded her. Mary flew across the room and crashed into a small table and lamp. Still conscious, she picked herself up as a small trickle of blood oozed from the side of her mouth. Her parents had not budged. Mary's mind was empty with dismay, and there was nothing she could think of that would change her father's mind. She did as her father commanded.

Later that night, with the little possessions that she could carry, Mary huddled behind a large rubbish bin with her eyes glazed over, tearless.

Mary spent some time in a homeless shelter as it was better than nothing. Eventually, the need for money became too great and she immersed herself in the trade that many in her situation had done before—prostitution. Mary knew it would not be long before her condition would become obvious, but it was long enough. With the earnings, she rented a meagre one-bedroom flat and bought some new clothes, and finally her prospects were looking brighter. After countless interviews, Mary got a part-time job in a factory. It was the graveyard shift, but it paid well enough to just live on, and it spelled the end of her current trade. Mary spent most of her daylight hours preparing for the arrival of her baby. Many hours were spent looking in baby shops at things she could never afford. But still, it was nice to dream.

On the way to the factory was a small temple. Mary often wanted to go inside but never had the courage. She felt she was not worthy and stayed away. But today, Mary was going in. Her parents were not overly religious, and she felt deprived in some way, but her child was not going to be. Mary walked along the low fence that bounded the temple grounds until she arrived at the small gate. The gate was open as usual. Mary turned and walked in. A few steps later, a sharp cramp crippled her, and Mary fell to the ground. Her six-month-old fetus felt like it was tearing at her insides. She gasped for air as the unrelenting cramp continued.

A priest appeared from the small side door and went to her aid. He helped Mary to her feet. 'Come inside and I'll call for a doctor.' The entrance to the temple was not far but with this cramp, it seemed leagues away. Mary turned back to the low fence to aid her stance. Mysteriously, the pain eased to a dull ache. She moved to the other side of the fence and the cramp completely subsided. 'Are you alright?' the priest asked.

'It's gone!' Mary replied in surprise.

'Do you want to come in anyway? I really think we should call the doctor.' He put his arm around her to help her in, but Mary would not budge.

'Thank you but I'm much better now.' She put her hand on her extended belly and massaged the origin of the cramp.

'Are you sure? Maybe just to rest your feet?'

'Thank you anyway. I think it would be best if I went home and lay down.' Why, she did not know, but Mary was sure that if she stepped passed the gate again, the cramp would return.

'If you insist. If you need anything else, our door is always open,' he said with a smile.

'I'll keep that in mind.' Mary never returned.

****

The next cramp doubled her over and she could barely get air into her lungs. The hospital was so close and yet so far, just like the door was to the temple three months earlier. Mary fell to the ground and writhed on the footway in agony. The stories of childbirth she'd heard from family and seen in films were never like this. The morning light around her grew increasingly dark and blurred as she started to go unconscious.

A loud voice rattled her senses. 'I'll get you inside and call for a doctor!'

Mary could only scream in reply. The next thing Mary knew, she was in a soft bed surrounded by luxury. The pain had passed for the moment. The voice that she had heard earlier rang in her ears again. 'What do you mean they can't come?'

Another more timid female voice replied, 'They said something about a bus load of gunshot victims or something. I'm sorry, I tried.'

'You obviously didn't try hard enough. Did you tell them who I am?'

'Yes mam, but it didn't make any difference.'

A blurred figure moved from Mary's side and out of view. 'I don't care how you get a doctor here, even if you have to kidnap one. Just get a doctor you stupid girl!' The figure returned to her side.

The face of the figure was clearer now. It was the face of a woman in her late thirties—she was remarkably beautiful. A thick dark head of hair grew from the well-defined face and her eyes were dark and exotic. The aquiline nose was strangely small, possibly due to cosmetic surgery. Her mouth was full, and her lips were painted ruby red. The woman held a cloth in her hand which she continually used to wipe over Mary's brow. Mary glanced down at her expensive white dress and wondered what the large red smear was across the front. 'Don't worry my dear, you will be alright. Is there anyone I can call? Your husband or your parents maybe?'

Mary shook her head; the woman's reaction was puzzlement. 'That's ok, I'll look after you. My name is Sarina, what's yours?'

'Mary. Thank you for ...' She gripped the bed sheets, another contraction taking hold. Mary groaned and lifted up her head and shoulders to push on the baby.

'No don't push yet. We must wait until the doctor arrives,' Sarina said with urgency.

'I can't help it ... I want to push ... so much I can't ... stand it!' Mary struggled to get the words out.

'I know, I know, but you must resist.'

'Arrrrrghh!' Mary cried out.

A loud bang shook the house, startling both of them. Sarina went to the nearest window and peered out. The daylight was almost drowned out by thick, black clouds. Heavy raindrops impacted with the side of the house, causing her to take a step back. The rain changed direction as depicted by the strong wind that buffeted the window pane. It was a mighty thunderstorm, quite unusual for this time of year. 'That's just great, what else could go wrong?!'

Mary screamed, drawing her attention away from the storm. Sarina went to her side as Mary shrieked at the top of her lungs. She glanced at Mary's pelvic region. From her vagina, a baby's backside was appearing. Sarina gasped at the sight. 'Oh my God, it's too late!' Blood gushed from Mary's tearing flesh—so much that it turned most of the lower half of the bed bright red. Mary shrieked again, only this time it sent a chill down Sarina's spine. She stood there staring in horror, helpless.

Suddenly, Mary went silent. The baby was out up to its shoulders, its legs wallowing in its mother's blood. Sarina acted without thinking and grabbed the baby's hips and pulled it out. It lay on the bed, still. She went to Mary and pressed her forefingers to her throat, but her neck was as still as the baby at her feet. Sarina slapped Mary's face a few times, then proceeded to perform heart massage as best she could. She knew very little about first aid. 'Come on Mary, your baby needs its mother! Don't give up, you hear?' she shouted as she pumped at her chest. Thirty seconds later, Mary was still motionless. Sarina stopped and looked at the baby, then realised what she had done. Quickly, Sarina lifted the baby by its legs and smacked its bottom ... nothing! She smacked the baby again and was rewarded with the crying of a healthy baby boy.

Despite the gore that covered him, Sarina cradled the baby in her arms. A smile grew across her face. 'Hello there.' Sarina just stood there marveling at the small miracle before her. She studied his face, tiny hands and tiny feet. He was perfect.

Sarina went back to Mary and pressed her forefingers on her neck again. Still there was no pulse. She brushed her hand over Mary's glazed stare to close her eyes. With a pair of scissors, she had doused in boiling water, Mary severed the boy's umbilical cord, freeing him from his dead mother. 'Say bye bye to mummy.' Sarina propped him up so he could see Mary and waved the boy's hand. His eyes were barely open. 'Bye bye.' She lifted him up to her own face. 'It looks like I'm your mummy now,' Sarina thought. 'Well, you have ten fingers and ten toes—and that's all a mother could wish for.'

For the past five years, Sarina and her husband John had been trying to have a family. It took two years before she discovered she was barren.

They researched several modern fertilisation methods, but it was impossible for them to have a baby of their own. The final resort was adoption, and they had been on the list for almost a year. Unfortunately, the list was long. Sarina looked into the baby's perfect new eyes and found the answer to all her problems.

'So, what are we going to call you? Hmmm ... I've always liked Judas. Hello Judas Salim.' John had been away on business for the past four months, which was an unusually long time as six weeks was the norm. John was the owner of two large import companies and the chairman of the board for two others. He was a key figure in the political circle and a man of great importance. Who was she to question his movements when he had given her so much wealth? But Sarina wanted more. She wanted to be a mother, and a bizarre sequence of events had given her what she had prayed for—a baby.

Sarina was sure she could give little Judas a good home and a standard of living few could match. If she went to the authorities, they may not believe her story. They may even think she killed Mary to gain the child. At the very least, she would never see him again. He would probably be sentenced to a life of misery in foster homes. Sarina would not allow that to happen. Who knew about Mary and Judas? According to Mary, there was no husband or parents to miss them, so the only other living person was that silly young girl Yentl. She was at the hospital trying to get a doctor. So Sarina had to think fast!

If she removed all evidence of Mary and baby Judas, then all Sarina would have to do was make up a story. 'I'm sorry doctor, I caught her sniffing some substance and she ran off. She's hallucinating. I'm very sorry to have troubled you. She will be severely punished!' *Yes, that is what I will say*, Sarina thought.

First, she wrapped up Judas in a soft towel and placed him in her own bed down the hall. She left him there as he quietly slept. Sarina wrapped up Mary's body in the bloody sheets and dragged her from the bedroom, down the hall, down the stairs, and into the garage. She unlocked the Mercedes boot and with all her strength, she hauled Mary into the boot. Sarina dashed upstairs and examined the bed. Fortunately, the mattress protector had lived up to its name and only it was stained. Sarina dashed downstairs again and threw the bloody mattress protector in the boot with Mary's body. Five minutes later, Sarina sat on a freshly made bed, exhausted. There was no visible sign of the gory nightmare that had gone on before.

Sarina went back to her bedroom and found Judas as she left him—quietly sleeping. She picked him up and cuddled him as she waited for Yentl's return.

Hours passed with no sign of Yentl. Eventually, the storm passed, and the sun went down, giving the city to the night. Sarina heard footsteps downstairs. She left Judas in her bedroom and went downstairs. There in the hallway, she found Yentl. Her clothes were soaked, and her face was awash with tears. 'Where in God's name have you been?' Sarina shouted.

'I begged them to come, but they wouldn't,' she sobbed. 'They kept saying the same thing—there are people dying here. No doctors can be spared. They told me to go to a local surgery and by the time I got there they had gone home.' She looked down at her feet. 'I didn't know what to do. I'm so sorry.'

This was better than Sarina had expected. Now there was only Yentl to convince, and that would be simple. 'You stupid little girl, it's all your fault. I told you not to come back without a doctor! I asked you to do one simple thing and even that was too hard for you.'

'I'm so sorry!'

'Shut up, just shut up! I was covered in that poor dead girl's blood. Did you hear me ... covered! She bled to death!' Sarina closed in, her stare cutting Yentl to pieces. 'And it's all because of YOU!'

Yentl's eyes widened as she poured out, 'Nooo, please nooo!'

Sarina pinned her against the wall, her face so close that Yentl could feel the words being breathed from her mouth. 'The baby died in my arms. Do you have even the slightest idea of how terrible that was?'

Yentl turned her face away as she wailed. 'God, please forgive me!'

Sarina released her. 'YOU'RE FIRED!' she shouted. 'Get out of my house, GET OUT!'

Yentl ran out the back door and into the night. 'God forgive me!'

Sarina stood in the hall with her heart racing. A muffled cry came from upstairs, redirecting her attention. 'Don't cry darling, Mummy's coming.' Later that night, Sarina disposed of Mary's body. She tied a car jack to her feet and dumped her in a river some miles away.

Two weeks later, John arrived home. 'Come this way, there is something I want to show you,' Sarina said. They went upstairs and into the bedroom where Mary had given birth to Judas. The bedroom had been redecorated into a nursery. John looked confused. 'This way.' She continued to lead him into the room and towards the cot in the centre. John peered over the side to see a little baby inside. He quickly turned back to Sarina. 'I don't understand?'

'He is your son.'

'But we can't have children! How? Where did he come from?'

'Remember that night about nine months ago, after we had dinner at Michael's house?'

A smile grew on John's face. His thick moustache lifted to reveal a set of white teeth. 'Yes, how could I forget?' he finished with a small snigger.

'I fell pregnant.'

His smile faded. 'But …?'

'Yes, I know what the doctor said. It's a miracle. He is a miracle. When I found out, I didn't tell you because I was afraid I would miscarriage. Then you went overseas, and I thought it would be best if you didn't know, just in case something went wrong.' Sarina was cautious. He may not believe her. She had spent the past three weeks carefully forging her story, and doubly making sure there was no loophole.

He looked down at the baby's small pudgy face and examined the large brown eyes staring back at him. They were so fresh and new as were his little nose and his red-lipped mouth. John turned back to Sarina and grabbed her, lifting her above his head. He spun around. 'A son, Sarina. You gave me a son!' He dropped her down and kissed her. 'It is a miracle. Besides, what do those quacks know anyway?' He hugged and kissed her again. Sarina couldn't stop smiling. 'From now on, there will be no more overseas business, not unless you both can come as well. I will resign from the two American company boards immediately.' He looked back at his miracle child. 'I don't want to spend even a moment away from him. Can I pick him up?'

'Off course you can, he is your son,' she pressed.

John gently reached into the cot and lifted him into his arms. 'Hello there,' he said in a soft voice. 'We have to name him.'

'I thought Judas would be a good strong name.'

'Judas, yes I like Judas,' John said as he gently rocked him back and forth. 'Hello Judas. I'm your daddy.' John joined Sarina's marathon smile.

****

John was good to his word and rarely left Judas's side. Judas was an exceptional baby. He was never sick, quick to learn and rarely cried. He was the perfect child. He took his first steps at nine months old and was walking with confidence at eleven months. He was able to string a complex sentence together at two and a half years of age, and by four and a half he was ready for school. His teachers could not speak more highly of him as his conduct was exemplary and his grades were all straight As. He was outgoing and keen to join in on any group activities. At the age of eleven he was the class captain. Judas was able to talk the other students, and even some teachers, into participating in whatever his latest activity was. Whether it was a school play or some project to raise money for the school, all would join in.

Samuel Harati was very large for his age. At sixty-five centimetres tall, he stood head and shoulders above the other students. To hide his limited intelligence, he resorted to being the school bully. His so-called gang of three friends clung to him at all times, each equally limited in brain matter. His friends nicknamed Samuel 'Goliath', and Samuel very much suited that name. Today, he had a special job in mind for Judas. Samuel approached him in the school quadrangle and as usual, his three mindless friends were close behind. Using his larger bulk, he pinned Judas to the building wall. 'Hi ya little shit! I hear you're pretty good with tests. Well, I've got a test for you to do—mine! Samuel's face was close enough for Judas to smell his vile breath. He put out his left hand and shook it at the smaller boy to his right. A few pieces of paper were thrust into Samuel's hand, which he then shoved into Judas's.

Judas was unusually calm. His usual active expression was replaced with one of utter blandness. He moved his face even closer to Samuel's and said softly, 'Look into my eyes and see what I have in store for you.' Samuel had no choice but to look into the monotonous stare of Judas's dark brown eyes. What Samuel first noticed was that his eyes were no longer brown but pitch black. The pupils were no longer a dull black, they were windows into his soul. With the closeness of Judas's face, Samuel had a stereo view that appeared as real as the world around him.

Inside, he saw his mother being eaten alive by a large black animal. He could not see what the animal was as the vision was from the animal's perspective. He could feel what the animal felt—it's strong heart pounding blood through its large body, primitive mind directing the body with a single thought—eat! Its gnashing jaws tore at his mother's flesh—the smell of gore, the taste of his mother's blood ...

The vision was so real that Samuel fell back from Judas like a hewed tree. Samuel's heart raced as his lungs struggled to oxygenate his brain. The vision terrified him so much that he got up and ran. The rest of the gang scurried after him, confused.

Judas watched the boys run as a satisfied smile grew across his face.

Later that evening, running across the dimly lit school oval, was Samuel with his gang close behind. Two of the smaller boys were carrying heavy pillowcases over their shoulders. Out of nowhere, a figure emerged and stood right in their path of flight. Samuel's heart nearly skipped a beat as he struggled to halt his speedy gait. The other boys crashed into one another and inevitably slid right into Samuel, bowling him over. The four of them peered up at the lone, pyjama wearing figure before them.

'Hi Goliath! I see you've been helping yourself to the school property again.' Judas said casually.

After the initial shock had passed, Samuel got up and confronted their antagonist. 'It's the little shit! For a moment there, I was worried. I'm going to do what I should have done a long time ago.' Samuel seemed less sure than he was earlier in the day. 'Okay, get him. I'm going to teach you some respect.'

The three boys, confident that they could overpower Judas, surrounded him to prepare for their assault. Samuel saw something shiny being produced from Judas's pyjama pocket. He sucked in a gulp of air to shout a warning, but it was too late. With supernatural speed, Judas slashed the blade in a full circle and returned to face Samuel. The three boys collapsed to the ground with their throats cut. Samuel gasped in horror as he watched his partners in crime writhe in their death throws. He turned back to Judas and saw that his eyes had turned black again. 'You ... you ... KILLED THEM!'

'You must know how amusing it was for me when you tried to threaten me. You still have no idea who I am, do you?'

'Some kind of psycho is what you are!' Samuel's heart raced as the fear built up in him like the pressure in an erupting volcano. He wanted to run but his legs failed to move.

'I shall reveal my true name to you as you have had the privilege of experiencing my first act of malice. You see, the soul within me is described by some prophets as being as black as the pits of hell, which is rather fitting as that is where I was forged. I am destined to rule this world with a rain of destruction that mankind has never seen before or will ever see again. When I am finished with the pathetic creatures of this world, they will all bow down to me. And you ...' Judas heckled him with a slight chuckle. 'You tried to bully me!' He turned his face to the sky. 'These humans are a waist of space. Why do you bother with them at all?' He turned back to Samuel. 'My father gave me some special gifts. The gift to lead the lost. The gift to master all that surrounds me and most of all, the gift to inflict agony on a level that your worst nightmares could not fathom. My father has many names—Satan, Devil, the Prince of Lies, and I am his divine son. I am the prince of darkness—I am the Antichrist! I have come to destroy your world and I shall start by TEARING YOUR HEART OUT!' He dropped the blood-soaked knife and lunged at Samuel. With his supernatural speed and agility, he was on top of Samuel before he could move a muscle. Despite his smaller frame, Judas knocked Samuel to the ground.

Samuel watched Judas's right arm pull back and with his long fingers forming a knife, thrust down into his chest cavity just below the collar bone. His fingers were hot like a branding iron as they cut aside the soft flesh. Nerves from his abdomen sent perilous messages of unbearable agony to his terrified brain. He felt the hand push aside vital organs to access its prize. Samuel was helpless. All he could do was watch as those black eyes absorbed the horror that the evil mind behind them created. He felt the hand grip his heart and pull it from its womb-like cavity deep within his chest. The tension of the hand pulling at his heart produced an unimaginable sharp agony as the major arteries were torn from their life-giving connections. In less than a second, Samuel's life had been torn from his body and presented to him like a trophy. The last images his optic nerves sent to his oxygen-starved brain was of Judas biting into his beating heart.

When he finished gnawing at the warm, dying heart, Judas stood above the carnage and reveled in the exhilaration of his kills. 'For you Father, four souls to torture as you will.'

The air around him became ice cold as a deep and sinister voice bellowed from the ground. 'These gifts I return to you. Your first act of malice should be celebrated. You may initiate their foreseen demise.'

An evil smile grew across Judas's face. Using the knife, he made a small cut on his forefinger and squeezed a few drops of his blood into the wounds of the four corpses. He stood back and watched.

The skin around the wounds of the corpses changed colour—to a dark shade of brown—and spread over the rest of the body. Flesh began to bubble and writhe as an unnatural chemical reaction began beneath the skin. The bodies contorted and flexed as muscle and sinew mutated to their new structure. The mutation was a violent one, and the clothes that covered the bodies tore away to reveal the rapid growth of thick, dark hair. The lifeless lungs sucked in fresh, cool air to release a sound that was far from human. The legs shortened until the thigh and shin bones were only a few inches long, and the foot was exaggerated to twice its length. The arms met a similar fate while the spine shortened and deformed. The jaw and skull extended and narrowed until it was that of a primitive carnivore, the ears becoming large and flaccid. Finally, the Antichrist stood over the newly formed bodies of four rottweilers.

'Stand my children, stand and greet your new master,' the Antichrist announced as he lifted up his arms. The four dogs came to life and stood at his feet. 'Now my children, go forth and destroy your families as I have foreseen. And when you're done, your service is no longer required. You shall then tear the supernatural lives from your own bodies. Except Goliath, as your fate will be more perpetual. You shall return to me and while that supernatural life still exists, you will serve and protect me. Until death do you part! Now off you go my children, off you go.' The Antichrist expelled a sinister triumphant laugh as the dogs sprinted into the surrounding darkness.

****

The next evening, Judas came home with what he claimed as a stray rottweiler. The dog appeared to have been well trained as it was very obedient of Judas's commands, but it seemed that John and Sarina were oblivious. 'Mum, Dad, can I keep him please? Please? Please?'

John wasn't convinced that it was a good idea. 'He must have an owner. He is obviously well trained. If the owner turns up, then we can't keep him.'

'But if he doesn't, then can we keep him?'

John knelt down to Judas and the dog. 'You will have to feed him, wash him and take him for walks. And only if the rightful owner doesn't come to claim him.'

'Great, thanks Dad.' Judas hugged his father. 'Come Goliath.' He turned and raced upstairs to his bedroom with the dog close behind.

'He has already named him. I hope he doesn't get too attached.

A dog that well trained will surely be missed,' John said with concern.

'And if not, he certainly has a great pet,' Sarina replied with a smile.

****

That same evening, reports of terrible multiple murders dominated the headlines of the local news.

****

Judas was asked to put up 'Lost Dog' posters and he reluctantly obliged. The weeks turned into months and no one came to claim the dog. Eventually, John said to Judas, 'You can take down the posters. It looks like Goliath is yours now.'

1

Discovery

Since his first act of anarchy, the years had passed without incident. Judas had continued his performance of righteousness to avoid any unnecessary attention. The wickedness within was very impatient; however, his ambition kept it under control. He had a will to succeed and could not afford to be discovered at this early stage in his life. Judas had kept it at bay, ignoring its writhes of torment as he counteracted the urges of his inner nature. His mental strength was forged with momentous resolve to survive his youth, and when he gained the power that was prophesied, the evil within his core would be unleashed.

To become a world ruler was no easy task—even with his special gifts. He would have to gain the best education possible and secure employment that would open the doors required for him to achieve his long-term goal. Language, his subject major in high school, was his tool to spread his influence across the Babylon that now stretched from pole to pole of the planet. His focus was on English, Spanish, French, German, Italian, Chinese, and his native tongue—Arabic. With these languages, he could communicate with over ninety percent of the world's inhabitants.

Since his birth, seventeen years had passed, and his final secondary school exams were only weeks away. The language teacher—Antonio Bertone—usually looked forward to teaching his class when Judas was in attendance. Judas was his star pupil, and in all his years of teaching, never had he seen anyone more gifted. Judas's ability to absorb words and articulate them correctly, was staggering. Following six years of high school, Antonio spent four intense years at university to reach his level of knowledge and skill. Judas, on the other hand, was only at the end of his secondary schooling, and already he was rivaling Antonio.

Judas's gift had now lost its wonder to Antonio. It was like having a second teacher in the class watching his every move, ready to pounce if he made a mistake. The excitement was gone, and with that, the joy of teaching. The last class with Judas had revealed Antonio's change of heart as he chastised Judas for the first time. It was the second minor mispronunciation he had made, and Judas had immediately corrected him. Judas himself had also changed his attitude somewhat over the last month as he reached the limits of Antonio's knowledge.

Antonio had been brooding over the incident since its occurrence two days prior, and after a second sleepless night he said to himself, 'No more!' He was going to put it behind him and move on. With his mind focused on the job, the chance of him mispronouncing a word would be minimalised, and another incident avoided. There were only three classes left and he would never have to teach Judas again. With his new resolve, Antonio walked into the classroom through its only doorway at the whiteboard end.

When he entered, the class of fifteen students was in its usual state of disarray. Most were engaging in a conversation while two at the back were throwing small paper balls to each other. The beige carpeted floor struggled to dampen the raucousness, while the large glass windows on the far side of the classroom provided much of the light and brightly reflected their menagerie of voices. As usual, Judas was seated at the front practising his written language skills. Antonio walked behind the desk and placed his folder of papers upon it. 'Bonjour class.'

'Bonjour,' the students answered as they made their way to their seats.

From the front of the classroom came a different reply, almost drowned out by the others. 'Salute.'

Antonio, ignoring Judas's rebellion, sat down and proceeded with the class. 'I expect you all have done your homework?' With no reply from the class, he continued, 'If that's the case, everyone can take out the passage I gave to you all last week.' Several moans were emitted from the students as they pulled out their homework from their bags and folders. With a huff, Judas sat back in his chair and displayed a bold expression of boredom. Since his adolescence, the hormones had relentlessly transformed his physic from the boyish figure to a more masculine frame.

Judas was now almost one hundred and eighty centimetres tall and his tame pursuits with sport had left his frame lean and muscular.

For the young girls of the school, he was a figure of admiration. His boyish charm clung on, softening the strong lines that developed from his new masculinity, leaving a vision of strength and luring softness that exuded a deep warmth. Judas's intelligence and sense of will forged the fame as the most wanted boy in school. However, his relationships were short and uneventful. If he were to give himself to the wiles of the inexperienced youth about him, only hideous death would remain as the berserker within would override the might of ultimate purpose.

Sometimes he felt the burning of sensual young eyes in the back of his head as he sat disjointed from their luring stares. But some eyes looked upon him driven by other emotions, such as envy and admiration. Many of the young men sought his friendship in hope that whatever emanated from him would rub off on them, making them more appealing to the eyes that sought Judas. Still, there were some that were ignorant of his presence, those that were typically physically gifted but mentally challenged.

A muscular young man at the back of the class whispered something to his friend beside him. Antonio knew Michael's skills lay only in his ability to kick a football, but still he wanted Michael to pay more attention. If Michael were to pursue a professional sporting career, language was one of the few courses that was advantageous. 'Michael, you can start.'

Michael looked back at his teacher with an expression of surprise that quickly changed to dread. He fumbled about for the passage in his backpack and eventually found it. He started studying the paper when Antonio interrupted him.

'Can you stand up please so we can hear you?' As he stood, his chair fell back against the wall and toppled over. There was a sudden roar of laughter as Michael lifted the chair.

'I hope you have more grace on the field,' Antonio said cheekily as a smile grew across his face.

Michael ignored both the comment and the settling giggles as he tried to decipher the hieroglyphics on the paper. He had a reasonable understanding of spoken English, but written English was another thing. Painfully, the words came from his lips, barely comprehensible. 'Accrooosss de meeaaddouw heee rode ... on ...'

'Thank you, Michael. I think we have heard enough. Petra, your turn.' As Michael sat down, all eyes turned to Petra.

Petra sat near the front behind Judas. She stood and began to read the passage. 'Across de meeaaddouw he rode on the wit stal ... stal ... stallion as de ... the ...'

At the front of the classroom, Judas's eyes rolled back as his frustration became unbearable. Where his hand gripped the timber desk, a splintering sound was emitted as he tried desperately to control his temper.

'... Gat ekho from de ... de ...' Petra paused as she struggled to pronounce the next word.

The years upon years of torment slowly chipped away at the strength of determination as berserk evil strove for freedom. Finally, for a brief moment, it breached the stalwart wall like a crack in a great dam, and loathing burst through as it tasted the sweet gratification of rage. Judas snatched up the paper before him and leapt to his feet, casting away his chair and table in a crash of violence. With a temper that mortal man would go mad in channeling, he roared out the words before him. 'ACROSS THE MEADOW HE RODE ON THE WHITE STALLION AS ITS GAIT ECHOED FROM THE WORN PATH BENEATH!' His impeccable pronunciation was highlighted by the surge of anger that drove out the breath from his lungs.

'We have harped over the same shit for months. We are graduating in a few months and all we can do is quote this useless poetry. When are we going to learn something useful? This course is a load of shit and you are a disgrace to your profession. And this ...!' Judas screwed up the paper and threw it at Antonio. '... is an insult to my intelligence!'

Antonio flinched as the paper struck his face. The extremity of Judas's outburst took him by surprise and his first reaction was a defensive one. He flew to his feet and pointed at Judas as he shouted, 'Get out of my class, NOW!'

Judas snatched up his bag and as left the room, he shot a look that would be embedded into Antonio's memory forever. With the rest of the class behind him, only Antonio was able to experience the sinister vision. The iris of his eyes turned pitch black as his incisors grew to an unnatural length. Bizarre lines impressed into his forehead and two small, bone-coloured horns protruded from his temples. Although the sudden and freakish transformation was terrifying enough, it was the sensation from those dead eyes that tore at the very core of Antonio's soul. Complete and utter evil shot from those wells of death, sending razor blades of nervous impulses down his spine.

For a moment, Antonio's stomach convulsed in an attempt to alleviate the sickening sensation of vomiting. Fortunately, the briefness of the moment enabled Antonio to control the regurgitation and re-swallow his partly digested lunch. As Judas disappeared, Antonio was left with a sickening taste in his mouth and a chill of cold steel in his bones.

It took some time for him to regain his composure. When his attention returned to the class, his gaze was met by a classroom full of stunned faces. Antonio was not alone when it came to the shock of Judas's outburst. Antonio had to act quickly to downplay the volatile event. He cleared the bile from his throat before speaking. 'Cleo, can you please read the passage for me?' As Cleo stood and began to read aloud the words before her, Antonio's concentration was shattered. For the rest of the lesson, he struggled to consider anything else but what he had just witnessed.

With the look of bitter anger upon his now human looking face, Judas continued his determined stride through the corridors of the school, knocking over anyone that was unfortunate enough to get in his path. The passage took him out of the school grounds and out into the streets of Jerusalem. That evening, ten unidentified bodies were found mutilated beyond recognition, the police declaring it an act of random violence by some crazed lunatic.

****

Antonio called in sick for the rest of that week. The ill feeling that struck during the incident had remained, and it was eating at the very core of his being. After several nights of no sleep and much deliberation, he decided to seek the counsel of his local priest. The police would not believe him—they would probably think he was mad and put him in an asylum. After what he had seen, he was sure he had experienced something supernatural so who better to turn to than the one person he knew was knowledgeable in the afterlife. That Sunday, he attended the morning service at the Church of the Holy Sepulchre.

The basilica was constructed in stages over a period of several hundred years, and with its Gothic architecture and lofting roof, it stood over the surrounding single storey buildings like a domineering parent. During the service in the main chamber of the basilica, Antonio felt the sickening sensation dissipate. Coincidence or not, it fueled his resolve to proceed with the counselling and the belief that Judas was no ordinary boy.

After the service, Father Michael held the confession. Antonio waited until he was the last before entering the small cubical. As he settled into a kneeling position, there was no sound from Father Michael on the other side of the tiny, barred window. 'Bless me Father for I have sinned. It has been three months since my last confession.' Antonio paused as he contemplated how he would tell Father Michael.

'Go on,' said the middle-aged man from the other side. There was a sense of boredom to his tone.

'I believe that one of my students is possessed by a demon.' As the words came from his mouth, Antonio realised how insane it sounded. He waited for the cynical reply.

'I don't believe that is a sin, unless you have harmed the boy in some way?'

The answer was unexpected. 'No, I have not harmed him, he harmed me.'

'In what way?'

'He looked at me and I have felt sick ever since—until I came to the service today.'

There was a long pause before Father Michael replied. 'This is not something for the confessional. Meet me in the vestry in ten minutes.'

Antonio struggled to speak. 'Okay.' Antonio left the confessional not knowing what to think. He sat on the pew not far from the confessional and waited nervously. After some time, Father Michael appeared from the confessional and walked briskly away towards the vestry. Antonio was surprised that Father Michael didn't look for him. He dismissed the notion and proceeded to follow, some distance behind him.

The vestry was in the right wing of the basilica behind an antiquated door. Antonio approached the door but it was closed. Not sure what to do, he eventually decided to knock. From within came the voice of Father Michael. 'Come in.'

Antonio opened the door to the moderate room and surveyed it for Father Michael. The room was formed with walls of stone like that of the outer wall, and it was lined with bookcases containing a countless number of old books. At the far end was a small stained-glass window that provided a moderate sample of light, leaving the room with a sense of darkened mystery. Beneath the window was an old, large timber desk at which Father Michael was seated. 'Close the door behind you,' he said without looking up. His attention was upon an old book that he carefully perused as it laid upon the cluttered desk. Antonio entered like a timid schoolboy who was in trouble for getting up to mischief.

'Have a seat,' he said as he found a page that took his interest. Antonio sat at the chair that was placed before the large timber table. Father Michael finally raised his head and looked at Antonio with an intense stare. Father Michael was in his late fifties and the years of study had had clearly taken their toll upon his body. His brown eyes required the assistance of the thin, metal-framed glasses that sat upon his large and slightly bulbous nose, the skin upon his face having had lost some of its elasticity, evident with the sagginess around his former strong jaw line. His full crop of clippered hair was now diminishing, its former dark brown colour now a silvery tone. His slight but tall frame was more rounded in the middle now, having gained quite a few pounds onto his normally stable weight of eighty kilos.

The man sitting opposite him was a good twenty years his junior, still retaining the raven coloured hair he was born with. Antonio's nose was as large as Father Michael's though it was much more slender, and from behind the fleshy protrusion were two dark eyes as clear and vibrant as the sole that possessed them. He stood taller than Father Michael's one hundred and seventy-seven centimetres but he felt very much at the mercy of this smaller, yet commanding, figure.

'Antonio, isn't it?' he asked as he tested his memory.

'Yes!' Antonio was surprised that he remembered his name. He was not a regular to the Sunday services and had only spoken to Father Michael once or twice over his years of attendance.

'You're a teacher at Jordon if I recall.'

'Yes.'

'I hear it's a fine school?'

'It is. I'm surprised you remember me?' Antonio had to ask.

'I never forget a face, or a name. What is it that you teach again?'

'Language.'

'Ahh. I remember now.'

Antonio was skeptical if Father Michael really did remember that much.

'So, tell me more about this boy,' he said as he removed his glasses momentarily and cleaned them with a cloth from his pocket.

'He is a fine student. In fact, he is the best I have ever taught. And very popular with the other students. But lately I have noticed a change in him. He is more aggressive and less tolerant of his classmates. I know he is frustrated with the lessons as he has reached the limit of the curriculum. He is more than ready for university. I'm afraid I cannot teach him anything more as he is as good as I, better in fact.'

'So, when was it that he, as you say, looked at you?' His glasses were returned to their former station upon his nose.

'Wednesday. I believe it had been building up for some time, then he just snapped. He became very abusive and disrespectful, so I sent him out of the classroom. A few months ago, I would never have believed this would happen. He was the perfect student back then but now he is my worst nightmare.' Antonio leaned forward as he continued. 'I know this sounds ridiculous, but when Judas looked at me on the way out, his face changed.'

When Antonio said his name, Father Michael reacted with a sense of nervousness. He quickly pulled his glasses off his face and asked, 'What did you say his name was?'

'Judas.' Antonio, unsure of what to make of the priest's reaction, continued, 'He had long teeth and horns, and his eyes were jet black. The worst part was the sensation those black eyes left behind. It made me feel physically ill. I'm sure I didn't imagine it.' He lowered his head for what he was about to say next. 'Am I going mad Father?'

Father Michael leaned back in his chair and quietly studied Antonio. Eventually, he replied. 'Unfortunately, no. I've seen madness before, and you do not fit the picture.' He gazed at the corner of the room for a moment as he chewed upon the arm of his glasses. What he was contemplating, Antonio could only guess. Father Michael returned his glasses to his face once more and sat forward to grasp the book on the table. He turned it around for Antonio and asked, 'Is this the face you saw?'

Antonio looked down at the open pages before him. The book was large and very old, the pages were made of parchment and on the pages was exquisite handwritten calligraphy. It was written in Latin and unfortunately for Antonio, Latin was a language he was not familiar with. On the second page was a meticulously hand-painted picture of a demon and its face is what struck Antonio with infinite terror. He leaped to his feet and turned away, clutching his stomach, 'Close the book!' He desperately searched for a receptacle and found a small round bin in the corner. Antonio rushed over and dispensed the contents of his stomach into the bin.

After he regained his composure, Antonio wiped away the remaining vomit from his face and looked back at Father Michael. He stood at the table and regarded him with the gravest of expressions. 'I must know, is that what you saw?'

Antonio just nodded. Father Michael moved from behind the desk to assist Antonio back to the chair. As he sat down, Father Michael apologised. 'I'm sorry about that, but I had to be sure.'

'Sure of what? That I'm telling the truth?' Antonio retorted as he looked up at him for any sign of credence.

'I knew you were telling the truth before you entered the room. I needed to be sure on what we are dealing with.' He crouched over to get a better look at Antonio. 'Will you be alright?'

'Yes. If you keep that book closed.' Antonio looked over and noticed the bold writing on its spine. Despite that it was written in Latin, he was able to recall some words from his days in college. The first word would best be translated as 'prophecy', the second was unknown to him, and the third and fourth he translated as 'Saint John'. 'What is that book?' Antonio asked.

'It's nothing.' Father Michael promptly snatched up the book and placed it in a drawer in the desk. 'I want to see this boy.'

'Judas?'

'Aaggrrhh! Do not speak its name!' He said with intense conviction.

'Why?'

'It will assist with its connection with your soul. You must disassociate yourself as much as possible. And never let it know you know what it is?' he said as he peered over the top of his glasses like a teacher from the old school.

Antonio became agitated by Father Michael's elusiveness. 'Why do you refer to him as it? What is he? What the hell is going on?!'

'It is best that you do not know. For now at least. When I have seen the boy, I will tell you more. But first I must get a look at it without it being aware of our intensions.'

'I may have a way,' Antonio announced as he stood with some refreshed vitality.

****

The next day, Antonio and Father Michael stood in the upper foyer of the new Majesty Hotel. Before them was a window that overlooked the oval at Jordon Senior College, and as they checked their watches, the ten o'clock bell rang from the school buildings beyond. 'He often comes out to the oval with his friends.'

The two waited impatiently as the students poured out from doorways leading to the oval. Antonio searched desperately for Judas among the many uniformed teenagers that littered the green of the oval. For the full fifteen minutes of the morning break, he searched and found nothing. As the bell sounded again, the students slowly left the oval and refilled the school buildings. When the last had left the oval, Antonio apologised. 'I was sure he would come out. Maybe he knows we are watching.'

'We will come back for the lunch break. He may come out then,' Father Michael said calmly.

They went downstairs to the café in the main foyer area of the hotel and talked while they consumed their cups of cappuccino. 'So, what made you decide to become a priest?' Antonio asked rather boldly.

'The jobs I had in my youth were never very fulfilling. Then, one day during a morning service I decided to enter the priesthood.'

'Just like that,' Antonio said with surprise.

'Yes, just like that,' Father Michael replied with composure.

'How old were you when you entered?'

'Thirty-two.'

'So, there was no divine experience, no heavenly calling?'

'That is something for me and me alone.' His answer was blunt, and Antonio got the clear message that he was probing an area where he was not welcome. Father Michael quickly changed the focus towards Antonio. 'So, what about you? What made you become a teacher?'

'Originally, I wanted to work in the field of foreign affairs. Maybe as an interpreter or as a consulate officer. To be able to interact with different cultures was always a passion of mine.' Antonio took another sip from his drink, then continued. 'I travelled as much as I could when I was studying. Mostly backpacking and working as I went as I had little money. When I tried to work in the field, there was little to choose from. Fate had a different idea for my future. I was well qualified for teaching and there was an abundance of employment opportunities. So, here I am, teaching possessed children.'

They proceeded with an idle conversation that never returned to a more personal nature. After discussing current affairs and the problems within Israel, the hours slipped away. The distant echo of the school bell returned their attention to more immediate matters. For Antonio, the urgency was lost, and as he strolled up the stairs with Father Michael, he was almost oblivious to the consequences of their mission. Father Michael's potent presence was rubbing off. They reached the second floor and went straight to the window they were formerly stationed at. The upper foyer was almost always deserted apart from the occasional person entering or exiting one of the elevators at the far end of the foyer.

They peered out over the expanse of green and watched the students fill the oval with the darkness of their uniforms. As time passed, Antonio became agitated again. He so wanted to solve this part of the puzzle so he could move on. Then he appeared.

At first it was difficult to get a clear view of him as he was surrounded by the masses upon the oval. Judas sat upon a small embankment with his friends and began to eat his lunch. 'There he is!'

'Where?' said Father Michael impatiently.

'He is the boy in the middle of the group sitting upon the grassy slope.'

'Yes, I see.' Father Michael removed a small vial from his pocket and said a prayer. 'Only with my eyes cleansed by holy water can I see the beast for what he truly is.' He poured the contents of the vial into his eyes as if he were attempting to wash away a toxin that could potentially blind him. Father Michael wiped away the excess fluid and returned his glasses to his face.

He slowly opened his eyes to behold a vision of pure evil. Its skin was blood red and scaly, and slick like oil. Upon each scale was a face of a tortured soul that writhed and screamed as the skin moved. Its bipedal body structure was supported by two hoofed limbs unlike that of any animal's, and the mighty thews adorned three fingered hands with long, black fingernails. Its face, sickening to Father Michael, had deep furrows that lined the creature's cheeks and jaw line. Its cruel mouth housed black, needle point teeth and a tongue forked like that of a snake. Upon the head were two sharp horns that curved up and towards each other. The most sinister of all were the creature's dead eyes—as black as the pits of hell—a preview of the horror of the soul within.

Father Michael knew that if he were to look directly into those horrid black orbs, his soul would be tortured in ways that only the damned could ever understand. The experience was too much for his ageing bones and he collapsed to the ground as prayers for salvation escaped from his trembling lips.

Antonio desperately attempted to catch Father Michael before he struck the ground but his slow reflexes failed to save the ageing priest and he landed with a thud, Antonio falling on top of him. Waves of fear flowed through his agonised mind as he struggled to connect with Father Michael. 'Father! Father! What's the matter? Are you okay?'

Father Michael recited every prayer he could think of to try and banish the memory that assailed his mind, but it was to no avail. It would forever be there, corrupting his sanity until such times as he was cleansed by the holy spirit—upon his death.

'Father Michael? What did you see?' Antonio was beside himself with terror. What was he to do now? He slapped Father Michael across the cheek to release him from the trance.

He immediately stopped babbling and focused upon Antonio as he replied, 'The spawn of Satan!' Antonio fell back as the words sunk into his mind. Father Michael reached out a trembling hand and pulled Antonio so they were face to face. Father Michael had lost the confidence that had proven so powerful up until now. Now, his face was more shaken than Antonio's. 'He will masquerade as righteous to lead the fallen, and with one look from his true eyes he can infect your soul. Only with my eyes cleansed by holy water can I see the beast for what he truly is. Saint John's prophecy has come true!' He pulled him closer and spat the words like he was exorcising himself. 'The boy is the Antichrist!'

Father Michael released Antonio, leaving him paralysed with the impact of the revelation. Moments passed before something pulled at his jacket. Antonio realised that Father Michael was standing over him, trying to get Antonio to move. 'We cannot say here. We must go … NOW!' Antonio stood up, his legs like jelly, and it took a few moments for him to regain his balance. Father Michael had returned to his former stalwart stature and dragged on Antonio's coat to make him move. 'Whatever you do, don't look back.'

As he heard the words, something compelled him to defy Father Michael's warning. Just for a moment, he glanced back at the Antichrist and to his horror, it was looking straight back at him. Its eyes channeled unbridled hate into Antonio's mind and left him with an ill that modern medicine could never hope to heal. Antonio turned away, the all too familiar nauseous sensation was back in his stomach.

****

Judas immediately sensed the prying eyes upon him. He scanned the horizon for the source and soon found it. From a distant window, a familiar face peered back at him—a face that displayed the horrific realisation of who he was. His unnatural eyes locked onto Antonio and gave him the gift of a slow, agonising death. But there was someone else with his former teacher, someone he was unfamiliar with. He must discover the identity of Antonio's comrade before he spreads the word. Judas projected his mind's eye to the far side of the oval where a large, black canine stood like a statue. Goliath's ears redirected towards his master as the command for 'search and destroy' filled his small brain. Goliath reacted instantly, sprinting to the Majesty Hotel.

Goliath was at the front of the hotel in a moment, and the pitter-patter of his small feet echoed from the stairs that led to the front entrance. The automated doors welcomed Goliath as he entered the front foyer of the hotel. Like a guided missile, he made for the stairs that led to the upper foyer.

The hotel concierge witnessed the intrusion in disbelief. In his ten-year career, he had never seen a dog enter a hotel like this— and with such a sense of purpose. He promptly directed two luggage handlers to chase down the dog and escort it from the premises.

When Goliath reached the upper level, he made his way to the window. Utilising his keen sense of smell, he detected the faint scent of two humans and locked them away in his memory. Following the scent, he went to the door of one of the elevators but the scent faded away. Goliath turned around and sprinted back to the wide stairway where he was met by the two men. With a deep growl and a display of his large white teeth, the two men backed away.

With his path clear, Goliath dashed down the stairs and back across the front foyer to the stairs that led to the underground car park. The concierge watched the dog's trek with great intent and wondered if it was looking for its owner. Moments later, the dog's two pursuers entered the main foyer and looked across to the concierge for direction. He pointed an agitated finger towards the other stairs and the two men followed, walking as quickly as they could without running. One rule they dare not break was that no one was to run in the hotel—especially staff.

At the base of the stairs, Goliath met a closed door. Despite the limited intellect at his disposal, some residue of the former human remained. At first, he pushed his sizeable bulk against the door in hope that it opened inwards, but it was not so. He had to turn the doorknob and pull it open. Using his powerful jaw, Goliath gripped the doorknob and turned his head to unlock the door. Stepping backward, he was able to open the door to the car park.

With the door open far enough to let go and still get through, his two pursuers arrived at the scene. The two stopped in their tracks as they stared in amazement at the ingenuity of the animal. The one on the left voiced what was going through both their minds. 'That's one smart dog!' They seized the moment to capture Goliath and charged the rottweiler, but his canine reflexes were too swift. He released the doorknob and slipped through the closing door. The two luggage handlers crashed into the closing door, falling in a tangled mess.

Goliath found the door to the lift and the trail once more. To his keen sense of smell, the invisible route of Antonio and Father Michael was a lit pathway leading directly to his prey. Goliath swiftly traversed the car park with his nose close to the ground, guiding his way. In moments he came to a vacant car space where the scent faded. Moments before, Antonio's heart was racing, his sweat glands reacting to the tension of the moment. For Goliath, human perspiration was detectable even when enclosed in a container. Soon his nose led him out of the vacant car space and towards the car park exit.

****

As Father Michael had no car, Antonio had to drive them to the hotel in his old C-Class Mercedes. Despite the cramping of his stomach, Antonio soldiered on. While he was paying the car park attendant the parking fee, he noticed a dark shape approaching in the wing mirror.
'That looks like his dog!'

'Whose dog?' Father Michael asked with concern.

'His dog!' Antonio exclaimed in an attempt to convey Judas's identity without saying his name.

The tone was enough for Father Michael to understand who he meant. 'Quick, we must go, NOW!'

Antonio slammed his foot on the accelerator, and they screeched out of the car park. The car park attendant stepped out from the small booth with Antonio's keycard still in his hand. 'Hey, you forgot your card!' The attendant then watched a rottweiler run past and chase the Mercedes down the street. He scratched his head in wonder as to what was going on. When the two luggage handlers jogged passed and stopped at the kerb, he couldn't resist the temptation to get involved. He shouted out to the two men that were now struggling to catch their breath. 'Did you two lose a dog?'

They turned around to look back at the parking attendant and nodded.

The parking attendant pointed down the street and said, 'He went that way!' Realising that the dog was long gone, they slowly walked back to the hotel foyer.

****

Father Michael shouted to Antonio. 'He's catching up, you must go faster!'

'But it's only a dog, isn't it?'

Father Michael shot a serious look at Antonio and answered, 'When it comes to the Antichrist, nothing will be as it appears.' He looked back over his shoulder and shouted again. 'Faster!'

The traffic was reasonably heavy, and it was difficult to negotiate the other vehicles at speed. Antonio watched the traffic lights ahead change to orange and he knew that soon they would have to stop. 'We've got a red light ahead, what are we going to do?'

'We must not stop, go through it,' Father Michael replied sternly.

Antonio stepped on the gas and swerved passed the cars in front. The front row of vehicles was already stationary and there was no way of getting past them. He pulled over to the wrong side of the road and swerved passed two cars coming the other way. He ignored their horns and shouts of abuse as he charged through the intersection. The vehicles on the cross street had just pulled away, leaving a small gap in the centre of the intersection for Antonio to negotiate. When they reached the far side of the lights, their hearts thumped loud and hard in their chests as adrenaline heightened their senses to the limit. With a clear road ahead, Antonio was able to speed away and leave their pursuer behind.

Goliath sprinted between the stationary vehicles and launched himself into the intersection. Cars from either direction flew by at lethal speeds, but Goliath was undeterred. Both his canine reflexes and outstanding agility enabled him to dash between the first stream of cars and then leap over the second. Despite his skill, he was unable to clear the second stream completely and his front legs were clipped by a passing car. His body was thrown into a spiral and his bulk fell back towards the ground. With unnatural skill, he landed on all fours and continued to chase after the Mercedes, oblivious to the close encounter with death. After a few hundred metres, Goliath came to a stop in the middle of the road. His prey had escaped, and the chase was over.

He growled and let out a bark, protesting his failure, before turning around and going back the way he had come.

****

Judas had remained on the oval after the bell had ended the lunch break. Most of the students had left to return to the classrooms with only a few stragglers still to be seen outside the school buildings. Goliath trotted up to his master and obediently sat before him. Judas crouched down, gripping the two sides of Goliath's large head, staring into his eyes. In a heartbeat, everything that had just transpired was conveyed to Judas. He patted Goliath on the head as a sign of his approval, then turned and went back into the school. Goliath trotted over to his former point of duty and remained there for the rest of the day—ready for the next decree.

****

Antonio struggled to retain his composure as he entered the cathedral with Father Michael. The pain in his chest was intensifying to an unbearable level. However, the drive to learn the truth overruled the need for a doctor and a soft bed. After they entered the vestry, Antonio collapsed in the chair in front of the desk.

Meanwhile, Father Michael paced back and forth muttering to himself. 'I thought it was a dream ... how could I have believed it to be real? I would never had believed that this would happen during my lifetime ... I must contact the Brethren and warn the Pope.'

'Father Michael. I have read *Revelations,* and what you have told me was not in it. So how do you know so much about the Antichrist?'

Father Michael stopped pacing and shot a look at Antonio. He moved over to his chair and sat down. By the intense expression on his face, Antonio could see that what Father Michael was about to disclose was going to be difficult. He cleared his throat and said, 'Earlier today you asked me why I became a priest. Well it had to do with a dream I had. Well, what I believed to be a dream.' Antonio thought it strange that he was now willing to disclose this personal information, but he was not going to interject. 'An angel dressed in white robes came to me and said, 'The Lord your God has sent me to deliver you a message. You are to enter the service of the Lord. And during your service, a man will come to you bearing the sign of the apocalypse. Do not turn him away.'

'Since this experience, I felt compelled to enter the priesthood. I studied at the Vatican and after four years, I was qualified and able to be ordained into the Church. One of the questions I was asked at the interview prior to ordainment was, 'Why do you want to become a priest?' Of course, I told them the story of the visitation. Later I would learn why I was accepted and the importance of my visitation.

After I was ordained, my first assignment was to work in a monastery near Florence, where I spent the next five years. It was then that Father Marcus came to visit. He was the cardinal in Jerusalem. To my surprise, he came to see me. I did not recall ever meeting a Father Marcus, nor had I ever heard of him. I was summoned to the main hall of the monastery where I found Father Marcus alone. I asked where the other Fathers were, and he told me that he requested a private council. Father Marcus then asked me to tell him about my visitation. It was then that it clicked how he knew about my experience; he was one of the interviewers during my ordainment. When I finished, he said, 'I have been searching for you all my life'. In his visitation he was told to search for the one who will discover the sign. He then showed me this.' Father Michael removed a book from a locked drawer in the desk and placed it upon the table. It was the book that contained the picture he had shown Antonio earlier.

'What is it?' asked Antonio.

'The complete letters of Saint John on *Revelations*. There are only six copies in the world, and the original is in the Vatican under the care of the Pope. It contains many things about the second coming that were long ago declared as too disturbing for common man. What is in The Bible is a cut down version with some of the more disturbing sections removed. The parts that were left out would be of no benefit to the general public. However, those parts are vital for the Brethren to identify the Antichrist.'

'Who is the Brethren?'

'Father Marcus was one of the members of the order. He was very old when we met, and I was chosen to take his place. The purpose of the Brethren is to protect *The Secret Book of Saint John*, and to stop the Antichrist. Father Marcus told me that my visitation was different from the others and believed that I was the one to discover the Antichrist. Although, at the time I didn't believe him. Then you came along.' Antonio doubled over in agony as the ill grew in strength. Father Michael understood the symptoms immediately. 'You looked back, didn't you?' Antonio nodded. 'I'll put you on a course of holy water, and you must remain within the church. The power of the Antichrist is humbled by consecrated ground.'

Antonio struggled to get the words out. 'What do we do now?'

'I must go to Rome immediately; the pontiff is in grave danger. It is written that upon the first sign of the apocalypse, the last of the blessed leaders will be slain.' He left the room for a moment then returned with someone in tow. 'This is Father Georgio. He will look after you while I am gone.' Father Michael went over to Antonio and placed his hand upon his head. 'God be with you my son. I shall pray for you.'

He turned and began to walk out the door when Antonio stopped him. 'Father Michael? Do you think you can stop him?' The look on his face was like that of a lost lonely child.

Father Michael bowed his head and replied, 'I don't know.' Then he continued out the door.

2

Pope's Plight

Rome, Italy

Father Michael, born Michael Etronio, was more certain now than ever before. At last, all that had gone before was now justified, and his clear sense of purpose fueled his resolve. He managed to get onto the evening flight to Rome and was in a taxi to the Vatican before midnight. As the taxi drove down Via della Conciliazione towards St. Peter's Square, memories of his student life came flooding back. In the distance, the majesty of St. Peter's Basilica rose from the surrounding metropolis as it defined the significance of the Vatican to Christianity. The sight of St. Peter's always fired his faith in the power of God.

Soon the view of the basilica was obscured as the taxi traversed the outer rim of the plaza to access Vatican City behind St. Peter's. The taxi dropped him off in the small side street Vaticano that partly bounded the vast grounds of Vatican City. Before him stood a twenty-foot-high stone wall that had been there for many years, protecting the interior. In the wall, a small steel door offered the only visible connection between the outside world and the inner sanctum of the Vatican.

Father Michael walked up to the door and pressed a small button positioned to one side. If there was a bell at the other end, he could not hear it and he wondered if there was anyone there to answer its call. He waited patiently in the cool evening air. Some time passed before the small hatch in the door opened to reveal an aged face. 'Yes?'

'I am Father Michael from Jerusalem. I have a message of the gravest importance for the Pope.'

The old face exposed the false teeth within as it chuckled, 'For the Pope you say?'

'Please can you give him this message? The Brethren are to unite.'

'The Brethren are to what?'

Father Michael thought this old priest was either hard of hearing or his Italian was getting rusty!

'The Brethren are to unite! Please, it is imperative that he gets this message immediately.'

The man's face lost its mockery as a more serious expression emerged. 'It is the middle of the night. It will have to wait until morning.'

'No! It cannot wait, it is a matter of life or death. Please, his Holiness is expecting the message.'

The mind behind the old face considered his words for a while before making a decision. 'You may enter, but this better be good.'

The sound of an old, thick bolt being released echoed through the metallic door before it opened outwards. Father Michael stepped in and the door was promptly closed again and bolted. They stood in a poorly lit corridor with a curved roof that was a little higher than the top of Father Michael's head. The old man was garbed in the traditional robes of a Vatican priest, his years of traversing these small passages clearly having had affected his posture. His curvature of the spine was not extensive but it was enough to make it difficult to get around and reduced his former stature to one that was more suited to the old Vatican corridors.

'How did you know about the rear entrance?' The priest asked as they turned into a long, curved corridor.

'I was once a student here many years ago. Although I was surprised that it was attended at this late hour.' The truth was that the pontiff himself had told him of its existence some years ago, but he decided that such knowledge was not for the ears of this old man.

'I don't sleep as well as I use to, the back you know. And students were never permitted in this part of Vatican City.' He glanced back at Father Michael to see his reaction.

'City walls have ears, and some of her secrets have been whispered to the forbidden, Father.'

Despite his age, the mind of Father Peitro was obviously still sharp, and Father Michael was not sure if he would accept his stretching of the truth. Father Pietro stopped outside a door and opened it. 'Wait in here.' The room was small and bare, with only an old worn pew to adorn the emptiness. If it were not for the single light hanging from the roof, the room would be cast in perpetual darkness as there was no window to provide an alternate light source. Father Michael entered and as he turned to speak to Father Peitro, the door was shut in his face and bolted.

It was obvious that Father Peitro distrusted him and whether he would give the Pope the message, Father Michael could not be sure. Either way, all he could do now was wait.

****

A little later, Father Peitro had reached the private chambers of Cardinal Jiovani, one of the senior advisors to the Pope. He knocked loudly on the timber door in hope that he would wake the cardinal. He waited a while then knocked again. From the other side of the door a muffled voice shouted, 'Alright, I'm coming!'

The door opened to reveal a priest in his early sixties with a mop of tangled greying hair that stuck out at all angles. 'Father Peitro, I know you have trouble sleeping but do you have to disturb those who don't?' His tone poorly disguised his annoyance towards the intrusion.

'Beg your forgiveness, but a young Father Michael requests an audience with his Holiness immediately.'

'What? You can't be serious. I am not waking him at this time of night for anyone.'

'He says it's a matter of life or death.'

'They always say that.'

'He said if you passed on the message, the Brethren are to unite, his Holiness would understand and accept his counsel.'

'The Brethren are to unite?' As the cardinal repeated the words, his expression changed to deep contemplation. 'Alright then.' He pointed a finger at Father Peitro and said, 'This better be good.'

'That is what I told him,' he replied with a smile.

****

In the private chambers of Pope Julius IV, the central feature was a magnificent bedroom suite that dated back to the early nineteenth century. In the centre of the expansive bed, and surrounded by numerous pillows, was the sleeping pontiff. Slowly, the bedroom door opened to release a modest amount of light into the dark, silent room. Cautiously, Cardinal Jiovani entered the room and approached the bed. The cardinal little more than whispered to the exposed ear of the Pope, 'Your Holiness, there is a man here to see you.'

He slowly stirred then opened his eyes. 'What is it?'

'There is someone here to see you, and he has a message.'

Pope Julius lifted his head from the mass of pillows and reached over to the bedside lamp. When he switched on the light, he momentarily protected his eyes from the direct light as he focused upon the face before him. 'Jiovani!' He sat up and rubbed his eyes. 'Who is he and what does he want?'

'A Father Michael. His message is that the Brethren are to unite, whatever that means.'

The cardinal could see the eighty-one-year-old pontiff struggling to access his memory. 'A Father Michael ... the Brethren are to unite?' Pope Julius's eyes came to life like two headlights in the night, and he stared at the cardinal. He shouted, 'Father Michael from Jerusalem!' He pulled away the covers and struggled to get to his feet. 'Help me up.' Before the cardinal could react, he changed his mind. 'No, no! Go and get him instead and bring him to the drawing room.' The cardinal appeared to be paralysed and stood there staring at the Pope. 'Go, go now!' With that, Cardinal Jiovani promptly left the bedroom.

****

Father Pietro had been gone almost half an hour, and Father Michael was beginning to wonder if he was going to spend the night in this room, only to be thrown out of the Vatican the next day. A menagerie of doom-filled thoughts passed through his mind while he waited. *I should have called first.*

The sound of the bolt being released startled him out of his paranoid trance. Father Pietro entered and close behind was another priest. Despite his scruffy appearance, Father Michael knew he was someone of importance as he had the robe of a cardinal thrown over him. 'Well, Father Michael,' stated the disorderly cardinal. 'This is your lucky day. His Holiness will see you.' The cardinal turned on his heels and left. Father Peitro directed him to follow the cardinal, so he left the room attempting to refuel his resolve for the task ahead.

The cardinal stormed through the Vatican at an Olympic walking pace, with Father Michael close behind. Father Michael hoped the pace would be less of a blurring speed as many of the corridors that they traversed were the first time for him. The narrow, bare stone tunnels were swiftly replaced with majestic, palace like hallways with great lofting ceilings and walls decorated with religious artworks from numerous great artists from the ages—Michael Angelo, Leonardo Da Vinci and Bernini, just to name a few.

As they stormed through the great halls, Cardinal Jiovani began to probe the stranger. 'I thought I knew all of the Pope's associates, but I have never heard of you. So how is it that the pontiff knows your name?'

Something that Father Marcus had made clear was that no one must know the existence of the Brethren—absolutely no one. His act of discretion with Antonio was to Father Michael a necessary one, as Antonio led him to the one the Brethren sought. For the cardinal, there was no reason in his mind that he should know of the existence of the Brethren. 'We are associates from long ago.'

'Tell me more.'

'We first met more than twenty years ago in a monastery in Jerusalem. Unfortunately, I have not had a chance to catch up with his Holiness since before his ordainment.'

The cardinal desisted his casual interrogation and remained silent for the rest of the trek.

They eventually reached the public area of the Vatican. Several guards patrolled the halls and every now and then they would be scrutinised by wary eyes. Having the familiar face of Cardinal Jiovani leading their way, no guards dared to stop them for questioning. As they entered the Sistine Chapel, Father Michael couldn't help but glance up at the famous mural upon the ceiling, but the cardinal's pace made it impossible to stop and absorb its magnificence. Finally, they came to the personal quarters of the pontiff. Outside were guards that parted to permit them access. They entered through the ornately carved oak door and strode down a short corridor. Near the end on the left was a half-opened door to a small room.

The cardinal led them into the room where they found Pope Julius IV seated in a large leather chair next to a small table. Immediately, Cardinal Jiovani introduced him in the appropriate formal manor. 'Your Holiness, I present you Father Michael from Jerusalem.'

Father Michael went down on one knee as his Holiness presented his hand for him to kiss the papal ring. He did as was the tradition for greeting the Pope and kissed the ring upon his hand. 'You may go Jiovani,' the Pope announced in a formal tone.

'Your Holiness, it is not wise to leave you alone in the company of an outsider.'

'I said go!' Pope Julius's voice croaked as he attempted to shout at the cardinal.

Reluctantly, Cardinal Jiovani backed out of the room. 'Yes, your Holiness.'

With the cardinal gone, the pontiff's tone changed to a less official tone. 'My old friend, how good it is to see you again. Please sit down.' He gestured Father Michael to a leather chair on the other side of the small table. He flopped down in the chair and let out a gasp of relief.

'You have travelled far my friend. Let us talk over a drink.' He pulled a small remote out of his pocket and pressed the only button on it.

A moment later, a priest appeared dressed similar to Father Pietro. 'Yes, your Holiness.'

'The usual, thank you.' The priest understood and promptly disappeared. Pope Julius turned back to Father Michael. 'Are you still preaching at the Church of the Holy Sepulchre?'

'Yes, I'm still there,' he said with a smile.

'So, you have some news for me?'

'Yes.' Father Michael sat forward and cleared his throat before commencing. 'I have seen it.'

'The Antichrist?'

'Yes.'

'Is the beast as it is written?'

'Yes.'

'Then all that has been foretold is about to be.'

'That is why I came here as soon as I could. We must get you to safety.'

'I am too old to run.'

'But we cannot leave you here, your life is in danger!'

'Satan's lure has caught many of those among us. I call them 'the fallen.' I expect they will be Satan's tool for my demise.'

'All the more reason to leave while you can.'

'There is one that I believe has not fallen to the temptation of the lust for power.'

'Who?'

The Pope leaned forward to convey the identity as quietly as possible. 'Cardinal Pius Bennedict.' He leaned back and continued, 'I believe he will be the next pontiff.'

'If he is to be next, then he must be the one to join the Antichrist in his evil crusade.'

'No, not Cardinal Pius. He is true of heart as any man could be. I have made the arrangements for Cardinal Pius to be inducted into the Brethren once I have departed.'

'But if we get you to safety then none of this will happen.'

'Ahh, I fear it will happen no matter what. It is written.'

'What is written can be changed. God helps those who help themselves. If we can prevent the chain of events, we may change the course of history—possibly foil the Antichrist in achieving complete power.'

The priest returned with a silver tray holding two small crystal glasses filled with port. He placed the two glasses next to each other on a small table between them, then left. As soon as they were alone again, the Pope replied, 'The world is as the Bible foretold. The heathen masses grow by the thousands each day. Maybe the apocalypse is to cleanse the world?'

'Yes, you may be right.'

'What can you tell me of the Antichrist?'

'He is still but a boy of seventeen years. His name is Judas Salim, a student at Jordon Senior College in Jerusalem.'

As the pontiff picked up his glass to take a sip of port, he asked, 'You have the current contact details for the Brethren?' He sipped on the ruby liquid.

Father Michael had no taste for port, so his glass remained untouched. 'Yes.'

'You must meet immediately, but not here.'

'What do you mean, you? Surely you are attending. You're the head of the order. Your presence is essential.'

'I cannot disappear to have secret meetings Father Michael, I am the pontiff. I have an entourage even when I go to the toilet. And the fallen will learn of the Brethren and jeopardise everything. No, I cannot attend.'

'Do you know which are already poisoned by Satan's lies?'

'I know some of their names, but there is one that is clearly the director of their bane.'

'Who?'

'It's ... it's ... Carrrrgghhh.' Pope Julius clutched at his chest as intense agony inflicted his aged face. It was like an invisible knife had been plunged into the heart of the pontiff. He writhed in agony before collapsing to the floor.

Father Michael fell to the floor next to the stricken Pope and rummaged through his robe to find the beeper. After a few moments of desperation, he found the electronic device and pressed the sole button. He then attempted to break through the Pope's agony and make contact. 'Your Holiness, what is it? Is it your heart?'

Between facial contortions, the pontiff nodded. Behind Father Michael appeared the Father that had formerly carried the tray. 'Call a doctor immediately, he is having a heart attack!' When the Father left, Father Michael watched as the Pope fell unconscious. 'Julius!' Despite his lack of formal training, he attempted to perform a heart message upon the pontiff. Positioning his hands over the estimated location of Pope Julius's heart, he began to push down on his chest in a rhythmical motion.

It wasn't long before a pair of Vatican paramedics arrived and one pulled Father Michael from the dying Pope. 'We'll take over from here.' Father Michael stepped back and watched in desperation as the paramedics fought to revive him. One placed a mask with a bag attached over the pontiff's face, while the other opened suitcase-sized electronic device with two paddles attached. He tore open the robe to reveal the pontiff's bare chest. The paramedic removed the paddles and placed them in strategic positions before yelling, 'Clear!' As soon as the other paramedic was no longer making contact, he pressed the button on the paddle.

The jolt of electrical energy made the Pope's body arch then fall limp again. The bag was immediately returned to the pontiff's face as they waited for the mobile defibrillator to recharge.

As the drama unfolded before him, Father Michael found himself slowly backing away. He was too late! The fallen had struck as was written by Saint John two thousand years ago. If he were implicated in the death of the Pope, he would be unable to warn the other members of the Brethren. He had to escape while he had the chance.

While the attention was still upon the pontiff, Father Michael slipped out of the room and fled the scene. Walking as swiftly as possible, he backtracked to the Sistine Chapel. This time he took no notice of the world-famous artwork above him. In the corridor beyond, he was met by two guards walking the opposite way. The adrenalin rush changed to a flood as his mind was besieged with a menagerie of desperate thoughts. What do I do now?

He maintained his brisk but controlled passage as he closed upon the two guards. At first, he thought, 'The Pope has been assassinated, why are they walking?' Then when he was almost upon them, he recognised the two faces; they were the guards he had passed earlier with Cardinal Jiovani. Father Michael glanced at them and met their suspicious gaze with a smile. The urge to say something was too great and he surprised himself when he said, 'Good evening.'

The two guards just nodded and kept walking at their casual pace. It was then he realised—they don't know! Luck was on his side, or was it the work of the Lord? Either way he was not sticking around to find out. Around the corner was access to the outside world and he made with all speed to the doorway. Fortunately, the bolts were accessible from the inside. He unlocked them and escaped to a courtyard at the side of St. Peter's Basilica.

Seconds later, the alarm was raised, and the Vatican was in lockdown like a prison.

Father Michael continued his swift gait passed the Basilica and onto the plaza. He allowed himself a brief glance behind but found no sign of pursuers. From there, he disappeared into the cool night.

****

The display upon the small television screen void of audio changed from the tragic scene within the drawing room to the gloomy bedroom of Cardinal Pius. As Cardinal Pius slept soundly in his modest bed, his deep sleep shrouded his senses from the presence of an intruder. The skulking shadow crept up to his bedside and dropped a small object into the glass of water upon his bedside table. The object fell to the bottom of the glass and began to dissolve in a flurry of tiny bubbles. When the intruder left the bedside of Father Pius, so did the visibility of the small object as it dissolved into the water.

When the surveillance equipment was switched off, the operator announced to himself, 'As last, I shall be Pope!'

****

When Father Michael returned to Jerusalem, Father Georgio had despairing news for him. The night before, Antonio had passed away in terrible agony. The sanctity of the holy ground only delayed the inevitable. With the authorities likely to be searching for him, Father Michael gathered up a few belongings to go into hiding. Before leaving his home for good, a suspicious letter arrived. As the letter brandished the hallmark of the pontiff, this he felt would contain important information for the task ahead. He didn't open it, but he kept it safe as he began contacting the other members of the Brethren to arrange the gathering.

3

The Brethren Unite

Near Salzburg, Switzerland

Some weeks later, the Brethren met for the first time in almost one thousand years. Each was aware of the other only by name and a current place of contact. The chosen meeting place was an abandoned monastery in Switzerland. The great structure sat upon a sloping hillside among the breathtaking views of the Swiss Alps, not far from Salzburg. The monastery was originally a castle several centuries ago and had since fallen into the ownership of the Catholic Church. At the turn of the twenty-first century, occupation of the monastery was ceased in favour of a more modern and economical residence. Its submission for sale had been mislaid and the monastery was all but forgotten. All except for one former resident and Brethren member.

The six men of the cloth garbed in their vestments and white collars gathered in what was once the chapel. The room was the largest in the building and still contained some of the furniture of its former design. Several pews remained waiting for a congregation that would never come, and to one side a pulpit rose up from the timber floor that once conducted many stern sermons. Upon the dais, its former occupant erected a small table and upon that he placed a golden crucifix. The ceiling was still cast in shadow as the light was insufficient from the three stained glass windows on either side. Outside, the morning sunlight broke through the ample cloudscape to shine upon the abandoned monastery. Excluded from the congregation within, the four apprentices were entertained by the magnificent countryside as the sun highlighted its serene beauty.

Despite the warm climate, the atmosphere within the old Chapel was still brisk. The Brethren formed a circle in the centre of the Chapel as they recited the Lord's Prayer. When finished, Father Michael commenced the meeting in the chosen common language of English. 'Welcome brothers. As we are unacquainted and know each other only by name, I suggest we introduce ourselves. I shall start. I am Father Michael from Jerusalem, and the instigator of this meeting.' He turned to the man on his left to indicate he was next.

'I am Father Paul from London.' Father Paul was well into his sixties, had little hair left and what remained, was as white as snow. Beneath a strong brow, stared two steel grey eyes that darted about providing some inkling of the sharp mind within. His nose was large and slender like his stature. Upon his nose sat a pair of grey, metal framed glasses over which he peered from time to time. 'My apprentice, Father Stephen, is one that waits outside.' He looked to his left to indicate the completion of his introduction.

The next man was somewhat younger, his fair hair still retaining some of its former colour. His accent gave a clear indication of the country he called home.

'Father William from Washington DC. I have no apprentice yet.' His blue eyes were as calm as his nature, and they somehow created a distraction from the extensive acne scarring on his cheeks.

'I am Father Hans from Salzburg. I have an apprentice as well, Father Emil.' His diction was less refined as the others though his conveyance was still clear. Father Hans was in his seventies and his eyes required the assistance of a pair of thick, brown-framed glasses. The original deep brown colour of his eyes had faded as did the original strength of his jaw line. Now, his visage was sagged and lined with deep creases. Whatever his former height was, his curved spine had reduced it to less than that of the brothers that beheld him. 'I hope you all find the accommodation here adequate. There is still running water though we no longer have power. I have some fond memories of this old place ...'

Father Hans was cut off by the next man in line. 'I am Father Thomas from Sydney, Australia. And thank you Father Hans for providing us with a such a fine choice of venue.' The immense stature of Father Thomas overshadowed the rest of the Brethren. The top of his broad shoulders was in line with the heads of his brothers, and his balding head was too far above for them to discern the beginning of his hair line. His brown eyes were still as fresh as they were in his youth, though the two deep creases extending from the corners of his nose to his mouth gave an inkling of his sixty years of age. 'I also have an apprentice waiting for us, Father Peter.'

'I am Father Alfred from Paris. I have an apprentice as well, Father Rene.' Father Alfred was the eldest of the Brethren and his forehead was well exposed after the receding of his grey hair. His original stature was not quite six feet and now his eighty-year-old frame was a good seven centimetres less. Two unassisted brown eyes peered from an exceedingly aged face that hinted at some illness that had plagued him over the years gone by. Despite the prompting from his apprentice, Father Alfred's stubbornness had kept him from a doctor and from an optometrist.

'Now that we are all acquainted, we can proceed.' Although he was not chosen as the chairman of the group, Father Michael felt obliged as he was the one responsible for the meeting. 'Firstly, I will brief you as best as I can on what has befallen, then we can decide on what to do with those outside. And finally, where we are to go from here.'

'Satan's child has been born and his name is Judas Salim.' Father Alfred and Father Hans both gasped at the mention of his name. Father Michael's gaze turned to a more intense stare as he said, 'Forgive me for uttering his name, and I hope you all heard me clearly for I will not speak it again. He is already seventeen years old and is a student at Jordon Junior College in Jerusalem.'

'Of course!' Father Paul stated. 'We should have expected him to start there. He mocks the Holy Land.'

'Yes. And more cunning than that, he is of Jewish decent! The acceptance by the Jews has been made easier.'

'How can that be?' Father Thomas asked. 'It is written that that this cannot be so. He cannot be one of God's chosen.'

'I realise this,' Michael retorted. 'However, he could be adopted as his looks show little resemblance to his parents. It is the only explanation. To my knowledge, he has killed at least once through unnatural means. The one who revealed the Antichrist to me was cursed by him, and after days of terrible suffering from a strange illness, his soul, I pray, is now with the Lord.'

Father William asked, 'Can you tell us how the Antichrist inflicted the curse?'

'He simply looked into his eyes,' replied Father Michael. Father Alfred and Father Hans gasped again, and both said a short prayer. 'My brothers, these are the gravest of times and we must fortify ourselves. For the task ahead will lead us into the lair of the beast himself, and only the bravest can hope to survive.' His look fell upon the elder members of the Brethren before he continued. 'My treatment of holy water and the sanctity of holy ground was successful the first time he was infected, but the second time he saw the truth and it was too much. The treatment only prolonged his agony.'

'We must find an antidote to his evil or we may succumb to his power as well. That must be one of our first priorities. As you know, our Italian counterpart has been assassinated by an unnamed force that his Holiness named 'the fallen'.

'How do you know it was an assassination? The news reports say it was a heart attack,' said Father Thomas.

'I know. Because I was there when it happened.' The looks on the others' faces was a mixture of surprise and suspicion. Father Michael continued, 'As soon as I was sure that it was the Antichrist, I made haste to the pontiff's side. As it is written, 'The last of the blessed leaders will be slain.' His Holiness told me of the ill that had infected the inner sanctum of the Vatican, and that he named them 'the fallen'. There was only one that he believed was pure of heart. A Cardinal Pius, who also died of a heart attack that same night.' He looked about at the Brethren as he said, 'Do you still doubt me?'

His question was met by silence.

'Good. It was upon sipping a drink during our meeting that the heart attack occurred. It was almost instant. I researched the possibility of a poison that can induce a heart attack and yet be undetectable. Apparently, there are at least three chemicals available over the Internet. And we must assume that the new pontiff Pope John, formerly Cardinal Jiovani, is one of them.'

Father Alfred gasped. 'The pontiff! Sacre bleu.'

Father Thomas's eyes narrowed as his suspicious mind read more into Father Michael's tale. 'You seem to know a lot about these poisons. What if you were the one to administer that poison?'

Father Michael just glared at Father Thomas before saying, 'Why would I claim that his Holiness was assassinated, when you all were told otherwise?' He paused for a moment before continuing, 'For now I am the only one you can trust.' Father Michael gave time for his words to sink in, then stated, 'We have all been chosen for this task. If there is one thing you can trust, trust God's judgement.'

'Our adversary is the most evil in human history, and only with our total and utter devotion to the cause and each other do we have even the slightest hope of succeeding. My brothers, let us cast out all doubt before it eats out the heart of the Brethren. We must not let such ill infiltrate us before we even start. I am more than willing to take a back step and another direct the Brethren. How about you Father Thomas?'

Father Thomas was less than keen to direct the Brethren, and Father Michael's words and logic were enough for him to begin to trust. 'Forgive my doubt Father Michael. My fear of the future has clouded my judgement. I do not yearn for the role and you are, in my mind, more than suitable to direct us.'

Father Michael continued, 'I too fear what is ahead. But we can use the fear to our advantage by ensuring that our decisions are without haste and free of imperfection. What of our young colleagues that await us? Father Paul, in your opinion is Father Stephen worthy of this most grievous of tasks?'

'In my opinion, yes.'

'And you Father Thomas; what of Father Peter?'

'I chose him because of his inner strength, and at times he humbles me. Yes, he is.'

'Father Hans?'

'Father Emil is worthy, otherwise I would have not chosen him.'

'My brothers, not only must they be worthy, but ready. So be careful in your decision.'

'Father Alfred? What of Father Rene?'

'I am not long for this world. Our task could span many years and I fear I will not still be here to fight the good fight. Ready or not, Father Rene is to be part of the Brethren.'

Father Michael announced, 'Good, then bring them in.'

****

In the small courtyard, the four apprentices waited. They presided near a low stone wall that bounded a ten metre drop to a lower level of the monastery, and beyond was the pristine valley. Each gazed in silence at the picturesque view, not knowing what to say to the other, or if they should say anything at all.

For Father Stephen, silence was not one of his virtues and eventually the sound of his voice filled the crisp morning air around them. 'So, what do you think they are talking about?' His question was not directed at anyone in particular. He only wanted the silence to stop.

'Most likely they are talking about us,' replied Father Peter as the cobblestone courtyard managed to reflect some of the resonance from his voice. 'Deciding if we are worthy of full induction into the Brethren.'

'My question is, is the induction a privilege or a curse?' Father Rene proposed more than questioned in his best English.

Father Emil stood erect as he spoke in an almost military style. 'For myself it would the greatest honour, and a cause that I would die for.' His clarity was impaired by his heavy Swiss accent, though it was refined enough for them all to comprehend.

'I'm glad one of us is keen,' said Father Stephen. 'I for one am not so enthusiastic about fighting the Antichrist head on. To experience the end of the world from a remote monastery is more my idea of fighting evil.' Father Stephen's hazel eyes peered back out upon the valley. Beneath his eyes was a substantial nose brandishing long, thin nostrils and underneath was a pair of thin, pink lips. His full crop of brown hair appeared more ginger in the direct sunlight, while his fair skin looked as white as snow. His youthful visage was showing the first signs of ageing as he was now in his mid-thirties.

'Be a coward if that is what you are. I for one have no fear as God is on my side.' The usual first impression of Father Emil is that of one who just stepped out of a time machine from Hitler's Third Reich. His fine Aryan appearance of fair hair, blue eyes, square jaw line, and tall stature, would confuse most especially when he announced that he was a priest.

'Coward he may be, though what the future holds for us would terrify the bravest. I too am not as, how you say, enthusiastic,' Father Rene said as he glanced at the large Arian with his dark brown eyes before returning his attention to the scenery. His raven coloured hair was highlighted with a few streaks of grey, providing an inclination to his fifty years of age. His small nose adorned a pale face and beneath was a mouth with full red lips. His stature was lean and small compared to those around him, though he had an indescribable presence that raised his standing to that of a much taller man.

'I'm with the locals on this one. I agree that we will be heading straight for certain doom, but I'm not one for standing around and waiting for the big bad guy to take over. I say we hit him quick and hard before he gains too much power.' Father Peter was not as tall as Father Emil though his physique was larger and stockier. His thick crop of brown hair and youthful features made it evident that he was the youngest among them. His slightly bent nose suggested his keen involvement with the local rugby team, as sport was a passion of his. Two clear blue eyes peered from beneath a strong brow, providing a contrast to the rest of his tough features.

Father Rene looked over at the maverick before him. 'Most of us will probably die in the attempt and in ways unimaginable. Our local brother may have the opportunity to prove that he is true to his word. However, if they grant me the opportunity to fight the Antichrist, I will still stand up and be counted. It is one war, no matter how terrible, that I will fight blindly.'

A voice from behind broke their attention on the conversation. 'Come inside, all of you,' shouted Father Paul from the narrow doorway. The four apprentices walked over to the doorway and entered the chapel. Within they found the rest of the Brethren waiting for them. They had formed a semicircle and the apprentices felt urged to complete the circle by standing opposite them. When the circle was completed, Father Michael addressed the newcomers. 'We have discussed your future in the Brethren and your mentors have nominated you all as suitable members. You are, under no circumstances, committed in any way to join our crusade. If you choose, you may leave now, and any connection between you and the Brethren will be terminated. You may live out the rest of your lives as if we never met. Although, you are still bound to the secrecy of the existence of the Brethren. No one outside this room is to know of our existence.'

'If you choose to join the Brethren, it will be final. You cannot change your mind later. Your service will be of the highest honour bestowed upon a papal since the foundation of the church. God has guided all of us to this point and we must trust in his judgement. Your task ahead will be the gravest and your very souls will be put to the test from here on in. So, make your decision wisely. We do not expect you to make your decision right now. You can give your answer tomorrow morning after breakfast. Unfortunately, we cannot wait any longer than that.'

Father Emil stepped forward first. His stance was in a military style of attention as he proudly spoke out. 'I made my decision many years ago and have been waiting for this day ever since. I accept your offer.'

'Father Emil, is it?' Asked Father Michael. He needed no introduction to the apprentices as their accents revealed their identities.

'Yes.'

'Are you certain of your choice?'

'Yes.'

Father Peter was next to step forward. 'Count me in.'

'Father Peter, are you certain of your choice?'

'This task may take many years and if that is the case the Brethren will need some youth on its side. Yes, I am very certain.'

Father Rene stepped forward and said, 'My brother has a point. Father Alfred will need a successor and thus my service is essential.' All eyes turned to Father Stephen as Father Michael said, 'Father Stephen, don't feel pressured to make your decision now. Please take your time.'

Father Stephen looked around at the Brethren and considered the minds behind the faces. He said, 'I see a group of foolish old men leading a few younger fools into the claws of Satan.'

Father Paul's jaw dropped. 'Father Stephen …'

Father Stephen put his hand up and interrupted his mentor. 'Wait, I haven't finished. The Brethren will need someone with some common sense and a sense of self-preservation to keep the rest of you in check. I could not live with myself if you all died on the first foolish attempt that you all haphazardly threw together. My service is more than essential, it is vital to the survival of the Brethren. Count me in.'

A smile grew on Father Michael's face as he said, 'Good to have your level head on our team Father Stephen.'

Father Paul's scowl faded to a more subdued expression as his offence to Father Stephen's opening words was marginally vanquished. 'Welcome brothers to the fellowship of the Brethren,' announced Father Michael. 'Now we are ten. To bring you all up to speed, the Antichrist is alive and living in Jerusalem. He is seventeen years old. The Pope's death was, as I have revealed, an assassination. The Vatican is infected by a group named 'the fallen', and I believe they are responsible for the pontiff's murder.' He gave no time for the apprentices to react to his revelations. 'The question now is, where do we go from here?'

'Assassinate the Antichrist,' Father Hans said confidently.

Father Stephen was next to express his ideals. 'We must have a contingency plan. It would be foolish of us to think we could avert the course of history by killing the Antichrist. That's if he can be killed by mortal weapons.'

'Father Stephen has a point. Especially about the mortality of the Antichrist,' announced Father Paul, feeling more confident in his apprentice.

'If we can alert the right people in the political circle, we could at least control his level of power,' stated Father William.

'But how are we going to tell these people without sounding like a group of crackpots?' retorted Father Thomas.

'Even if we initially appear to be, how you say, crackpots, the idea will be planted.' Father Rene paused as he gathered his thoughts. 'For example, if I were to reveal to you that one of us was a murderer, you would outwardly dismiss the claim as ridiculous. But within, there would always be some doubt. And if some evidence were to indicate the rumour as true, the doubt would grow to suspicion. It may be enough.'

'Who shall we tell?' asked Father Alfred.

'The president of the United States would be a good start,' suggested Father Michael.

'The president of the United Nations?' added Father Hans.

Father William retorted, 'Actually, the presidents may not be such a good choice. Presidents are in office for only a short period of time. We need someone in a career position, like a senior member of the Central Intelligence Agency.'

'Good point. Who else?' Father Michael asked.

'A Senior member of MI6,' said Father Paul.

'Yes. What about Russia?'

Father Emil replied, 'We could contact a high-level secret police officer.'

'How are we going to make contact with them?' asked Father Stephen.

After a moment of silence, Father Peter said, 'One of my old school friends is, or was, a bit of a computer hacker. He might be able to help us contact them and still remain anonymous.'

'Sounds like a lead,' Father Michael replied before changing the course of the meeting. 'Now, how are we going to stop the Antichrist?'

His question was met by silence until Father Hans asked Father Michael, 'Do you know if the Antichrist has ever been injured?'

'To my knowledge, no.'

'Does he have any sentinels in place yet?' asked Father Emil.

'At least one. It is in the form of a large black dog.'

'I believe he can at least be injured by mortal weapons,' announced Father Alfred as he kept his focus upon the crucifix on the altar beyond the ring.

Father Hans queried his revelation. 'And what do you base this upon?'

'Two things: one, he requires the protection of sentinels and two, it was revealed to me during my visitation,' retorted Father Alfred.

Father Michael looked around at the Brethren before he stated, 'I too have had a visitation. Has anyone else?' As his eyes scanned the group, his gaze was met by a succession of nods.

'Our visitations are what set us apart from the others, and those visions may contain vital information. Now I believe is the time to put our cards on the table. I will start. My visitation told me I would be approached by a man who would lead me to the Antichrist.' He looked to his left to indicate he was finished and the next to take over.

Father Paul said, 'My visitation revealed to me that I would have to do what is unjust to achieve the just cause.'

'My visitation revealed that I must not lose hope even when man is on the edge of extinction,' Father William said calmly.

'My visitation revealed to me the message, *the guardians will fall under the honed cross cleansed by the holy spirit*. However, I am at a loss as to what it means,' Father Hans added.

'I believe I can help with that,' replied Father Michael. 'Correct me if I am wrong, but the guardians represent the sentinels. The phrase, 'cleansed by the holy spirit' refers to the cleansing by holy water, and the honed cross could be a crucifix shaped to form a knife.'

'Ah, of course!' exclaimed Father Hans. 'That has baffled me for decades. I was never good with cryptic messages.'

'Here is a cryptic message for you all,' announced Father Thomas. 'Alas the cause will be in vain, though still necessary. Do not lose hope.' He looked at Father Michael then the others for a solution.

'Was there any indication as to the cause?' questioned Father Michael.

'No.' He looked around again before saying, 'Does it mean that we will fail?'

'Then why send us on a task that is doomed?' queried Father William.

'It does say that the cause is still necessary. So, whatever the outcome, the need for its deployment is still important,' Father Rene added.

'We can discuss this in detail later. In the meantime, let us move on,' instructed Father Michael.

'You already know of the subject of mine. The power of the beast is without mortal measure, but to walk the upon the earth is to be mortal,' Father Alfred said as he dismissed himself.

'My visitation revealed this—impetuosity will feature among your brothers. Let providence be your name.' Father Stephen paused to look around at his colleagues before continuing. 'Now you know why I have chosen to be in the Brethren.'

'I think we all know the meaning of your message Father Stephen,' Father Michael added.

The look upon Father Emil's face became very grim as he said, 'Doubt will test your faith. Let not his lies temper your resolve, for your path ahead will be arduous.'

The Brethren all stared at Father Peter to compel him to announce his prophecy. Peter cleared his throat then said, 'In the end, the last of the brothers will stand against the beast. His cause, though in vain, will bring unity to the apocalypse and prepare the world for what is to be. Be strong of heart and faith, for the Lord is with you.' Silence met his prophecy.

The Brethren stared upon each other as the words sank into their baffled minds. Eventually, Father Stephen broke the silence. 'So, we are all about to embark on a crusade where only one of us will make it to the end. And to top it off, it will all be for nothing. Sounds fun!' he retorted sarcastically.

'Our crusade may be in vain but our actions are not,' Father Michael countered.

Father Peter added, 'Our actions must have some significant effect on future events, and that effect is necessary for God's plan to unfold.'

'We must proceed no matter how futile our task,' announced Father Emil in his usual totalitarian way.

Father Stephen's eyes narrowed at Father Emil. Was it he that his prophecy was directed at? He wished it were one of the old members of the Brethren, at least they had the excuse of old people's single mindedness. It was then that a new thought popped into his mind he felt worth sharing. 'It did say in *The Secret Book of Saint John* that the beast's reign would last one score and seven?'

'Yes,' said Father Michael. 'For several us, old age will take our lives well before the end of the apocalypse. It may be that it will take us the full seventeen years to execute our plan to stop the Antichrist, but I hope that we can deliver our solution quicker than that.'

Father Alfred then deduced, 'And who can say when his rule starts. Is it from birth? Or is it when he reaches full power? And when would that be?'

Father William scanned the Brethren before announcing, 'This crusade will take time and will be costly. Without the direct support of the Vatican, how do we hope to find the funds?'

'Good point Father William,' injected Father Alfred. 'And as you say Father Michael, the beast, though mortal, is in the possession of unearthly powers. My question is, what are they and how do we overcome them?'

'Father Michael, your friend died just by looking upon the beast,' Father Rene declared before continuing, 'We must find a way to protect ourselves from his evil.'

Father Michael removed an envelope from his jacket pocket before saying, 'A few days after the murder of our good friend, I received this letter. It is from Julius.' He opened the letter and began to read it.

'My dear friend, I hope all is well and life is good in our Lord's homeland. Unfortunately, things are not so good here. Several cardinals have become drunk with greed and power, and we few of clear mind have chosen to apply an appropriate name for them, 'the fallen'. The fallen are gaining in numbers and power, and despite being the pontiff, I am regretfully powerless to stop it. It is spreading like a disease throughout this once decent establishment. I fear that one night soon I will not wake to see the sun rise again over the Vatican. A long time ago I had a dream that warned me of this. An angel appeared in my dream and conveyed many terrible things that were to unfold and what I should do.

This letter I write to you is what should have been delivered to the new pontiff after my natural passing, but I doubt that my death in this current environment would be anything but. In the event that something untoward should happen to me and to the dear Cardinal Pius, who I believe will be my successor, I have instructed my contacts outside the Vatican to have this letter sent to you instead of the next pontiff. I have also instructed that the original of The Secret Book of Saint John be destroyed to withhold its revelations from the fallen. If you have this letter, then my wishes have been carried out, and I dare say, I have met an untimely end.

For in my dream, I was warned that I would witness the fall from grace of the Church, and it would signal the coming of the beast. Please pass onto the Brethren this: My brothers, you must leave your churches and go into hiding. The beast will seek you out to destroy you, for you are the few that actually threaten him. And to do this you will need finances. For the past several hundred years, each pontiff has been secretly building a nest egg to help the Brethren fight the beast. I dare say it would be quite a sum by now. You will need to go to the Swiss National Bank in Geneva in Rue François-Diday Street. The account to access is in the name of the Brethren, account number is one and the password is my nickname for you, Father Michael, when we were much younger. Ah to be young again. The beast is not without his special talents and to thwart him you will need to be extra vigilant. In my dream was a clue as to how to combat his unnatural skills.

Now would be a good time to reveal to you what was in my dream. The church that the faithful have built in the Lord's name will fall from grace before you, and your reign will be the last of those that serve the Lord. For the beast has come to corrupt the world. Folly is the task set upon your brothers, but the task is the will of the Lord most high. Powerful and cunning is the beast and to face such evil is the purest of bravery, but the beast is not without weakness. The prophecy of John that remains concealed, disguises what your brothers seek. Three, seven and ten hold the key. The beast fears only those that hold the key, and those that hold the key will be sought and destroyed. Be strong through this darkest of times for the Lord is with you. In the end, all will be as it is written. Well my brothers, that is all and I pray it is enough to get you all started on this most holy of crusades. God bless you all. Your friend and pontiff, Julius.'

Father Michael returned the letter to its envelope and put it back in his pocket. 'Julius has come to our rescue.'

'We were at college together. I do miss his dry sense of humour,' announced Father Hans.

'We will all miss him,' added Father Thomas. 'We were on a mission together for four years in Ethiopia providing food for the homeless. I feel that if any modern Pope were to be declared a saint, it would be Julius.'

'He was my student many years ago,' proclaimed Father Alfred. 'He was a bit mischievous but had a sharp mind and a good heart. He was one of my favourite students.'

'Where do we go from here?' queried Father Rene to the rest of the Brethren.

Father William injected, 'We should strike as soon as possible before he is too powerful. I don't fancy waiting around to the end.'

'I cannot agree more,' Said Father Michael before continuing, 'I will go to Geneva to investigate this account.'

'I will join you,' said Father Hans. 'You will need a local who can speak Swiss.'

'I think we should always travel in pairs,' declared Father Peter. 'And from here on in we should disappear from society and become invisible. Break all ties with our past but leave our past in a way that won't attract attention.' Father Peter looked around at the elders that surveyed him and met their stares. 'You all heard Pope Julius. We must go into hiding immediately. The beast will soon be after us. I also feel that we should separate. All of us in one place gives the beast the opportunity to finish us all in one move. We must find a way to communicate and yet not lead to our whereabouts. The Al-Qaeda cells have been an effective system and one that I think we should adopt.'

Father Peter's speech left the Brethren silent. It was moments before Father Michael spoke. 'Father Peter, you have surprised us all.
Your youth is apparently no measure of your wisdom. I for one am in agreement with your proposal. Father Stephen, as our resident sanity check, what are your thoughts on Father Peter's proposal?'

Father Stephen carefully considered the plan of attack before saying, 'Father Peter has an excellent grasp on the situation we are in and has a good proposal. The terrorist cell methodology is a very successful one and a good way forward. And may I say, a good irony.'

'To fight evil with its own devise, very clever Father Peter, very clever,' added Father William.

Father Michael then concluded, 'But before we can all disappear, we need funds. May I suggest that first Father Hans and I go and see what dear Julius has for us. And while we are gone, you can work on the game plan.'

Father William added, 'I feel that we are safe for the moment, and we should take this time to prepare ourselves as best possible for once we are in hiding, communication will be difficult.'

'Are we in agreement?' announced Father Michael. He scanned the circle and watched each of the Brethren nod. 'Good. Come Father Hans, we have a gift to collect.'

4

The Oldest Bank Account

Geneva, Switzerland

Later that day, Father Michael and Father Hans were walking down *Rue François-Diday* Street in Geneva's city centre, looking for the Swiss National Bank. As they came to a street corner, Father Hans pointed to the recently renovated, two-storey building opposite them and said, 'There it is.'

They crossed the street and entered the building. The foyer was very modern in its decor but the walls contradicted the twenty-first century refurbishment. The walls were adorned with 18th century features that had been renovated and repainted in an attempt to match the rest of the modern design. The main contrasting features were two marble busts of dignitaries from times past.

Their shoes clicked on the new stone floor as they approached the queue for the teller. They waited patiently for the lady who was already at the counter, to finished being served. A moment later, she walked away from the teller and Father Michael and Father Hans approached.

'Guten Tag,' said the teller in a rather robotic tone.

Father Hans spoke to the teller in Swiss. 'Hello, we would like to check the balance of an account.'

'Certainly Sir, do you have your key card?' she replied politely.

'Sorry, no,' Father Hans replied.

'That's ok Sir, what is your account number and the account name?'

Father Hans glanced back at Father Michael before replying to the teller, 'The account number is one and it is in the name of The Brethren.' The teller looked up from the monitor at the two men before her and noticed they were wearing collars of the clergy. She then said, 'Sir, the account number is an eight-digit number.'

Father Hans turned back to Father Michael and translated, 'She said the account number has to be eight digits.'

'Eight digits!' exclaimed Father Michael with a perplexed look on his face. He thought for a moment then said, 'Maybe the account number is seven zeros followed by a one?'

Father Hans turned back to the teller and counted with his fingers while saying, 'Try zero zero zero zero zero zero zero one.'

The teller looked back at the two priests in dismay before saying, 'Okay then. Account number zero zero zero zero zero zero zero one!' She typed in the number and pressed enter. Her eyes widened and her mouth gaped open as she stared at the monitor. To her amazement, the details for account number one were before her. 'Well how about that? Account number one!' Her eyes scanned the screen to where she read a special note. 'Excuse me Sir, I will be back in a moment.' The teller disappeared around the corner and a moment later reappeared with a middle-aged, balding man in tow. The two stared at the screen for a moment then looked up at the two priests before them.

The balding man peered intently at them from over his small spectacles before saying, 'Just one moment gentlemen.' He disappeared around the corner again, leaving the teller staring at them. A click sounded from the wall to their left and the balding man appeared from behind a door. He approached Father Hans and stretched out his right hand before saying, 'I am the branch manager Mr Stein.'

Father Hans shook his hand and asked, 'Is there a problem?'

Mr Stein then shook Father Michael's hand as he replied, 'On the contrary, this is a great honour. Please come with me.' He led them up the old sweeping staircase to the second floor of the building. The second floor was sectioned into a few small offices and other office amenities. Mr Stein then led them to the largest office and sat behind a large antique desk. He gestured at the two seats facing the desk as he said, 'Please take a seat.' He took a deep breath before saying, 'I cannot tell you how excited I am. If only my grandfather was here ...'

Before he could continue, Father Hans cut him off. 'Sorry Mr Stein, do you speak English? My friend does not speak Swiss.'

'English it is then,' he replied in English with a strong accent. He leaned in a little closer as he continued. 'Five years at the London office.

But before we can begin, we have to make sure you are the rightful account holders.' After a few button clicks of the mouse attached to the computer terminal on the desk, he turned the monitor and keyboard around to face the two priests. 'Please enter the password.'

Father Michael leaned forward and typed in the word 'Romeo', then pressed enter. Father Hans looked at Father Michael in surprise. Father Michael turned to him and said quietly, 'I wasn't always a man of the cloth.'

Mr Stein turned the screen and keyboard back to him and checked the details. All was in order. He let out a brief gasp before stating, 'I don't believe it! I never thought I would live to see the day.'

Father Michael and Father Hans glanced at each other before Father Michael asked, 'We don't understand what all the fuss is about?'

Mr Stein looked puzzled. 'You don't know?'

'Know what?' replied Father Hans.

Mr Stein continued, 'How could you not know?'

Father Michael felt it was time to add some explanation. 'The account was a gift.'

'From a good friend,' added Father Hans.

Mr Stein sat at his desk stunned. His mouth remained gaping until he announced, 'Are you telling me that someone just gave you the oldest bank account in the world?' The two priests nodded. 'Just like that, just gave it to you?' They nodded again. His eyes narrowed for a moment then he asked, 'I don't believe I have your names?'

They glanced at each other before Father Hans said, 'I am Father Hans, and my colleague is Father Michael.'

Mr Stein stared for a moment then sat back in his chair. 'Well you do have full access to the account, and why am I so surprised considering the account's history? Have I got a story for you …'

Mr Stein leaned forward and made himself comfortable to tell his apparently exciting story.

'Sometime during the fifteenth century, the first bank account was opened in the oldest bank in the world, Banca Monte dei Paschi di Siena. It is unknown who opened the account as there were few records kept during those days, but when they did start keeping records in the sixteenth century, this account was given the number 'one'. We can't be sure it was

the first account but must have been the oldest account at the time. Every month a moderate sum was deposited into the account and rarely by the same person, but usually by a member of the Vatican clergy. This obviously gave rise to the theory that it was the personal account of the Pope. In all that time no one ever withdrew funds, never in four hundred years! Totally unprecedented. And made it impossible to determine the owner of the account. But we could not close the account as the account was always active through the deposits. And while it was open, the bank could profit from the balance through using the collateral for trade.

Then in 1941, during the second world war, the account was moved from the Banca Monte dei Paschi di Siena to this very branch of the Swiss National Bank by none other than President Mussolini. Now that threw the Pope theory into turmoil. However, it is well documented that Pope Pius XII was well acquainted with Mussolini and could have requested Mussolini to move it for him. It was no surprise that the account was moved to here as little was safe in Italy during the war. It was my grandfather that was approached to create the account here and of course, given the account's history, he ensured the account number remained as number one. And here it has remained for the past eighty years. Every month, without fail, a moderate deposit was made by persons who are certainly not connected directly with the account, until today.'

Mr Stein paused for a moment to give time for his story to be digested. He then asked, 'So gentlemen, can you please lay to rest once and for all the mystery of account number one. Is this the personal bank account of the Pope?' He stared with great apprehension at the two priests before him.

The two priests stared back, silent. After an uncomfortable pause, Father Michael broke the silence. 'The account belongs to those whom the account is in the name of—The Brethren.' Father Hans flicked Father Michael's leg with his hand in a way as not to alert Mr Stein, but to convey his approval of Father Michael's answer.

Mr Stein stared at them for an unbearable length of time. Finally, he asked, 'And who is the Brethren?'

Father Hans replied, 'We are.'

The look on Mr Stein's face was one of frustration and disappointment. He knew they would not reveal any more to him. 'Well,

I wasn't born yesterday, and I can tell when I have reached the end of the line. Mind you, it does leave a nice air of mystery, don't you think?'

The two priests looked at each other for a moment before gazing back at Mr Stein. Mr Stein decided to move things on from the stalemate. 'I suppose you want to know the account balance?'

'That is what we came here for,' stated Father Hans.

Mr Stein pressed a button on the keyboard then turned the screen around to display it to the new account owners.

The two priests leaned forward to view the account balance. Father Hans squinted at the screen in an attempt to focus on the digits, and in frustration he said, 'I cannot work out how much that is. Is it one hundred thousand?'

Mr Stein leaned forward and replied, 'No Father Hans, it is one hundred million!'

The two priests looked up at Mr Stein, wearing expressions of utter shock. They looked at each other as Father Michael let out, 'Holy mother Mary of ...!' Father Hans gasped, 'All the blessed saints!'

Mr Stein turned the monitor back to him and stated, 'One hundred and three million, seven hundred and fifteen thousand, eight hundred and twelve euros and ten cents to be precise. Gentlemen, you are now millionaires!'

'Millionaires!' stated Father Michael in continued disbelief.

'What on earth are we to do with that much money?' added Father Hans.

Mr Stein was quick to reply, 'We do provide some very effective investment plans.'

The shock soon began to fade as Father Michael's practical mind took hold. 'Mr Stein, would you please excuse us for a moment? I would like to have a private word with my colleague.'

Mr Stein replied with a quick nervous smile, 'Certainly gentlemen, I will be in the next office if you need me.' He stood up and left the office, closing the door behind him.

A soon as they were alone, Father Hans turned to Father Michael and asked with a gasp, 'What on earth are we going to do with that much money? We don't need a hundred million. Let's give most of it to our charities.'

'Hans, I would love to give it all away, but we don't know yet what we need to stop you know who. And we don't know how long it will take. It could take decades.'

Father Hans stared at Father Michael for a moment and soon his posture stooped as the realisation of the weight of responsibility fell on his shoulders. 'I suppose you're right.'

Father Michael continued. 'We need to break the money up into separate accounts for each of us. Then we can talk with the others to see what to do next.'

The anxiety of the situation was taking its toll on Father Hans. He felt overwhelmed. He hadn't the strength to argue and so, he nodded in agreement. 'Okay.' He thought for a moment then said, 'We cannot create accounts for the others as we do not have all their details.'

'You are right, we have to create the accounts in our names,' concluded Father Michael. 'But we have ten accounts to create and there are only two of us, so five each.'

'Not if we keep account number one,' stated Father Hans.

Father Michael considered the idea then said, 'Too risky. The fallen could trace the account to us. We must cover our tracks.' Father Hans nodded in agreement and Father Michael continued, 'So, five each?'

Father Hans retorted, 'Just one account is enough to make me woozy.'

'Okay, I will go and get him.' Father Michael got up and left to go and find Mr Stein. A moment later, the two returned to the office cubical and seated themselves as before. Father Michael said, 'We would like to open some new accounts.'

'Sure, how many accounts, two?' replied Mr Stein, adding his assumption.

'Ten,' returned Father Michael.

'Ten!' Mr Stein said it so loud that it was almost a shout. He could see that they were serious about their request, so he continued with a business-like demeanor. 'Ten accounts it is then. Who shall I make the account out to?'

'Five accounts to me and five to Father Hans, and we would like the funds evenly distributed among them.'

Mr Stein looked concerned as he asked, 'So what do you want to do with the old account?'

'Close it,' replied Father Michael.

Mr Stein's eyes widened. 'Close it! You can't close the oldest bank account in the world. This bank's reputation has been built around this account.' His aggression quickly subsided and it was replaced with a more subservient tone. 'Please don't close it. Is there something I could do to change your mind?'

Father Michael glanced at Father Hans before saying, 'On one condition. You delete the records of the transactions to the new accounts.'

Mr Stein glared at them as he said, 'But that is against the law and I could lose my job!'

'Fine, then close the account,' Father Michael said sternly.

Mr Stein continued his glare as his eyes darted between the two priests. An uncomfortable moment later, his demeanor stooped and he relinquished. 'Okay, okay, you win. I'll blame it on a computer error. It wouldn't be the first time we have lost data. But to keep the account open, a small balance will need to remain, say ten euros?'

The two priests looked at each other and shrugged. Then Father Hans replied, 'That sounds okay.'

'Okay then, let's get to it,' stated Mr Stein.

Some thirty minutes later, the accounts were created, and the transfers made. Mr Stein announced, 'There you go gentlemen, all done. Now is there anything else I can help you with?'

'No, I think that will be all,' said Father Hans confidently as he looked at Father Michael before turning back to Mr Stein.

Mr Stein stood up and extended his hand. 'Good. Well gentlemen it has been a pleasure meeting you and a pleasure doing business.' After shaking hands, he continued, 'Let me escort you to the door.'

As they left the bank, Father Michael asked, 'So Hans, how does it feel to be a multi-millionaire?'

'To be honest, I want to throw up!'

5

The Secret Book of Saint John

Near Salzburg, Switzerland

'Three, seven and ten hold the key?' stated Father Thomas as he paced back and forth in the chapel.

Father William looked a little annoyed as he said, 'It doesn't matter how many times you say it, it won't help solve the riddle.'

Father Thomas looked up at Father William and apologised.

'Do pardon me Father William, I was never good at riddles.'

'I still think it is the position of letters,' Father Peter declared.

'But in what position?' Father William retorted. 'Vertically, horizontally, word, sentence, paragraph? The combinations are endless.'

'Well, I'm tired of just sitting around trying to figure it out,' Father Peter announced as he stood up from the old pew. 'Has anyone got a copy of the secret book with them?'

Father Alfred glared at Father Peter as he retorted, 'Dear boy, the book has remained secret because no one would be foolish enough to walk around with it in their pocket!'

A moment later, a small cough came from the mouth of Father Rene. 'Ah, I have a copy on my phone,' he announced sheepishly.

Father Alfred turned to Father Rene with a look of astonishment as he shouted, 'Sacré bleu! Are you out of your mind?'

'It is password and bio ID protected. It is safe,' replied Father Rene as he defended himself. 'Besides, even if someone were to gain access to the file, they wouldn't know what it was or of its importance.'

'But the fallen would understand its importance,' Father Alfred explained. 'And if it were to fall into their hands, they would know what we know, and they could thwart us. That is why the Brethren have kept it secret over the centuries.'

'Yes, I understand that, but the general public are so ignorant these days. I don't see them as a threat to us,' Father Rene countered.

Father Alfred started to babble under his breath in French when Father Peter interjected, 'Sorry to interrupt your debate but could I see the book.'

'Yes, yes,' Father Rene said as he pressed buttons on his smart phone and handed it to Father Peter.

Father Peter started to read the book then asked, 'Has anyone got a pen and paper?'

There was a moment of silence before Father Emil said, 'There could be some in the vestry, I will go and look.' He walked off to the rear of the chapel and a short while later returned with a pen and paper.

Father Peter accepted the pen and paper and quickly began writing. 'I'll start with the third, seventh and tenth letter in each row.' Slowly, the others began to gather around him while he sat on the pew writing out the letters. A minute later he stopped writing and had the message, 'TDBINTITBBKFGNDKSCRJFFSSDT'. Father Peter announced, 'Okay, so it's not that. How about the third seventh and tenth word?' He began writing down the words and after the tenth word he stopped. Before him he had the sentence, 'Of the Lord has beast God for thus to to'. 'Okay, so it's not that either.' He thought for a moment then said, 'How about the third word of the seventh line of the tenth verse.'

He began reading the letter for the first word when Father Alfred said, 'No it can't be that. No one verse has seven lines.'

Father Rene challenged his mentor. 'How can you be sure?'

Father Alfred looked at his apprentice and stated with great confidence, 'Because I memorised the letter.'

'All seventeen pages?' exclaimed Father Thomas.

'Of course,' replied Father Alfred in a matter-of-fact manner.

Father Peter looked at Father Alfred and said, 'Okay, so that doesn't work either.' He thought for a moment then said, 'How about the first word of every third, seventh and tenth line?'

'We could be here for weeks. I think we are wasting our time,' Father Alfred protested.

Father Paul peered over his glasses at Father Alfred as he said, 'Give the boy a chance. In my experience, persistence gets you everywhere.'

Father Peter wrote a few words, paused for a moment, then began writing more down with great vigour. Soon he stopped and sat back from the piece of paper before him. The onlookers peered down at the paper on the pew. On the paper was the message, 'The beast is most mortal when on holy ground and still no mortal weapon will penetrate. Only then can silver cleansed with the holy spirit pierce the heart of evil.'

Father Alfred started babbling in French then stopped himself and restarted in English. 'He's done it!'

Father Paul said quietly to himself, 'Here endeth the lesson.'

'On holy ground, a church!' deduced Father Rene.

'So, we need to get him into a church and then kill him with a silver bullet washed in holy water,' said Father Thomas. He then added sarcastically, 'Sounds easy.'

'I don't know about the rest of you but I have never shot a man,' Father Alfred announced. His voice was old and crackled but his speech was clear enough for his audience. 'Even if it was the Antichrist, I would find it hard to pull the trigger.'

Father Emil stood up straight as he said, 'If it were the Antichrist before me, I would pull the trigger.'

Father Peter stood next to Father Emil as he said, 'I would too.'

'Who said that we had to pull the trigger?' Father Paul crossed his arms as he continued. 'Why don't we hire a hitman?'

Father Rene was kneeling on the pew in front of Father Peter, but the hard seat began to make his knees ache. He stood up before saying, 'Good idea, but we do not have much money and I would expect a hitman would be very expensive.'

The afternoon sun filtered through the colours of the high stained glass windows across the chapel. Where the beams of coloured light cut through the warmed air, millions of dust particles danced about as if to celebrate the brief moment of sunlight exposure. At the far side of the chapel, the two-and-a-half-metre-high, right-hand entrance door creaked open. More sunlight shot into the chapel, triggering more dust to dance about in the light. Two silhouettes briskly entered.

Behind them the large door closed, and the renewed dark concealed the figures as they approached the congregation of priests. It was not until the faces of the two figures were captured by the beams of light from the stained-glass windows that the Brethren could see that it was Father Michael and Father Hans.

The two priests stopped in the middle of the aisle, then knelt briefly as they crossed themselves. When they rose to their feet again, they faced the rest of the Brethren. The congregation studied the two for signs of an indication as to what had transpired. But their examinations met conflicting expressions—one of confidence and one of fear.

Father Paul broke the silence. 'Well brothers, what news do you have of the gift of our good friend and pontiff?'

Father Hans seemed overwhelmed by some great invisible burden when he said, 'I need to sit down.' He plonked himself down on the pew opposite the others.

Father Michael glanced at Father Hans then stood erect as he announced, 'Well my brothers, we are all now multi-millionaires!' He scanned the audience for their reaction and found a series of gaping mouths and shocked expressions. He decided to continue on the path of revelation. 'Father Hans and I have created ten accounts, each with a balance of over ten million euros.' The expressions became more dire as more mouths gaped and eyes widened. Father Emil ran from the congregation to the presbytery to vomit.

Father Stephen was the first to push words from his gaping mouth. 'You did say ten million, didn't you?'

'Yes, I did,' he replied calmly.

Father Thomas and Father William crossed themselves as Father Alfred asked, 'So much money. What are we going to do with it all?'

Father Michael was quick to add, 'We have a long road ahead, and I expect we will need every euro to succeed in our crusade.

'Money is the root of all evil,' Father Paul injected. His eyes narrowed as he declared the challenge to the confident priest before him. 'Such temptation will test us all. Are you ready for it, Father Michael?'

Father Hans couldn't help but add, 'In my life I have never been in the possession of any more than a few hundred euros. To be in the possession of millions is unthinkable. I can feel its deviance already working its evil on my soul and it has only been a few hours.'

Father Alfred sat down on the pew and said, 'Think of how many people we could help with this money—charities, missions, orphanages. I say we give most of it away.'

Father Peter stood from his pew as anger boiled up within him. An expression of great fury marked his face as he bellowed:

Listen to yourselves! A few hours ago, you all stood here declaring your allegiance to the crusade against the Antichrist, and now that we have the means to fund it you are all cowering away from the task ahead! This is not some dictator; this is the Antichrist! For all we know, we could be spending the rest of our natural lives fighting this monster. I for one will be doing everything I can to foil his devise, day after day, week after week, year after year. And I absolutely will not stop, ever! We will need money to buy weapons, information, even assassins; and God knows what else. We will face far greater perils than just greed. If the thought of money scares you then you're not up to the task. He is a living, breathing, real life monster. Billions are foretold to die under his reign, and all you can focus on is the few. We need to do far more than just help the needy, we need to save the whole world!'

He pushed past the gathering and stormed up to the dais. He fell to his knees before the gold crucifix on the table.

As Father Emil returned wiping his chin with a towel, Father Thomas felt the need to speak up after his apprentice's outburst. 'I must apologise, he can get a little hot-headed.'

'I could not agree more with Father Peter,' announced Father Michael. 'Our path ahead is unknown and will be no doubt costly.' Father Peter turned his head slightly and looked over his shoulder to listen. 'I believe that the Lord has answered our prayers and granted us this gift, and this gift is no more and no less than what we need to get the job done.' Father Michael's eyes scanned the Brethren and he looked into the eyes of each as he continued. 'Every cent is needed. Not one is to be wasted. We will not be giving anything away until the job is done. And we will continue to live as we have done. Not like millionaires but like ordinary middle-class people. We must blend in and disappear.' He walked over to Father Peter and stretched out his hand to him. 'Forgive us Father Peter, we just need a little time to adjust.'

Father Peter looked up at Father Michael to let him see the frustration fade away. He then took his hand and let Father Michael help him to his feet.

Father Michael turned back to the Brethren and continued, 'Remember what our dear friend Julius told us, we must leave the church and become civilians. We will no longer be servants of the church, but we will still be servants of God. We may even need to get a job to help us blend in.' Father Hans and Father Alfred looked at each other to study their expressions of dismay. Neither had known anything except life in the church. 'And Father Peter is correct. I have seen the beast with my own eyes. As it is written in *The Secret Book of Saint John*, only with my eyes cleansed by holy water can I see the beast for what he truly is. This adversary is like nothing we have battled in the past. His power is truly not of this earth. From here on in, we need to become archangels. So, Father Paul, Father Alfred, Father Hans, are you up to embarking on the crusade?' As Father Michael spoke each of their names, he looked squarely into each of their eyes, meeting each of their stares.

Father Paul looked down his long nose and over his glasses at Father Michael as he stated, 'Yes brother, I am up to the task.'

Father Michael stared at Father Alfred. Father Alfred stood erect for a moment as he said, 'Wealth does not tempt me, but to live outside the church is beyond me. I have been a monk for most of my life and I know little else.'

Father Rene put his hand on Father Alfred's shoulder. 'Dear Teacher, I have learnt so much from you. Now I can return the favour. I will help you in your new life.'

Father Alfred looked up, smiled briefly and said, 'Okay then. It will be hard, but I am willing to try. As Father Peter said, the whole world is depending on us, not just those in need.

Father Michael turned around to face Father Hans. The others followed his gaze. Father Hans was still seated on the pew with his head bowed but soon realised everyone was watching him. He looked up for a moment to confirm their stares then bowed his head again. 'I left the world behind and sought the sanctuary of the church to protect myself from my own weakness. There, money was scarce and so my weakness could not take hold. I lost everything. Day after day I would gamble, always hoping for the big win that would save me. Of course, it never came.' He stared up at the afternoon sunrays beaming though the dusty air above. The Brethren could just make out the tears that welled up in the corners of his eyes from behind his thick, brown glasses. 'My dearest Angelica. She put up with me for two years until my weakness broke her heart, then it broke mine. After she left, I lost my job, and I began to drink heavily. I was penniless, then homeless. It was then that I found the church, or should I say, it found me. And then God saved me, and so I devoted the rest of my life to him.' Father Hans looked squarely at Father Michael. 'But my weakness still plagues me, every day. I cannot be trusted with this money.'

Father Emil kneeled down before him and met his gaze. He said quietly, 'I too owe so much to you. You have been like a father to me, the father I should have had. I have no temptation of money. I will look after the money for both of us. It will be an honour.'

Father Hans smiled for a moment, then put his hand on Father Emil's shoulder. 'Thank you, dear boy. You cannot trust me, not even for a moment. Are you sure you want to do this?'

'Very sure,' replied Father Emil.

Father Hans stared into his eyes for a moment then nodded. 'With the help of Father Emil, I will defeat my weakness and serve the crusade as I promised.'

Father Michael smiled and patted Father Hans on the shoulder. 'Very good Father Hans, very good.'

Father William, having had remained seated though much of the recent events, stood as he asked, 'Well, if we are to separate, then we need a means of communication without revealing our identities.'

'Good point Father William,' stated Father Stephen. 'Any ideas?' he asked of the congregation.

'What about email?' said Father Rene. 'It is virtually anonymous, and it is free. If we use a global service like *myMail*, it would be hard to determine where we are living.'

'Sounds like a plan,' concluded Father Thomas.

'Does anyone have any better ideas?' Father Michael asked. He looked around and was met with silence and head shakes. 'Well, email it is.'

'I can create the accounts on my phone. That way we know what the addresses are,' added Father Rene.

Father Paul peered over his glasses as he asked in a facetious tone, 'Does your phone also make a nice cup of tea?'

Father Rene glared at Father Paul for a moment then replied, 'No but I can order one on home delivery.' He continued pressing buttons and tapping the screen with his thumbs until he stopped and asked,

'What is the address of this monastery?'

Father Hans asked, 'Why do you want to know the address?'

'I need a valid postal address, or I cannot create the accounts. And I doubt if anyone can trace us from here.'

'Good idea Father Rene,' declared Father Michael.

Father Hans produced the address like it was burned into his memory. 'Bourg-Saint-Pierre 1946 Switzerland.'

A few more thumb presses later, Father Rene asked, 'Okay, I now need some names for each email address, maybe a nickname? Father Michael, shall we start with you?' He glanced at Father Michael before returning his attention to his phone screen.

After an embarrassing pause Father Michael said, 'Romeo.'

The Brethren looked at him with stares of surprise until Father Hans announced, 'He wasn't a priest all his life you know.'

The Brethren turned their attention to the unassuming old man seated on a pew with equal surprise.

Father Rene raised his eyes from his phone screen and looked at him as well. 'Father Hans?'

Father Hans shuffled his seated position and cleared his throat before stating, 'Black hole!' His statement was met with silence.

Father Rene felt the need to clarify his chosen name as it was clear that the audience felt uncomfortable with his choice. 'Are you sure brother?'

Father Hans straightened his bent back as best as he could as he replied, 'I am what I am, and I must not forget that. It will help me keep my focus.'

Father Rene returned to his phone screen and performed another thumb dance. He paused again and made his next choice, 'Father William?'

Father William had his arms crossed as if to protect his ego as he announced. 'Popeye.' There was a pause as he gauged his audience's reaction, before explaining, 'I like spinach!'

Father Rene continued his routine then said, 'Who's next, Father Thomas?'

Father Thomas's intense brown eyes peered down at Father Rene as he said, 'Little John.'

Father Rene began his routine then stopped. 'It is already taken.'

'Well I can't use the nickname that I was given at school,' Father Thomas announced.

'How bad could it be?' asked Father William.

'Bad enough,' Father Peter declared.

Father Thomas felt the need to add some clarification. 'Little John became Just John, with my first name at the end.'

'What is so bad about John Thomas?' asked Father Emil innocently.

The English members all glared at the blank face of Father Emil until Father Peter said, 'It is a colloquial term for a man's genitals.'

Father Emil said, 'Oh!' A smile grew on his face and he let out a little snicker. The rest of the Brethren, apart from Father Thomas, were all doing their best to contain their schoolboy smirks. Father Emil's reaction broke their steely expressions and a moment later the chapel was filled with the sounds of laughter.

Father Thomas let the jocularity flow for a moment before deciding that they had all had their fill. 'Okay, okay, that's enough.' The laughter reduced to a few snickers and Father Thomas continued. 'It would appear that we are all in need of a little laughter, be it at my expense. So, Father Rene, try John Thomas, one word.'

'Are you sure brother?' Father Rene asked.

'Quick! Before I change my mind,' replied Father Thomas.

'You are in luck. John Thomas is available,' Father Rene said in a serious tone, a smirk growing across his face. Soon, a new barrage of laugher exploded from the Brethren. When the raucousness died down, Father Rene continued his routine. 'Father Alfred?'

Father Alfred was wiping away the tears of laughter from his old fading eyes when he said, 'Donkey.'

The snickering stopped dead. Father Rene looked up at his mentor and asked the question that was on all of their minds. 'It wouldn't have anything to do with the subject of Father Stephen's that gave us so much amusement?'

The Brethren was all ears. Father Alfred looked around him at his brothers and tried to focus on their blurred faces. His eyes, like his knees, were failing him but he would not accept that they needed assistance. 'No, it is because I can be rather stubborn. Though I think I am rather malleable for someone my age.'

Father Rene cleared his throat nervously to mask his true feeling on the subject. He owed a great deal to Father Alfred, but more than anyone he knew how difficult Father Alfred could be. He continued his routine of entering details via his smart phone and stopped for the details of the next email address. 'Father Peter?'

'Wallaby,' Father Peter announced.

Father Thomas and Father Peter looked at each other, then broke out in the chant, 'I wanna wanna be a walla wallaby!'

As the smile left his face, Father Thomas explained. 'Father Peter was once in the under eighteens Australian Rugby team. I wasn't into rugby much until we met and now, I too am a keen fan.'

Father Rene entered the details before announcing the next participant. 'Father Paul?'

'What was it they used to call me behind my back at college, Father Stephen?' He peered over his glasses at Father Stephen like an old school master.

Sheepishly, Father Stephen replied with the demeanor of a schoolboy in trouble. 'The Gov'ner'.

'Gov'ner will do fine Father Rene,' he declared.

'Okay, gov'ner it is.' He resumed his routine and paused once more for the next participant. 'Father Stephen?'

Father Stephen looked at Father Paul with a smile as he said, 'Father Paul can answer that for you.'

This time Father Paul replied with a warmer tone, 'Rodney!'

Several the European Brethren looked at the two of them with expressions of confusion. Father Stephen looked around and realised it needed an explanation. 'You know, Rodney, from *Only Fools and Horses*? The TV show from the eighties!' Still a number of blank faces stared at him. 'Apparently I look a bit like him.'

Father Rene continued his routine once more and stopped for the last name. 'Who is lucky last? Ah, Father Emil.

Father Emil looked rather embarrassed when he said, 'I have never had a nickname that I can recall, and I can't think of anything suitable.'

Father Hans stood and placed his hand on Father Emil's shoulder, 'Well we will have to think of one for you.'

Father Stephen was quick to the mark. 'What is *yes* in Swiss?'

'Ah, *yah*,' Father Emil answered cautiously.

'How about Yahman?' Father Stephen proposed confidently.

'Why Yahman? What does it mean?' Father Emil was cautious of the name's implication, considering recent choices of the other members.

Father Stephen didn't mean to offend Father Emil, he just felt it was a good name for him. 'Well you are such an agreeable fellow.'

Father Emil thought for a moment and studied the faces of the others for signs of disagreement but found none. He took a chance and decided to go with his first ever nickname. 'Okay, Yahman it is.' Father Rene added the name and said, 'All done.'

'Aren't you forgetting someone?' Father Michael stated.

'Who?' he asked.

'You!' Father Michael replied.

His eyes widened for a moment as he said, 'Oh, of course.' He pressed a few buttons then said, 'Napoleon.'

Father Rene looked up from his screen for a moment to see the reaction from the rest of the Brethren. The audience stared at him as they scrutinised the little French man. Quickly, their faces showed the realisation of why he chose that name. His small stature, dark hair and slight features—he was a look-a-like.

Father Stephen couldn't help not being facetious. 'Makes sense. Sure you're not related?'

Father Rene shot a look of disapproval as he replied, 'Definitely not!' He pressed more buttons then stopped as he said, 'Okay, I will email the addresses to all the email accounts so we know what they are. Best not to delete this email for future reference in case you forget an address.' Some more button presses then he announced once more, 'All done.'

'Well brothers,' Father Michael began, 'Now that we have a form of secure communication, we should remember to not use our real names or talk about where we live or what we do for a living. Especially any details on a plan to thwart the beast.'

'And I suggest not using the same computer when sending emails,' Father Rene added. 'They can be traced.

'Thank you, Father Rene. Your computer skills have been invaluable,' Father Michael said with a warm smile. 'Anything else before we separate?'

'Just one thing,' declared Father Paul. 'We are all paired with our apprentices, but you are not. May I suggest you and Father William join forces in Israel as this is the current home of the beast.'

Father William turned to Father Michael. 'How do you feel about having a guest?'

Father Michael replied with another warm smile, 'My door is always open for my brothers. It would be a pleasure.' He scanned the Brethren as he said, 'Unless there is anything else, I believe it is time for us to part our ways. We will keep in contact via the email accounts, thanks to Father Rene. Good luck my brothers, and God bless you. Shall we finish with a prayer?'

The nods from the congregation signaled the go ahead. They all bowed their heads as Father Michael continued:

Dear heavenly father most high, be with us and protect us during this crusade against the greatest evil. Give us the strength and wisdom to serve the difficult task you have set for us. Steady our hands and our resolve to do what is needed to be done. We ask this in the name of our Lord and saviour, amen.'

After raising their heads, each said goodbye to the other before quietly parting from the chapel.

6

The Crusade Begins

Sydney, Australia

At the front door of the Sydney suburban house, a hand grabbed the knocker and clanked it firmly against the door. The two figures stood quietly, listening carefully for sounds of someone coming to the front door. A moment later, there was some muffled shouting in Cantonese followed by shuffling footsteps. There was a pause before the door opened slightly and a middle-aged Chinese face peered through the narrow gap. The woman asked, 'Hello, can I help you?'

The young man before her said, 'Mrs Ho, it's Peter, Winston's friend from school.'

Mrs Ho looked Peter up and down as she tried to match the figure before her to her memory. Her expression quickly changed to a large smile and the door was flung open. 'Peter!' Mrs Ho gave him a big hug before stepping back to view all of him. 'Look at you! You have grown tawrrer.' Her eyes narrowed and her chin disappeared into her neck as she asked, 'Where your collar?'

Peter touched his neck and replied, 'We're off duty. This is a personal call. Oh, and this is Father Thomas.'

Mrs Ho smiled politely and shook Thomas's hand, which he had presented to her. 'Come in, come in. We find that troublesome boy of mine. He probably playing games on his computer.' Mrs Ho led them down a narrow hallway and up a flight of stairs. 'I tell my Winson, why can't you be more like your friend Peter? He a good boy. He became a priest!' The narrow stairway echoed her voice, making her ranting clear to the two men in tow. 'But he not listen. He want to be political instead and get in big trouble. Now he only play games and be good for nothing.'

Mrs Ho led them along a small hallway to a door on the left. From the other side of the door came muffled music. She banged on the door with her fist and shouted, 'Winson, Winson, your friend Peter here to see you! Winson, Winson!'

The muffled music faded away and was replaced with the sound of objects being shuffled about. The door was opened abruptly to reveal an Asian man in his twenties. His hair had streaks of electric blue through it and his cheeks bore faded ache scars. 'Mum, I'm not deaf.'

'How can you hear me over that racket in there without me shouting?'

They began an argument in Cantonese and after a few moments, Winston stopped and glared at Peter. 'G'day Pete!' He grabbed Peter's hand with one hand and shook it, while hugging him with the other. They separated and Winston continued, 'Mate, how long has it been, two years?' Winston spoke fluent English without any Asian accent; a product of being born and raised in Australia.

'Almost,' Peter replied. 'And this is Thomas.'

'G'day Thomas,' he said as he shook Thomas's hand.

'Nice to meet you Winston,' Thomas replied politely.

Winston directed them to his room as he said, 'Come in guys.'

Peter and Thomas walked into Winston's bedroom and he followed. Before Winston could shut the bedroom door, his mother stuck herself in the way and said to Peter, 'You talk some sense into him. Tell him to get a job.'

Winston retaliated. 'Mum I told you, I have a job.'

'That not a real job, it playing computer games. Why don't you work for your father, he give you a proper job?'

Winston put his head in his hands as he said, 'Mum, we've gone over this a thousand times!' He looked at her again and continued, 'I have a job, I like my job, and I'm not working for my dad! Ever!'

Mrs Ho glared at him for a moment before turning to Peter. 'See what he like? Maybe you can talk sense into him.' With that she stormed out of the room and shut the door.

Winston rolled his eyes before saying, 'Sorry guys.' He sat on the edge of the computer desk and gestured for them to take a seat on his bed. 'Please sit down.'

The bedroom was small with a single bed, computer workstation and a built-in wardrobe. The room was littered with dirty clothes, computer magazines and computer component boxes. Thomas and Peter pushed aside some of the litter to sit down on the bed.

'So, what are you up to these days?' Peter asked as he scanned the untidy room.

'Despite what my mum says, I have a job with a computer gaming company, bug fixing their latest games. I'm currently working on Unreal Tournament - The Beginning. Wicked game, you should have a go. How is the priesthood?'

'Good, very busy as usual,' replied Peter. He cleared his throat before saying, 'We have a favour to ask.'

Winston looked a little puzzled as he said, 'Sure.'

'Do you think it would be possible to send an email that is untraceable?' Peter looked at Winston unsure of what his reaction would be. Thomas sat quietly beside Peter, feeling comfortable not engaging in this conversation.

Winston stared at them both, puzzlement ruling his expression. 'Why would you want to send an untraceable email? You're priests!'

Peter glanced at Thomas before replying, 'We'd rather not say.'

Winston's eyes narrowed as he tried to fathom what they were up to. 'How untraceable?'

'Utterly untraceable,' Peter replied.

Winston pursued his interrogation. 'Federal police untraceable or CIA untraceable?'

Peter answered, 'Better. Hacker untraceable.'

'Hacker? I don't know what you guys are up to, but it definitely isn't kosher.' His eyes widened as an exciting thought flashed into his mind. He jumped to his feet and said, 'Wait until I tell my mum. Finally, I can get her off my back!'

Peter put his hands out as if to wipe away Winston's thought. 'No, no. You can't tell her. You can't tell anyone. Especially your mum!'

'Come on, you can't do this to me. You throw me a lifeline and you don't want me to catch it!' Winston retorted.

'Sorry mate,' Peter apologised. 'You know what your mum is like.'

Winston dropped his head and said reluctantly, 'Yeah I know. Tell my mum and the whole world will know by the end of the week.'

'Look, I promise to talk to your mum after this. See if I can take some of the heat off you,' Peter added.

'She will listen to you. Thanks,' said Winston.

Thomas knew nothing about Winston and sure had his reservations about his credibility. Knowing more about Winston's eventful past would either ease his concerns or elevate his fears. 'Ah Winston, would you mind me asking what happened that got you into so much trouble?'

Winston and Peter looked at each other with expressions of unease. Peter decided to answer but initially kept his eyes on Winston for any signal to stop. 'Winston found a loophole in the security of the servers in the Australian Secret Intelligence Office, ASIO. He repeatedly attempted to warn them, but as he was only seventeen, no one took him seriously.'

Winston decided to take over from Peter in telling his story. 'So, I used the loophole to spam their network with emails and website banners that told them their network security was crap!' Both Winston and Peter were now looking at Thomas, signifying their unity, as Winston continued. 'But despite my warnings, they didn't take too kindly to me hacking their network. Fortunately, I was too young to go to jail or they would have sent me there for a good few years. I didn't do any real damage, but I still had to do two years of community work—serious drag.'

'So, did they fix their security in the end?' Thomas asked.

'Eventually,' Winston replied. 'Their hacker experts are behind the times.'

Winston stared Peter in the eyes as he said, 'So you want to send an untraceable email? Okay, you're in luck. A loophole has been found in the core code for the management of the IP stack on most routers. A friend of mine showed me a test case only a few weeks ago. With a clever script built into the payload of the packet, you can erase the source address as you transit each router.'

Peter and Thomas looked at him with blank faces. After a lengthy pause Peter asked, 'So it can be done?'

'Yes,' Winston replied confidently.

'No chance of tracing the email?' Peter confirmed.

'Totally untraceable. I can build the script and email it to you. All you need to do is create the email, add the recipient, and run the script. It will do the rest.'

'Thanks Mate. We really appreciate your help,' added Peter as both he and Thomas stood up. 'There is one other thing. Do you have the email address for the prime minister?'

Winston stopped in his tracks and glared at them. 'What on Earth are you two up to?' He put up his hands as if to stop an invisible assailant. 'No, don't tell me. I don't want to know. And if anyone comes around asking about you two, I will deny everything. I don't want any more trouble in my life.'

Peter reassured him. 'Mate, we will treat this meeting as a confession. That way we are sworn to secrecy.'

Winston glared at Peter for a moment then said, 'Well I was going to email him about the security issue but then I decided to do you know what. When I was raided by ASIO they took my computer, but they couldn't take my memory. His personal email address is probably still good as I didn't use it. It's peter.geraldton@mymail.com.au. But I never told you that and we never had this conversation. Okay?'

'Okay,' replied Peter.

Winston opened the bedroom door for them and said, 'Now that the easy stuff is done, it's on to the hard stuff—you convincing my mum I'm not useless!'

****

Jerusalem, Israel

Michael sat at the computer in the small, two-bedroom flat he had bought a few weeks before. Standing behind him was William. Since their abrupt departure from the church, neither had worn the garb of a priest. William wore a plain white T-shirt and jeans, while Michael remained in more formal gear with a collared, striped shirt, and tan trousers.

Michael looked closer at the computer monitor and said, 'This one looks good. A private investigator with twenty years' experience and ten years with the CIA. Very professional, very discreet.' He glanced at William. 'What do you think?'

William looked closer at the monitor to read the rest of the advert. 'Looks like a potential candidate. Let's give him a call.'

Michael picked up his mobile and dialed the mobile number in the advert. He put his mobile on loudspeaker and placed it on the computer desk so William could listen in. After a few rings, a deep voice answered. 'Shalom.'

Michael replied in a nervous tone, 'Ah Shalom. Is this Pri Eye Services?'

'Yes, it is,' answered the deep, rough voice.

'We are looking at your advert and we are interested in hiring you.'

'Sure. What service is it that you require?' His accent was a strange mix of American and Israeli.

'We require surveillance on an extremely dangerous individual.'

'I've performed surveillance on many dangerous individuals—especially during my CIA operative days.'

'Not like this one. He must never know you are watching him.'

'I have a perfect record for being discreet. No one has ever detected my presence unless I choose to be detected.'

Michael needed to be sure that this man knew what he was up against, so he decided to go out on a limb. 'The subject has telepathic powers and can sense if he is being watched.' Michael glanced at William for some level of reassurance. William just crossed his arms and stared at the mobile phone on the desk.

His comment was met with silence. Then the rough voice answered. 'I once was required to monitor a psychic. It did take some unusual methods, but I was successful in the surveillance for over three months. So, what sort of surveillance are you after?'

Michael and William looked at each other and nodded in approval. Michael answered, 'We are just after a record of his coming and goings. Where he studies or works. Where he goes out to. Where he likes to spend his time. If he plans to go overseas and where, that sort of thing.'

'Okay. So how long for?'

Michael answered with a definitive tone. 'Indefinitely.'

'Indefinitely! You have seen that I charge by the hour, haven't you?'

'Yes. We were hoping you could fix a monthly rate?'

'Monthly rate! Hmm, hope you're good for the cash because it won't be cheap.'

'Yes, we are good for the cash,' Michael said confidently.

'And I want monthly upfront payments—in cash.'

Michael looked at William and William nodded his approval. Michael replied, 'That is fine with us.'

'Okay. I am on a job now until the end of next week. After that I am free to start.'

'Okay,' Michael confirmed.

'You can register on my website and I'll send you the monthly rate and my account details. So, what is the target's name?'

'We cannot say his name out loud, but I can spell it out to you.'

'Okay, go ahead.'

'J, u, d, a, s ... s, a, l, i, m,' Michael said slowly and as clearly as possible.

'I've got it. I don't need an address. I can find that easy enough.'

'I will email you my first report in six weeks.'

'Great, shalom.'

'Shalom.' After hanging up, Michael looked up at William and said, 'We now have a private eye!'

'Good. We need to start planning on how we get him on holy ground and then ...' William was interrupted by the computer. An alert popped up on the screen. 'You have a new message!'.

Michael clicked on the alert and watched the email message appear before him. It was from the contact 'Wallaby.' The email read, 'G'day Romeo, hope you are well. Our contact here has built the tool we needed. It is in the attached zip file and has the instructions in the *readme* file. We are about to use it to contact our local head of state. If you have any problems, let me know. I have also attached an example of what we plan to say in our email, in case you wanted to align the messages. Good luck, Wallaby.'

Michael clicked reply and typed, 'Hi Wallaby. We are all well here and thank you for the tool. We are going to contact both our respective head of states once we figure out how to. All the best, Romeo.' Michael turned around to William and said, 'We have the key, we just need the email address.'

William put his hand to his chin as he voiced his thoughts. 'I doubt very much any email address that is supposed to be for our glorious leaders will be read by them initially—or at all. What if we tried a blanket approach, email as many officials as possible and hope that it is enough to spread the word to the top?'

Michael stared across the lounge room and out the opposite window as he contemplated William's proposal. 'It could work. And every senator has their email address on their office website.'

'Let's go for it,' William announced confidently.

****

Canberra, Australia

At The Lodge in Canberra, Prime Minister Peter Geraldton sat on the lounge with his laptop. He glanced up at the clock on the wall—11: 49 pm. He then returned his gaze to the screen before him. He devoted half an hour each day to reading his personal emails. As the political leader, he was a very busy man so time for his personal life was reduced to the last hour of the day. His eyes scanned the inbox where fifty emails waited to be read. Ten emails down, one caught his eye. The subject read 'For the PM's Eyes Only'. A stern gaze formed on his face as he opened the email. He had made a considerable effort to separate his working life from his private life, and any breach of his private life was totally unacceptable. How did someone get a hold of his personal email address and how dare they abuse it for business purposes! He noticed the 'From' field was blank. Peter clicked on the 'Open Email' button and scrolled down to the bottom without reading it to see who the email was from. To his frustration, the email was unsigned. He scrolled back to the beginning of the email and started to read it in hope that it would reveal whom it was from.

> *'Who we are is inconsequential, but the message we convey to you is of paramount importance. The Antichrist has been born! He lives in Jerusalem and is seventeen years old. We are notifying all political leaders of the western world so they can be ready for the coming apocalypse. Be warned, the Antichrist is not a mortal being. He has unearthly abilities and cannot be killed by mortal weapons alone. He is attractive, charismatic, and highly intelligent—the perfect tools to deceive the unfaithful and lead them into the war that will end all wars. Our mission is to do what we can to counter his devise in an attempt to minimise the death that he will inflict upon this world. Our first step is to inform you of what is about to unfold so you can prepare the security services for the long battle ahead—it is foretold that this war will last at least seventeen years. Let's hope we can reduce that. All the best in your future leadership. And the Antichrist's name is Judas Salim.'*

Peter stared at the email, his eyes reading the words *Antichrist* and *apocalypse* over and over. His mind was at loggerheads. Was this just the ravings of a mad man or did it have some foundation of truth? Either way, he needed to know who they were and how they got his email address. He forwarded the email to his work email address where he planned to forward it to the security team first thing the following morning.

****

Jerusalem, Israel

Michael finished proofreading what William had written in the draft email. The email was ready to be sent to all the leading politicians in Israel and the USA. The email was just waiting for the 'Send' button to be pressed. Michael pulled at his chin as he said, 'All looks good but I'm not sure about putting in a reference to the Brethren.'

William, who was sitting next to him, looked at Michael with an inquisitive expression. 'How could they find us by that? We have no official link to the name, and to add to the mix, it is well used by the monks.'

'True. But still, there could be some remote chance. Maybe we should consult Father Stephen as he has been nominated as our resident consultant for rash decisions.'

William looked back at the monitor screen where the email was displayed. 'Okay, I'll delete it.' He selected the text to be deleted and pressed a key on the keyboard. A message displayed on the screen. 'Email Sent!'

'What? But I pressed delete!'

Michael grasped his head as he yelled in anger. 'Aaggrrhh! You must have bumped the 'enter' key sending the email!'

'What? Noooo,' William retorted.

'Well, it's too late now!' Michael added with a tone of futility.

'What are we going to do now?' William asked in a calmer tone as he stared at the words, 'email sent'.

'Start a new email,' Michael stated with a reluctant tone. 'We need to warn the others.'

****

New York, USA

Senator James Richardson was trawling through the countless emails sent to his office Dropbox. There were too many for him to read so he picked out ones of interest. Fifty emails down he saw the subject 'For Your Eyes Only'. He clicked on it and began to read the email. When he got to the end, his eyes went back to the words, 'The Antichrist has been born!' James pondered over the email for a moment then picked up the phone on his desk. His large office, on the fifty-first floor, had an uninterrupted view of the New York city skyline. He pressed one of the speed dial buttons and spun around to look at the view from the expansive window. After a few rings, the phone was answered. 'Hello?'

'Hi Frank, it's Jim. How you doing?' James said in his pure New York accent.

'Ah Jim, not so well,' Frank replied, deliberately leading him to a more detailed discussion. Frank's accent was very west coast.

'What's up buddy?' James asked with a tone of concern.

'It's Amy again. She's been caught DUI.'

'Oh no. Sorry to hear that.'

'It will be all over the papers tomorrow. My PR man is running around like a chicken without a head.'

'Election is only five months away.'

'Yep.'

'Oh man, not good.'

'Tell me about it. Who knows, maybe the voters will sympathise with me.'

'Could do. Who hasn't had a kid in trouble? What about my David?'

'True. Anyway, enough about me. So, what's new?'

'Well, for once David has been on the straight and narrow—no grass for him.'

'Sounds like mine has taken over where yours has left off.'

'Yeah, but I doubt that my troubles are over. One other thing. I got an email in my senate office account, from an unknown sender, claiming they sent a similar message to other senators. I was just wondering if you got one too?'

'I haven't had a chance to get to my email today. Hang on, I'll open it and have a look.' A few moments passed as the sounds of mouse clicks echoed from the phone handset. 'Ah, what's this? For Your Eyes Only.'

'Yeah, that's it. Have a read and tell me what you think.'

Some time passed before Frank replied. 'Okay, sounds all doom and gloom. Most likely some crackpot. But he has named the guy. Rather out of the ordinary. Ever heard of this Judas Salim?'

'No, that's what's bugging me. Why make a big deal about a nobody?'

'You're not suggesting that it's legit, are you?'

'No, but there is something else. I had a dream two nights ago—a very weird dream. I dreamed that I was fighting World War III, and I was up against the Antichrist. And get this—his name was Salim!'

There was a pregnant pause before a voice, surrounding rather uncomfortable, sounded in his ear.

'Okay, now you're really weirding me out. So, what do you think we should do?'

'Don't know. Normally we would ignore the message or have them locked up. We have a meeting of parliament in two weeks. I might ask around and see if any of the others have had the same message. If so, then I may bring it up with the boss.'

'Okay, but be careful, they might throw you in the nuthouse instead.'

'Okay, will do. Later.'

'By now.'

James spun around on his chair and put the handset down. He was in his late thirties and was one of the youngest senators to be voted in. His clean-shaven face poorly reflected the late afternoon sunlight that filled his office. However, the white of his brown eyes did respond to the bright orange glow around him. His short, dark brown locks couldn't resist the brilliant glow, and flecks shone in concert with the light song of the sun. James was a devout Christian, and his strong beliefs stirred within him. If it wasn't for the dream, he would have happily dismissed the email. But an uncomfortable pressure pressed upon his soul. 'Is this real?' he asked himself. The subject kept playing on his mind. He had a strong belief that his appointment as senator was a gift from God, and he felt driven to honour that gift. He read the email again, sucked in a gulp of air and steeled himself again on what he was about to embark.

****

Three months later

President Rebecca Bailey was going through the morning paperwork in the Oval Office. The morning sunlight, filtered by the curtains, filled the office with a soft glow. Her concentration was broken by the phone ringing. She pressed the 'Speaker' button and said, 'Yes?'

'Mrs President, Mr Stone is here to see you,' said the female voice on the other side of the phone.

'Ed? Okay, send him in.' Rebecca returned to the document before her to minimise the loss of time for whatever Ed Stone was coming to discuss.

A few moments later, a door at the far side of the Oval Office opened and a tall greying man entered. 'Mrs President.'

'Come in Ed. I'll be with you in a moment.'

'Yes Mam,' he replied like a schoolboy before the head mistress.

Rebecca finished reading the page before her and looked up. She was in her mid-sixties and the first female to become president. Not only that, but Rebecca was also the first black female president— something she was very proud of.

Ed however, was very old school and it took some time to adjust to a female president. The former president was a stickler for protocol, and he retained some of the older values. But the current president was not, and Ed was still struggling with her casual manner.

Rebecca looked up at Ed over her half-rimmed glasses like a head mistress would. 'Now Ed. Did you get my email on the informal meeting protocol?'

'Ah, yes Mam,' he replied cautiously.

'Then you will know that I don't like being called Mam.' She looked up at the ceiling as she said, 'It makes me feel so old.' Her gaze returned to the tall man before her. 'You can call me Becky.'

Ed shuffled on his feet as he said, 'Yes Becky.' He hated calling the president by her nickname.

Rebecca sat back in the big leather chair and took off her glasses. 'Take a seat.' She gestured towards one of the black, leather clad chairs in front of her desk. When Ed sat down, Rebecca continued. 'So, what brings the head of security to me this morning?'

Ed made himself comfortable and crossed his legs as he started. 'There has been a number of emails, on the same subject, sent to many of the heads of state across the western world. All with more or less the same content. We believe they have been sent by some sort of faction or extremist group.'

Ed paused for a moment and gave Rebecca time to inject. 'Doesn't sound like something I need to get involved in.'

'The emails were all untraceable,' Ed added.

'I thought all emails were traceable?'

'So, did we and other intelligence agencies across the world. They were able to exploit a floor in the way routers process the IP stack. Very clever stuff. And in the end, we were not able to trace the emails.' Ed scratched the side of his thin, shaven face and bumped his frameless glasses as he did so. 'Also, this faction was able to gain access to the private email address of the Prime Minster of Australia. I was wondering if you had received a similar email titled, *For Your Eyes Only?*'

'No, I don't recall any such email,' Rebecca replied. 'Nor do I recall any from my public email addresses.'

'You did receive such an email in one of your public email addresses, but your staff declared it a prank and deleted it. We were able to retrieve the email from our backup systems. We were concerned that they had infiltrated your personal email.'

'No, my personal email is fine, but you say they infiltrated the emails of the Prime Minister of Australia?'

'Yes, we think the faction could be based there. Our Aussie counterparts are investigating the possibility.'

'So, what was the email about, can you forward it to me?'

'I have a printout.' Ed removed a folded piece of paper from his coat pocket and handed it to the president.

Rebecca unfolded it and put her glasses back on to read the email. When she finished, she said, 'It all sounds very realistic. And they named him. So, what do we know about this Judas Salim?'

Ed crossed his legs the other way and answered, 'Not much. He is seventeen, lives in Jerusalem, no criminal record. Rather ordinary boy.' Rebecca looked over the top of her glasses at Ed. 'Why would somebody in Australia have it in for a boy in Jerusalem?'

Ed's eyes narrowed for a moment as he replied, 'Good question. I had our psychoanalysts look at this and they feel that whoever these people are, they honestly think this boy is the Antichrist!'

Rebecca's eyes returned to the email. 'So, they call themselves the Brethren. Any leads there?'

'Only the emails sent to the US and Israel had the name the Brethren. The rest were unsigned, but the content was almost the same. So, we believe they are all part of the same faction. As for this Brethren, we have no firm leads. There are numerous Brethren groups across the globe—all tied to monasteries. However, when searching against the term 'The Brethren', we did get one interesting hit. The pentagon has been converting all the documents from World War II into a database. One of our new research tools picked up some interesting data on a Swiss bank account that was opened by the Vatican in 1941 under the name, 'The Brethren'. We then found out that this account was the oldest bank account in the world and, because it was so old, whoever originally opened the account is unknown. But it has been kept open by the Vatican by way of regular small deposits.'

Rebecca looked up at Ed again. 'The oldest back account in the world? How is that possible when banks existed well before 1941?'

'The account wasn't opened in 1941, it was transferred from another bank. The account was established sometime in the 1500s and was originally managed by ...' Ed removed another piece of paper from his coat pocket and read it out, '... The Banca Monte Dei Paschi Di Siena in Italy—the world's oldest bank.' He folded the paper and returned it to his coat pocket. 'The account was given the number 'one'. According to some banking fraternity blogs, it still exists. One blog suggested that a few months ago, unknown persons made a withdrawal from this account. This apparently was the first withdrawal since the account was opened.'

Rebecca's eyes narrowed for a moment as she said, 'If the account has been deposited into for five hundred years, who knows how much would be in it? Possibly hundreds of thousands.'

'Or millions,' Ed added.

'Well, if it is their bank account it should be easy to ID this faction?'

'Normally yes. However, this is no ordinary account. Our hackers found that the Swiss bank does not have an address or a name on the account. So, we hit a dead end. Still, this faction could be well funded as well as ingenious. Who knows what they are capable of?'

Rebecca took off her glasses and began to chew the end of one of the arms. 'It sounds to me like a group of Catholic priests have decided for some reason that this boy is the Antichrist. If that is the case, then the only real threat is to this boy. No, my instincts tell me that this faction is not what we need to be concerned about. What we do need to be concerned about is if this faction has it right—if this boy is who they say he is—we all have a real problem.'

Ed sat forward as he asked with concern, 'You don't honestly believe what this faction is claiming.'

Rebecca stared at Ed for a moment. She was a devout Christian and concerns that she would live to see the end of the world plagued her mind from time to time, but never did she dream that it could happen while she was president. Rebecca sat forward as she replied, 'Ed I didn't get to become the president by assuming anyone was right or wrong. I've learned to always keep my options open. And you have to agree that this case is out of the ordinary.' She sat back in her chair and continued, 'Get the boys in the CIA to see if they can dig anything else up on the Brethren. And I want a file opened on this Judas Salim, with an annual report on what he is up to, where he lives, what career path he takes, that sort of thing.' Rebecca sat forward again, pointing her glasses at Ed in an aggressive manner. 'I do not want a whole team of agents watching this kid 24-7. We are finally making some headway on the national debt and we need to keep a lid on our spending. So that's desktop surveillance only. Am I clear?'

Ed sat back in his chair as if her words were wielded with punches. He replied, 'Yes, crystal.'

'Anything else?' she asked in a calmer manner.

'No, Becky.' Ed stood and walked from the oval office.

Rebecca read the email again and said out loud to herself, 'Who in their right mind would ever name their son Judas?'

****

Jerusalem, Israel

Samuel Asher was in his early sixties and after retiring from performing contracts for the CIA, he decided to try out being a private eye. The role was much the same, but the subjects he gathered intelligence on were less powerful and less dangerous—and it often paid better. Samuel was born in Jerusalem and lived most of his life there, apart from eight years in the United States where he learned his trade. He had put on quite an amount of weight over the past ten years and felt too old to try and lose it in the gym. His thick, dark mop of hair had withered and gone grey, and the fine lines on the sides of his mouth had grown into deep furrows. Sometimes, when he looked in the mirror, he could still see the young man that he once was. More often now though, he could not recognise that young man at all. He had never married, and thanks to the long hours and dangerous nature of his career, he only had a few failed relationships to account for. His mother was always hopeful that he would find someone—even on her death bed. He could remember her frail words so clearly—'Find yourself a good woman and settle down and have some children or you will regret it.' Nowadays he absorbed himself in his work feeling it was his only contribution to society.

Sam, as his few friends called him, sat in front of the television watching the footage from the surveillance camera while listening to the recording from a long-range listening device. He had set the surveillance platform on top of a nearby building near where the subject lived. One thing he had learned from his days working for the CIA was that psychics could not detect remote surveillance. What he was watching and listening to was all of a few hours old. Sam had gained a great deal of knowledge on this Judas Salim and so far, he had seen nothing out of the ordinary. Judas appeared to be a normal teenager about to enter the big wide world.

Sam made himself comfortable in the large leather chair, ready to spend the next few hours perusing the surveillance for the day. He twisted off the bottle top of his beer, took a handful of crisps from the bowl next to him and fed his face. Sam had synchronised the audio and the video, but it was the audio that he paid closest attention to. The video rarely displayed anything of interest, just the street scape outside the home and the daily comings and goings of its residents. He briefly listened to the beginning of the recording then pressed fast forward on the remote and skipped several minutes. Sam wasn't going to listen to every dull moment of the subject's life. He stopped fast forwarding to listen for anything interesting. He heard the typical sounds of the toilet flushing and the constant drone of the television. Sam fast forwarded a few minutes and stopped again to play. A great bellow of noise startled his senses, making him drop his beer. 'Shit!' He quickly pressed pause and picked up the beer bottle. He pressed rewind, backtracked a few minutes, then pressed play again.

There was no shouting this time, just the sound of the TV and people moving around in the kitchen. The time on the counter read 7:56 am.

The voice of Judas's mother Sarina came through clearly. 'There is a letter here for you.'

'Thanks,' replied the voice that Sam had identified as Judas. There was the sound of ripping paper, followed by an unfolding rustle. A moment later, Judas announced with excitement, 'Yes!'

'What is it?' Sarina asked.

'I have been accepted into the Sapienza University of Rome!' His voice was filled with joy.

There was a moment's pause before Sarina shouted, 'But we decided you were going to stay here in Israel to study!'

'No, *you* decided I was staying here,' Judas shouted back.

'You don't need to go anywhere else to study, the universities here are perfectly fine!' There was a distinct falter in her tone as she fought off the tears.

'I cannot stay here forever Mum; I need to get out into the world!'

There was a pause before Sarina continued, 'Just wait until your father gets home! He will never agree to you going to Rome.'

Judas sounded forcefully calm as he said, 'I'm not a child anymore. You need to let me go.'

Her voice wavered and quivered as she forced out her protest. 'No, I forbid it. You cannot go!'

The voice of Judas boomed through the speakers in an unnatural tone and at an unnatural volume. 'YOU CANNOT STOP ME!'

Sarina's voice quivered, 'B-but I am your m-mother.'

His voice was more human this time as he stated in a clear and concise tone, 'You are not my real mother!' The sound of footsteps on a tiled floor came through the speakers, followed by an opening and a slamming of a door.

All that was left was the sound of Sarina sobbing.

Sam sat forward in the chair to look closer at the high-definition video footage on the television. Judas appeared from the front door, turned right and began walking down the street. As usual, the boy had his dog in tow. Everywhere Judas went, so did the large black rottweiler—and the dog was always well behaved. For a moment Sam thought, 'Maybe I should get a dog.' The motion detection system captured Judas's movement and zoomed in on him as he walked along. Sam could see his face; he was clearly wearing a very dark expression.

Just then, Judas stopped. His head turned towards the camera and he began to stare. For a moment, Sam's heart skipped a beat. Had he detected the small surveillance station?

What happened next sent a chill down Sam's spine. Judas's eyes went black and the soft features of his face blurred before transforming into sharp lines and sunken cheeks. His teeth lengthened and sharpened to the shape of needles. It was then that Sam experienced true terror.

Those black pools for eyes drew in his stare like a moth to a flame, swallowing his consciousness. Within those black pits, horrific and grotesque images poured into his mind as though a bucket of evil was being poured over his face. Then the most ear-splitting scream bombarded his ears. In desperation to block the flood of vile insight, he threw his left arm over his eyes and fumbled for the remote. But the onslaught was too great. Sam fell to the floor like a rag doll and sent the remote skidding across the polished floorboards. His face contorted as the excruciating pain filled his mind. Sam desperately crawled across the floor to the waiting remote. His vision was impaired by a dark fluid that filled his tear ducts—the location of the remote was about to go beyond the limits of his vision. With the searing pain in his head, every moment seemed like a year in hell. Sam dug his fingernails into the hardwood floor to produce the grip he needed to move his bulk. He could no longer see, and the only hope to find the remote was to slap his outstretched hand on the floor and try to locate it by chance. Finally, his hand slapped on top of the remote. Sam wildly pointed the remote in the general direction of the television, pressing any button his thumb could find. Suddenly, the suffering stopped. The scream faded in his head and the television went blank.

Sam rolled onto his back panting, his heart racing like the chugging of a fully throttled steam train. He felt something oozing down the sides of his face and the back of his neck. Gradually, the ichor drained from his eyes and his vision returned. The ceiling became visible and soon he could make out features of the light that hung from it. He dabbed his hand in the ichor that oozed down his cheek and looked at his fingers—they were red with blood.

Slowly, Sam sat up, waiting a moment till he felt well enough to stand. He staggered to the bathroom and grasped the sink for support as he looked in the mirror. He looked like hell. Blood streaked from his eyes and ears. He turned on the tap and frantically splashed and washed away the marks of his torment. He looked in the mirror again—this time he looked a little better. Sam's stomach began to churn and contract, and a great volume of vomit traversed his oesophagus and exited his mouth. Finally, when his stomach was empty, he gasped for air and coughed out the remains of the vomit. Sam washed his face again until he felt cleansed. Exhausted, he staggered to his bedroom and collapsed on the bed.

Some time passed as he attempted to grasp what had happened. Never had he experienced anything like this—ever!

Sam reached over to the cordless phone on the bedside table and picked it up. He scrolled through the received call list until he found the unidentified mobile number from three months ago. Sam received so few calls these days it was easy to find. He pressed the 'Talk' button and waited. After a few rings, the vaguely familiar voice answered. 'Shalom?'

'What in the hell is that thing?' Sam said in a very blunt tone.

There was a long pause before the voice answered, 'You have seen his true face, haven't you?'

'Yes!' Sam replied.

'Did you look into its eyes?'

'You didn't answer my question.'

This time the voice was more assertive. 'Did you look into its eyes?'

'YES! It nearly killed me. I can't believe it could reach me through video footage that was nine hours old. It was like it was in the room with me.'

'You were lucky. The delay must have been enough to conceal you, so he hit you instead with a full blast of his malice in the hope that it would finish you off.'

'I certainly don't feel very lucky.'

'Now listen to me very carefully, your life depends on it.' The male voice at the other end was very serious. 'Are you a religious man?'

Sam didn't expect a question like that. 'Ah, not particularly.'

'Well, you are about to be. Go to the Basilica of the Agony at the foot of the Mount of Olives. Towards the back of the Basilica, on the left, you will see a stone font. You should find it filled with fresh holy water. Wash your face and eyes well with the water. This should cleanse away the remaining malice. Then ask Father Luke to bless you. Stay in the Basilica until you feel better. Go NOW!'

'You still didn't answer my question!'

The pause on the phone seemed an eternity before the voice said, with great conviction, 'It is the Antichrist!'

The words echoed in Sam's head as if to permanently burn them on his memory. It was not the answer he was expecting and if it wasn't for what he had just been through, he would never have believed it. One thing was for sure though—that boy was far from normal. 'In case I don't make it, he has been accepted into the Sapienza University of Rome and from what I heard, he will definitely be going.'

'Thank you. Now please go.'

Sam hung up and laid there for a moment, contemplating the situation he was in. It was all so surreal. Considering recent events, Sam decided to take the advice he had just been given. He got off the bed and went to church.

****

Michael hung up and put the mobile back in his pocket. When Sam had called, Michael and William were on the small, two-seater lounge discussing where they could launch an attack on the Antichrist.

William looked at him with concern. 'Is he okay?'

'Yes. At the moment. But he will need all of our prayers if he is to survive. He did say that you know who is on the move. He is off to university in Rome.'

William's eyebrows raised as he said, 'Rome? What evil is he planning in the home of our church?'

'Only the Lord knows.'

'True,' replied William. 'Come, let us pray for him.' They bowed their heads and began to pray.

****

Sam parked his old C-Class Mercedes Benz near the Basilica of the Agony. After locking the car, he strode towards the entrance of the Basilica. He had definitely felt better than he did now. There was a constant dull ache in his head and a nauseous sensation in his stomach. Maybe this would make him feel better. He walked up the few steps to the Basilica and entered through the small side door next to the main doors that were large enough to drive a bus through.

The moment Sam stepped inside, he felt worse. The pain in his head increased and the nausea made his stomach cramp. He pushed forward down the centre aisle holding onto the chairs as he went. His concentration zoomed in on the stone font at the other end of the Basilica. At this late hour, the Basilica was empty of worshippers, and not a soul was about to assist. Every step, taking him closer to the font, only increased the agony. The font was only a few feet away, but it might as well have been kilometres. The last steps were almost impossible. Sam had to concentrate on every muscle in his legs to force each step.

A male voice came from somewhere to Sam's left, but he didn't look as his only objective was to get to the font. 'Are you okay?'

Sam lurched at the font and grabbed its sturdy structure that was able to support him. He plunged his face into the pool of holy water and began to drink it. His stomach heaved and his eyes stung. Sam lifted his head for a moment to take in air. Through his blurred sight, he could see a priest before him wearing an expression of great shock. From Sam's eyes and ears oozed black ichor, and as it dripped into the font, it sizzled like oil on a hot plate. He plunged his face in again and drank once more. Sam took several gulps of holy water before raising his head again. This time the heaving sensation in his stomach was too great and he vomited up black ichor on the stone floor.

As Sam coughed out the remains, the priest scooped up a handful of holy water and poured it onto the black ichor on the floor. They both watched as the holy water burned away at the malice that lay before them. The ichor writhed and sizzled as the pure water neutralised its evil substance. In moments, the ichor had completely evaporated.

The priest before Sam asked again, 'Are you okay?'

This time Sam answered. 'I think so.'

'Come, sit down,' the priest said.

They sat on the nearest wooden folding chairs and Sam rested his head in his hands, his spinning senses regaining control. 'Are you Father Luke?' Sam asked while giving a brief glance at the priest next to him.

'Yes,' Father Luke answered.

'Could you bless me? I think I will need it.'

'I think you need more than a blessing. Are you baptised?'

Sam glanced at him again as he said, 'I'm Jewish. Not a practising one though.'

'God's people are most welcome in our church. How do you feel about converting?'

Sam lifted his head from his hands, expelled a sigh, and said, 'I think I will be okay.'

Father Luke leaned forward. 'If I can baptise you, I can give you Holy Communion. It is the most purifying act you can perform.'

Sam was never much of a believer in anything except humanity, but recent events had him questioning his take on the world. There was certainly something about this church and its ability to combat the ill that inflicted him. He nodded in acceptance.

Father Luke got to work and performed the ceremony of baptism on Sam. Father Luke was expecting something unusual as he performed the sign of the cross on Sam's forehead, but Sam didn't react. Father Luke then performed Holy Communion—he blessed the bread and the wine as usual before presenting the bread wafer to Sam.

Sam, kneeling before Father Luke, took the bread and ate it. Father Luke then presented the wine goblet to Sam. As Sam opened his mouth to drink the wine, black smoke billowed out. He took a good gulp of the wine and handed the goblet back to Father Luke. A great cramp inflicted his stomach and he cried out, 'Ooohh!' From his mouth came a great black cloud that writhed and wriggled above him, shrieking. The cloud made for Father Luke, but he immediately brought the goblet to his lips and finished off the blessed wine.

With no soul to bear it, the black cloud of remaining malice slowed and fell to the floor. It sizzled and writhed on the stone until it was no more.

Father Luke helped Sam to his feet. 'I declare that you are now cleansed of the demon. How do you feel now?'

Sam stood straight and with clear eyes. He felt better than he had in years. 'Great!'

Father Luke put his chin down so he could see Sam through the upper section of his bifocal, thick-rimmed glasses. He wore an expression of satisfaction as he said, 'Good. Now tell me, how did you come about to be cursed by this demon?'

Sam took a moment to study the priest before him. Father Luke was in his seventies with a stocky build and remarkably, a full head of grey hair. He was taller than Sam and had a distinct presence that for reasons Sam couldn't put a finger on, but it made him a figure of certainty. His almost calm attitude to the seemingly unfathomable events that had recently taken place, gave Sam the feeling that he was in knowledgeable hands. Still, reiterating the revelation of how this all came about was not going to be easy for him. 'You wouldn't believe me. I can hardly believe it myself.'

Father Luke stared at Sam with great confidence as he said, 'Try me!'

Sam couldn't look Father Luke in the face as he said, 'A boy looked at me.' Once he got the words out, he felt comfortable enough to look at him again.

'Must have been some boy. Yours is not the first possession I have seen. I was present at two exorcisms in Africa. Many years ago, of course—when I was younger and more cavalier. But neither were as definite as yours. So, who is this boy?'

'I cannot tell you his name. Probably best that I don't. But I can tell you *what* it is.'

Father Luke's stare became more intense as he asked, 'So *what* is it?'

This time Sam looked Father Luke in the eyes as he replied, 'The Antichrist!'

Father Luke stared at Sam for some time, studying his face. He said, 'I believe you.'

Sam raised his eyebrows in surprise. 'You do?'

'You believe in what you say, and from what I have just seen, why should I not?'

'Fair point.' Sam couldn't argue with his logic.

'There is one thing that puzzles me though—how we were able to cast out the demon so quickly. In my experience, they can be very stubborn. It may be our location that has given us the upper hand.'

'Being in a church?' Sam guessed.

'Yes, the church is hallowed ground but where we are is incredibly special indeed. This is the location where our saviour held communion with Moses and Elijah. See the exposed rock there in the centre? That is where it all happened two thousand years ago. Even after so long, the Lord's spirit can still leave its mark.' Father Luke smiled to himself for a moment then continued. 'It might be best you stay a while, just in case you have a relapse. There is a mid-week midnight service on in an hour, you are welcome to stay and join us.'

Sam wasn't willing to leave the safety of the Basilica just yet. 'I think I might take you up on the offer.'

'Great,' Father Luke smiled.

****

When Judas was angry, his strength welled up like a volcano about to erupt and his supernatural senses heightened. As he strode down the street from the house, his senses detected prying eyes. He scanned the far side of the street for a sense of the spy but could not pinpoint it. His anger reached boiling point and in frustration, he sent out a burst of his malice. If someone were spying, they would be dead in a day.

That was six hours ago, and he had spent the last several hours calming down. Judas could have easily slaughtered the woman that calls herself his mother, but her usefulness had not expired—not yet. Besides, he was off to Italy in a few weeks and he would no longer have to suffer her pathetic attempts to dominate him. He could keep her at arm's length and use her if the need arose. His so-called father was a different story. He had some respect for John. John always said what he meant and was rarely clouded by emotions. However, weakness lay in John's love for Sarina, and Sarina could play his heart strings like a maestro. He would have to play his cards carefully to maintain the status quo and promote his studying in Italy.

Judas approached the house as the fading sun gave way to dusk. He slowed as he surveyed the lights coming from the front windows. It wasn't clear if John was home yet, but he was due home today after a three-day business trip—perhaps not until later that night though.

Judas walked up to the front door and Goliath, as usual, obediently followed. He unlocked the door and entered the house. The drawing room was the first room to the right of the front door and Judas could see his mother seated, waiting for him. Sarina wore an expression of great resolve, something he didn't see on her very often. Judas walked into the drawing room ready to confront Sarina, but it was then that he saw John standing on the other side of the room.

'Hello Judas. Your mother told me what happened,' John said in a calm voice. He had his hands in his pockets, possibly to hide his fighting fingers from sight. 'Why would you say you such a terrible thing to your mother?'

'A woman came to see me. She told me about my real birth and who my real mother was.' Judas stared into Sarina's eyes as he said, 'Her name was Yentl.'

Sarina's eyes were like saucers. She covered her mouth to stop her gasp from being heard. John's eyes went from Judas to his wife and the expression on her face was not what he expected. John's eyes narrowed as he said to Sarina, 'What is Judas talking about?' He first thought it was some cruel lie to get his way, which was something out of character for Judas, but not for a teenager. However, Sarina's reaction gave him doubts.

Sarina's eyes welled up with tears and her hands began to shake. Through trembling lips, she spat, 'That's a lie!'

Unfazed by her retort, Judas stared at her with dead eyes as he said, 'And my real mother's name was Mary.'

His words were like a knife opening an old wound. Sarina was not expecting this. 'How could you possibly know any of this? She left the country and never came back!'

Her reaction for John was devastating. He stood there staring at Sarina, dumbfounded. His practical mind slowly regained control and he strode over to Sarina. Raising her chin slowly with his hand, he asked, 'Is this true?'

His dark brown eyes burned into Sarina's with such conviction that they were like a truth serum. Her eyes welled up more and tears streamed down her cheeks. Slowly, reluctantly, she nodded.

John closed his eyes and bowed his head for a moment. Judas remained quiet, almost statuesque. John raised his head and looked at Judas. 'If you really want to go to Rome to study, then you have my blessing. But know this, your mother and I may not be your biological parents, but your natural parents we are, and nothing will change that. Meanwhile, if you will excuse us, your mother and I need to have a little chat.'

Judas stared at them for a moment, then turned and went to his bedroom. Mission accomplished.

****

Michael and William had been researching the Sapienza University of Rome for opportunities to strike down the Antichrist.

'Look there,' William announced. 'There is a church on the grounds.'

'Yes!' Michael retorted.

William's excitement was overflowing. 'If we can get him into the church, we could strike him there.'

'But how?' Michael asked. Michael's mobile rang and he answered. 'Hello?'

'Well, that was interesting,' said the voice.

Michael recognised the voice and put it on speaker phone so William could hear. 'I have to say, I am relieved to hear your voice. How are you feeling?'

'Much better thank you. Your friend Father Luke was extremely helpful. Now that I am aware of who we are dealing with here, I will be more diligent.'

Michael looked at William in surprise before speaking to the voice coming from the mobile. 'So, you are okay to continue the surveillance?'

'Yes,' said the voice in a matter-of-fact way.

William placed his hands together in a gesture of prayer, looked up at the ceiling and mouthed the words, 'Thank you'.

Michael stated, 'I thought you may have been deterred by recent events.'

'On the contrary, now that I know the magnitude of this job, I am all the more determined. By the way, the reason for the call is that I have some more info for you.'

'Yes?' Michael asked.

'His real mother died at birth. They are not his natural parents.'

William looked at Michael with a startled expression. But Michael took the news more sedately. 'This was suggested to me before, but there was no proof.'

'Sarina admitted it. Apparently, a girl named Mary was the mother but died during birth at the house. Sarina disposed of the body and took the baby as her own. There was no mention of the father.'

'Wow, sounds like something out of a soap opera.'

'Yes, in my line of work I see a lot of this sort of thing. I should become a soap scriptwriter.'

Michael and William let out a brief chuckle.

'Well, it looks like I am destined for a trip to Rome. I will make contact once I am set up and the subject is under my watchful eye.'

'Okay, bye.'

'Bye.'

Michael hung up the phone and said, 'We are back in business. I think it may be time to hand this over to our friends in Europe. What do you think?'

'I agree. A fresh set of minds would be good,' answered William. 'I will send the email.'

7

A Fool's Hope

Rome, Italy

Three months later, the two former monks sat in the back of the church on the campus of the Sapienza University of Rome. Emil was dressed in jeans and a T-shirt to blend in with the other students. Hans on the other hand, looked very out of place as he wore a suit jacket and a tie. Still, the other students took little or no notice of him. Emil wondered if they thought he was a lecturer.

'According to Michael's source, he passes this church most days,' Hans stated. 'But how to get him in here?'

'If we make up a good enough reason to invite him, maybe he will just walk right in.'

Hans stared over his thick-rimmed glasses at Emil. 'I hardly think so.'

'It was just a thought,' Emil shrugged.

'He should be passing by any moment now; his next class starts in five minutes,' Hans added.

'Let's get into a good position where we can see him but he can't see us,' Emil said as he stood up. 'What about over there?' He pointed to a part of the church that was out of the direct rays of sunlight beaming through the large, open doorway.

'Yes, that looks like a good spot. We have a good view down the street, and we should be able to spot him.'

The church was deserted at this time of the day as the resident priest was on morning duties elsewhere, and all the students were moving from lecture to lecture. Just to be on the safe side, in case someone *did* walk into the church, Emil and Hans stood facing each other to masquerade a conversation. They positioned themselves so that either could turn his head slightly and see down the street.

A group of students appeared some distance away, all in an inaudible conversation. Hans and Emil studied the group as they approached to identify the youth named Judas. Hans stated what was going through both of their minds. 'This is so hard without knowing exactly what he looks like. If only we had a photo.'

'Well, we don't as it could provide him with a link to us. All we know is that he is 1.9 metres tall, he has short, black hair, is good looking, and carries a red rucksack,' Emil said to remind Hans as well as himself.

The group was close enough now to see them all clearly, but Judas was not among them. A second group of students appeared behind them and the two inquisitors studied the group for a potential match. Again, there was no student that matched the description. As the group turned passed the entrance to the church, there were two young men walking together. The one on the right matched the description right down to his red rucksack.

Hans gasped and covered his mouth, then looked back at Emil.

Emil straightened his back and his eyes narrowed before he turned away and returned Hans's gaze. 'It's him.'

Hans dared not look back at the Antichrist, but Emil did. Hans whispered, 'Don't look at him, he might ...'

Emil watched the two young men turn and continue down the street, almost directly outside the doorway to the church. He studied the face of the young man he sought to kill, then quickly turned back to Hans. Judas took no notice of the two men in the church or the one that had surveyed him.

Hans dropped his hand from his mouth and asked, 'Are you okay?'

Emil took a moment to answer. 'Yes, I am fine. Strange though, he seemed oblivious to our presence. I looked right at him and he didn't see me. I would have thought his supernatural powers would have detected us.'

'You took a great risk. We could both be dead right now,' Hans protested.

'I wonder,' said Emil as he looked around at the church. 'I wonder if being on consecrated ground protected us.'

Hans did the same and surveyed the church. 'Holy ground may not only weaken him, it could completely rob him of his powers.'

Emil looked out at the street scape where Judas was and said, 'What if being close to holy ground makes him almost mortal? What if ... what if I just pushed him in here?'

Hans glared at Emil. 'No. It couldn't possibly work!'

'Why not? If he is mortal, or near mortal, it would be easy to push him right into the church. Then it would be just one against two. The odds will be on our side.' Emil was oozing enthusiasm as his heart raced with excitement.

Hans moved so he could stare Emil in the face. 'You're not planning to do it yourself, are you?'

'Why not?' Emil's determination was swelling.

Hans was in complete contrast to Emil—full of doubt, full of caution. 'It was agreed that we would get a professional. We are monks for heaven's sake!'

Emil just looked out at the scene where he planned to do his sinful deed. 'Not anymore. We are now archangels.' He looked back at Hans, his steel blue eyes mirroring his metal within. 'Are you with me?'

Hans continued his protest. 'We need a gun, and we need silver bullets. Where would we get such things?'

'I know where,' Emil said confidently.

****

Emil and Hans walked into a small café in Rome. It was just after the lunchtime rush and most of the office patrons had returned to work. A handful of late comers were still finishing off their meals. Emil and Hans sat at a small table for two in the centre of the café. When they settled, Hans grabbed a menu and started searching for something he liked. Emil, on the other hand, kept his eyes on the small door leading to the kitchen. A moment later, a dark-haired young man came through the small door carrying two plates filled with steaming pasta. After placing the plates on a nearby table where two women sat, he came over to Emil and Hans. He kept his head down as he pulled out his ordering PDA and said, 'Ciao, cosa desidera ordinare?' When he looked up, his eyes went to Hans who seemed more eager to order.

Hans replied in English. 'A toasted chicken sandwich with avocado, and a cappuccino. Thank you.'

The waiter looked over to Emil and said, this time in English, 'And you sir? Emil!'

'Mario! How are you my friend?' Emil said while shaking Mario's hand. 'Good, six months out of the lockup and still clean.'

'That is great news,' Emil replied cheerily.

'My cousin set me up with this waiting job.' Mario lowered his voice for a moment while saying, 'Pay is crap, but the hours are good and many bellissimo women come here—they love the Mario!' Mario smacked his hand on his behind and the two women at the table he had just served glanced over at him. He bent down towards Emil and Hans and said, 'See?' Mario was in his late twenties and had raven black hair, striking brown eyes and a large nose. His two-metre-tall stature was made more prominent by his slight frame.

'I didn't recognise you without your robes. I think it suits you. You know you're in danger of cramping my style,' Mario said with a wink. He glanced at Hans then looked back at Emil.

'Where are my manners?' Emil exclaimed. 'Mario, Hans. Hans is my mentor at the monastery.'

Mario reached out and shook his hand. 'I am honoured.'

Emil asked, 'So when do you have a break?'

Mario glanced around the café and said, 'From the looks of things, as soon as you two have finished.'

'Great, we can catch up then,' Emil declared.

Mario took Emil's order and returned to the kitchen.

Hans leaned towards Emil and asked, almost whispering, 'How do you know this guy?'

Emil replied in a tone that was almost as quiet as Hans's. 'You remember some years ago when I went to a prison in northern Italy to console the inmates as part of my training?'

'How could I forget? Didn't one of the inmates try to strangle you?' Hans replied.

'Yes, but I did have one success—Mario.'

'So, what was he in jail for?' Hans asked with a distinct tone of concern.

'Armed robbery,' Emil replied casually.

'Armed robbery!' Hans said as he raised his voice.

'Sshhh!' Emil said while looking around to see if they were overheard. Fortunately, no one looked over at them. 'He was the getaway driver; he never held a gun in his life! It was his older brother that was the real villain. Mario was a great driver and his brother talked him into driving the getaway car. The robbery went horribly wrong, his brother shot a guard. The police caught them all. His brother is in for life, but Mario served only four of his eight-year sentence—for good behaviour. I could see straight away he didn't belong there, and I made it my mission to help him get back on track. He was my greatest success, and the reason why I chose to commit my life to the church. He even goes to church on Sundays.' Emil lowered his voice as he said, 'It was during one of our communions that he told me about a man that makes custom-made guns. One of the gang members lost his trigger finger during a fight, and he needed a custom-made gun. I was thinking he could be our man to make us what we need.'

Hans sat back in his chair and said, 'Sounds very risky. What if this guy doesn't like us and guns us down in cold blood? These are hardened criminals remember.'

'Yes, I know, but we have to try. It's our only lead,' Emil stated with a sense of urgency.

'We must be careful. We are way out of our depth here.'

'I know, and we will be careful.'

Later, when they had finished their lunch, Mario came over to them. 'There is a small park around the corner, I like to go there on my breaks. Shall we go there?'

'Sounds great. Okay,' Emil replied.

They followed Mario and in a few moments they had reached the small park that Mario told them about. In the centre, was a patch of grass and benches placed in points that caught most of the sunshine. The weather was mild and sunny as autumn was settling in before winter.

Mario sat down on the grass and Emil sat next to him. Hans slowly bent down, and Emil grabbed his elbow to steady his descent.

Once they had all settled, Mario asked, 'So how did you find me?'

Emil answered, 'It was me who convinced your cousin to give you the job.'

Mario smiled. 'Ah my friend. You always look after the Mario. One day I hope to return the favour. So, what brings you to my beautiful city of Roma?'

'We have business near here. We have an exorcism to perform,' Emil said in a matter-of-fact tone.

Hans darted a look at Emil as he had no idea where he was going with this. Plus, Emil telling a lie was something new to Hans.

Mario leaned forward, the subject taking him by surprise. 'Sounds dangerous. I saw the movie *The Exorcist* and I still have nightmares.'

Emil continued, 'Yes this is a profoundly serious case. So serious that we need special protection.'

'Like what?' Mario asked.

Emil then said with great conviction, 'A gun that fires silver bullets!'

Mario's brown eyes darted between the two priests, then fixed upon Emil. 'No, no, no, no. I know where this is going, and the answer is no!'

'But we only need his contact details, that's all,' Emil stated while trying to calm Mario down.

Mario protested. 'Luccio works for the mob and only the mob. There is no way that he will even see you.'

'We must try,' Emil continued his defence. 'A young man's life is at stake; we cannot let the monster that possesses him win!'

Mario pleaded with them. 'Please don't ask this of me? I have severed all ties with them, and I want to keep it that way.'

Emil wasn't going to give in. 'I know, and I wouldn't ask this of you if it weren't such a serious matter.'

'You don't understand,' Mario persisted. 'The only way he will see you is if I am with you. Otherwise, he will shut the door on your faces.'

'Then that will be as far as your involvement goes. You introduce us and then leave, and don't look back.' Emil stared at Mario in the hope that his words would change his mind.

Mario stared back, silently. Moments passed without a word being said. Then, through trembling lips, Mario said, 'You will do exactly as I say, exactly. If I say we go, we go. No arguments!'

'Absolutely,' Emil replied.

Mario's tone changed as he said, 'Will you pray for me?'

Emil's tone changed to mirror Mario's. 'Every day.'

'It would seem it is time for Mario to come to your rescue. Meet me at the park entrance over there next Tuesday at 6:00 pm.' Mario pointed in the direction they came from.

Emil and Hans both nodded.

****

Emil and Hans arrived at the small park entrance at the agreed time. This time they were dressed in their vestments and not in civilian garb. Hans insisted they wear their priestly garb as it may prevent them from being shot. 'Not every criminal has the heart to kill a monk,' he proclaimed.

They waited for about a minute before an old, red Fiat 500 pulled up. Mario alighted from the car and pulled his driver seat forward so one of them could get in the back. 'Hello, my friends,' he said with a big smile. His work uniform—a black shirt and black jeans—was replaced by a black T-shirt and faded blue jeans.

After Hans protested that his arthritis would prevent him from ever getting out again, Emil got in the back. Hans happily sat in the front next to Mario. That was until Mario took off like he was in a Formula One race.

They darted through the narrow streets of Rome at breakneck speed, Hans and Emil hanging on for dear life at every corner. They quickly resorted to bracing themselves against the doors and the roof while Mario's intense gaze matched that of a professional racing car driver. From time to time, Hans noticed Mario's skillful gear changes and heel toe racing action on the pedals. The scene outside was mostly a blur, only becoming clear when a sharp corner came up. A pedestrian at a crossing bravely stepped out in front of the car thinking it would stop. But Mario had no intention of slowing down or stopping for the pedestrian. Instead, he performed a well-practised driving manoeuvre, drifting the car around the pedestrian and around the following corner.

The only thing Emil saw of the pedestrian was her saucer-like eyes as her face darted passed the back window. Neither Emil nor Hans had any idea of where they were. The street scape flashed so quick they could not make out any landmarks. Soon, the inner-city scene was replaced by a suburban landscape with longer and wider streets, which gave Mario the opportunity to drive even faster. The dash to their destination continued for another ten minutes before he hit the brakes. Emil and Hans lurched forward in their seats, only their seatbelts preventing them from being launched through the windscreen.

Mario looked over at Hans then back at Emil and said, 'Uh, uh! Is Mario not the greatest driver in the world?'

Hans sat clutching his chest, waiting for his heart to beat again. Emil stared at Mario, speechless. A few moments passed before Hans said, 'I think my heart has started again.'

'At least we know who to call if we need to get somewhere in a hurry,' Emil added.

'Are we here? Please tell me we are here,' Hans pleaded.

'We have stopped, haven't we?' Mario stated. He got out of the car and let Emil out from the back seat. Hans slowly alighted and closed the door behind him. They stood in a typical suburban street with homes lining the footways. The home before them had a high wall across the frontage with a high wooden gate in the centre. Mario walked up to the gate and was about to open it when he turned to the others and said, 'Now remember, do exactly as I say. If I say we go, we go immediately, okay?' Emil and Hans both nodded.

Mario opened the gate and the others followed. Behind the fence was a courtyard lined with pot plants, and in the centre a large water feature—a statue of a nude female holding a jug of water that poured continuously into the surrounding pond at her feet. They walked to the opposite end where the main house stood. Mario walked up to the front door and swung the large brass knocker three times onto the door.

A few moments passed before a small hatch slid open in the door. From behind the small hatch an old face appeared. 'Si?' All that they could see of the face was a bent nose and two fading brown eyes peering at them.

'Luccio, it's Mario.'

'Mario.' His eyes narrowed. 'Where is your brother Roberto, isn't he still in the lock up?'

Mario's head dropped momentarily as he said, 'Si.'

'You know I only do business with very particular clients—and you're not one of them. Arrivederci.' Luccio's face disappeared and the small hatch was closed abruptly.

Mario shouted at the door. 'Luccio please, the church needs your help!' Nothing happened for several seconds, then the hatch reopened.

Luccio's face reappeared. 'The church wants nothing to do with me or my family. Why do you say this?' His eyes seemed more intense than before.

'Look, they are here to see you, see?' Mario stepped aside so Luccio had a clear line of sight. Luccio's beady eyes studied the two men before him. Another small hatch opened at waist height and a gun barrel appeared from it. 'Who are you and what do you want?'

Hans stood behind Emil's tall stature and poked his head out to see what was happening.

Emil's eyes widened as an explanation poured from his mouth. 'I am Father Emil, and this is Father Hans.' Emil looked back at Hans briefly before continuing, 'We are from Switzerland. There is a boy that is possessed by a terrible demon, and we are about to perform an exorcism. We are not confident that we can free the boy of this demon and there is a danger that it could possess one of us during the ritual. The only way to rid the boy, or us, of this demon is a silver bullet to the head. Though we hope it does not come to that, we must be prepared.'

Emil paused for a moment to let his words sink in before continuing, 'Please, you are our only hope to make such a weapon.'

Luccio stared, eyes like a master painting, at the priests before him. He summed them up before saying, 'Silver bullets are difficult to make, and extremely expensive. I assume cost is not an issue?'

Emil shook his head. 'No.'

Luccio's eyes changed to a more pleasant expression as he asked, 'Can either of you perform a baptism?'

Emil and Hans looked at each other, then back at the face in the hatch. They nodded.

'Can you do it now?' Luccio's question felt more like a demand.

Emil replied, 'We don't have a service book with us, but we could go and get one.'

'No need, I have one here,' Luccio said. The gun disappeared as did his face from the small hatch. Several latches could be heard being unlocked before the door opened inwards. In the doorway stood a man well in his sixties with only a band of grey hair across the back of his head. His thin lips encircled a set of rather misaligned teeth, stained from many years of smoking. He wore a pale blue, short-sleeved shirt and a pair of brown trousers that seemed too big for his legs, but barely fitted his portly waist. 'Come in,' he said with an out-of-character, friendly tone.

Behind Luccio was a long hallway with a tiled floor, and within the walls were several closed doors. They walked the length of the hallway and at the end it opened out into a large living area. Across the far wall was a floor-to-ceiling glass window that overlooked a landscaped garden with ornate water features. Luccio gestured for them to sit down on the designer leather lounge suite that dominated the living area. He then left the room.

'Mario whispered to Emil, 'Good that you wore your uniform or else we may not have got in.'

Emil nodded and Hans wore an expression of self-satisfaction.

Luccio returned with a woman in her late twenties. She was wearing black jeans and a white blouse, and she was holding a baby that appeared to be around six months old. The woman sat down in the remaining vacant lounge chair and stared at the three before her. Her features were much softer than that of Luccio's and her eyes were more intense, but her nose and jawline were unmistakably like his.

Luccio remained standing as he said, 'Apparently one of my customers had a run in with the local cardinal, and now no priest in the country will perform any ceremony for me or for any of my family. Not even a baptism for my beautiful grandson. My wife wants to divorce me, and my daughter Sophia hardly speaks to me.' He gestured towards the young woman before them. 'But how is that fair on them? They did nothing wrong. But they can't punish me so instead they punish the innocent—my family—and my innocent little grandson.' He turned towards Sophia, who redirected her stare at him. 'But see, I fix. I will not let you be punished because of me.'

Sophia stared at her father, her dark orbs penetrating his soul. She turned to Emil and Hans and asked, 'Are you real priests?'

Luccio quickly butted in. 'Of course they are real.'

Sophia's eyes darted to her father. 'I am talking to them, not you Papa.' Her stare returned to Emil and Hans.

Hans answered, 'Yes my child, we are from a monastery in Switzerland.'

'What would two priests from Switzerland have to do with my father?'

Emil answered, 'Your father is helping us to forge a weapon that can exorcise a demon.'

Sophia stared at them for a moment before saying, 'You can't be serious?'

'Believe me, we are very serious,' Hans replied. Emil's tactic was very clever—the way he phrased the answers was essentially the truth, but it gave Hans the comfort to join in. 'This demon is the worst we have ever come across and it is the most dangerous.'

Sophia stared again as she summed up the two before her. 'Okay,' she said. 'I believe you.'

Luccio, bursting with excitement, hugged his daughter and said, 'Thank you, thank you. You see, I fix, I fix.'

Once Luccio ended the embrace, Sophia said, 'You're not off the hook yet Papa. You were lucky I was here when they turned up. If you called and told me about this, I would not have believed you.'

Luccio's demeanor became more sombre as he said, 'Still, you were here, and I fix. I go get the service book.'

Hans added, 'And could you please bring a bowl of fresh, clean water?'

'Si, si,' Luccio said as he left the room.

Hans performed the baptism and Emil assisted. When the ceremony was over, Luccio led them to back to the front door. As he ushered them outside, he said, 'Come back in two weeks, the items will be ready.'

****

Two weeks passed and as instructed, Emil and Hans returned to Luccio's house. They waited a few minutes until Mario arrived, and as expected, it came with the smell of burned rubber. The three entered the front gate, Mario leading the way. He knocked on the door and a moment later, Luccio's face appeared from behind the small hatch. 'Si? Ahh, come in, come in.'

Luccio led them down the corridor and through the lounge where they had spent most of their time during their last visit. They were led down another hallway that bordered the internal garden courtyard, to a door at the end. Luccio opened the door and they all entered.

Behind the door was a room that traversed the width of the property. Most of the room was set up as a firing range, but at the end where they had entered, there was a small metal workshop. Upon the work bench in the centre was a lathe, two vices, a small box, and a handgun.

After they had all entered, Luccio closed the soundproof door behind them, walked up to the bench and picked up the handgun.

Hans and Emil's eyes were glued upon the weapon as Luccio removed the magazine and said, 'I chose the Kahr MK9 9mm pistol for you. It is a favourite among my female clients and is perfect for first timers like yourselves. It's small, light and easy to fire. You are new to this, are you not?'

Emil and Hans both nodded.

'Here, try it out. Feel the weight and balance.' Luccio handed the pistol to Emil first.

Emil took the weapon and stared at it for a moment as if it were an alien. Holding it more naturally, he began having flashbacks from a Dirty Harry movie he once watched on TV. 'I have the urge to say, 'Go ahead, make my day!'

'This is not a forty-four magnum, but it is untraceable—no registration numbers,' Luccio stated. 'Come over to the firing range and get a feel for it in action.' They walked over to the firing range and Luccio took the pistol. He showed Emil how to load the magazine then he gave the gun back to him.

Emil raised the pistol to his eye line and aimed at the cardboard target some six metres away. He fired the gun. Both Hans and Emil flinched from the sudden bang, but Luccio remained unfazed. A small bullet hole appeared at the top, right-hand corner of the target.

Luccio said, 'Cup your left hand under your right to steady your aim. Try again.' Emil did as Luccio said and fired the pistol again. This time the bullet hole that appeared in the target was near the centre.

'Good. Very good. You are a natural,' Luccio complimented. 'Now you have a go.' He signalled to Hans.

Hans timidly took the pistol and aimed at the target. As he pulled the trigger, he closed his eyes—the bullet completely missed.

Luccio protested, 'You must keep your eyes open when you pull the trigger—and cup your left hand under your right to steady it.' Hans tried again, managing to keep his eyes open. A small hole appeared near the bottom left of the target. 'Better,' said Luccio. 'Have another go.'

Hans and Emil fired the pistol a few more times until they had had enough. They returned the pistol to Luccio. Luccio removed the magazine, emptied it of bullets and reinserted it into the pistol.

He walked over to the bench and picked up the small box. 'Here is the silver ammunition. A box of twenty-four. Each custom made in solid silver and guaranteed to work every time—no jamming.' He placed the box back on the table and said, 'Now it is just a matter of payment—500 Euros for the pistol and 14,000 for the ammunition.'

Mario gasped. '14,000? Mamma mia!'

Luccio shot Mario a look before stating, 'A fair price for untraceable, solid silver bullets.'

Emil pulled out his smart phone from his pocket and said, 'The price is fine. What is your bank account details? I will transfer it now.'

Luccio gave Emil the details and he made the online transaction on his phone. 'There, transfer completed.'

Luccio handed the pistol and ammunition to Emil and shook both the men's hands. 'All the best with your exorcism.'

'Thank you,' Hans replied.

After leaving the house, Emil said to Mario, 'Thank you for your help. We couldn't have done this without you.'

'Anything for my friends. Good luck.' Mario said as he waved goodbye and got into his car. With a screech from the car tyres, Mario was off down the street in a flash.

Hans turned to Emil. 'Well, we have the tools for the job. Now it is up to us to finish this.'

Emil's eyes narrowed as he said, 'Yes, and finish it we will.'

****

The following Tuesday, Emil and Hans returned to the church on the university grounds. To be less conspicuous, they wore their civilian clothes again.

Hans was in the position he was in the previous time where he could see out the doorway and down the street. Emil was standing near the door, with his back against the wall, looking at Hans. Apart from the two wannabe assassins, the church was empty. The night before, as directed by *The Secret Book of Saint John*, they had washed the bullets in holy water and blessed them with a crucifix.

The scene was set, and their hearts raced. The plan was simple—Hans would nod to Emil when the moment was right. Emil would jump out, grab the Antichrist and drag it into the church. Once inside, he would immediately shoot him in the heart. The plan was so simple Emil was sure it would succeed. Hans had to agree, it was a simple and precise plan with little chance of failure.

Hans began to perspire, and his palms became wet. He had to keep wiping his hands on his trousers.

Emil's concentration steeled him against his impending sinful act. He kept whispering to himself over and over, 'He is not a real person, he is evil. He is not a real person, he is evil. He is not a real person, he is evil.' The seconds passed like hours; the minutes passed like days. Emil changed his chant to the *Lord's Prayer*, reciting it over and over in his head.

Hans looked at his watch again and again, checking to see if the moment had passed, the Antichrist was a no show, and they had managed to avoid the whole deadly event. But no, there was still time. The dread in his head made his stomach feel like it was digesting a rotten meal. Then the target appeared, casually strolling down the street. And to make his stomach wretch even more, he was alone. Hans waited for the right moment, his heart racing frantically. Could this be the moment where they save the world from the apocalypse? He dared not dwell on the frail hope of success. Still, they must try for the sake of the world.

It seemed liked forever before Hans showed any sign of the impending pinnacle moment, then his expression suddenly changed. His eyes widened and his mouth gaped. The moment of all moments was nigh. Emil began thumping his right fist into his left hand as if he were about to start a fight—and a fight it would no doubt be. 'You are an Archangel fighting pure evil,' he thought.

Hans watched the young man walk closer and closer until he was only a few steps away from the church entrance. Slowly and deliberately, Hans nodded.

Emil sprung into action, so fast he even took Hans by surprise. The target had just passed the entrance—Hans's timing was perfect. Emil was upon the target in a heartbeat—he grabbed the backpack strap and a fist full of T-shirt and threw the young man into the church entrance. The target slid along the polished marble floor well into the church.

Before the young man had time to turn over and face his assailant, Emil was already over him with the gun trained on his forehead.

Just like that! It was so easy—too easy. Emil stared into the face of the young man before him, a face that revealed utter shock.

How could this rather unassuming person be the dreaded Antichrist?

Emil expected a battle, an unholy and unearthly battle. But none came. He hesitated. For the time it took for his heart to perform its rhythmical beating—*thump, thump*, he thought, 'Is this the right guy?' But that was the limit of his hesitation. If he was the Antichrist, he had to shoot him—right here, right now. His finger began to squeeze the trigger.

But Emil's millisecond hesitation was all that Judas needed. Before Emil's finger could complete the trigger action, Judas kicked the gun from Emil's extended arm, sending the pistol across the church floor. He rolled thrice in the direction of the pistol; his hand landed precisely on the gun as he completed his third roll. In the time that Emil's heart had completed two beats, the tables had been turned.

Unlike Emil, the Antichrist did not hesitate, and he immediately pulled the trigger. The sound of the gunshot seemed quite antiquated and almost harmless to Hans's ears. It was more like the sound of a small firecracker going off, but the result of the seemingly harmless noise was lethal—Luccio had chosen well. The gun was small but effective, and his crafted munition was straight and true.

Hans looked at Emil and noticed a small, dark hole appearing in the middle of his forehead. A slow flow of dark red ooze came from the hole and travelled down the bridge of his nose and onto his right cheek. Then, like a falling tree, the great frame of Emil struck the marble floor face first.

Hans stood there paralysed, staring at the prostrate corpse of Emil. He didn't even notice the large black dog that had appeared at the church entrance. The dog did not enter, it just stood there, growling in a low and sinister tone.

The voice of the Antichrist broke Hans's trance. 'Too late Goliath, you missed all the fun.'

Hans looked at the figure before him and expected a gun to be trained on him, but there was none. The gun hung innocuously in Judas's left hand, by his side.

The Antichrist casually walked up to Hans, brutishly grabbed his face and began studying the old man's features. He stated in a tone bloated with contempt, 'Is this the best your God can do? An old man and a fool?' He glanced over at Emil's body then returned his gaze to Hans. 'Don't know why he bothered.' His expression changed to an almost unnatural form of anger and his voice was strained with intense passion. 'I am the most powerful being to walk this Earth! A nation's army would have been more appropriate, not just the two of you.' His expression morphed again in concert with his wildly changing emotions. Now, his face wore a more pleasant expression. 'Though you have done your homework. Attempting an ambush from within a church. And let me guess ...' He raised the pistol so that it was next to Hans's face, pointing towards his head. 'Silver bullets? I hope you cleansed them with holy water.'

For a moment Hans gained some inner strength and said defiantly, 'You are not the most powerful being to walk the Earth. The son of God is!'

Judas's eyes widened at the insolence of his captive. 'What, him? You believe the hype too much.'

Hans sensed he had hit a raw nerve and his confidence grew enough to continue his crusade. 'Your arrogance will be your downfall!'

The Antichrist's eyes widened even more, and his expression became intensely dark. 'And your foolishness yours!' He grabbed Hans by the back of the neck and pushed him towards the entrance. 'Let's get out of here. This place sickens me.' As they neared the entrance, Goliath stepped back but growled even louder and bared his teeth. 'No Goliath, this one is mine!' Judas spat through gritted teeth.

As they left the church, Hans felt the strength of the hand on the back of his neck increase unnaturally. With the sanctuary of the church walls behind him, Hans was now at the mercy of the full power of the Antichrist. He was led around the side of the church to a spot that was obscured from onlookers. The Antichrist threw the frail frame of Hans against the wall and began to sniff his face like an animal, its expression turning to one of revulsion. 'You stink of baptism!' Its tone then changed to disappointment. 'Shame, it means I can't have as much fun with you as I would like. Still, I'm sure I can find something to entertain me.' It sniffed him again and a smile appeared. "Ah, you have been suppressing your true self. It cries out to me like a starving beast! You really need to let it free, let yourself be who you truly are. Here, let me help you.' The white of the Antichrist's eyes turned black and his pupils became doorways to the epitome of evil.

Hans felt all his inner strength drain from his soul like water out of a bottle. His craving for gambling swelled into a great bubble in his mind. He tried to avert his eyes from the unholy stare, but the Antichrist pulled his face back in line. It was over in seconds. Hans was weaker now than he had ever been—even during his darkest days. Not satisfied with destroying all of Hans's inner metal, the Antichrist subjected his mind to inhuman sounds and images that left his mind in a weakened hypnotic state.

The Antichrist gripped Hans's shirt with both fists and said to him, 'Go and fulfil your sinful desires and when you have reached the absolute bottom of your pathetic existence ...' His left hand let go of his shirt and returned the gun to Hans's face. '... end your miserable life!' He threw Hans to the ground and dropped the gun on him. The Antichrist walked away with Goliath in tow. Goliath paused for a moment to turn back and give Hans a goodbye growl, before returning to follow his master.

Hans's eyes, wide with madness, darted about like a pair of small fruit flies. An insane smile grew across his face as he let out a short, quick giggle, then another and another. Finally, he burst into a flurry of laughing madness.

****

Sam flinched so much he dropped the remote. The sound of the gunshot echoed in his ears well after the speakers had produced it. For months, everything was as dull as dull could be. He had set up two surveillance stations outside the two places that the subject spent most of his time. One was across the road from the luxury one-bedroom apartment the subject rented in the city centre of Rome, and the other was atop a tall building that overlooked the university campus. From the top of that building, Sam had a clear view of most of the streets in the campus.

He watched Judas walk down the campus street and turn the corner on his way to the next lecture as he had done many times before. All was as normal until that gunshot. Many would mistake that sound to be the backfire of a car or some other less eventful sound, but Sam knew all too well what that sound was. He picked up the remote from the floor and pressed the 'Rewind' button. He went back two minutes and resumed play. Sam sat forward in his chair and watched the ultra-high-definition television intently. Although the view of the campus was from a point some distance away, he was still able to make out figures walking around the campus, and he was just able to identify the subject of his surveillance.

There, he appeared from behind a building and was walking down the centre of the street, as all the students did. He turned the corner out the front of the church and began walking down the second street to his next lecture. A figure darted from the church, grabbed the subject, and threw him into the church. From what Sam could make out, the figure was a tall young man dressed like a student. Seconds passed before the gunshot rang out. Moments later, the subject's dog came up to the church entrance and stayed there. The dog seemed reluctant to enter the church and seek its master.

Some time passed without anything happening. Sam was about to press the 'Fast Forward' button when two figures appeared. This time the subject was led by an old man from the church. But the two figures were very close together—unnaturally close. Although Sam couldn't make out the weapon, he could tell by their postures that the subject had a gun in the old man's back. They walked around to the side of the church, to an obscured place, and stayed there for a short time. Despite Sam's vantage point, he could not see the two figures. Eventually, the subject reappeared without the old man and went on his way to his next lecture as if the interruption had never happened.

Sam fast forwarded until he saw the old man reappear, which was some time after the subject had left. The old man walked down the university street, in the opposite direction to the subject, and disappeared. Sam sat there staring at the television, wondering what the hell had just happened. The young man that first appeared and grabbed the subject, was not seen again. While Sam's mind went through numerous fatal scenarios involving the young man, the old man reappeared on the television screen. This time he was just across the street from the surveillance station. Sam could see him clearly and hear him as well.

The old man was muttering to himself and his eyes were darting about frantically. He hailed a taxi and got in. 'Ciao. 153 Viale Giulio Cesare,' said the old man to the driver.

'Si,' the driver answered before taking off.

Sam fast forwarded until he saw a robed man enter the church. A few moments later, he came running out shouting, and waving his hands.

Sam fast forwarded again until he saw the police and an ambulance. He then watched as a body was removed on a stretcher in a body bag.

Sam paused the recording, mesmerised by the static scene before him. Was that the man that had employed him? Or was it the old man that had left in the taxi? Was it someone else? His head was full of questions. He rewound the footage to just before the old man got in the taxi. He studied his face. Did that face match the voice on the phone? Sam wasn't sure. He picked up his mobile and dialled his employer. The phone rang and he listened intently before hanging up. What if the police had the phone and were monitoring the calls? And now he had hung up after three rings, in a suspicious manor. Had he just made himself a suspect for murder?

His mobile started playing his favourite U2 song—*Sunday Bloody Sunday*. He looked at the caller ID and it was his employer.

Sam froze. Could it be the police? He had to answer the call because either way, the police would find him. 'Hello?' Sam answered nervously. His heart was racing, and his palms became moist with sweat.

'Hello, you called.' Sam sighed in relief; it was the voice of his employer.

'Was that you?' Sam asked.

'Sorry, I don't understand,' Michael replied.

'Was that you that tried to attack the subject?'

'Attack? No, it wasn't. Tell me what happened.'

'A young fair-haired man and an old man with a bent back tried something with the subject in a church. The subject killed the young man, did something to the old man, then let him go.'

Sam heard a gasp in the background, and it didn't sound like his employer.

There was a moment's silence before Michael said, 'Holy Mary mother of ... the old man, did you see where he went?'

'I have an address. 153 Viale Giulio Cesare.'

'Okay, thank you.' Michael hung up and looked at William. William stood staring at Michael, his hand covering his mouth to mute the great gasp he had let out earlier. They had just finished a cup of coffee and William was returning from the kitchen after putting the cups in the dishwasher.

Michael was sitting on the lounge, his mobile on loudspeaker when Sam had delivered the terrible news.

William regained his composure and removed his hand from his mouth. 'Dear Emil, how horrible.'

Michael stared out the large glass window that overlooked the small balcony. For a moment, the shock muted his mind, before kicking it into gear again, allowing him to think forward. 'I am worried about Hans. Whatever the Antichrist did to him, it could not have been good. We must tell the others the bad news. Our friends in France can get to Hans faster than us. Let's hope they find him before it's too late.'

****

Rome, Italy

Eighteen hours later, a car pulled up out the front of the last known address of Hans and Emil. Rene had driven overnight to Italy while Alfred slept in the passenger seat next to him. They first heard about Emil's death while watching the evening news. They saw a report on an unknown man being shot in a church in Rome's La Sapienza University, and it rang too many alarm bells. Rene immediately checked his email for any messages and sure enough, there was one from Romeo.

They were on their way in thirty minutes.

They alighted from the car and walked up to the entrance of the hostel at that address. They entered through the glass door and into the foyer of the hostel. The foyer was a rather plain room with little decor to brighten it up. There were two old chairs in one corner, both in good condition. It was obvious the owner of the hostel knew that spending money on an establishment where the clientele were mostly students, was not a good investment. To the right was a plain reception desk where a very scruffy and bored looking man sat. He took no notice of the two men that had just entered and continued to slowly turn the pages of the newspaper on the desk.

Alfred and Rene approached the desk and waited for a response from the man, but none came. Alfred cleared his throat. 'Huckhum.'

The middle-aged man with a stubbly chin continued to read the paper and said, 'Si?'

Alfred responded in Italian. 'Some friends of ours are staying here. A tall, fair-haired young man and an old man with a bad back.'

Finally, the man raised his eyes from the paper. 'Does this look like a hotel?'

Alfred was taken aback by his curtness but was determined to press on. 'We just want to know what room they are in?'

The man rolled his eyes before replying in exasperation, 'Room 12.' He returned to his paper.

Alfred and Rene remained standing in front of the desk and after a long pause the man looked up at them and said with great exasperation, 'What now?'

Alfred asked very politely, 'Where is Room 12?'

The man slammed the paper on the table and pointed behind them. 'Up the stairs and to the left!'

'Grazie tanto,' Alfred replied.

They left the grumpy man behind, walked up the stairs and turned left at the top. Before them was a short corridor lined by doors. Alfred and Rene walked down the corridor, reading the numbers on the doors. The last door on the left bore the number twelve.

Alfred knocked on the door and they waited. With no sign of an answer, he knocked again. Again, there was no reply. Alfred looked at Rene. 'He appears to be out.'

On the off-chance that the door was not locked, Rene turned the doorknob and the door opened. He pushed the door open and said aloud, 'Hans?'

They entered the small double bedroom. The room was a mess; clothes and garbage littered the floor, and the only pieces of furniture were two single beds with matching bedside drawers and a television on a small stand. On one of the bedside tables was a laptop, the other containing a glass that Alfred assumed was for Hans's false teeth. Next to the glass was a small box that took Alfred's interest. He opened the box and gasped.

Rene came to his side and asked, 'What is it?'

Alfred showed him the contents. 'Bullets!'

'Not just bullets Alfred, they look like silver bullets!'

'How on Earth did they get such a thing?'

'Don't know, but don't leave them lying around. We will need them. Give the box to me." Alfred was more than happy to be rid of the box and gave it to Rene.

Rene walked to the only other door in the room that led to the small bathroom. It too was a mess but was void of any occupants. 'He could be anywhere,' Rene stated.

Alfred turned to Rene. 'Maybe there is a clue on the computer.'

'Worth a try,' Rene replied. He sat on the bed, opened the laptop and turned it on. He looked at the desktop for any files of interest but found none. He then checked recent files. Again, nothing stood out. Rene checked the browsing history and launched the last viewed page. He stared at the page for a moment then turned the laptop around so Alfred could see it. 'You're right, it was worth a try.'

Alfred bent over to view the screen better, then looked down through the bottom half of his bifocal glasses. Across the top of the webpage was the banner 'Casinò di Venezia'. He looked back at Rene. 'I've always wanted to visit Venice, though the casino would not be on my site seeing list.'

'We should take the laptop with us. It shouldn't be left just lying about,' stated Rene.

'Good idea. I'm surprised it's still here,' Alfred said as he glanced around.

'Come on, let's go,' said Rene.

****

Venice, Italy

That evening, Alfred and Rene stood outside the oldest casino in the world. To blend in, they wore appropriate evening attire—collared shirts, trousers, and suit jackets. They entered the casino, trying to look casual and as though they had done this many times before. But to the observant eye, they looked extremely uncomfortable.

Alfred and Rene were surprised to see so many people in the casino. It wasn't as full as what the staff would see on a weekend, but for midweek, it was a good turnout. The ground floor was full of poker machines and at approximately every second machine, there was some poor soul hypnotised by its spinning symbols.

They zigzagged their way through what was like a small maze until they had covered the whole floor.

'Let's try upstairs,' Rene suggested.

The next floor was full of roulette wheels and craps tables. Every table had a small group of gamblers surrounding it.

Alfred asked, 'Don't these people have homes and families to tend to?'

'Apparently not,' Rene replied.

Again, they covered the whole floor with no sign of Hans. 'One more floor to go. Let's hope it's our lucky floor,' Rene added.

Alfred struggled up the second flight of stairs, his old knees beginning to ache.

Rene stepped patiently behind Alfred so as not to rush him. At the top Rene said, 'Let's take the lift back down.'

They scanned the floor before them, this one devoted to blackjack. At the far side of the floor was a raised level; two security guards stood at the roped off entrance.

Alfred and Rene walked casually through the blackjack tables looking for Hans. When they reached the end of the room, they stared at the sectioned off table. At the end of the table was Hans—a glass of Scotch in one, and cards in the other.

Rene said, 'Remember he has been touched by the Antichrist. We must be careful.' Alfred nodded.

They approached the entrance and the two security guards. The muscular guard on the left said in Italian, 'Sorry this is a VIP area.'

Alfred said, 'Our friend is on the table.'

'You will have to wait until the current hand is played, then your friend can leave the table and arrange for your access.'

They waited, wondering why this table was so special. Then they heard the dealer say, 'The Signor has raised to fifty thousand. House will match the bet.'

Alfred and Rene could not see his cards, but they could see Hans's eyes. They darted about from his cards to the table, to the dealer—over and over. The unnatural motion sent a chill down Rene's spine.

Hans placed his cards on the table and the dealer announced, 'Twenty.' The dealer flipped a card on the table before him and said, 'Blackjack! House wins.'

The other players got up from the table while Hans remained with his head in his hands. The security guards opened the rope across the entrance to let the players out; the last to leave was Hans. He walked right passed Alfred and Rene and headed towards the bar.

Rene caught up to him, put his hand on his shoulder and spun Hans around. 'Hans, it's us—Rene and Alfred. What are you doing here?'

Hans stared at Rene for a moment before his eyes began to dart between Alfred and Rene. 'Getting a drink.' He turned around and continued towards the bar. Alfred, getting a strong waft of alcohol from Hans's breath, waved his hand in front of his nose.

Rene grabbed Hans by the arm and said, 'No I think you need some fresh air instead.'

Alfred grabbed Hans by the other arm, and they escorted him to the balcony. Once they stepped on the balcony, Rene checked if they were alone. There was a couple at the far end of the balcony—out of ear shot.

Rene grabbed Hans by both shoulders, stared into his mad eyes and said, 'What happened yesterday? What did it do to you?'

Hans's eye kept darting from side to side. 'Who did what?'

'The beast! Remember? Do you remember what happened?'

'Remember? Remember?' He gasped, began to hyperventilate and finally he screamed, 'Aaggrrhh!' Hans reached into his coat pocket, pulled out a small handgun and raised it to his head.

Rene was quick to grab the gun from Hans's weaker grip and hand it to Alfred. Alfred quickly hid it in his coat pocket.

Hans struggled against Rene's restraint and cried, 'No, no don't let me live. Kill me, kill me!'

'What happened?' Rene demanded.

Hans began to whimper then collapsed to his knees and said, 'The beast was mortal in the church, but it was still very quick. It shot Emil. Outside its power is unimaginable and it knows of us now. We have failed! It then … it took away my strength! Look at me, look at what I truly am. Please don't tell my dearest Angelica?'

Rene said calmly, 'She will know nothing of this. Come, let's go.'

Rene and Alfred got Hans to his feet and they walked to the doorway that led back into the casino. Rene noticed the couple at the end of the balcony was staring at them.

Before Rene and Alfred could react, Hans turned on his heels, ran to the balcony railing and leaped over it. Rene and Alfred turned and reached for a leg, but he was too quick. They watched their brother fall to his death.

'Hans!' cried Alfred as he looked over the balcony. Rene glanced at the body on the road below then turned his head away. Alfred followed suit.

A scream from the couple at the end of the balcony was loud enough to alert security. Two musclebound men ran onto the balcony to attend to the woman who had screamed. Alfred and Rene quietly ducked back into the casino and took the lift to the ground floor.

By the time they reached the front doors of the casino, a crowd had formed around the bloodied body of Hans.

Rene began to head towards the crowd when Alfred stopped him. 'No, we must leave. Now!'

They walked down the street to the car, but Rene couldn't help but look back from time to time. He felt like a deserter.

Alfred said, 'If we are linked with Hans, the police could link us to what happened with Emil, and then who knows where it could lead.'

What Alfred said made sense. Just before they turned the corner towards the car, Rene saw the two security guards looking for them in the crowd. They would certainly have been questioned, names and addresses recorded, and questions would have been asked about why they were there and how they found Hans. The more he thought about it, the more comfortable he became about leaving Hans.

The next day while driving back to France, the news was filled with the story of the mysterious deaths of two monks. When they arrived back in France, they had the regretful task of emailing the Brethren to inform them of the loss of not just one, but two brothers.

8

Assassin's Plight

Six years had passed, and the Brethren had not made any other attempt on the life of Satan's spawn; and since then, Judas was more cautious of being near holy ground. The surveillance from Sam had confirmed this as Judas kept to the other side of the road when walking past the university church. The Brethren was at a loss as to how to get the beast on holy ground again.

Judas however, knew exactly where he was going. He finished his studies and returned to Jerusalem to practise law. He completed the bar exam in record time and was quickly snapped up by one of the leading law firms in Israel. It wasn't long before he was winning high profile cases.

Sarina and John could not be prouder of their adopted son. John was nearing retirement, and the disappointment in not having a bloodline heir had long since passed. John felt comfortable that his family name was in good hands. Judas had not returned to the family home and was living in a lavish one-bedroom apartment in an exclusive area of Jerusalem. Both John and Sarina knew it was time for Judas to make his own way in life. Her precious Judas was all grown up. Her opportunities to be a mother were reduced to the moments when she and John would visit Judas, and Sarina could give advice on how his apartment could be better decorated.

Not far from the luxurious and successful life of Judas, was the empty lives of two much older men. The futility of their existence was becoming unbearable—to William in particular. More absurd were his proposed solutions to the problem. 'No, we can't break into his office and consecrate it! There is too much security, we would never get away with it,' Michael protested.

'We must do something. Every day he gets stronger and us weaker,' William retorted.

'Yes, I know but we must not be foolish either,' Michael took another mouthful of cereal as his eyes focused on the television.

They sat at the table in the small dining room of their apartment in Jerusalem. The morning news was on the television and the current hot topic of the day was the extensive drought that had befallen the country. 'Ten years since our last good rainfall,' the newsreader declared. 'We only have two years of water left. The government's project to build two desalination plants is still three years away from completion, and there are great concerns that the project is too little too late. Other breaking news, the US has been struck by another super storm over the Gulf of Mexico. The earthquake in Turkey has now claimed the lives of five hundred and officials expect the count to continue to rise.'

William turned the volume down and added, 'The first horseman of the apocalypse has already broken the first seal. Drought plagues us, massive earthquakes, and super storms. What next?' He dropped the remote on the dining table before continuing, 'We must do something, anything! I am tired of just sitting around trying to think of something to stop all this.'

Michael ignored him, picked up the remote and turned the volume back up.

The reporter had returned to the main story of the day. 'The drought has now begun to affect businesses. Companies that depend on water, like window washers and cleaners, have been laying off staff as they are unable to source their basic tools of the trade. A new category of water restrictions came into force yesterday, Level Six, where fresh water can now only be used for drinking and showering. Most car wash companies have closed as their access to fresh water has been cut.'

Michael turned the volume down and said, 'Do I need to remind you of what happened in Italy?'

William jumped to his feet so fast the dining chair he was sitting on almost toppled over. 'I certainly do not need reminding! I was the only one willing to take the risk of attending the funeral.'

'My dear William,' Michael said calmly. 'Father Stephen was right. If any of us were to attend, the police would be onto us. The risk was far too great. Besides, I have an idea.'

William folded his arms and glared at Michael. 'And I suppose your idea will be better than any of mine?' he asked in a sarcastic tone.

'How about you hear my idea first and then tell me if you think it will work,' Michael replied in his continued calm tone.

'Okay then, let's hear it.'

Michael glanced at the television and said, 'We get jobs as cleaners.'

William looked at the television to see a cleaner being interviewed over the water shortage report. He looked back at Michael. 'Go on.'

'He lives in a very expensive building complex, which would no doubt employ its own cleaning staff. Cleaning staff usually have access to all areas. Once we have keys to the vault so to speak, we consecrate his apartment. As he is usually at work all day, we would have plenty of time to complete the service; and there's no security to get in the way. But we should not attempt the assassination ourselves. I don't want a repeat of last time. We need a professional.'

William unfolded his arms to count on his fingers the points he was about to make. 'One, we don't know any assassins. Two, there is a drought— in case you haven't been listening—and cleaners are losing their jobs!'

Michael stood and began to pace the dining room. 'Yes, we don't know any assassins, but our private eye might. As I recall, he said he worked for the CIA. It will take some time to infiltrate the cleaning service, possibly years, but it will be worth the wait.'

'What if he moves before then?'

'Then we will form a new plan.'

William stared at Michael for some time before saying, 'Okay, you win. But the concept is still much the same as mine, just with fewer flaws.'

Michael smiled. 'Certainly. I just added a few finishing touches.'

William looked uncertainly at Michael, not sure if he was being facetious. Either way, he wasn't bothered because finally, he could start focusing on a solid plan. William smiled and let out a small chuckle. 'Okay, you can contact the PI and I will research the cleaning company.'

****

Sam had slept in. He was at his niece's wedding last night and had drunk a bit too much. His mobile phone woke him up. His first reaction was to check the time on the bedside alarm clock—9:48 am. Sam was normally up by 7:30 am but today he was not so much bothered by his late start, but more by the fact that he had been woken up on a Sunday morning. He picked up his mobile from the bedside table and said in a groggy and crackly voice, 'Shalom?'

The familiar voice was clear and purposeful. 'Shalom. Sorry to disturb you on a Sunday morning, but we are hoping you could help us.'

As Sam replied, his voice cleared to its more natural tone. 'You are my best client, so just name it.'

'Would you know of any assassins?'

The question took Sam by surprise. He sat up in his bed and cleared his throat. 'So, you have a way to make him mortal?'

'Yes,' the voice answered.

'Well, that is encouraging news. Hmm, there was a guy I met once about ten years ago. He was extensively used by the CIA, and successfully I might add. But he doesn't like people looking for him, and for those who do, often end up dead.'

'Oh, well is there anyone else?'

'No. But he knows me, so I have a good chance of finding him and not ending up in a coffin!'

'If you are okay with tracking him down?'

'By the way, assuming I do find him, he will want to know the details of the job. I know who and where, but the when and how I don't know.'

'We will let you know exactly when at a later date, but the how would be best from a distance. And he will need special bullets.'

'What type of bullets?'

'Silver.'

'They are not easy to come by and they may take some time to source.'

'That's okay, we already have some. The box says they are 9 mm bullets.'

Sam smiled as he thought, 'This guy is full of surprises.' Sam then continued, 'Great. I'll let you know if I find him.'

'Shalom.'

'Shalom.'

****

Three weeks later, Sam found the mobile number of Gerrard Bejoux. He knew that Gerrard never answered his mobile as he screened every call.

Sure enough, the mobile rang out and Sam was diverted to voicemail with an automated voice, 'Leave a message after the tone.'

'Gerrard, it's Sam from the Israeli mission we did back in 2009. Hope you remember me. To jog your memory—Operation Hammerhead. I have a job for you if you are still in the business. Call me back on this number.' Sam hung up and waited.

Two hours later, his mobile rang while he was leaving the local supermarket after picking up some groceries. The number was not recognised by his mobile address book. 'Shalom?'

A rough voice sounded in his ear. 'What was the cover name of the girl that manned the hub for Operation Hammerhead?'

Sam began to rub the top of his head in a psychosomatic gesture to recall the old memory from his head. 'Ahh, oh yeah, how could I forget? Shelly Beach.'

The voice replied in a less gruff tone, 'Hello Sam, long time no speak.'

'Ten years I figure. How have you been?'

'Had a double bypass two years ago. Too much fast food while on the job. Now it's all salad sandwiches. Taste like crap but it will keep me alive. How about you?'

'Been well, lots of walking has kept the doctor away. Are you still in the same business?'

'Freelance now, much better. I get to choose the jobs so it's only true villains for me, no political bullshit. I even sleep at night sometimes now.'

'That's good to hear. Well, I have a real villain for you if you are interested.'

'What's the M.O.?'

'He has killed several people, and I was almost added to the list.'

'Okay, I will need a list of the victim's names and whatever details you have on the target.'

Sam paused for a moment before he said, 'There are some things you should know about the target first. They may change your mind about the job.'

'Okay, like what?'

Sam paused again then cleared his throat before saying, 'He can't be killed by normal munitions, but silver bullets can kill him.'

His statement was met with silence and Sam felt compelled to justify it. 'I know it sounds crazy, but I have seen this guy in action— he is far from normal. All he did was look at me and I nearly died. I'm telling you, he's a freak, an extremely dangerous freak!'

The silence continued for what seemed like minutes, but only a few seconds passed before Gerrard asked in a tone mixed with sarcasm and nervousness, 'So what is he, some sort of werewolf?'

'No, worse. My client claims he is the Antichrist, and after my close encounter, I believe him.'

'That is some claim.'

'So, what do you think?'

'Sounds challenging. The silver bullets will take some time to source.'

'No need, we already have them—9 mm.'

'Okay, so what is the offer?'

'You name it.'

'Send me the details and I'll let you know.'

'Okay, good to speak to you.'

'Salut.'

'Shalom.'

Two days later, Sam received a text message saying, 'I am in. Price five million Euros. Half up front and half when the job is done. Account details are attached. Let me know who to contact for the bullets.'

****

Paris, France

The midday sunshine beamed down upon Alfred and Rene as they walked along the Avenue Pierre Loti. Before them was the great iron monolith of the Eiffel Tower. Its dull paint ignored the brightness of the day and only reflected a flat beige colour. Two days ago, Rene received a text message telling him to rendezvous underneath the Eiffel Tower. The message was from an unknown number, but he knew very well who it was from as an email from Michael and William some days ago had forewarned them.

Both Alfred and Rene wore casual clothes—jeans and T-shirts—to blend in with the crowd of surrounding tourists.

Alfred was not in a good mood. 'Why does he want to meet us? Why can't we just post the bullets to him?'

Rene answered, 'I don't know why, but if he wants to meet us in person, then meet I will.'

'He is a professional killer. I have no desire to meet such a man.'

'As I said before, you do not have to do this. I am happy to meet him by myself.'

Alfred glared at Rene. 'I meant what I said. We stick together, no matter what.'

They walked under the massive structure to the centre, as instructed. Both Alfred and Rene couldn't help but look up and marvel at the impressive superstructure. When they reached the middle, they looked at the sparse gathering of tourists around them to see if they could spot the assassin. Everyone looked very normal, for tourists at least.

'What are we supposed to do now?' Alfred grumbled.

'Wait I guess,' Rene shrugged.

Rene's mobile beeped. He pulled it out of his pocket and read the new text.

'Cross the river and go to the centre of the park on the left.'

Rene announced, 'He wants us to cross the river.'

'What?' Alfred protested. 'Why did he tell us to come to the wrong place? What sort of fool is he?'

'He is watching us, and it is to see if we are being followed,' Rene concluded.

'Why would anyone follow a pair of old priests?' Alfred declared.

They walked to the Pont d'Léna that crossed over the Seine river. As they crossed, both Alfred and Rene looked down at the silvery reflection of the sunlight on the water. The blackness of their sunglasses reflected the silver shimmering of the water before them, and for a moment they forgot about their mission and enjoyed the stunning view.

Once they had reached the end of the Pont d'Léna, before them was the Palais de Chaillot and its fountains. The water danced about in the sunlight, oblivious to the seriousness of the two that surveyed it.

To the left was the park. Alfred and Rene crossed the road and entered it via the wide path that met the intersection. They reached the centre of the park and found a large, rectangular section of manicured lawn. Several people were sunning themselves on blankets, some in engrossed an almost indecent public embrace with their partners.

Alfred and Rene scanned those on the lawn for anyone that looked like an assassin, but neither knew what an assassin would look like. Nevertheless, no one looked suspicious.

Rene's mobile rang and he pulled it out of his pocket and answered. 'Bonjour?'

A rough voice answered, 'Go to the park bench on your right and sit down.' Then hung up.

'He wants us to sit down,' Rene relayed.

They sat down as instructed and began to scan the surrounding area for the assassin. Minutes passed with no sign of him, and Alfred was becoming more and more agitated. 'This is ridiculous.'

'But necessary,' said a rough voice behind them.

Alfred and Rene both flinched from the surprise.

The rough voice continued. 'Do not turn around or it will the last thing you ever do.'

They both froze.

'Do you have the bullets?', asked the voice.

Rene gathered the courage to answer. 'Yes.'

'Put the box on your right shoulder.'

Rene did as instructed. As soon as he placed the box on his shoulder, a hidden force removed it from his grasp. Alfred was on his right and from what Rene could gather, the assassin was standing behind the bench and between them.

Alfred's frozen state was only brief as his bad mood was heightened by wafts of stale cigarettes from the voice behind him. 'Why must we meet? We could have posted the bullets.'

'I wanted to know if it was true and the best way is to hear it for myself, face to face, or should I say, back to face,' Gerrard said in his low, deep voice.

'Know what is true?' Alfred snapped.

'That he is what you say he is,' Gerrard replied.

'What? You already know who he is? The Antichrist?' Alfred stated abruptly.

There was a brief pause before Gerrard said, 'You honestly think he is the Antichrist.'

Alfred's temper was swelling. 'Well, of course he is. You know what he has done, and you know what he can do. Do we have to go through all the gory details again?'

'You are very brave for a priest,' Gerrard said with some restraint. 'Such an attitude could result in you being very dead!'

'You don't scare me. I am at the end of my life, so the treat of death is pointless!' Alfred stated firmly while straightening his posture.

Rene grabbed Alfred's arm in a gesture to halt his dangerous avenue, then asked tentatively, 'How do you know that he is a priest?'

'I know you are both priests and you both disappeared from the church some years ago. You now live together in a small Paris apartment. Rather strange behaviour if you ask me. And all I needed was your mobile number!'

'Try taking on the Antichrist and then see how strangely *you* behave!' Alfred retorted.

Gerrard ignored Alfred's comment and said, 'I will contact you when the job is done, and the remaining funds are to be transferred within forty-eight hours.'

'Wait, it's not as simple as that,' Rene interjected. 'It will take more than a silver bullet to stop him.'

'Not even one straight through the head?' Gerrard stated confidently.

'He was created in the underworld, and the only one of his kind to be born into this world. No, a bullet by itself will not suffice,' Rene said sternly. 'He must be executed in his apartment but only after we have prepared it. Only then will he be mortal. We will contact you when we have done our part, but you must be ready to act immediately. The instant he steps into the apartment is when you need to take him out, not a moment before and not a moment after. And it must be through the heart, not the head. If you fail, he will be after you, and I can only pray for your soul for what he will do to you.'

'I have never failed to complete a job, and I don't plan on starting with this one.'

'If you succeed, you will save mankind from destruction. If you fail ...'

Behind them was a sudden emptiness, as if a presence had left, and Alfred could no longer smell stale cigarettes. They both slowly and cautiously looked over their shoulders; behind them was no one.

'Didn't even say goodbye, very rude!' Alfred said grumpily.

Jerusalem, Israel

****

In August, the drought in Israel broke. But it was replaced with flooding and torrential downpours. Michael and William had applied for their cleaning licences, and William began his campaign for them to be employees of the First Class Cleaning Company.

It took some months but eventually they had some success. Michael was awarded the job, but William was passed over.

'I can't imagine what I did wrong. It's a cleaning position for goodness' sake,' William grumbled.

Michael said, 'All I can think of is that you are American. It is uncommon for someone from the US to apply for a cleaning role in Israel. It doesn't matter anyway, we need only one of us to be on the inside.'

Michael and William were in a local coffee shop not far from the apartments where Judas lived. The sky was a blanket of grey and the threat of another rainstorm was considerable. They chose to stay under the cover of the shop awning, but they still had a clear view of the clouds above.

'Never in my life have I seen it like this. Look at how dark those clouds are!' Michael declared.

'And it is going to get worse,' William said with a grim expression on his face as he looked at the sky. He turned his gaze upon his companion. 'So, what is the latest with accessing the apartment?'

'Not good. I am assigned to the main facilities—pool, gym. The apartments are assigned to the more experienced cleaners, and the woman that cleans his apartment rarely takes a day off.'

'So, another waiting game,' William said with reluctance.

'Unfortunately,' Michael replied.

Michael added, 'Yes, and I have to get ready for work.'

****

It was mid-November on a Tuesday morning, and William's mobile rang. He looked at the caller ID—it was Michael. 'Michael, what's up?'

Michael replied in a low voice, 'We are in!'

'What? In as in—we have access?!' William said with excitement.

'Yes, all this rain has made her children sick, and now her,' Michael replied quietly.

'YES!' William celebrated.

'Make the call, then meet me at the rendezvous point as planned.'

'Okay.' William hung up and selected his contact, 'Deliverance'. He pressed the 'Dial' button.

****

Gerrard sat out the back of his favourite café in Rome, reading the latest news on his tablet. Vapours flowed casually from the coffee mug on the small table before him, while the smoke from his cigarette flowed in a more sinister manner up into the small umbrella above. Gerrard chose this café for two reasons: it was one of the few cafés left that accommodated for smokers, and the secluded rear garden had more than one exit—just in case he had to make a quick getaway.

His mobile began to vibrate on the small table while playing his favourite Puccini concerto. He picked up the mobile and saw the incoming call was from one of his diverted IP phone numbers. Gerrard had set up a series of secure lines that were difficult to track in case someone was trying to locate him. This line he had allocated to his current job. 'Oui?'

An unfamiliar American voice sounded in his ear. 'All will be in place this evening when he gets home.'

'Okay, I will be waiting for him.' He hung up.

Gerrard was in his late fifties and was still in reasonable shape considering the abuse he had inflicted on his body over the decades. His medium height and build were useful for blending into crowds after completing a mission. His grey receding hair was cut short to expose a well-tanned, olive-skinned face beneath. From his two alert, brown eyes extended a large aquiline nose and further below was a thin-lipped mouth. As Gerrard took a sip of his coffee, his protruding Adam's apple bobbed up and down as he swallowed.

He wore an expensive dark grey suit but had made his attire more casual with a T-shirt. He picked up his tablet and selected the app with a tile that looked like a bull's eye.

A week after meeting Alfred and Rene, Gerrard was in Rome preparing for the job. No one took any notice of a satellite repair man entering the apartment block across the road from where the Antichrist lived. The apartment block Judas lived in was three storeys high, and he lived in the penthouse suite. That evening, a new grey service enclosure had appeared on top of the air conditioning unit on the roof of the two storey building. There was a direct view from the small dark aperture in the enclosure to the floor-to-ceiling windows of the penthouse.

Within the grey enclosure was a custom-made, remote-controlled rifle, a high-definition video camera, and a backup power supply. The custom-made weapon had two barrels and two separate triggers. As it was common to shoot through glass windows, Gerrard had had this rifle made to his specifications by the greatest custom weapons expert in Europe— Luccio Andreonio. The first barrel would fire a quarter of a second before the kill shot, to break the glass and create a clear path for the lethal munition. As window glass can often be laminated, the first bullet could get deflected off the target. So, to make a successful kill, a second shot is often required. With his custom-made rifle, the two shots were automatic.

Was Gerrard ready? He was ready a week after the meeting in the park in Paris.

He pressed the app that looked like a bull's eye and waited a moment for the screen to display the view from the video camera in the enclosure. Gerrard spread his fingers over the screen to zoom in on the back of the apartment door. 'Ready when you are,' he said.

****

As arranged, William stood at the back of the apartment block, near the security door, and tried his best to look as casual as possible. However, to the observant, William appeared very agitated. William looked at his wristwatch—it was 10:02 am—two minutes after the time that Michael was supposed to unlock the door. 'Where is he?' William said under his breath. Then the door clicked open, but it was only ajar to appear as though it was still closed. William looked around to see if he was alone. The rear alley was void of occupation. He looked at his watch, waited thirty seconds, then opened the door and entered.

Before him was a short corridor with marble floors and clean, slate coloured walls. He walked to the end and turned right, then proceeded across the foyer to the lifts. The foyer was furbished in expensive marble tiles and crystal chandeliers, and at the centre was a lonesome leather lounge. William pressed the 'Up' button on the lift and waited a few moments for it to arrive.

He wore a suit jacket and an opened collared shirt to try and look like a guest of one of the wealthy residents. His false apparel clearly worked as the occupant that exited the lift when it arrived, took no notice of him. William pressed the top button labelled 'P' for penthouse. Soon the doors opened to reveal a short but wide corridor that accessed the only two penthouse apartments. He walked down the corridor to the apartment door on the left labelled 'P1'. The door was ajar. William entered the apartment and found Michael setting up for the consecration.

'Ah good, you made it. Any problems?' Michael asked. He was wearing the cleaner's uniform—blue overalls, and William still found it odd to see him wearing this attire despite him having had done so most days for the past several months. 'No.'

'Good, then let's get started.'

****

Gerrard flinched as he saw the apartment door open. The target was not due home for hours. He quickly zoomed in and saw that it was the cleaner, but he had not seen this one before. Out of interest, he watched the cleaner closely.

The cleaner was not following the usual cleaning routine. He pulled a bag from a drawer in his cleaning cart. The cleaner emptied the contents of the bag onto the coffee table and didn't seem to take much care in doing so. There was one object that made Gerrard sit up in his café chair—a crucifix!

Was he one of the priests from the park? The apartment door opened again, and another unknown man walked in. He was dressed in casual clothing.

Gerrard watched the two men change into priestly robes and perform some kind of ritual in the apartment. He wondered, 'How many more of them are there?'

****

Michael had hidden the required items for the consecration in the cleaning trolley—including the ceremonial gowns. William brought the service book. They went through the ritual of consecration, each performing their part. They included several hymns, just to make sure, and after an hour, they had completed the ceremony.

William commented, 'Do you feel the atmosphere in here has lifted somewhat?'

'Yes, it's like the air has become lighter,' Michael replied. 'Last time I performed a consecration, the church was full of people. It was way too busy to be able to take in the fresh atmosphere. Well, now it is up to our hired gun. I wonder if he is watching us right now.' Michael stared out the floor-to-ceiling wall of glass opposite them. 'I expect he is,' William replied.

****

That evening, Judas parked his Mercedes in the secure parking at the bottom of his apartment block. For Judas, this was like any other day in his life over the past several years. Raising his profile was a daily task. As several court cases involved the defence of questionable politicians, he soon became the representative of choice for the leaders of the country. Judas was now the name on all the lips of the rich and powerful who were in trouble with the law. For Judas, losing a case was an experience he was unfamiliar with. Some of his clients suggested that he turn to politics, and that was his plan.

The time for change was almost upon him. The political landscape was perfect for his induction and once executed, the world would never be the same again. He pulled up into his parking spot, turned off the engine, and got of the car. He waited a moment for Goliath to embark from the passenger seat before closing the door behind him. Goliath was with him almost twenty-four seven. Only when Judas was in the office was Goliath away from his side.

There, Goliath remained obediently in the office car park, and the car park attendants would spend much of their spare time playing with him and bringing him food and water. The car park attendants couldn't believe how obedient and well-natured Goliath was.

Judas walked down the short but wide corridor to the front door to his apartment, Goliath in tow. He unlocked the door and let Goliath in before entering and closing the door behind him.

****

Gerrard was back at his rented apartment and had been monitoring the view from the tablet computer all day. In the old days, he would be on location staring down the scope until the moment had come to make the kill. But with current technology, he could perform the task remotely. He looked at the digital clock on the wall—8:21 pm—the only sound emanating from the apartment being the low tones from the radio. During his surveillance over the past few months, he had learned that the target often arrived home around this time. A flutter of suspense inflicted Gerrard's stomach. He rubbed his eyes and stared at the tablet computer screen again.

The door opened!

Gerrard's heart began to race as he focused on the screen. He watched the large, black dog enter the apartment ahead of the target, before the door was closed and the target turned to face the apartment. Gerrard aimed the cross hairs at the middle of the target's heart and thought, 'Now!'. He tapped the screen.

****

Judas turned, a wave of weakness flowing up from his feet and wash over his entire body.

Goliath growled, facing the expanse of window opposite.

What unfolded next happened in a heartbeat. One of the windows broke—a small hole appeared, surrounded by numerous cracks. Goliath leaped from the floor as if to catch something, but a thud echoed from his large, black abdomen as he fell to the floor—limp.

Judas felt a hidden fist strike the base of his neck, followed by a red hot poker piercing deep into the impact point. He fell to his knees then onto the floor while clutching the wound in his neck.

The high-powered rifle had sent the bullet straight through Goliath's shoulder region. It missed the bone and exited the other side, straight into Judas. Goliath's bulk was enough to deflect the path of the bullet from Judas's heart to his neck.

****

Gerrard stared at the tablet computer screen looking for any movement, but all was still. Goliath's large, black body was obscuring his view of the target. He could not change the position of the rifle as it was fixed, and frustration began to swell in him.

Gerrard zoomed in further on the small extremities of the target that were visible, but all remained motionless. He zoomed out again to gain full view of the target. His heart nearly stopped. A bloodied arm had extended above the still mass of Goliath, unlocking the front door of the apartment.

Gerrard quickly moved the cross hairs onto the extended arm and tapped the screen firmly. He watched as another small hole appeared in the window and then in the front door where the arm had been. Gerrard watched the door being opened wide by a hidden force. He aimed back at the still form of Goliath and fired two more shots. Goliath's corpse flinched twice as the silver slugs penetrated. He caught a glimpse of a figure moving behind Goliath, but it was almost completely obscured. In desperation, Gerrard took another wild shot at a small section that was exposed and saw a small spattering of blood explode from the impact point. The movement behind Goliath stopped. Gerrard scanned the scene for any more movement but saw none. He realised in horror that the figure had crawled out the door and out of sight.

****

The stabbing sensation in Judas's neck was intense. If he stayed here much longer, he would die and with that, his father's plans for the apocalypse. He must get out of the apartment. He kept pressure on the gory wound with one hand and reached for the door handle with the other. To his surprise, he turned the doorknob without being shot again. As he dropped his arm to the bottom of the door, another bullet impacted just where his arm had been. Judas opened the door as wide as he could and carefully crawled out the door, keeping as low as possible. As he rounded the corner of the door, another bullet struck his shoulder. An intense piercing pain radiated out from the new flesh wound and he was no longer able to maintain pressure upon the wound on his neck. Judas dropped his hand from his neck and used both arms to drag himself the rest of the way.

When he was finally clear of the doorway, he sat up against the corridor wall, blood oozing from his wounds. The burden of weakness drained from his body like water from a pouring jug. The wall was the spiritual boundary between hallowed ground and the unblessed. In seconds, the full might of his evil was pumping through his veins again. The blood from his wounds stopped flowing as scabs formed to seal off the flow.

Slowly, he dragged his frame to its feet—and there his form mutated. His lightly tanned skin was replaced by blood red flesh, and his mouth became a snout bearing needle-like teeth. The raven black hair on his head faded into blood red flesh as two great curved horns grew from his skull. His legs became hoofed, twisting into beastly proportions, and his hands formed two fingers and a thumb, brandished with long, black talons. His beautiful dark eyes became black lifeless pits that descended into hell itself. His Armani suit, struggling to contain the unnatural form of the monster, omitted the sharp sound of minor tearing.

The real form of the Antichrist is indescribable and far more alien than the monstrous form that it had just become. It chose this vision from the deepest depths of humanity's nightmares—it was the pinnacle of human fear, horror, and terror.

His wounds bubbled, letting off toxic vapour as they healed. Just before the last of the wounds dissipated, the bullets were pushed out through the healing flesh.

What pushed the bullets out was not some unnatural motion of flesh and blood, but the force of countless tiny, withered hands. For the Antichrist was not one being, but millions. Each lost soul was a slave to its master, and the master was the spawn of total evil. It was through the mastery of so many lost souls that the Antichrist was able to command so much supernatural power.

The Antichrist stepped back into the doorway and spat onto the floor of the apartment. The floor sizzled and writhed as the surface was bereft of holiness. It then set its gaze upon the small, dark window on the small enclosure on the roof opposite. Another bullet penetrated his forehead, making his skull flinch—but that was all. A moment later, the bullet was pushed out onto the floor with not a drop of blood being spilled.

From behind scaly lips, a sinister needle-toothed smile grew before the full force of its evil was cast out and into the eyes that watched from so far away.

****

Gerrard's heart thumped like the hooves of a racehorse on the track. How could he have missed? He never misses! How did the dog know he was about to fire? Why didn't anyone warn him about the dog?

He scanned the open doorway, looking, hoping for the target to reappear. Moments passed with no sign of movement. What now? Should he abandon the mission and flee, or take the target on at close range?

Then a figure appeared in the doorway. Not just a figure, but a monster. A real, living, breathing horror. Gerrard's heart stopped!

He could not believe his eyes. What he saw was like something straight out of the most terrifying horror movie—and utterly horrific. But to view this monster with his own eyes—in real life—was far more terrifying than any movie.

The initial urge to cast the tablet computer away from his sight was overwhelming. But Gerrard's well-honed instincts took control and he quickly took aim then tapped the screen on the tablet computer. The view on the screen was crystal clear, the monstrous figure filling it with its grotesque apparition. Gerrard watched its hideous head flinch as the bullet penetrated its forehead. A chill travelled down his spine as he saw the bullet being squeezed back out by unnatural forces.

The monster smiled—a smile of utter contempt. It was then that the real horror hit.

Gerrard fell into those empty black pits for eyes. Though he was a few kilometres away, Gerrard might as well have been standing face to face with the creature. What his brain perceived blurred before morphing into him, plummeting him down an old dark, dank, cold, wall-less well. The sensation of falling continued for an unnatural period before stopping abruptly. It was like he was alone at the bottom of the deepest trench in the deepest part of the ocean. No light, no sensation, no feeling—just an endless black abyss. Searing pain struck every nerve ending in his body. He screamed uncontrollably but no sound came from his invisible mouth. Something was eating him alive. A glow formed around his body, formed by a thousand mutant iridescent creatures. They looked like spiders. Gerrard feared only one creature on Earth, and they were eating him alive! Although his physical body was disappearing from under the teeth of the spiders, he knew it was not his body being devoured, but his soul. And it was his soul that was making them glow.

He felt his childhood memories disappearing, then his youth. They had removed his limbs and were starting on his abdomen. His working life began to fade from thought and soon only the most recent memories remained. Physically, all that remained was most of his skull and some of his spinal cord. Then the pain stopped, and the spiders scattered into the inky blackness.

Gerrard was almost void of any identity—he been erased.

A pin prick of light formed in the distance, growing brighter and brighter, larger and larger, until he was fully consumed by its brightness. He was back in his apartment, lying on the floor. Blood oozed from his ears, out over the tiled floor. Gerrard sat up abruptly and screamed. This time his scream was audible. He became an apparition of a screaming lunatic. Then he stopped. He was now under the control of the voice in his head, 'Come, come to me!' He stood up and left his apartment.

****

Judas sat on his lounge, sipping a glass of fine Scotch whisky while listening to the soft tones of a Mozart opera. A pale figure entered the apartment and robotically strode over to the lounge and sat opposite Judas.

Judas took no visible notice of the intruder and kept staring out the large expanse of window opposite. He said, 'I suppose you're thinking right now, 'Why didn't I retire earlier?' A brief smile appeared on Judas's face before returning to a more sombre expression. He redirected his gaze to the one seated opposite. 'You did well though, I have to say. Destroyed my sentinel, wounded me. Oh, as you can see, I am a very fast healer,' he said, pointing at his neck. 'Did you enjoy my little pets? I had them made especially for you I hope you know.' Gerrard stared blankly at Judas.

'You see, they can only feed on those that are not baptised. And …,' Judas leaned forward and sniffed, 'Oh dear me, if only your mother was more religious!' Judas sat back and continued, 'If you were baptised it would really restrict what fun I could have with you.' His expression became very dark as he said, 'And I don't like being restricted!' Judas's expression calmed again. 'Goliath was such a loyal dog; I was becoming rather fond of him. Never mind, what's the point of a sentinel if it isn't expendable? So, I am now in need of a replacement, and I think you will fit the bill quite nicely. But before you commence your service, I have a job for you. Your partners in crime are becoming rather tiresome, and I want you to track them down and eliminate them all. I left you with your more recent memories and that part of you that makes you such a successful killer, so you should have no problems in completing your mission.' Judas returned to gazing out the window. 'You are dismissed. Now run along.'

Gerrard stood and walked back to the door but before he reached it, Judas said, 'And one other thing ...' Gerrard paused his gait to listen. Judas kept staring out the window as he said, 'Make it slow. I want to enjoy it.'

****

The surveillance station Sam had planted was only a few metres away from where Gerrard had placed his. Sam watched the events unfold with intense interest. For a moment, he hoped that the prophecies of old were to be proven wrong. However, his hopes were soon dashed when a monstrous apparition appeared on his television screen. The horrific sight instantly sent a chill through his whole body. He immediately turned the television off. Sam was not going to risk being cursed again.

He quickly picked up his mobile phone and called the client. A few rings later, the familiar voice answered. 'Shalom?'

'We failed! It's still alive. We are all dead!'

Michael replied, 'We will be on the first plane out of here. I suggest you do the same.'

'Roger that. Good luck to you,' Sam replied.

There was a pause before Michael said, 'God bless you and keep you safe.' He hung up.

****

Michael placed his mobile phone on the coffee table and looked at William with an expression of dread.

William said, 'We are dead!'

'He will have to find us first,' Michael stated. 'Let's get out of here!'

In case they failed, Michael and William had already packed their bags. Within a few minutes, they had left the apartment and were in a taxi on their way to the airport. William kept looking behind to check if they were being followed. 'So far so good,' William thought.

The last flight to the United States was at 10:30 pm and they had only an hour to get to the airport and catch the flight.

Michael told the taxi driver they were late for their flight and immediately the taxi driver accelerated. The taxi darted through the streets of Jerusalem at an alarming rate, and in fifteen minutes they had arrived at the airport. William paid the driver and told him to keep the change, which was considerably more than the required fare. As the taxi drove away, they could hear the driver repeating over and over, 'Toda, toda, toda!'

Michael and William scurried through to the automated luggage check-in bay. They entered the pin numbers from their tickets into the terminal and attached the printed labels to their luggage handles. They placed the luggage onto the end of the conveyor belt and watched their bags disappear into the luggage distribution system.

They raced through customs and jogged to the gate where the aircraft was stationed. When Michael and William arrived, they found a large crowd of people waiting to board.

An air hostess that was stationed at the gate desk pressed a button on the desk and spoke into a microphone. 'Ladies and gentlemen, there has been a short delay. However, we will be boarding in approximately five minutes. Israel Air apologises for any inconvenience.'

Michael and William stood panting, like athletes at the end of a sprint. It took a minute for them to catch their breath, and William said, 'I need to take a leak.'

'Me too,' Michael added.

They walked over to the nearby toilets and went in. After relieving themselves, they stood at the wash basins washing their hands and Michael said, 'I think we may survive this.'

William replied, 'I'm feeling optimistic as well.' William felt a sharp pain in his back as if someone had thrust a knife into it. A heartbeat later, Michael felt the same searing sharpness in his spine. His ability to feel his legs was replaced by agonising pins and needles. Michael collapsed to the floor next to the prostrate figure of William.

Standing over them was a thin-faced man with a large aquiline nose, wearing a cleaner's uniform. In his right hand was a pistol brandishing a long black silencer.

He said in a strong French accent, 'I'm afraid you are both very wrong!'

Gerrard dragged their immobile bodies into the cubicle at the far end of the cubicle row, leaving a smear of blood behind. As Michael and William lay prostrate on the cubicle floor, Gerrard said in a calm tone, 'The bullets have severed your spinal cords. You are now both quadriplegics. You know, if you had left your mobile phone behind, you would have been far more challenging to locate. You see, mobile phones are easily tracked if you didn't know. But you are wondering how I got your mobile number so quickly, right? A simple phone call to the cleaning company pretending to be the resident you wanted me to kill.' Gerrard put his hand to his head to imitate talking on the phone. 'I can't find my memory stick. It was on the coffee table and the cleaner has moved it somewhere. The next minute I have your mobile number and shortly after, you!

Unfortunately, my new master wants this to be slow and painful, and what master wants, master gets.'

Gerrard produced a knife, stuck it into the back of their heads near the base of their necks, then wiped the knife on Michael's clothes before returning it to his pocket. Michael and William flinched from the pain but were unable to move or scream. 'You are both now completely paralysed. Soon the severed nerves will send false pain messages to the brain and it will feel like your entire body is on fire. After several minutes of excruciating agony, your brains will shut down the nerve receptors and you will fall into unconsciousness. Death will quickly follow. Before I go, I need your mobile phone.' Gerrard searched them and found Michael's mobile in his pocket. He pressed a few buttons and said, 'Ah, one call received after the kill attempt. No doubt one of your accomplices. Au revoir gentlemen!' Gerrard left them and began to mop up the bloody smear off the floor. A man entered the toilet before he was finished, and Gerrard casually pointed at the sign blocking the entrance that read 'Closed for Cleaning'. The man left promptly without any protest. When Gerrard had finished mopping the floor, he casually left the toilet leaving the two doomed occupants behind.

****

Sam zipped his luggage closed and heaved it off the bed to the floor, then extended the handle and walked it to the lounge room. Sam was not prepared for this quick departure and had spent the past few hours getting his things together. He didn't feel the need for great urgency as his involvement in this was completely anonymous. Still, he was not going to stick around to find out if that monster could locate him.

He picked up his keys, wallet and mobile. He stared at his mobile for a moment before deciding to turn it off. 'Just in case,' he said to himself, before leaving the apartment.

Sam approached his Mercedes Benz in the rear private car park of the apartments, and it obediently unlocked itself so he could enter. He threw his bag in the boot of the S-Class and got in. He always enjoyed getting into his Merc. He had wanted one since he was young but could never afford it. But thanks to his current clients, his dream had come true.

As he reached for the 'Start' button, he saw a figure in the passenger window. The figure was wearing black overalls and was holding a pistol with a silencer. Immediately, the window shattered, and Sam felt a searing pain in his abdomen. He doubled over onto the steering wheel, but by the time he was able to take the pain and look for his assailant, Gerrard was sitting next to him. Sam lashed out with his left fist in a futile attempt to gain the upper hand, but Gerrard expertly blocked his fist and thrust a knife into the back of Sam's neck, near the base of his skull. Sam sagged to the steering wheel like a dropped rag doll.

Gerrard wiped the knife blade on Sam's shirt and returned it to his pocket. 'You are paralysed. You cannot scream or signal for help. My new master has ordered for your death to be slow and painful, and so it shall be. Goodbye.' Gerrard got out of the car and left yet another victim behind to die slowly and painfully.

****

Paris, France

'Why have we not heard from them I ask you? Because they are dead. We have failed!' snapped Alfred.

Rene's deep brown eyes stared into the distance as his mind fought through the myriad of scenarios that could explain the delay in communication. Finally, he said, 'I know. It doesn't look good.'

'Brother Michael clearly stated they would email us immediately on their success or failure. It was supposed to happen yesterday. It is now 6:00 pm!' Alfred leaned closer as he said, 'We need to run—now!'

Alfred and Rene were seated for dinner in their favourite local restaurant, and their orders were on their way to their table.

Rene said, 'Not until I have had my last serving of escargot. And here it is.' A big smile grew over his face.

The waitress placed their meals on their table and as she left, she said, 'Bon appétit.'

'At least we will start our running on a full stomach,' Rene added.

'This is madness,' Alfred protested. 'The Antichrist is after us. Not some crazed lunatic. The Antichrist! Any minute now it could walk through that very door.' Alfred gestured towards the front door of the restaurant. 'And here we are eating escargot!' He stabbed a snail on his plate with his fork and put it in his mouth. After a few chews and a roll of his eyes he gasped, 'An utterly superb escargot.' He continued chewing.

After swallowing a mouthful of snail, Rene said, 'We have left our church and have been in hiding for how many years? All we have done is wait and plot, and until now we have been too cautious to make a move. Now we have finally acted, and if we have failed and we are about to die, then so be it. If the Antichrist were to walk in that door, we couldn't stop it anyway. At least I will die with a great taste in my mouth.' He stuffed another snail in his mouth and continued with a carefree tone, 'Our bags are packed, we have a safe house to go to, and we will be on our way straight after this. Now eat up and enjoy.'

They finished their meal and left the table; the bill was paid, and a handsome tip left on top.

They walked out of the popular outer suburb Paris restaurant and headed back to their apartment.

Soon, they were back at their apartment block and approaching the front door.

Alfred stopped Rene before he put the key in the door. 'Wait! What if he is inside waiting for us?'

Rene looked at Alfred and said casually, 'Then we are about to die.' He proceeded to unlock the door and open it. Rene pushed the door wide open to expose the small lounge and dining room. The room was lit by a small lamp in the corner, giving the scene a warm glow. The furnishings were cheap and basic as the men had resisted the temptation to splash out on quality products. Neither knew what a quality product was anyway, or the reasons for buying one. But they did decide on a large flat screen television as Alfred had such poor eyesight, or maybe that was the excuse Rene had used to justify the expense.

There was no scuffle or sound of gunfire as Rene surveyed the apartment. Alfred cautiously peered over Rene's shoulder and scanned the room too. They found it unoccupied.

Rene said, 'Looks like we get to live for another day.'

'The day is not over yet,' Alfred said pessimistically.

They entered the apartment and Alfred closed the door behind them. But the door did not close properly—it stayed ajar, blocked by something caught in the door jamb.

Alfred and Rene both noticed the distinct lack of a clunk of the door closing. They turned around and stared in stunned silence as the door slowly swung open again. In the doorway stood a tall, thin man wearing black overalls and holding a pistol with a silencer.

He fired the pistol twice in quick succession and Alfred and Rene collapsed to the floor. Gerrard stepped into the apartment and casually closed the door behind him. He approached Alfred first and kneeled down next to him to examine his marksmanship. The bullet had passed through Alfred's neck and he was now drowning in his own blood. Gerrard said casually, 'You were right. The day is not over yet, but it is over for both of you.' Gerrard stood up and continued, 'Fortunately for you old man, your death will be quick. My bullet was ten millimetres too far to the left and I missed your spinal cord.' He looked at the nearby bleeding prostrate figure of Rene, staring at him through eyes of anguish. 'However, your death will be slow and painful, as requested.'

Alfred managed to gurgle the words, 'Why ... did you do this ... we paid ... you?'

Gerrard replied in a cold and matter-of-fact tone, 'The person you paid has been erased. Only this shell remains and some of his knowledge and skills.' He paused for a moment before opening his mouth wide as if he were about to shout, but only a hollow exhale left his body. 'The remains of that person want to scream, but my master forbids it. The torment pleases my master.'

He looked down at Alfred and said, 'My master wants to know why you persist when all the armies of the world could not defeat him? What hope do you have?'

The strain on Rene's face looked unbearable but he could not say or do a thing.

Alfred spat out some blood before answering, 'Where we fail, ... our Lord ... will succeed!'

Gerard stared coldly at Alfred and said, 'Your Lord is no match for my master.'

Alfred gasped with his failing breath, 'We shall see.' The last gasp of air exited his lungs as life left his body.

Gerrard took one more look at Rene and said, 'Enjoy your slow death.' He turned and left the apartment.

All Rene could do was stare at Alfred's dead body through dry eyes as agony bombarded his brain. Screaming was impossible, and the knowledge of impending death was his only comfort until a certain end.

****

The next evening Judas was seated on the lounge in his apartment, working on his laptop. He was still in his black business suit but had taken the liberty of removing his tie. The evening news was on the TV, but the volume was down low so he could focus on his work. For no apparent reason, Judas looked up from his work and stared at the front door to the apartment. A moment later, Gerrard walked in and closed the door behind him. He was no longer in his black overalls, but in jeans and a black shirt. His casual dress clashed with the robotic nature of his mannerisms and he did little to hide them.

Judas said in a smug tone, 'Good dog! You obeyed your orders well. Now we just need to make you one.' His tone abruptly turned venomous. 'Into the kitchen!'

Gerrard obediently walked into the open plan kitchen and stood waiting for his next command.

Judas walked casually over to the kitchen bench and grabbed the largest blade from the knife stand. He plunged the knife into Gerrard's chest and watched him collapse to the tiled floor.

All that escaped from Gerrard's mouth was a faint gasp. Blood oozed from the wound in his chest and over the shirt before pooling onto the cool tiles. Just as his heart made its final low pressure beat, Judas cut his palm with the knife and let a few drops of his blood fall into the open weeping wound. Judas watched the cut seal up and the blood flow stop as if there was an invisible zipper on his flesh. He stood back from the gory figure on the floor and watched. Gerrard's body began to steam, then bubble, then sizzle. His arms and legs retracted and deformed into short bent limbs. His fingers extended and fused into big paws while his skull looked like it was inside an invisible vice as it narrowed and extended. His jaw line extended, his teeth grew into fangs and his lips transformed into jowls. Thick, short, black hair sprouted all over his body as his rib cage deformed into a long, narrow structure. His clothes fell loose following the final stages of the mutation, and the sizzling and bubbling ceased. It took but a minute for the human body to become the great black body of a rottweiler.

The dog lay on the floor for a moment as still as death, before it opened its eyes. The eyes were not like a dog's, they appeared very human. It got up on all fours and sniffed the blood on the floor.

Judas looked down his nose at his creation and with a spiteful tone said, 'Lick up that mess you made, and when you have finished take those rags to the bin downstairs.'

The dog obediently began licking up the blood but every now and then it would gag on it.

'If you vomit, I will punish you, and you will have to eat your own vomit. And I don't want to see a drop left!' Judas crossed his arms while he watched the dog lick up the red ichor. 'Now, what are we going to call you? Hmm, how about Zeus? Yes, Zeus will do.'

When Zeus finished licking the floor clean, he picked up the clothes in his mouth and trotted to the front door, then waited.

Judas walked over to the front door and opened it for him. Zeus trotted out the door and headed for the lift. Judas left the door ajar so he could get back in, and he returned to the lounge and his work.

A few minutes later, Zeus returned through the ajar door and closed it behind him. He went straight to Judas's side and sat. Judas patted him on the head and gave him a smile. 'There's a good boy. See? If you do as you are told, we are going to get on fine.'

A news report on the TV caught Judas's attention. He looked up and watched the segment on the Prime Minister of Israel. The news reporter said into the camera, 'The prime minister has just left the peace conference with the leader of the State of Palestine saying that the negotiations have broken down again. This is the second peace summit to fail and now many are asking if there will ever be peace in the region ...'

Judas stroked Zeus's head as he said, 'Zeus, it would appear that the world is now ready to be introduced to me!'

9

Rise of the Antichrist

Judas became a member of the federal opposition party as it was gaining strength following the failed attempts for peace by the prime minister.

Using his extensive political connections, Judas was able to knock out the current local representative for the area in which he lived, then run for that seat in the forthcoming election. It was a landslide victory for the opposition party as it gained a seventy-two percent majority over the former government.

Judas again used his political connections to be nominated for prime minister. His charm, good looks and eloquent speeches made him a very strong candidate. And there was one other trump card he had up his sleeve—the president's daughter. Although the president was little more than a figurehead, he still had the power to choose who could be nominated for prime minister. Judas had used his legal contacts to get a drug charge overturned and out of the courts—for the president's daughter. And the president had promised him that if there was ever anything he needed ... well, that time had come.

When the president announced the nominees, one name surprised many—Judas Salim.

Suddenly, the spotlight fell on Judas and the Israeli media went into a frenzy. The youngest nominee, and the shortest and most miraculous political career of any politician. Interview offers flooded in as everyone wanted to know who this upstart was. After several television and newspaper interviews, everyone knew who Judas Salim was, or at least the public version.

It was time for the parliament to vote for the new prime minister. There were three other candidates. Two had a minority support from the elected parliament, but the remaining was a strong contender. Shimon

Weizman had been in the political arena for nearly two decades and had many loyal party members. However, the fifty-nine-year-old veteran had also made a few enemies over the years. Judas had not been around long enough to ruffle the feathers of other party members and he had a good chance of taking the top job. But a good chance was not good enough, so Judas set about to turn the odds strongly in his favour.

****

After a long day at the office, Safra Bluwstien walked through the underground car park towards her car. Her employer was still at work at 10:30 pm but had sent her home saying, 'I've almost finished the speech. You go home and we will review it in the morning'. Safra was the personal secretary for Shimon Weizman. She was in her early forties and had been working for Shimon for the past five years. Safra was very beautiful in her youth—silky long, raven black hair, fine features, and smooth olive skin. Much of her former beauty remained and still caught the eye of many a suiter. Her marriage of ten years had fallen apart just three years earlier after her husband's long-term affair. It had taken most of those three years to get over the divorce and Safra had recently began dating again. In some ways she was now glad that her ex-husband was against having children, as at least only the two of them had been affected and not an innocent child.

Safra approached her car and pressed the remote to unlock it. It was then that she noticed the figure staring at her in the shadows nearby. Safra turned and looked straight into the eyes that were more of a window into hell. She screamed!

The shriek stopped abruptly, and her expression dropped to one that was mute, dull, and lifeless. Safra's eyes glazed over, and she turned on her heels and got in the car.

As her car left the car park, the shadowy figure of Judas walked casually from the basement car park.

****

Emergency phone operator, Jude, took call number 1204. 'Shalom, what is the address you are calling from?'

'He tried to rape me!' said the traumatised voice on the line.

'What is your name?' Jude said in a half warm tone.

'Safra, Safra Bluwstien. He tried to rape me!'

Jude added more warmth this time. 'Where are you darling?'

There was a pause before Jude heard the words, 'I'm at home.'

'Who tried to rape you?' Jude did her best to say it with as much professionalism as she could, but all she wanted to do was to give the voice a big hug.

The frail voice on the line said between sobs, 'My boss ... Shimon ... Shimon ... Weizman.'

Jude paused for a moment. Did she hear correctly? 'The Senator?' Jude composed herself and returned to her duty. 'What is your address?'

The line went dead.

Jude stared at the computer screen for a moment as she watched the last call entry read, 'Disconnected'. She quickly typed up the details of the call into the next field on the action window. Under the field, 'Follow up action', Jude typed 'Send unit to home address'. Jude stared once more at the screen momentarily as the thought went through her mind, 'We have your name, and we know you are at home. The police will be there very soon, just don't do anything silly. Hang in there!'

****

Safra had just hung up from the emergency call as she stared at the view of the night sky from her third-floor apartment. The charade was over as well as the tears. Safra became a lifeless figurine waiting for its owner to play with it. Then the next command thundered in her head, 'Run!'

Like a puppet on strings, Safra stood and ran straight ahead to the balcony. The voice said, 'Jump!' Safra obeyed and jumped off.

****

Judas took a sip of his coffee as he watched the morning news. He was half dressed in his business suit but was still barefoot. Zeus had his head deep in his food bowl in the kitchen.

The anchorman stared down the camera as he read the auto cue, 'The personal secretary for Senator Shimon Weizman was found dead last night after falling from her third-floor balcony. The police believe the death of forty-two-year-old Safra Bluwstien is a suicide after reports of a disturbing phone call she made to emergency services only moments before she fell to her death. In the phone call, Miss Bluwstien claimed that Senator Shimon Weizman had attempted to rape her. At this point there has been no statement released by Senator Weizman over the allegations, and the police have detained the Senator for questioning. Considering the seriousness of the allegations, party officials expect Senator Weizman to withdraw his candidacy for prime minister and possibly even provide a full resignation from government.'

Zeus trotted up to Judas's side and sat. Judas patted him on the head as he said, 'Your master is about to become prime minister!' Zeus looked up at him with his big brown eyes but with an empty expression. 'What, not satisfied?' He grabbed Zeus by both ears and rubbed in an affectionate manner. He then said as if he were talking to a baby, 'You want me to rule the world, don't you? All in good time Zeus, all in good time.'

****

On 12 November, Judas Salim was announced as the new prime minister of Israel. At the fledgling age of only thirty, there was much hope placed on the new prime minister to add a breath of fresh air to the parliament and new ideas on solving the ongoing threat of war with Palestine.

Abba Ameir sat on a fine leather chair with his legs casually crossed as he prepared to talk to the studio camera. Being the star reporter for *The World This Morning* television program, he had the choice of interviewing the top celebrities. Today, Abba was to interview the new Prime Minister of Israel. 'Shalom. *The World This Morning* has a special guest today—our new Prime Minister Judas Salim.' Abba turned to his guest and said, 'Welcome Prime Minister.'

The camera flicked over to Judas as he said, 'Thank you, it's a pleasure to be here.'

Abba continued, 'Your career has been, to say the least, miraculous. Secured a position in one of the top law firms in Jerusalem. Successfully defended many high-profile cases. Only two years in the political arena and now the top job of prime minister. What next, world domination?' Abba finished with a smile. Judas just casually laughed before Abba continued. 'What is the secret to your amazing story of success?'

Judas mimicked Abba's pose as he replied, 'Integrity. If say you are going to do something, then do it. Unwavering determination and a lot of hard work.'

Abba looked up and down at the well-dressed, good-looking young man and felt rather unattractive comparing his additional fifteen years of age, larger nose, and receding hair line. 'According to the latest Internet polls, you are now the most eligible bachelor in Israel. I am sure that many of our female viewers are dying to know—is there a special woman in your life at the moment?'

Judas smiled and replied, 'Unfortunately there hasn't been much time for anything else but work. So, no.'

Abba looked at the camera and said, 'Well ladies, you heard it first on *The World This Morning*. However, ...' Abba focused his stare on Judas. '... There is one special woman that we know of, and we have her live on Skype.' Behind them the large projection screen came to life and displayed an image of a greying woman in her seventies. 'Sarina, shalom.'

A big smile grew across her face as Sarina replied, 'Shalom.'

'What would you like to say about your son on national television?'

Sarina beamed as she said, 'Judas, I just want to say how proud your father and I are of you. Israel could not have a better leader.'

The camera flicked over to Judas. For a moment, his expression was strained but it soon changed to a warm smile. 'Thanks Mum.'

****

London, UK

'I think I am going to be sick!' Stephen announced as he watched the delayed broadcast.

Paul said in a matter-of-fact tone, 'I don't know why you are so surprised.'

Stephen and Paul were watching *Sky News* as they sipped their morning cups of tea.

'He is the Antichrist for goodness sake! And look, they all think he's wonderful!' Stephen added.

Paul continued his matter-of-fact tone. 'We know who he is, the world does not.'

'How long has it been, ten years? And here he is, the political leader of the Holy Land.' Stephen slammed down his cup as he declared, 'We have let God down. We have not done what we set out to do.' He glared at Paul as he said, 'We must stop him. We have to stop him now—right now,' Stephen said as he pointed his finger at the floor.

Paul said calmly, 'What do you suggest we do, there are only four of us left now?'

Stephen didn't react to Paul's question, he just stared at the television screen and said, 'At least now we know what he looks like. He's got such a baby face.'

'Makes sense,' Paul stated. 'Look at all the worst serial killers— baby faces. If they look harmless then people will be more trusting. Makes them more affective predators.' Paul took another sip of tea and added, 'Besides, we are too late to act now, he has risen to power. The prophesies are all coming true.'

'It's not too late.' Stephen stood and began pacing the room of the small London apartment. 'There has to be a way.' The last ten years had widened Stephen's waist and dashed some grey in his hair. His slight frame was more muscular across the chest than in his youth as his trips to the gym to avert the steady growth of his waist, had mostly improved his upper body strength. His face was less youthful as the years had taken some of the elasticity from his skin. His companion however had no visible signs of ageing from the last decade.

Paul finished his tea and put it on the low coffee table before him. He looked over the top of his new rectangular, frameless glasses as he stated, 'It would appear that you wish to do something rash, and I thought you were the cautious one.'

'If we had more details of the last attempt, we could identify what went wrong and we could avoid the same mistake.'

Paul rolled his eyes before saying, 'We went through what we had a hundred times and found nothing. Only the dead can answer your question.'

Stephen stopped and stared out of the lounge room window. It was turning into a very cold winter and the sky outside was very grey. 'This time we must have a foolproof plan, one that cannot fail.'

'Well, I'm open to any foolproof ideas you may have,' Paul said with an air of sarcasm.

Stephen crossed his arms and stared at Paul. 'I'm not an ideas man, never have been. How about you?'

'No, I would say I wasn't either. But one thing is for sure, we can't do much from another country, we need to get closer.'

'But a pair of British lads in Israel! We would stand out like elephants in short grass. No, we need to blend in, we will need to wait for him to come to us. Sooner or later, his prime minister role will take him to a western country, and then we can strike. But how? How would we get close enough to have a chance?'

Paul rubbed his chin as he thought out loud. 'Well, if he does come here, or say the US, then those that get near him are police, secret service, foreign office staff, prime minister staff. And if he were to attend an event here, then the event staff would be a good choice as well.'

Stephen sat down on the single seater lounge opposite Paul. The reflection of the dull light from the lounge window in Paul's glasses managed to obscure some of his steel grey eyes from Stephen's stare.

Stephen said with some excitement, 'We're not the secret service type, or the police for that matter. But public service or event management is not out of the question.'

Paul sat forward and looked over his glasses at Stephen. 'It sounds like we have some research to do. Who's firing up the laptop, and who is on tea making duty?'

****

Judas was not expecting this—*I will not tolerate surprises!* His parents were now a risk. His controversial start to life must not become public, and the only way to ensure this was to eliminate his parents. Now was not the right time but soon though, very soon.

Abba changed the subject back to politics as the screen behind them returned to the program logo. 'Prime Minister, what will be on top of your agenda for your first term as leader of Israel?'

'Meeting the Palestinian president to resolve the differences between our two states once and for all.'

'That is a bold statement, and you seem so confident.' Abba said with an air of skepticism.

'I am confident because I will succeed where the others failed. Besides, how could he refuse my charm?' Judas added with a smile.

Abba grinned as he added, 'Of course, who could? Unfortunately, we have run out of time. Thank you for coming on our show Prime Minister.' Judas nodded, 'My pleasure.'

****

Two weeks later, Judas arranged a one-on-one with the Palestinian President Mohammed Abbas, and the president nominated the neutral location of a hotel in Cairo, Egypt. The choice of location had no bearing on Judas as he strode along the hotel corridor towards the penthouse where the president was waiting. Judas just wanted to meet him face to face as soon as possible and get this seemingly impossible situation resolved. Judas wore what was becoming his signature uniform of a black suit, black shirt, and a red tie.

In front of Judas was a secret service man dressed in a company issued black suit and black tie. Behind him were two other secret service men, and behind them was the rest of his entourage: his personal secretary, two personal advisers, two ministerial gofers in the form of university graduates, and the foreign minister.

The secret service man in front stopped at the penthouse door where two armed men stood in thawbs and keffiyehs. The armed men holding the AK-47s were the president's personal guards.

Judas stopped next to the secret service men and the other two stopped on the other side of Judas. The rest of the entourage cued down the corridor. The secret service men eyed off the armed guards, and the armed guards eyed off the secret service men who no doubt had pistols concealed in their chest holsters. No armed man blinked or moved, for if any one of them did, an all-out fire fight would be inevitable.

Judas stepped forward and knocked on the penthouse door. A moment later, it was opened. One of the secret service men entered the penthouse first, then Judas, then his entourage. Two of the secret servicemen stayed outside opposite the armed guards to continue their Mexican standoff.

The penthouse was expansive, with polished marble floors and high decorative ceilings. The walls were decorated with fine classic Egyptian artwork and the furnishing was all imitation Egyptian pharaoh artifacts. The curtains to the penthouse were all drawn, blocking the panoramic views of Cairo and the Egyptian pyramids in the distance. Still, the bright sunlight filtered through the curtains to illuminate the penthouse in a bright warm glow. In the centre of the living area was an expensive lounge suite placed upon what appeared to be a large genuine Persian rug. There was a figure seated upon one of the single seat lounge chairs, but they were obscured by the two armed guards standing in front. Behind the seated figure was his own entourage of several thawb-dressed officials.

The secret serviceman in front of Judas and the armed guards eyed each other off for a moment, then simultaneously stepped aside to enable Judas full view of the president.

Mohammed Abbas was in his late fifties, and his former darkhaired goatee and moustache was now becoming grey. His skin was rather dark from the many years in the hot middle eastern sun, and several wrinkles had formed around his eyes. His head of hair was fully concealed by a keffiyeh that was pure white and held in place by a black head band. When he smiled, a mouth of bright white teeth shone from behind dark, tanned lips. 'Prime Minister, please come and join me,' Mohammed said with an air of disdain. His right arm appeared from under his white thawb and he gestured to the three-seater leather lounge next to him.

Judas casually walked over to the lounge and sat down. He reached out his right hand and said in a warm tone, 'Mr President, how good to meet you.'

They shook hands briefly before Mohammed stated in a bored manner, 'So you wish to negotiate. However, I doubt you can offer anything else that others have not. Because what we want, you won't give, and what you want, you can't have.'

Judas crossed his legs before replying, 'Well I beg to differ. But before we start, do you think we could discuss this in private? There are so many people here with different thoughts and concerns, I doubt any agreement could be reached. How about just you and I sit down and discuss the issue like two civilised gentlemen?'

Everybody in the room glared at Judas. This was unprecedented—no advisors, no bodyguards? A member of the entourage bent over and whispered something into the president's ear, but he was dismissed by a wave of his hand. One of Judas's advisors outwardly protested, 'Prime Minister, I beg you to reconsider.'

Judas took no notice as he just kept his gaze trained upon the president.

'Well Prime Minister, this is highly unusual.' Mohammed stared back at Judas as he thought:

What could he do to me, kill me? That would lead to all-out war, and he would be tried for murder. No, he is too smart for that. Besides, I am a veteran of the Palestinian Army and have fought in many bloody battles, he has not.

He has had no military training, which is highly unusual for an Israeli. How did he avoid the mandatory service? Maybe his rich parents were able to cut a deal with the right people. He probably doesn't even know how to use a knife. Yes, he is young and fit, but that's no match for skill and experience. So, what is it that he wants to propose that he doesn't want his advisors to hear? Hmm, this is worth the risk.

Mohammed said casually, 'Agreed.'

Murmuring came from both entourages before they reluctantly left the penthouse. The last to leave were the armed guards and secret servicemen, all with a nervous last look at the two leaders.

When the door finally closed, Judas said casually, 'Now we can talk, man to beast!'

For a brief moment, Mohammed's eyes widened as he thought the term 'beast' referred to him. But he soon realised that Judas was talking about himself.

Judas's stare locked onto Mohammed's eyes and began to bore into his soul. The whites of his eyes went black while the deep brown of his iris turned to red flames. Excruciating agony struck Mohammed's nervous system, but he could not scream. Only a slight gurgle and a gasp escaped his constricted throat. It was then that Mohammed's vision of the fiery eyes turned to a bottomless pit, and he was falling into it. All the while, agony inflicted his senses, yet no release of a scream was possible to make sense of the terror.

Judas's fiery stare remained transfixed on the president as he casually said, 'Mr Abbas, I'm a busy man. I now have a country to rule and I still have a world to conquer. So, I don't have time to sit here and listen to you say no. Fortunately, your murderous past gives me the opportunity to expedite the negotiations.'

Mohammed began to drool from the corner of his mouth as it gaped opened in his zombie-like state, but his eyes remained transfixed upon Judas.

'So, this is what you are going to do. You are going to agree with everything I propose, and if anyone opposes what I want, you will have them eliminated. First of all, we are going to break down the border between our two states, then we are going to allow anyone to own land from either side. Again, if anyone resists, or kills someone from the other side, they will be shot on sight. Then ...' Judas continued his list of commands and when he finished, he said, 'Obviously those outside doing their best to eavesdrop, failing in the process mind you, will not expect us to come to a reasonable conclusion so soon. Let's stay a while and enjoy the great facilities.' Judas stood up and made himself a Scotch on the rocks with the eighteen-year-old whisky in the room. The president continued to stare at Judas's seat as if he had never moved. Judas soon returned with a full glass in his hand. He looked up and down at the drooling zombie before him, then with a look of abhorrence he said, 'Hell you're disgusting!' His face changed to a more tedious expression. 'So Mr Abbas, we have some time to kill, but you're such a bore. How can we liven this up a little? I know, why don't you tell me your deepest darkest secrets?'

Judas shook the glass to mix the melted ice with the Scotch, then looked at Mohammed with a rather bored expression.

****

Three weeks later, the highly fortified wall between Israel and Palestine was opened to allow anyone and everyone to pass through. There was much furious debate among the media and the politicians as everyone expected a bloody conflict—but none came. As much of the conflict was over access to land, once the borders were down, those that wanted land in the other state offered a handsome price and many accepted the offer. No underground militia showed any resistance, and no one had to be shot. Judas became an overnight sensation, and almost a saintly figure in the eyes of the public. His approval rating as prime minister was at a record high of ninety-five percent, and the following year Judas was awarded the Nobel Peace Prize. Sections of the wall itself were eventually removed, and within a few years the former boundary between the two states was all but erased.

Political leaders across the world wanted to meet Judas, as did movie stars, sports stars, and religious leaders. However, some leaders though full of praises for his great achievement, were not knocking on his door to meet him. They were the leaders of England, Australia and the USA. Conspiracy theories were rampant as some claimed the west was secretly fueling the conflict of admiration for political purposes.

But the figurehead that was on the top of Judas's list was the Pope. Judas declined the offer of meeting the Pope in the Vatican but offered to meet the Pope in his home state—the Holy Land—and the Pope accepted. Cardinal Jiovani Vieneto became Pope John XIV on the day of his inauguration. His term so far as Pope had been well received as he had a more contemporary view on religion than his predecessors. He had declared the use of condoms within a marriage acceptable, and that the non-physical act of homosexual love was not a sin. Though the traditionalists were not a fan of the latest Pope, as his relaxed view on such subjects was very much frowned upon.

Judas had arranged to meet the Pope at the recently refurbished Parliament House for a brief tour, then a photo shoot with the media. He stood at the entrance to the small art gallery that occupied one of the annexes of Parliament House. It contained a fine selection of works by Jewish artists. Behind Judas was his usual entourage of advisors and gofers. To either side of the gallery entrance was a collection of camera men and reporters ready to capture the moment when they first met. Judas wore one of his typical tailored designer black suits with a thin blue tie, and much of his entourage had also taken up the very western form of attire.

There was a sudden flurry of camera flashes and reporter activity to announce the arrival of the pontiff. The first of the Pope's entourage of cardinals came into view, dressed in the signature black tunic and red sash, then a second appeared. Behind the two cardinals walked the Pope in his unique white tunic and short, red and white coat. Pope John continued to walk towards Judas and smiled as he approached. Judas stepped forward, shook the pontiff's hand, and said in Italian, 'Welcome your Holiness.'

A flurry of camera flashes exploded around them as Pope John replied, 'Thank you Prime Minister.' The Pope replied in Hebrew, 'Please let us talk in Hebrew. I don't get to use it much and I wouldn't want all those years of studying the Holy Land language to go to waste.'

Judas smiled and replied in Hebrew, 'Certainly.'

The Pope's former curly dark locks had long since disappeared and were now a thin grey wisp. His strong facial features had sagged and wrinkled, and his once deep blue eyes were now a faded steel grey; but they still retained some of their former liveliness.

During the camera flashlight show, for a split second, the iris of Judas's eyes flashed flame red and the almost blinding camera flashes around him completely concealed the brief transformation. In that fleeting moment, Judas looked deep into the soul of the eighty-three-year-old man before him and saw all that was wicked. A soul that lusted for fame, riches, and most of all, power.

As it was so swift, and with the added distraction of the flashing cameras, Pope John was totally unaware of the mental intrusion that had just been inflicted on him.

Judas thought as they finished shaking hands, *'You have been a very naughty boy Jiovani, murdering your predecessor, and not repenting for it. That means your mine, all mine!'* A big smile grew across Judas's face as he directed the pontiff into the art gallery. 'Come this way. We have a fine selection from some of our best local artists. This one is by Aharon Avni.'

'Yes, very nice,' Pope John replied as he squinted to see the detail in the painting. 'Unfortunately, I don't have my reading glasses with me. You see, I didn't come here to see art, I came here to meet you.' They moved slowly onto the next painting while the camera flashes continued. 'Please, I must know, how did you get the Palestinian president to agree?' Judas smiled again, 'You are not the first person to ask me this your Holiness. As I said before, we just sat down and had a good talk. You know, we both wanted the same thing—peace.'

Pope John looked at all the crowds around them and said, 'The camera flashes hurt my old eyes, do you think we can continue on alone?'

'Certainly.' Judas called over one of his advisors and whispered something to him. The advisor turned and began herding the crowd of journalists and cameramen away. Pope John nodded to a group of cardinals and they also left. Finally, they were alone to talk. Pope John asked, 'Prime Minister, can I call you Judas?'

'Sure,' Judas replied.

Pope John stared intently at Judas as he stated, 'Judas, I had a dream, and in that dream I was told that I would meet a man, a man that could perform miracles, a man that will change the world. Are you that man?'

Judas smiled and said, 'My father is very resourceful.' Judas returned the intense stare and asked, 'What does your heart tell you?'

Pope John's expression changed to one of great humility. He then fell to his knees and kissed Judas's right hand. 'My Lord, have mercy on me.'

Judas gazed down at his first disciple with great satisfaction as he stated, 'Mercy! You will be a made great in my kingdom on Earth. We have so much to do and many miracles to perform. The only thing I require is …' A smile grew on his expression. '… Your soul!' Judas's eyes turned to flames as he began the consumption of the soul at his knees.

Pope John screamed and writhed in agony as the Antichrist consumed him. Finally, he collapsed on the marble floor.

The scream echoed through the gallery and in moments the entourage of bishops and reporters were upon them. They found Judas over the Pope, wearing the direst expression.

Judas shouted, 'Get a doctor quick!'

One of the Pope's entourage pushed through the crowd and shouted back in Italian, 'I am his Holiness's physician, move back!' The middle-aged man was carrying a briefcase, which he promptly placed on the floor and opened. He pulled out a stethoscope and began examining the pontiff. The papal doctor said with some restraint, 'His heart has stopped!' The doctor began CPR while the crowd watched in deathly silence.

No one noticed the single smirk in the crowd as the drama unfolded before them.

A minute passed and the Pope still had no heartbeat. The doctor stopped CPR and tore open the Pope's vest to expose his bare, grey haired chest. He turned to his briefcase and flicked a switch on a machine inside, then lifted two white paddles from the case that were attached by curled power cords. The briefcase emitted an ever-increasing pitched tone while the doctor rubbed the two metal surfaces of the paddles together. The increasing pitched tone stopped and was replaced by a constant beeping. The doctor strategically placed the paddles upon the pontiff's chest and yelled, 'Chiaro, clear!'

The immediate crowd stepped back slightly but continued to stare at the spectacle. The Pope's body lurched slightly as the high voltage current surged through it. The doctor looked at a small screen in the briefcase that displayed the heart rate of the body the paddles were pressed against. But the screen showed only a straight red line with no sign of life. He pressed a button on one of the paddles to reset the charge and once recharged, he yelled again, 'Chiaro!'

Again, the pontiff's body lurched while the doctor studied the heart rate monitor. The monitor continued to display a straight red line. He repeated the process and again no result.

The doctor returned the paddles and began to rhythmically punch the pontiff's chest while saying in Italian, 'Live your Holiness, live!' After several blows, the doctor stopped, his own heart was racing like an

Olympic athlete. Finally, the doctor bowed his head and shook it, and said, 'He's gone!'

Gasps emitted from the crowd, followed by the muttering of prayers from the bishops. One of the reporters began to sob in mourning.

It was then that Judas stepped forward and said, 'Let me through!' The crowd parted for the prime minister as they expected him to utter some sort of a memorial speech. Instead, he knelt beside the pontiff and opposite the devastated doctor. He assumed a prayer-like kneeling position and laid his hands upon the Pope's chest. Judas closed his eyes and tipped his head back for a moment, then looked back down at the prostrate body and said, 'Breathe!'

Judas's eyes flashed red for a millisecond and with his head down, looking at the Pope, no one witnessed the fleeting incident. The Antichrist returned just enough of the Pope's soul for him to regain life but not enough for the Antichrist to lose control.

The Pope drew breath!

Suddenly, there was a barrage of camera flashes as video cameramen fought to get a clear shot of the Pope breathing.

Next, Judas stood over the Pope, extended his hand and said, 'Get up!'

Pope John opened his eyes as consciousness returned. Slowly, he raised his head from the marble floor and tried to focus on the scene around him. He fixated on the helping hand that was extended to him and grabbed it. The splitting headache began to fade as he looked upon the face of Judas.

One of the bishops declared to the crowd, 'He brought his Holiness back from the dead! It's a miracle!' Following the declaration was a great wave of cheers and gasps from the crowd.

In Pope John's right ear, the familiar voice of his doctor shouted over the commotion, 'Your Holiness, we need to get you to a hospital immediately!'

As his mind began to clear, Pope John was able to utter, 'No! Not yet.'

He began to sway but Judas steadied him. Pope John looked up at Judas again, then at the crowd about them and stated in a concise loud voice, 'Listen to me!' The raucous quickly faded. 'We have all witnessed a miracle today, and it won't be the last. Before us stands more than just a saint, but the saint of saints. I had a dream that I would meet a man that would change the world, and that man stands before me. I declare, the one that stands before me is the Messiah! I bow down to his majesty.' With some frailty, the pontiff dropped to one knee and bowed his head before Judas.

The bishops all stared at the Pope for a moment, before following suit and obediently bowing before their new spiritual leader.

It was undeniable that what had just transpired was miraculous. Slowly, some of the reporters fell to their knees, then some of the cameramen. Finally, the entourage fell to their knees, but this was more peer pressure than anything else.

In complete exhalation, Judas raised his arms in a gesture that welcomed all at his feet. 'There cometh a New World Order, and I will be at the forefront, directing the revolution. And my ministry starts here with you.'

10

Britain's Recourse

London, UK

Stephen and Paul were transfixed by the BBC news report on the miraculous resurrection of the Pope. The news presenter, James Stuart, continued his report. 'Doctors have examined His Holiness and found him in good health. We are at a loss to explain how the Israeli Prime Minister was able to resurrect the pontiff.' The presenter was replaced with a scene of a speech podium and a doctor answering questions from the media. 'We are men of science, but what happened today is currently without explanation.' The presenter returned. He was in his late forties and had only secured the role of the prime-time anchor role a few months before. 'After the Pope's declaration that the prime minister is the Messiah, many devoted Catholics and other Christian religions are supporting his Holiness's view. We have here in the studio a very special guest, the Archbishop of Canterbury Arthur Peterson. Archbishop, thank you for joining us this evening.'

The camera turned to a middle-aged man wearing his vestment. 'Thank you.'

'Archbishop, being second in charge of the Church of England, after his royal highness King William, what is your take on today's events?'

The archbishop shifted to a more comfortable position before saying, 'Well it has been a very eventful day. For the first time, a miracle has been recorded on live television, involving none other than the Pope. One would ask if it were the divinity of the prime minister—or the divinity of the Pope—that created the miracle, or more likely the divinity of God himself. However, it does state in the Bible that the Messiah will bring peace and unity to the Holy Land, which Mr Salim has done. It also states that he will unite the world under a new ministry, which Mr Salim too has declared. What doesn't align with the prophecies is the Apocalypse. The Messiah is to return, cast out the Antichrist and bring forth the end to the most terrible of wars. This, as we know, has not transpired.'

James sat forward to emphasis his next question. 'So, you disagree with the Pope's declaration?'

'It's more a case of the jury still being out on this one,' Archbishop Peterson replied with a brief smile.

'Many believe that World War II was the Apocalypse?' James asked in a manner that was more like a statement.

'Yes, but Mr Salim was born fifty-five years after, and there is no evidence to declare World War II as the Apocalypse.'

James sat back in his armchair to close off the interview. 'Either way, these are very exciting times. Thank you, Archbishop.'

Paul sipped on his cup of tea then stated, 'At least he hasn't been fooled as well—yet.'

Stephen buried his head in his hands while saying, 'Why can't anyone see him for what he is? It's so obvious!'

Paul said in a calm tone, 'Any action by us now will have complicated ramifications.'

Stephen sat back in the lounge chair and stared at the screen. 'Undoubtedly, but we can't give up. At least we have succeeded in one area—event management. My job at World Stage Productions, the company of choice for the government, was a great windfall.'

'We are making progress in the infiltration of Number 10 too,' Paul said with confidence as he looked over his glasses. 'I have an interview next week for a job as a part-time clerk you may remember.'

'Yes, but it is still a long shot that you get in. You're no spring chicken, you know.'

Paul sipped his tea again before adding, 'I'm sure something will turn up. I am happy to leave it in the Lord's hands.'

'You are right there, only a miracle would get you in.'

****

The following Wednesday Paul sat in a waiting room wearing a dark suit and blue tie. The window opposite allowed what little light there was outside to illuminate the room. A lamp on a table near the door assisted in brightening the room enough to be able to see clearly. Although more than seventy years of life had passed his eyes, Paul had kept himself in good physical shape and looked much younger for his years. He had shaved off what little grey hair remained on his head, leaving a persona that was age indifferent.

The room was in a building adjacent the famous 10 Downing Street, where the prime minister resided. Paul pondered for a moment over what the room was originally built for—maybe a lounge or a dining room?

A door opened opposite where he had entered, and a woman who appeared to be in her late thirties said, 'Sorry to keep you waiting, it's been a very busy morning. Please come in.'

Paul got up and approached the woman. When he was close enough, she extended her hand and added, 'Paul, is it? I'm Rachel, nice to meet you.'

They shook hands as Paul replied, 'Hello, nice to meet you too.' Paul stepped into a small office where an antique looking desk was positioned opposite the door. Before the desk was a lone armchair and behind it an office chair. Paul made his way to the armchair and Rachel headed for the office chair behind the desk.

Rachel had a very slight frame and shoulder length blonde hair that was tied up in a ponytail. Her bright blue eyes were obscured by a pair of black-framed, designer glasses that sat near the end of her nose. As Rachel sat down, she instinctively pushed her glasses back towards her face. 'Thanks for coming in Paul. I'm the head clerk for the foreign office and the recruiting manager for the role. As you understand, this is a part-time role with a maximum of thirty hours per week. You will have access to full government benefits as if you were a full-time employee. The office is a quiet and concentrated environment—does that sound like something that would suit you?'

Paul replied with approval, 'Oh yes, that does sound well suited to my idea of an ideal working environment.'

Rachel continued, 'Good.' She picked up her tablet computer lying on the desk and said, 'I see from your CV you have the necessary computer skills, and most of your career was in the Catholic Church. So, what is it that has attracted you towards politics?'

Paul recited his well-rehearsed speech. 'I have always had a great personal interest in politics and since my retirement from the church, I felt it was a good time explore a career that involved my interest.'

'Good,' Rachel said with a smile. 'Tell me about your career in the church.'

'Well, I was first inducted when I was twenty-four and lead my first congregation when I was twenty-seven. I held positions in West London, Milton Keynes, Maidenhead, and Norwich.'

Something seemed to spark Rachel's interest. 'So, whereabouts was the position in Maidenhead?'

'At St Joseph's.'

Rachel's eyes narrowed as she asked, 'When was it that you were working at St Joseph's?'

Paul stared at Rachel for a moment trying to fathom her line of questioning. He did not want to go into dates and highlight his age, but he could not lie to her. He took a leap of faith and told her the truth. 'From 1992 to 2004.'

Rachel sat back in her chair and stared at Paul as she said, 'Your Father Paul from St Joseph's—you baptised me! I remember going to Sunday school and at the end we would go into the church to catch the end of your sermon.' A smile grew on her face as she said, 'Wow, what a small world.'

The anxiety in Paul eased, giving him room to search his memory. A smile grew across his face. 'Little Rachel Simons! How are your parents, James and Tina?'

Rachel's expression became sombre as she replied, 'Mum is good, but Dad has prostate cancer. It's okay, he is responding to the chemo.'

'Oh, I am sorry to hear that, I will say a prayer for him.'

'Thanks.' Rachel's expression became more open. 'Paul, this position is not a high paying role, and it has little chance of career opportunities. It's not a role that would suit many people. You see, often the minister has administration needs out of normal office hours, and we need a skeleton staff on hand during those hours. These hours could include late at night or weekends. Would that be suitable for you?'

Paul smiled then replied, 'Sounds perfect. It's often during the odd hours that I am most active. I'm not a big sleeper you see, so why not make those hours useful?'

'Excellent!' Rachel stated. 'I think we have found a perfect match. When can you start?'

'Next week is fine with me.'

'Great. Come here next Monday at 5:00 pm, we have a late-night television interview to prepare for.' Rachel stood and put out her hand. 'Welcome aboard!'

Paul shook her hand, smiled and said, 'You have made an old man very happy.'

****

Later that day, Stephen returned from work to find Paul sitting on the lounge watching the afternoon news, cup of tea in hand.

Stephen dropped his work backpack on the floor near the front door and walked over to Paul. He stood staring at Paul, hands on hips. 'Well?'

Paul glanced up at Stephen and said casually, 'Well what?'

Stephen rolled his eyes and replied with an annoyed tone, 'How did the interview go?'

Paul continued in a blithe tone, 'Oh that. I told you the Lord moves in mysterious ways. Her parents were once members of my congregation ... oh, and I baptised her when she was a baby. I start Monday.'

Stephen, making a fist with his right hand and pulling it into his body as if he just caught an imaginary ball, said, 'Yes!' He sat in the lounge seat adjacent Paul and added, 'We are in business!'

'Maybe, maybe not.' Paul placed the empty teacup on the coffee table in front of him. 'We don't know if I will be privy to any real intel. We will just have to wait and see.'

'It feels good to finally have a game plan though. I think this is how the others felt when they went into action. Do you?'

Paul looked at Stephen over the top of his glasses and replied, 'As long we don't end up *feeling* like the others—dead!'

****

Washington DC, USA

James Richardson had won the last election to become the next president of the United States. He had been in office for only a few months and had delivered on his first election promise—to prevent further development of coal-fired power plants, and ensure all future power was provided by the way of green energy. With the increasing extreme weather events over recent decades having scared many of the American people, they wanted change—and they wanted it now! Jim, as he preferred to be called, delivered as promised and congress backed him wholeheartedly. Jim, now in his early fifties, sat at the desk of the Oval Office, reading through a document. The morning sunlight, filtered by the curtains on the windows, brightly lit the office. Jim's brown locks had faded to grey and his brown eyes had started giving way to the erosion of time. Upon his nose sat a pair of frameless reading glasses, to aid his deteriorating vision. The lines on his face had deepened, further emphasising Jim's age. Before he had finished reading the document, a knock on the door distracted him.

The door opened and the face of his personal assistant appeared from behind the door.

'Mr President, the prime minister is here.'

Jim answered, 'Thanks Nancy, bring him in.' Jim stepped out from behind the desk to greet his guest—the Prime Minister of Britain. This was the second time he had met the British Prime Minister. The first time was at the G20 Summit where there was little time to have a good talk and get to know each other. There were so many things Jim wanted to talk to the prime minister about, the first one being the recent events in Israel.

Luke Churchill walked into the Oval Office as Nancy quietly closed the door behind him. Luke was taller than Jim at almost two metres and he was nearly ten years his junior. Luke had raven black hair with bright blue eyes and a large nose. His lips were not as full as Jim's, but he still cut a fine line in many a woman's eye.

Jim extended his hand to meet Luke's. 'Welcome Prime Minister, hope you had a good flight.'

'Thank you, Mr President. Yes, the flight went well.'

The two looked each other up and down to see that they were both wearing the same black suit, but Jim had chosen a blue tie over Luke's red.

Jim said in jest, 'Glad our wives got us to wear different ties or else the fashion police would hammer us in the tabloids.' Luke laughed as Jim continued, 'I must apologise for not meeting you at the plane, but things have been rather crazy of late.'

'No need to. I understand completely.'

'Has the weather in London warmed up at all?'

'A little, but it still feels like a Nordic winter.'

'Shame, I spent a few weeks in England during summer some years ago and had a wonderful time—the weather was quite warm. Sign of the times I'm afraid. Anyway, we can discuss global warming later. Please take a seat.' Jim directed Luke to the antique lounge suite that occupied the centre of the office.

They sat down but before they could say another word, there was another knock on the office door. Nancy entered carrying a tray of coffee, tea and biscuits. She placed the tray on the coffee table before the seated leaders and quietly left. Luke noticed some differences between his own personal secretary and the president's personal assistant. Nancy was a well-dressed, rather attractive women in her early forties, with fashionably tied up blonde hair and striking blue eyes. Her figure-hugging, sky blue suit and matching high heels showed off her obviously well-exercised physique. Oliver, his personal secretary, was a man in his early fifties who suffered from baldness and classic middle-age spread.

'Earl Grey I understand is your preferred brew?' Jim asked as he gestured towards the cup of tea in front of Luke.

'Yes, thank you,' Luke replied with a smile.

'I'm a more avid coffee drinker,' Jim said as he took a sip from the coffee mug embossed with the presidential seal.

Luke gazed around the room for a moment then said, 'I can't believe I'm in the famous Oval Office. Mind you I still sometimes can't believe I am the prime minister,' he said before taking a sip of tea.

Jim smiled and said, 'I'm still in the denial stage too. I wake up each morning wondering where the hell I am! So, this is your ah, ninth month in office?'

'Yes, a tough nine months.'

'I met Barack Obama last week. What a great guy. He's my favourite president. Barack said that it was about a year before it all seemed normal for him. And it just gets harder as well he said.'

'Great, that's cheered me up,' Luke said sarcastically.

'Now Luke, I know there are a number of things that we have on the agenda to discuss, but there is one thing I would like to add that is off the record.'

Luke's eyes narrowed for a moment as he pondered the possible subject. There was one thing that had been on his mind as well and Luke took a gamble on whether Jim was on the same wavelength.

'Recent events in Israel?'

'Yes,' Jim replied. 'What is your take on it?'

Luke deduced that if the president had raised the subject, then it must have been weighing on his mind as well. 'There is something not right about the whole thing if you ask me.'

'I agree. I would have thought that the arrival of the Messiah would have been more, well, eventful,' Jim added.

'And having the name "Judas" also bothers me,' Luke said cautiously before sipping his tea.

Jim took a sip from his coffee and said, 'I'm going to go out on a limb here.'

Luke paused, took another sip, and put the cup down. 'This could be interesting,' he thought.

'When I was the Senator of New York several years ago, I received an email from an unknown source.' Jim turned on the tablet computer that was sitting on the coffee table and handed it to Luke. Luke perused the email for a few moments then said, 'I've seen this before. A former PM had an MI6 file created and they have been watching him ever since.' Luke took another sip from his tea and continued, 'When I first read the email, there was something very disturbing about it. It seemed so … definite.'

'That is what I sensed as well,' Jim stated.

'Do you have any intelligence on the Brethren?'

'Nothing concrete, but what we believe is that they are a very old society that appears to have originated from the Catholic Church. And potentially well-funded. We have not been able to shed any further light. The Vatican denies any knowledge of course,' Jim replied.

'Well-funded?'

'Ever heard of the oldest bank account in the world?'

'Can't say that I have.'

'Look it up, it is an interesting read. In short, the account was opened by the Vatican in the first bank in Italy back in the sixteenth century. Deposits have continued ever since but there has never been a withdrawal. Some blogs claimed it was the Pope's private account and is worth millions. The account was moved to a Swiss account during World War II and has remained there ever since. Ten years ago, it was claimed that a pair of priests withdrew most of the funds. Unfortunately, we could not confirm any of this with the bank. The Swiss are very tight lipped as you know. But one blog claimed that the account was held in the name, 'The Brethren'.

'So, if they are well funded, it makes you wonder what else they could be up to.'

'True, but all this is unfortunately unsubstantiated. I was hoping you could shed some more light.'

'Sorry, I now know as much as you,' Luke said with an air or regret.

'We have digressed. Back to the events in Israel?'

'Yes, when he became the PM of Israel, MI6 immediately showed me the email and his file. And I have to say, he has been a model citizen so far. So, do you think he is you know who?'

Jim put his hands to his face in a subconscious gesture to hide what he really wanted to say, but instead a political response came out. 'I don't know.'

Luke picked up his cup again and sipped his tea before adding, 'So the big question is, what can we do? That's if he is, you know, the big bad "A". For some reason, I don't feel comfortable saying …' Luke leaned forward and whispered, '… "Antichrist" out loud.'

Jim, puzzled, stared at Luke for a moment before replying, 'I hadn't thought of that. If he is the big bad "A", then he could have supernatural powers. Either way, I don't think there is much we can do right now. His popularity is skyrocketing, and many Arab nations are becoming followers. The Jewish community is much the same.'

Jim's eyes narrowed for a moment as he asked, 'You're Church of England, aren't you?'

'Yes, but not an avid follower. And Jim, you're Catholic?'

'Yes.'

'How do you feel about the Pope?'

Jim took a sip from his coffee mug and said, 'He has been a decent Pope so far, and he has a more modern take on things compared to his predecessors, but there is something about him that bothers me too. And I'm not the only one who thinks so. Father Joseph, my parish priest has said nothing about the Pope's declaration. The whole thing stinks to high heaven if you ask me. Let's face it, the writing is on the wall.'

'What do you mean?'

Jim raised his hands and gestured, 'The Christians on one side and …'

Luke nervously completed his sentence. '… non-Christians on the other. Division between Christians and non-Christians.'

'Yes,' Jim added, sitting forward on the lounge in a more engaged position.

'This could blow up into something catastrophic if we are not careful,' Luke said while retaining his casual posture. 'But the Pope supports him so surely most of the Catholics will as well?'

'No, I don't think so. There could be a split in the church over this. Our sources in the Vatican say that all is not well between the cardinals and the Pope. And considering that my parish priest doesn't appear to agree then there could be insurrection at many levels of the church.' Jim briefly rubbed his hands over his face in an attempt to wipe away the stress.

'We need to find out who we can trust.'

'The French seem quiet, as do the Germans,' Luke interjected.

'Add the Aussies to the list, not a peep from Down Under. Any others?'

Luke stared across the room for a moment before saying, 'No. The Russians are definitely out. The president already announced to the media he wants to meet him.'

Jim, scratching his head, said, 'We need to confirm if they are believers or not, without sparking off an international incident.'

'I am meeting with both the president of France and the chancellor of Germany next month at the European Summit. I should have a chance to speak to them discreetly.'

'Good,' Jim added. 'I will speak to the Prime Minister of Australia, been planning to anyway.' Jim finished the remains of his coffee just as there was another knock on the door. Nancy poked her head inside and said, 'The media are ready Mr President.'

'Thanks Nancy.' Jim stood and said, 'Time to face the wolves. Got your best smile ready?'

'Always,' Luke replied.

****

Jerusalem, Israel

Abba Ameir was seated on the stage ready for his guests that were about to join him. Normally Abba was cool, calm and collected before an interview no matter who the guest was. However, today was different. Today he was interviewing the Messiah. Normally it would be a closed set, but today a small audience was permitted. Abba looked around at the anxious faces before him and felt the radiation of excitement. He cleared his throat before starting his standard greeting. 'Welcome back. Today we have two very special guests on our show, and I have to say, I'm a little nervous.' Abba extended an open hand in the direction of the two vacant chairs opposite him and added, 'Ladies and gentlemen, I have the great privilege and honour to present Pope John and Prime Minister ... or should I say, *Messiah* Judas Salim.'

The two entered the stage and Abba stood as they approached. Pope John was not wearing his usual papal vestment, but rather a smart suit and red tie. Judas had also cast aside his usual designer outfit and was wearing a white thawb. The audience clapped and cheered but only the Pope waved to recognise the welcome. Judas's face was stony. Abba wasn't sure what to do as a suitable greeting, so went down on one knee and bowed his head. Both Judas and Pope John touched him on top of his head before sitting.

Abba quickly stood and returned to his seat. The applause from the crowd faded and Abba composed himself with a deep breath before saying, 'This is such an honour to have you on our show.'

Pope John smiled and waved, but Judas remained steely.

Abba continued, 'This has been quite a few weeks, hasn't it? Pope John, I noticed that you are not wearing your usual vestment. We understand that there has been some resistance to your declaration within the Catholic Church, but is there something more that has led you to wear civilian clothes?'

Pope John replied, 'I have cast off the shackles of devotion to the church and am now fully devoted to the Messiah and his quest to save the world.'

Abba's expression went flat as he realised that a world scoop was about to unfold before him. He said carefully and concisely, 'Are you suggesting that you are leaving the church?'

He answered, 'Have left! I denounced my position as head of the Catholic Church this morning. You can simply call me *Jiovani*.'

The audience gasped while Abba's jaw dropped. It was at that moment that Judas interjected, 'The role of the Pope has become redundant. A new world is to be born and the roles of the past are mute. For I too have resigned from my position as prime minister. I met with the president not half an hour ago.'

Again, the audience gasped. Abba's jaw remained agape as he couldn't believe what was unfolding before him. He did think it was unusual for the prime minister to request a small audience for the interview, but he didn't expect this.

'Wow, so the Catholic Church needs a new Pope, and we need a new prime minister.' Abba turned to the camera and stated, 'And you heard it first on *The World This Morning*.'

'There is no need for a Pope or a prime minister. There is no need for ruling parties, politicians or dictators,' Judas said sternly. 'Man has segregated himself for too long. Why do we need borders, why do we need countries? The answer is—we don't!'

'But who will make the big decisions?' Abba asked.

'If there are no country borders then there is no need to run it. Look at the European Union. People pass between each country every day and no one checks their passports anymore. And look at how strong the European Union has become now that the borders are more or less gone. The need for regional management is becoming less and less. Imagine if the world was one—imagine how great it would be. There would be no more wars as there would be no more countries to fight each other.' Judas's gaze fell upon the small audience. 'Imagine a world without war. Peace and unity are the cornerstones of the world I want to live in. How about you?' Judas asked as he looked at the audience.

The audience erupted in a round of applause.

Abba was out of his depth; serious political journalism was not his forte. All he could come up with was, 'It does sound wonderful, but easier said than done.'

'All we need is the will to do it, and it will be done,' Judas replied with certainty.

Abba was keen to change the subject to one that was more in his scope—sensationalism. 'We do have a special guest in the audience, one who is very keen to meet you. Come out Fahid.'

From the shadows emerged a young woman wearing jeans and a T-shirt. She pushed a wheelchair into the stage lights, and upon the chair sat a cloaked figure. The young woman stopped at the foot of the stage, fell to her knees before Judas and said, 'Please, help my father?'

The bright lights seemed to irritate the cloaked figure, causing him to raise his left hand over his face, exposing his flesh to the onlookers. Half of his fingers were missing, and his skin was covered in sores.

The audience screamed!

Abba almost leaped from his chair. He had seen this before but only from other journalists' coverage—it was leprosy. Judas had asked for this man and his daughter to be invited as special guests, but if Abba had known the father had leprosy, he would never have had agreed.

Some of the audience near the front scurried to the back of the small stand. The stage crew took a few steps back while the cameraman backed away, having to zoom back in so the stage was back in frame.

Jiovani's reaction was also one of shock as Judas had not mentioned this as part of the big announcement. He distinctly leaned back and away from the cloaked figure before him.

Judas stood before the young woman and said with authority, 'Mika, what disease is it that ails your father?'

The studio went silent and the boom operator lowered the microphone as close to the women as he dared.

Mika kept her head bowed and did not look up at the imposing figure above her. With a soft voice she answered, 'Leprosy.' Judas's expression was one of stern judgment. 'Louder!'

This time the woman lifted her head, looked into the eyes of Judas and shouted, 'Leprosy!' Tears were flowing from her deep brown eyes and down her pale cheeks.

'Can he be cured?' Judas demanded.

She almost sobbed as she answered, 'No.'

'Then why did you ask me to cure him?'

Mika answered softly, 'Because I believe in you.'

Judas's eyes became more intense. 'Louder!'

This time she shouted, 'I believe in you!'

Judas's gaze fell upon the semi-cloaked figure and in a soft tone he said, 'Fahid, show your face to me.'

Slowly, two ruined hands pulled back the cloak to reveal a head covered in pockmarks and a face with no nose. Fahid resembled a ghoul more than a human, and the unveiling resulted in a wave of gasps and muttering from the audience.

Judas looked out upon the audience and announced, 'Behold the impossible!' He reached back and grabbed Jiovani's right arm and dragged him to his feet, then forced his hand upon the left diseased hand of Fahid. He grabbed Fahid's right hand, forming a small circle.

Jiovani's expression was of loathing but he dared not let go for fear of disobeying Judas. Judas's face was utterly intense as a faint red glow illuminated the pupils of his eyes.

The Antichrist had no ability to heal, only the ability to destroy. He needed to access the little piece of God within Jiovani to perform this miracle. Unlike Jiovani, the Antichrist was born of hell and had no divinity within him.

Fahid's body went rigid and he threw his head back to reveal an expression of intense anguish. The pockmarks began to boil, steam emitting from them as though they were miniature volcanoes. Fahid's fingers and nose began to sizzle and reform as if time had been turned back to before the disease took hold.

Gasps echoed from the audience and the stage crew. Abba stared in wide-eyed horror while Jiovani's eyes were like saucers, mirroring the blend of shock and terror that was inflicting his brain. Judas stood over the event like a master puppeteer; his eyes lavishing the glory of the spectacle. Mika's face was alien to the rest; it was one of exaltation.

Finally, Fahid drooped unconscious in the wheelchair and Judas let go of his hand. Jiovani let go as if he were touching a red-hot iron. Mika fell upon her father's limp frame and shouted, 'Father, Father?' She studied his face for signs of life but Fahid remained comatose.

Judas stood like a monument over the two figures at his feet, the look on his face causing some of the audience to avert their eyes away from the scene before them. Silence fell upon the studio like a thick blanket.

Fahid groaned, then stirred.

Mika said with excitement, 'Father!'

Fahid's head was leaning against the wheelchair handle at an angle, and when he opened his eyes the studio lights made his pupils rapidly contract. Bringing his left hand up to cover his face, he saw his hand. He stared at it for a moment, then surveyed it by rotating his hand so he could view it from all angles. Fahid brought his right hand to his face and surveyed it as well. His hands were complete. He started rubbing them together, relishing the sensation of touch as his fingers had been numb for decades. He brought his newly healed hands to his face and began to feel his full nose and smooth, unblemished skin.

Fahid gasped. He looked into his daughter's eyes and cried, 'Mika, it's a miracle!' The two embraced as tears flowed freely accompanied by cries of joy.

The audience stood, giving an ovation, and shouting words of praise. From the back of the audience came the chant, 'Judas, Messiah! Judas, Messiah! Judas, Messiah!' In a moment, the whole audience had joined in as well as some of the studio crew.

Abba joined the chants and clapped in harmony with the audience. This was beyond his wildest dreams. This was the show to end all shows. This could be his big break to launch his own program. The biggest smile of all grew across Abba's face.

Mika fell to her knees at Judas's feet, followed by her father, then finally Jiovani.

Judas was like a monolith before the audience; his arms out with his palms facing them like that of a deity statue. He put his head back, closed his eyes and bathed in the flood of positive energy.

****

Sydney, Australia

Thomas and Peter watched the spectacle on the lounge room television in Thomas's apartment. The event on Israeli television had been broadcast all over the world and had been uploaded to *YouTube*. Peter replayed the high-definition footage again as they commenced another round of analysis.

'It's like watching a scene from a horror movie,' Thomas stated.

'I still can't believe what I am watching.' Peter supported his head in his hands, elbows on his knees while he stared trance like at the screen.

Thomas leaned forward and asked, 'Why does he need to involve Jiovani?'

'Good question,' Peter said.

'There must be something that he lacks that requires assistance from him,' Thomas added.

'The Antichrist was born in hell, so he would not have a soul like ours—if any,' Peter said turning to Thomas. 'Maybe he is not capable of healing.'

'Yes, makes sense. He is only capable of death and destruction and probably needs a human soul to do good.'

'I still can't believe the Pope. How could he be party to this?' Peter stated as he turned back to the *YouTube* footage.

Thomas sat back in the lounge chair and said, 'Pope Julius was right about the fallen, and there is no doubt now who the ringleader was.'

Peter stood and walked to the window overlooking the balcony. Before him was a spectacular view of—Sydney Harbour and the beautiful orange sunset bathing the sailing boats in a warm afternoon glow. Even the Opera House and the Sydney Harbour Bridge had joined in, appearing like a painting of summer colours with hues of pink and mauve. Some of Peter's youthfulness had faded from his face, a few fine lines having formed around his eyes. He turned back to Thomas and said, 'We need to contact our British counterparts. We have to try again to stop him.'

Thomas stood and walked over to join Peter on the balcony. 'We have failed twice so far, and we will fail again, no doubt.'

Peter spoke into Thomas's ear as Thomas stared out at the view. 'But we have to try—and now. If we wait much longer, it will be too late!'

Thomas leaned on the balcony rail, bowing his head for a moment. He looked out at the magnificent view again. 'All this will be gone, it's such a shame. Better to have tried and failed than to never have tried at all, I always say. Let's join forces and stop this monster.'

A smile grew across Peter's face as he said, 'I'm on it.'

****

London, UK

Stephen and Paul sat on a bench in Green Park, throwing a few bits of stale bread to the pigeons before them. If they turned their heads to the left, they could see Buckingham Palace between the leafless trees. It was early March and Britain had just experienced the longest and coldest winter on record. With much of Scotland and Northern Ireland still covered in snow, additional gritter trucks and snowploughs had been brought in from Europe to compensate. Scientists were waiting on the results of the study on the Gulf Stream. They believed the unusually cold winter was the result of the Gulf Stream stopping its warm water flow to the Northern Atlantic. Without it, Britain was destined to become like Nordic countries.

Thick grey clouds covered the skyline, and a gentle icy wind blew across the park. Both Stephen and Paul were rugged up in thick woollen coats, beanies, scarves, and ski gloves.

'Whose bright idea was it to meet in the park?' Paul protested. 'We could have done this in the pub.'

'Mine,' Stephen replied. 'It is less conspicuous, and our conversation won't be overheard.'

'Four chaps meeting in the park to feed the pigeons when it is minus five and about to snow, sounds very suspicious to me! They better hurry up or we will freeze to death.'

As there was another park bench positioned back-to-back with the one they sat on, Stephen has strategically chosen this spot so they could all talk while pretending not to know each other.

Paul threw out another handful of stale bread to the very cold looking pigeons when they heard a voice from behind their backs.
'Governor, Del Boy.'

Without turning around, Stephen replied, 'Wallaby, John Thomas.'

'About time, another five minutes and we would have been a pair of icicles,' Paul complained.

Thomas said, 'Very, sorry. We got off at the wrong tube station then we got lost on the way here.'

'We did just come from the other side of the planet, you know,' Peter added.

Peter and Thomas were not as well garbed for the weather as Stephen and Paul. They wore thick coats and gloves, but they had no beanies or scarves to really rug up. Paul asked, 'So where are you staying?'

'At the Hilton,' Peter replied.

'On Hyde Park? Nice,' Stephen said.

Peter asked, 'Any reason why we are meeting out here in the freezing cold?'

Paul glanced at Stephen before replying, 'It's so we can be inconspicuous and have a private conversation.'

Thomas turned his head around enough to see the backs of their heads and said, 'We are the only people out here. How much more conspicuous can we be?'

'We passed a nice warm pub on the way here,' Peter said as he rubbed his gloved hands together. He hugged himself and said, 'I say we go there. I could use a stiff cup of coffee.'

'I will need something stronger to thaw my old bones,' Paul declared.

'So where was the pub?' asked Stephen.

Peter replied, 'I think it was called Henry's, and it is on Piccadilly Road on the way back to Green Park Tube Station.'

Stephen continued his direction, 'Okay, we should go separately just to be safe. We will go first and you two follow two minutes after. Hopefully, there will be a private table for us.'

Paul immediately got to his feet, began stamping them and said impatiently, 'Come on, let's go.'

Paul and Stephen left in a brisk gait in the direction of Green Park Tube Station.

Thomas turned to Peter and said, 'This is the first time I have been to England and I have to say, I don't think I will be recommending it.'

Five minutes later, Thomas and Peter entered the pub and looked around to find Stephen and Paul. After a minute of searching, they found them seated in a booth in a secluded corner. Peter indicated that he and Thomas would get a coffee first before joining them. A few minutes later, they returned with their cappuccinos and sat down opposite Stephen and Paul.

Thomas looked down at Stephen and Paul's lowball glasses and asked, 'So what poisons have you chosen to thaw your bones?'

Paul answered first. 'A double shot of Scotch whisky, single malt. Perfect for a day like this.'

Stephen said, 'Cointreau, double, I have more of a sweet tooth.'

Peter took a big sip of his coffee and wondered if he had made the right choice of beverage. 'So, what have you two been up to of late?'

Stephen replied, 'I am working for an events company and Paul is working for the foreign office. What about you?'

Peter answered, 'I have been working for a sailing company and Thomas manages a vintage bookstore.'

Thomas said, 'Your choice of occupations is very intriguing. Sounds like you have a plan.'

Stephen and Paul glanced at each other before Paul answered, 'Yes.'

There was a lengthy silence before Peter said, 'So, let's have it!'

Stephen looked around to see if anyone could be listening before giving Paul a 'the coast is clear' nod.

Paul cleared his throat before saying in a low and barely audible tone, 'Now that he is a major celebrity, at some stage he will meet our prime minister. There will likely be some sort of grand meet and greet. We thought that if one of us joins a major events company and the other the foreign office, we could have a chance at getting him.'

Thomas asked in a full voice, 'Getting him, how?'

Stephen said, 'Shhh, keep your voice down.' He looked around to see if anyone heard. Everyone else seemed very disinterested in the four men in the corner booth.

'Sorry,' Thomas added.

Paul continued, 'We haven't figured that part out yet. We were hoping you could put some ideas on the table.'

Peter said, 'Well we know that directly taking him on failed, and using an assassin failed. So those ideas are out.'

'We need to use a remote form of attack,' Stephen said.

'What, like a bomb?' Thomas interjected.

'Maybe,' Paul replied.

'Does anyone here know how to make a bomb? I don't!' Stephen whispered.

Peter said, 'Then we learn how to, like off the Internet.'

Stephen sat up straight and said, 'The government would certainly have systems logging and locating whoever types in the word "bomb".'

'Then we steal a bomb,' Peter said boldly.

Thomas glared at Peter, but Paul spoke first. 'Listen to us. I can't believe the words that are coming from our mouths!'

Peter seemed unfazed by Paul's disgust and continued his steely stare upon the others.

Stephen spoke to break the frostiness of the conversation. 'Maybe there is some other way that doesn't involve a crime.'

Peter added, 'Did you hear the news today? Syria and Jordan have now joined his …' He raised two fingers from each hand in the air and curled them in a manner that represented quotation marks. '… New World.' He lowered his hands. 'And Libya is likely to be next. His reign is spreading like wildfire across the east. The Apocalypse is nigh!'

Thomas then said with conviction, 'The library!'

'The library?' Peter asked as he gazed at Thomas, puzzled. His expression then changed to one of realisation. 'The library!'

Stephen was next to catch on. 'Of course! We can research whatever we want in total anonymity. No one can monitor what books you read in a library, especially if you don't take the book out.'

'Still, being able to find a book that will tell us what we want to know won't be easy,' Paul declared. 'The library is not likely to keep books on making a bomb.'

Peter said, 'What about books on World War I and II and the weapons used? That could be a good start point.'

Stephen said, 'We have the next few days off, so it looks like we will be spending them in the library.'

'Fine with me, I love the library,' Thomas declared. 'It's really the books that I love. The peace and quiet of the library are great too.'

'I've never been in a library, so this will be a first for me,' Peter added.

'So where is the nearest library?' Thomas asked.

'The London Library,' Paul replied. 'It's only a short walk from here.'

'Walk!' Peter protested. 'If I am going to walk in the bitter cold out there again, I am going to need one of those.' He pointed at Paul's double Scotch whisky.

Thomas glared at Peter before saying, 'I don't think that is such a wise idea.'

'I'll be okay. I have been clean for years and it doesn't have its hold on me like it used to,' Peter responded.

Thomas's glare intensified. 'Okay, but I will be keeping an eye on you.'

Paul and Stephen looked at Peter, surprised by the revelation that he had a prior drinking problem.

Thomas added, 'I'll have the same.'

****

Peter and Thomas walked into The London Library about five minutes before Paul and Stephen. Stephen decided it was best they continued the charade that they were not acquainted, and that they should perform their research in two separate groups. As Peter and Thomas entered the Victorian building, they took a moment to take in the classic architecture and décor, and the traditional aisles of shelved books. Thomas thought about how sad it was that very few books were still being produced in hard copy since the ebook revolution killed the paperback industry. Thomas did not see the ebook as progress, but a lifeless digital substitute. Peter's only thought was how they were going to find the right books. They found a vacant table on which to place their excess winter wardrobe, and Thomas led Peter to one of the library database terminals.

As Thomas typed in the search subject, Peter announced, 'Ah, so that's how you find a book!'

When Paul and Stephen arrived, they chose a table as far away as possible from Peter and Thomas and used a different terminal to enhance the charade.

Paul and Stephen began with World War II, and Peter and Thomas with World War I. Every now and then they would pass each other in the library and discreetly show each other what book they were about to read.

Peter was surprised by how many people were in the library as he expected it to be deserted. It was occupied by several quiet people, mostly senior citizens.

After a few hours, the two teams discreetly swapped notes. In the notes were the Mills bomb, jam tin bomb, and pipe bomb. They had dynamite ingredients that included peanut oil, and discovered that gun power is made from sulphur, charcoal and potassium nitrate.

By closing time, a note was passed between the teams saying, 'Meet back at the pub.'

Shortly after, the four met at their previous meeting booth and discussed the day's progress. The pub, now filling up with office workers and becoming noisy, was perfect for muffling out their conversation from unwanted listeners.

Peter said, 'Well it seems plausible for us to build a small grenade of some form, and access ingredients to make the explosive.'

'Yes, something like either a jam tin bomb or a pipe bomb could work,' Stephen added.

Paul said, 'But we have to make the bomb so that it will only kill the beast.'

'Easier said than done,' Peter replied.

'Still, I won't be party to a deed that could harm anyone except the beast himself,' Paul protested.

'Here, here,' Thomas endorsed.

'And it will have to be undetectable by sniffer dogs. They will no doubt be casing the venue for any such devices,' Stephen added.

Peter sat back in the booth and rubbed the top of his head as he racked his brain for a solution. Paul took another slp from his Scotch whisky while Thomas and Stephen stared at each other silently.

Peter began staring at the downlights illuminating the bar, then sat forward and said, 'What if it were up high, away from the ground where the dogs would be searching?'

'How do you mean?' Stephen asked.

'Assuming we have access to the event's setup, we could put the device in a spotlight. Most spotlights will be pointed at the podium, and our target.'

'But we were looking at making something that went *boom*, not *bang* like a gun,' Stephen stated.

'What if we have been looking at this the wrong way?' Peter continued. 'Look at what we are trying to achieve here. We need to fire some blessed silver into the body of the beast while it stands on holy ground. We don't need to blow it up into tiny pieces.'

The booth went quiet as its occupants waited on the next word from Peter, but it took Thomas to prompt him to continue. 'Go on.'

'What if we built a device that just shot a handful of silver pellets in a narrow field at the podium? A least one would hit the target. And while he is making a speech, he should be all alone so there is little risk of hitting anyone else.'

There was a moment of silence before Paul said, 'It could work.'

Stephen interrupted, 'Wait, *The Secret Book of Saint John* said that only silver cleansed with the holy spirit can pierce the heart of evil. I think we need to get him in the heart.'

They all sat back in the booth and stared at each other for a while. Thomas finally broke the silence. 'What if we added an aiming device?'

'How?' Peter asked.

'Using a webcam.' Thomas sat forward, the stare of his brown eyes becoming more intense in an unconscious display of excitement. 'One of my regular customers at the bookshop showed me how he monitors what happens in his garage … from his phone.'

Paul asked, 'Why would you want to monitor your garage?'

Thomas continued, 'He has a rare British sports car and he had two recent attempted break-ins. He installed a motion sensor and linked it up to the webcam somehow. So, when something moved in the garage, it would activate the webcam and send him a text to warn him.'

'It sounds rather complicated. We could be overstretching ourselves,' Stephen said with apprehension.

'On the contrary, he was not a very technical man. Apparently, it all came as a kit. I think it's worth a try,' Thomas retorted.

Peter said, 'What we will need is one of the stage lights.' He looked at Stephen as he asked, 'Do you think you could get your hands on one?'

Stephen screwed up his face and said, 'I don't know, possibly not. The gear is closely tracked when it leaves the warehouse. What I could do though is get the brand and model number then you could see if you can source one from the supplier.'

'Okay,' Peter replied.

'So where do we go from here?' Paul asked.

Peter replied, 'Well we need to do more library research. But after that Thomas and I could work on the weapon and aiming device while you two continue your roles. That way we can be ready if he arrives in the country.'

'But won't both of you have to go back to Australia? You must only be on a holiday visa.' Stephen said.

Peter replied, 'No, we can stay as long as we like. We applied for permanent residency and we got it.'

'How?' Paul asked.

Thomas smiled and said, 'The world is your oyster when you have a big bank balance.'

'Typical,' Paul said in disgust.

'But that also means that if we need to set up base in another country, we could,' Stephen added.

Peter said, 'Email me the light details and we will let you know when we are finished, but it could take a while though.'

'Let's just hope he doesn't arrive here any time soon,' Thomas added.

Peter stood and said, 'Time we headed back to the hotel. Will we see you in the library tomorrow?'

While Thomas slid across the booth seat and stood next to Peter, Stephen and Paul looked at each other for a moment and nodded to themselves. Stephen replied, 'Yes sure. See you then.'

****

Near Cairo, Egypt

Judas stood in the wing of the large temporary stage that had The Great Pyramid of Giza as a dramatic backdrop. The organisers predicted that nearly one hundred thousand would attend the formal acceptance of Egypt, Iraq and Yemen to the New World. Apart from the rich and the very powerful, it was standing room only.

Judas wore what has become his signature white kaftan with a red sash. Beside him stood Jiovani, who had taken to wearing a black kaftan with a red sash to display his allegiance to Judas. Behind them was an entourage of willing staff in signature black suits, black shirts and red ties, all ready to do their master's bidding. One of the members of the entourage approached Judas and asked, 'My Lord, is there anything I can get you before you go on stage?'

Judas raised his hand in a signal of rejection and the young woman obediently returned to the entourage, blending in again.

Jiovani poked his head around to catch a glimpse of the crowd outside. All he could see was an ocean of heads. He looked up at Judas and said, 'My Lord, your dream is finally coming true.'

A small smile grew across Judas's face. Jiovani was right—his dream was coming true, but not the dream that Jiovani envisaged. The Antichrist had but one dream—world domination and the destruction of all who opposed it.

A man wearing a wireless headset looked over at Judas and signalled to him it was time to go on stage.

Judas cleared his throat and strode forward onto the stage. Jiovani followed him on stage but only as far as the edge of the podium. Judas stepped up and gazed upon the sea of followers before him. The crowd burst into life and a soundwave of cheers hit the stage like an invisible tsunami.

Judas raised his arms in a poetic gesture that symbolised him catching their approval. The many microphones mounted on the podium quivered from the vibrations of the roaring crowd. It took a full minute for the cheers to die down so that Judas could commence his speech.

'Thank you, thank you. Welcome to the New World!' The crowd exploded again, and it took almost another minute before he could say his next word. 'Your countries—Egypt, Iraq and Yemen— have come to join the new brotherhood. You have already seen the first signs of the new prosperity. Better jobs, better pay, better schooling for your children—and this is only the start. No longer will you be isolated by borders and persecuted by greedy governments and dictators. You are now all free, free to live the life that you deserve. Free to share the wealth and prosperity of all nations. You will have new passports, new currency, and a new nation that you can truly be proud of. This is my gift to you.'

As Judas paused, the audience cheered again. He waited until the raucousness had died down before continuing. 'My treasurer told me just before coming on stage that the New World dollar has just gone up by two percent over the rest of the world currencies. You have all just become a little richer.' The audience cheered again, and Judas raised his right hand in a gesture to quieten them. 'There are still some people that doubt who I am.' The audience became deathly quiet. 'So, I will prove once more to those who doubt.' Judas stepped off the podium as an Egyptian woman dressed in casual clothes came onto the stage. The woman appeared quite withdrawn and she had her left hand concealed in the pocket of her jeans. Judas beckoned her over as he said, 'Come closer, do not be afraid.'

The woman approached Judas and stood beside him. She took a brief glance at the sea of people before her then set her gaze upon Judas. Looking at the crowd seemed to make her uncomfortable but looking at Judas created a greater reaction as she fell to her knees before him.

'What is your name?' Judas commanded.

'Anna,' she replied softly. The small microphone on her T-shirt made her faint voice loud and clear to the audience.

'Why do you kneel before me?' Judas's gaze was intense.

'To ask you to heal me.'

'What is it that you want me to heal?'

Anna removed her left hand from her pocket to reveal only a small stump. A low murmur emitted from the audience.

'How did it happen?'

'At work. I am ... was ... a machine operator.'

Judas looked out at the audience and stated loud and clear, 'To those who still doubt, doubt no more!'

Judas looked back at Jiovani, and Jiovani knew what to do. Judas grabbed hold of Anna's severed limb, and Jiovani grabbed her right hand as well as Judas's left hand, to form a ring. Anna remained on her knees, gazing up at the two imposing figures—but mainly at the handsome figure that was Judas. Pain inflicted her mind as if she was being electrocuted. Waves of energy pulsed up her arms and heated her whole body as beads of sweat quickly formed on her olive skin and brow. Anna threw her head back as the agony filled her mind, but through the wall of anguish she felt the stump on her left arm tingle. Soon, the intense wave of pain subsided and all she could sense was the tingling sensation in her left arm.

Anna felt as if she had just plunged her left hand into a bucket of freezing water. Her fingers stung with the sensation of pins and needles, but how could that be when she had no hand? Anna opened her eyes and looked at the stump on her left arm—it was no longer a stump! Bones had grown from her stump like a young plant grows in time lapse photography. Tendons, muscles and nerves were forming over the bones. It was then that she noticed the scene behind the incredible display of her reforming hand—a sea of wide-eyed people staring in utter amazement. Anna felt the nerves in her fingers come to life, a feeling of warm air passing between them. With her hand now fully reformed, she could not take her eyes of the new appendage.

Judas let go of Anna and stood back. Jiovani followed suit.

Anna studied her new hand closely, moving her fingers around and opening and closing her hand to make a fist. She touched her face, then her clothes, revelling in the sensation. Anna stopped abruptly and looked at Judas. He appeared drained but not as much as Jiovani who had to sit down on the edge of the podium to rest.

Anna fell at Judas's feet and wept. Between the sobs she uttered, 'Messiah!'

That single word triggered the vast audience to chant, 'Masih, Masih, Masih ...'

Judas threw up his arms and bathed in the soundwaves of glory.

****

APOCALYPSE - RISE OF THE ANTICHRIST

Washington DC, USA

President Richardson pressed the 'Video Call' button on the computer software and waited for the multipoint conference to begin. The computer was stationed in the Oval Office and ran a hack-proof video call program written by a CIA programmer. This was the first time he had used the system and Jim recalled confirming with the programmer that it was in fact hack proof.

'How can you be sure that this is hack proof?'

The young, pimple-faced geek retorted abruptly, 'Because I designed and built it! The software has been written in a coding language that I invented, and it runs variable 12-bit encryption that I also invented. Only we know it exists and only I can crack it. As an extra insurance, I custom built the operating system for it and right now there are only two computers in the world that have it—one is in your office, and this is the other one. The operating system cannot access the Internet, only the webcam software has that ability so there is no back-door access. And the final nail in the hacking coffin is a minimum fifty-character password, or should I say sentence, that locks the system down so that not even I can gain access!'

During the retort, Jim noticed how his eyes kept darting around the room and they never fixed on his or anyone's face. He was warned that the boy was a little abrupt and that he suffered from Asperger's Syndrome, but he was also told that the boy was a programming genius.

All Jim could say at the end of the boy's rant was, 'Okay, you've sold me.'

The first face to appear on the secure video call was Luke Churchill, the British Prime Minister.

'Luke, good evening.'

'Good morning to you Jim. It is still morning, isn't it?'

'Just.'

'I see we are the first online. Wait.' Luke watched a new window appear on his computer screen that was identical to Jim's. In the new window, the face of a man in his late forties appeared. He had greying black hair and sharp brown eyes. He wore rimless glasses and what appeared to be a pyjama top. 'Matthew, how are you?'

'It's 4:00 am, best I don't say.'

Luke smiled before asking, 'Jim, have you met the Australian Prime Minister, Mr Turner?'

'How ya doin' Matthew? Not had the pleasure yet but we have spoken on the phone.'

'G'day Jim. So, when are you coming down to visit our big old island? We are all keen to show you around,' Matthew said.

'Early next year is looking good at the moment. Looking forward to seeing that beautiful country of yours.'

Two more windows appeared—one of a woman in her late forties, and the other of a balding man in his late fifties. The woman had shoulder length, dark hair that was immaculately groomed and almost certainly dyed, and it was in contrast with her bright red lipstick. The older man wore rimless glasses that sat upon his large nose. He had fading blue eyes and his receding hairline retained little of its former blonde hue.

Now that all the attendees were present, labels appeared for each window. The woman was identified as the French President Gabrielle Pasteur, and the man was German Chancellor Johann Schiffer. In a heavy German accent Johann said, 'Hello Luke, Jim, and Matthew. Good to see you all.'

Gabrielle was quick to follow but her accent was softer. 'Hello gentlemen.'

The others replied, 'Hi Gabrielle, Johann.'

Jim said, 'Welcome to the first fully secure webcam conference.'

Matthew asked, 'So how secure is this system?'

'Well, I asked that same question to the developer and believe me he made it very clear that it was hack proof,' Jim replied.

'We had our security team check it over,' Gabrielle added, 'And they were very impressed with the design.'

'Good,' said Jim. 'Now, we are here to discuss the events in the Middle East, and as I understand it, we all have similar concerns.'

'Ya, the New World has already surpassed the EU as an economic power and is on the way to surpassing even China,' Johann stated.

Gabrielle added, 'And I don't see how we can prevent it from continuing to grow. Turkey and Morocco are talking about joining now.'

Luke said, 'We have a significant number of New World supporters here in Britain and there is a lot of pressure to at least publicly accept the New World concept. They have formed their own New World political party and are pressuring the government to invite

Judas to the country.'

'We are having similar pressures,' said Gabrielle.

'So, what is the sentiment Down Under?' Jim asked.

Matthew replied, 'There isn't quite the same support down here for the New World so no immediate concern. Still, there have been a few protests over my government's lack of open support.'

Jim asked, 'I assume you have all seen the email from the Brethren. So, what are your thoughts about Judas being the Messiah? Or more importantly, the exact opposite?'

Matthew was blunt in replying. 'Opposite!'

Gabrielle then added, 'Opposite.'

Then Johann, 'Ya, opposite.'

Luke decided to embellish on his answer. 'Whatever he is, there is one thing that is very clear. He is rapidly becoming the most powerful figure on Earth. And that makes him a great threat to the status quo and world stability.'

'Yes,' Matthew agreed. 'Heaven help any country that upsets their Messiah.'

Jim said, 'You can now add Iran and Pakistan to the list.' There was a moment of silence as Jim's words sank in.

Matthew was the first to verbalise their thoughts. 'Then the New World is about to become a nuclear power!'

Gabrielle uttered under her breath, 'Merde!'

'So, what can we do to stop him?' Johann asked.

Matthew said, 'I don't know about the rest of you but I for one have not stopping thinking about that. Unfortunately, little has come to mind apart from revealing who he really is.'

'And we will sound like a bunch of crackpots in the process,' Jim added.

'Ya, we would need solid proof that he is you know who,' Johann said.

'Does anyone have any worthwhile intel on him?' Gabrielle asked.

'Not us,' Matthew replied.

'Squeaky clean as far as we know,' Jim said.

'The only thing we found was that four boys disappeared from his school when he was eleven,' Luke said. 'And there was no evidence to link him with the disappearance.'

'To be honest, it would take a lot to prove to his followers that he is anything but a miracle man,' said Jim.

'Agreed,' Johann added.

The expression on Luke's face hardened as he said, 'What if he were to have, say, a fatal accident?'

The audio on the conference went quiet.

Luke said, 'You can't tell me you all haven't romanced the idea?'

Jim replied, 'We may have thought it but to act on the thought is another story.'

Johann said with conviction, 'If such a thing were to happen, it would have to be perfect, or we will be looking at World War III!'

Matthew said, 'And if I am correct, no such action has ever been perfect.'

Gabrielle said, 'It may be something we could consider in the future but right now I don't see it being an option.'

'I just wanted to put the idea on the table. Happy to bin it,' Luke said in a more submissive tone.

'So, we are back to discrediting him?' Gabrielle announced.

Jim said, 'I think we need to go back and dig a little deeper. There must be something in his past that could put a dent in his armour.'

'I will talk to my people and see if there is anything else that we could have missed,' Luke said.

'Agreed,' added Gabrielle.

'Okay, how about we reconvene in eight weeks and see where we are at?' Jim proposed. The others all nodded in agreement.

Jim closed off with, 'Thank you all for your time, and see you again soon.'

****

Jerusalem, Israel

Judas bathed in the warm spring sunlight as he laid back in the poolside deck chair. Apart from a pair of black board shorts, all he wore was a pair of Ray-Ban sunglasses and a very content expression.

Two very attractive, bikini-clad women were attending to his manicure and pedicure while Judas sipped on a refreshing cocktail.

Jiovani lounged in a deck chair to Judas's right but was not receiving the same attention. Jiovani wore a T-shirt and light cotton trousers, and mimicked his Lord in wearing the same brand of sunglasses. That was the extent of the duplicity as he was engrossed in a novel on his tablet computer. At the head of Judas's deck chair sat Zeus like an ancient sentinel, forever vigilant.

The newly built mansion in the hills overlooking Jerusalem was a gift from the Israelis and the Palestinians for delivering them from perpetual war. The four-hectare estate included a ten-car garage, a four-room pool house, ten-bedroom servants' quarters, and a twenty-bedroom mansion.

From the pool house strode a black suited young man with a clear conviction of urgency. When he reached Judas's side, his conviction faded as his nervousness increased. He fell on both knees and bowed his head before saying, 'My Lord please forgive me. I have an urgent request from the Defence Minister.'

Before the communications assistant could say another word, Jiovani put down his tablet computer and said scornfully, 'How dare you disturb the Messiah on his only day off! Once a month all he asks for is some peace and quiet and you have the audacity to disrupt that serenity.'

Judas raised his left hand in a gesture that made Jiovani halt. The beautician that was working on Judas's left hand scowled briefly at the young assistant.

Judas said in a calm tone, 'My dear Jiovani, you are correct as always, but let me hear what the issue is first.'

Jiovani returned to his novel as the communications assistant said, 'Thank you my Lord. The Defence Minister wanted to know your thoughts on the badge design of the uniforms?'

Judas placed the cocktail glass on the small table beside his chair and said, 'Now you see Jiovani, not all requests are unpleasant. Now I have already given this some thought. The number six is seen as a symbol of prosperity and happiness, and if you turn it upside down you get the number nine, which symbolises magic and power. Rather fitting don't you think, Jiovani?'

'Yes, my Lord,' Jiovani replied with an air of disinterest.

'I want the three sixes inside the sun.' As Judas described the design, he drew the image in the air. 'The sun of course represents myself, and the three sixes represent my people. The sixes will be in a circle so two of the sixes will always appear upside down to the observer and you will always have a nine in the same symbol.'

'Thank you, my Lord. I will tell the Defence Minister,' said the communications assistant before standing and walking back to the pool house.

Although Jiovani continued to stare at his tablet computer, his expression was not of contentment. Instead, his face was an intense expression of anguish. It took a few moments for Judas's words to sink in, and it was then that Jiovani realised what Judas was describing— the mark of the beast! His hands began to tremble, and he was forced to put the tablet computer down. The Antichrist had taken much of Jiovani's soul but not all of it. Enough was left behind to enable Jiovani to function but not enough for free will. Jiovani was the puppet, and the Antichrist was the puppet master. While Judas displayed all the signs of being the Messiah, Jiovani was accepting of the notion.

However, Judas describing the mark of the beast was too clear a sign to ignore even in his current state of mental incarceration. First sign was this mansion, then the rock star lifestyle, and now the mark of the beast. How many times had he read about it in the Bible, posturing over how symbolic the text was or how literal it could be? Now he knew that it was very literal, and finally his weak mind began to question. Was Judas the Messiah after all, or was he the monster of all monsters? Jiovani accosted himself; what an old fool I have been.

Judas didn't look at Jiovani as he laid back in the deck chair. 'Now Jiovani, I can sense the turmoil within you, but there is no need for it. Think of all the wealth and power you have gained, and this is not the end of it. Soon your former piety will seem meagre. That is what you craved, isn't it?' Judas turned his head to Jiovani and commanded, 'Look at me!' Jiovani reluctantly obeyed. Judas's eyes flashed red as a little more of his soul was devoured by the beast. 'Jiovani, you are spoiling my day off, and I was having so much fun. Now you sit there and read your book like a good Pope.'

Jiovani obeyed.

The two beauticians passed a brief look of confusion between them but kept silent to not draw attention.

Judas continued his monologue with indifference to his audience. 'Your usefulness is almost at an end, but not yet. I still have some need for you. Until then you can remain my obedient sidekick.'

Zeus let out a brief woof before returning to his continuous panting.

Judas reached behind and patted Zeus on the head as he said, 'Yes Zeus, you will have your play friend soon enough.'

Judas stood up abruptly, leaving the beauticians lost for a client. He said, 'Girls!'

As their sight fell upon the soft facial features of Judas, they also looked into the eyes of the monster of all monsters. Their natural human expressions faded to a blank canvas as their eyes went dull like that of a mannequin's. 'It has been a long time since I have fed, and you two will do nicely in breaking my fast. Come.'

The beauticians obediently went to his side so he could wrap an arm around each one as he led them to the mansion. Zeus followed close behind, maintaining his sentinel personification. Beneath the mansion was a bunker, and when in there, no sound could escape—including the screams that derived from an unimaginable torture.

Buckinghamshire, UK

Stephen received an email from Wallaby the previous day, which read: *Meet tomorrow at 76 Ellesborough Road, Wendover, Buckinghamshire at 10:00 am. We have something to show you.'*

Stephen drove down the country road and slowed as he approached the location marked on the Mazda3's satellite navigation.

Paul, Stephen's passenger, said, 'There it is.' He pointed at an open gate with the number *76* painted on it.

Stephen pulled onto the driveway and drove slowly down the narrow gravel access. They soon came to a cottage and he parked the car out the front. They approached the front door of the cottage and Paul rang the doorbell. They waited. As the warm summer temperature had been replaced with a wintery cold snap, Stephen and Paul both wore their Gore-Tex jackets and beanies to stay warm.

Paul thought, 'At least it's not as cold as last winter's blizzard.' About a minute passed and there was no answer at the door.

'We do have the right address, don't we?' Paul asked.

'I think so,' Stephen replied. 'We are slightly early. It has just gone 10:00 am.'

'Let's give it another minute then we will try around the back,' Paul said.

'Guys, this way,' said a familiar voice to their right. It was Peter.

'We were starting to wonder if we had the right address,' Paul said.

'Sorry, got held up with some last-minute adjustments,' Peter apologised.

Peter led them behind the cottage to a small studio about ten metres away.

Peter said, 'The previous owners used this as an art studio. It is ideal as it's very private.'

Stephen looked around at the two-hectare property and concluded that it would have been a working farmhouse and stables until recently.

Peter escorted them into the studio where an open fire warmed the air to a more pleasant temperature. Peter immediately took off his coat, but Stephen and Paul left theirs on while they thawed.

'Cup of tea?' Peter asked.

'Yes please,' Paul and Stephen replied.

'How do you take it?'

'White with one,' Stephen replied.

'White, no sugar,' Paul added.

The studio had a small lounge with a fireplace, and a kitchenette on the end. Near the front door was an internal door leading to a second room, which was most likely the studio itself.

It took a few minutes for Stephen and Paul to thaw out enough to be willing to take off their coats.

A moment later, Peter handed them each a mug of tea. 'Warmed up now?'

'Yes thanks,' Paul said.

'I often wonder if I will ever see warm weather again!' Stephen exclaimed.

'You both should come and visit Down Under, much warmer there. Though the humidity in summer is hard to bear,' said Peter.

'Sounds like a stellar idea,' Paul concluded.

'Follow me.' Peter led them through the internal door and into a spacious room cluttered with tools, wires, scrap metal, and two work benches.

Thomas, drill in hand, stood at one of the work benches. 'Morning gentlemen, nice trip up?' he said as he placed the drill on the table.

'Yes, thank you,' Paul replied. 'Nice country drive up to the house. Shame it wasn't a little warmer.'

Thomas and Peter, obviously quite warm from their workshop activities, were wearing T-shirts and jeans, while Stephen and Paul were less casual in shirts and trousers.

In the centre of the room, there was a stage light on a stand which pointed at a paper target on the wall opposite. Stephen went up to the light and said, 'This looks familiar.'

'Careful, it's loaded,' Peter announced.

Stephen stepped back from the light and stared at it intensely. 'But it looks just like a real light!'

'That is because it *is* a real light,' Thomas said confidently.

'It works?' Paul added.

'Yes. We figured that it would have to work both as a light and as a weapon,' Peter stated. 'The hard part was to find the right type of thin, clear plastic lens that worked both as a light diffuser and as something we could see through.'

Thomas said to Stephen, 'Here, catch.' He threw him his mobile phone.

Stephen caught it and looked at the screen. He could see Paul standing in the room just to the left of the target on the wall.

Stephen said, 'That is amazing!'

'Not bad for a pair of ex-Aussie priests,' Thomas said confidently.

Paul waved his hand in front of the light and watched it move on the mobile phone screen in Stephen's hand. 'Stellar effort if you ask me.'

Thomas said, 'Most of it went together quite easily except for the lens as Peter said. That took a good two months to solve.'

Peter added, 'While the light is on you can't see through the lens, but once it is off the lens is see through.'

'Like a two-way mirror,' Paul concluded.

'Yes,' said Peter. 'But that meant we had to also install a remote on/off switch for the light. Pass me the phone.' Stephen handed Peter the phone, and Peter touched a small virtual button on the screen. The stage light came to life, the brightness forcing Paul to shade his eyes.

Peter tapped the virtual button again and the light went off.

Stephen declared again, 'Stellar job!'

'To be honest ...' Thomas said. '... most of the gear we found on the Internet, and all we had to do was put it all together. The switch for the light was straight out of the box as was the servos for the aiming function.'

'Servos?' Stephen asked with curiosity.

'Here.' Peter handed the iPhone back to Stephen. 'Now move your finger over the screen and keep an eye on the small graticule in the centre.'

Stephen looked at the screen and the small red dot in the centre, then moved his finger over the screen. The image moved in line with his finger movements. 'Wow!' Thomas injected. 'We couldn't figure out how to build in a virtual crosshair on the screen, so we just used a permanent marker and placed a dot in the centre of the webcam lens.'

'Clever!' Paul added.

Peter said, 'Do you want to see it in action?'

'Absolutely,' Stephen replied.

'Stand behind the light.' As Paul and Stephen joined Peter and Thomas behind the light, Peter said, 'We have built a target on the wall; it is made of plasterboard. Aim at the centre of the target.'

Stephen moved the small black dot over the centre of the target. He could just make out the sound of the servos moving the weapon inside the light. 'Okay, now what?'

Peter said, 'See the orange button on the top left?'

'Yes,' Stephen said with apprehension.

'Press it.'

As Stephen pressed the button, both he and Paul braced themselves for a loud bang. But all that happened was a red button appeared in the top right of the screen.

'That reveals the trigger—a safety precaution Thomas added after I accidentally fired the weapon.'

Thomas confirmed his statement with a momentary discerning scowl before saying, 'Fortunately I wasn't standing in the firing line at the time!'

Peter continued with, 'Now press the red button.'

Stephen tentatively pressed the red button as he and Paul winced for the impending bang. All that was heard was a small crack that sounded more like a party popper going off. They all glared at the target and viewed the new gathering of small holes around the bullseye.

'It worked!' Stephen declared.

'I was expecting something more ... eventful,' Paul stated.

Stephen asked, 'Is it powerful enough?'

'We're not sure yet, but we think so,' Thomas answered. 'The pellets go through three layers of plasterboard and embed themselves well into the timber backing.'

Peter added, 'We want to test the system using a pig's carcass. An idea I got from watching an old episode of Mythbusters.'

Stephen asked, 'What is its range?'

'Of the weapon or the remote?' Thomas asked.

'Well both?' Stephen clarified.

Thomas replied, 'The weapon is good up to about fifteen metres, and the remote can be operated either by WiFi or over the Internet. Over the Internet you could be anywhere in the world, but via WiFi the range is about thirty metres.

'That should be okay,' Stephen said. 'I will be required to stay for the duration just in case a light goes on us. But if it does work over the Internet, I will be elsewhere when I fire it.'

'Wise move,' Thomas added.

Paul asked, 'So what did you use for the explosive?'

Thomas said, 'Match heads!'

Paul said, 'You can't be serious!'

Peter answered, 'When we researched what chemicals would be good for a small combustible material such as phosphorus, one of the common items listed was matches. So, all we had to do was buy a few boxes of matches, scrape off the match heads and pack it into our homemade gun barrel, which Thomas made on that old lathe over there.'

Stephen and Paul looked over at a bench with a large metal contraption on it.

Stephen said, 'Amazing!'

'So, when do you think it will be ready?' Paul asked.

Peter said, 'If it passes the pig carcass test, in a week or two. We still have a few minor tweaks that we want to make.'

'Well, that is about all the time you will have,' Paul announced.

'Is he coming here?' Thomas asked.

Paul continued, 'Yes, the government has finally succumbed to public pressure. I found out last night that he is planning to come over next month and will be making a speech at Wembley Stadium.'

Stephen added, 'My company is one of the contractors that supports Wembley Stadium, so all is looking good so far.'

Peter and Thomas both looked at each other as their colleague's words sank in. After a moment Peter said, 'We have some work to do.'

Paul said, 'It looks like you are on top of things here, we will keep in touch when we know more. In the meantime, happy pig shooting!'

****

London, UK

Prime Minister Luke Churchill sat in the study of 10 Downing Street reading from a box of government documents on his lap. Two lamps illuminated the study with a soft light that was bright enough to make out the time on the vintage, wood-framed clock on the wall. It was 11:15 pm. There was a knock on the door and Luke said aloud, 'Come in.'

A middle-aged, balding man opened the door to the study and without entering the room fully, said, 'Prime Minister, Agent Smith is here to see you on an urgent matter. It is late, shall I tell her to see you first thing in the morning?'

'That's okay Oliver, let her in,' Luke replied.

Oliver disappeared behind the door as a woman in her early thirties entered the room.

Luke placed the red box of documents on the floor next to him as Agent Smith approached. 'Prime Minister, we have a potential lead on the background check you requested.'

Luke took a moment to survey the woman before him. Agent Smith wore a black business suit with a knee-length skirt and a white blouse. Her natural blonde hair was tied back in a ponytail and Luke noticed that her athletic legs were not adorned with any stockings. He was impressed with how natural and perfect her skin was along with the rest of her features. The soft light from the lamps in the room gave her fresh soft skin a warm glow. Luke looked into her bright blue eyes, pondering her background. 'Agent Smith, is it?'

'Yes, Sir.'

'Your name isn't really *Smith*, is it?'

Agent Smith seemed unfazed by the prime minister's question and did not answer. Instead, she just stared at him.

Luke sat back in the large leather chair, crossed his legs and said, 'You don't look like a typical MI6 agent.'

She shifted her weight to her right leg, put her hand on her hip and said in an annoyed tone, 'So, what is an MI6 agent supposed to look like?'

Luke replied bluntly, 'Cold.'

'Well, I'm not your typical agent.'

'I can see that. So, what do you specialise in?'

'Finding people!' she said with confidence.

'Are you any good?'

This time his blunt question seemed to hit a nerve and her answer had more passion behind it. 'The best!'

Luke changed to a more official tone and asked, 'So what is the potential lead?'

Agent Smith appeared to relax somewhat with the change of subject and returned to her initial stance of military attention. 'The subject's parents employed a maid up until the subject's birth but dismissed the woman immediately after. We think she could have some information of interest.'

'Sounds like a bit of a long shot. Is there anything else?'

'Not at this time Prime Minister.'

'So, do we know where she is?'

'Not yet, but we will find her.'

'Okay, see if you can track this maid down, but don't put too many resources on it. I don't want to waste taxpayers' money on a possible dead end. So, what is this maid's name?'

'Yentl. Yentl Ustinov.'

****

New York City, USA

Abraham's Patisserie on Broadway, New York, was a well-established business with some of the best pastries in the city. The family-owned patisserie was managed by the matriarch—a mother of two sons, who also doubled as waiters. The business specialised in pastries but also served coffee, tea and freshly made sandwiches.

As Yentl's middle-aged body was no longer able to handle long hours on her feet, she ran the till instead. Most of the small shop was taken up by a collection of small tables where the customers often sat to enjoy a coffee and a freshly baked croissant. Yentl had put on some weight since her youth, but her active lifestyle of running a small business had helped her retain some of her former figure. The biggest telltale of her years was the grey streaks in her hair and the lines now visible from the corners of her deep brown eyes. But her eyes were still very bright and clear.

It was 11:00 am and the usual morning rush had finished so the staff had time to prepare for the forthcoming lunchtime crowd.

A tall, attractive woman entered the shop and sat at a table near the till. She began to read the menu.

Yentl's eldest son Marcus approached the woman to take her order. 'Good morning, what would you like?'

'Ah, a cappuccino and one of your nice muffins—apple and cinnamon, thanks,' the woman replied.

'One cap and muffin coming up,' said Marcus as he headed back to the kitchen.

The woman got up and went to the small table next to the till where several papers and magazines were laid out. As she reached for the women's magazine on top, Yentl said, 'You don't sound like a local, whereabouts are you from?'

'England actually,' the woman replied.

'England? Never been there. I hear it is very cold.'

'Yes, it is these days.'

'Have you always lived in New York?' the woman asked.

'No, I grew up in Israel. I left when I was only nineteen and came to stay with my aunty here in New York. I fell in love with my handsome George and have never looked back.'

'So, where is George?' the woman asked.

A sadness appeared on her face when she said, 'He is with God now, cancer got him.'

The woman's expression changed to reflect Yentl's as she said, 'Oh, I am sorry.'

'That's okay, it has been nearly five years. Still, I have my two beautiful boys. Marcus who served you and Jonah who is on a break.' Yentl looked over at the young man in the corner who was busy texting someone.

He took the time to look up, wave his hand and say, 'Hi.' He returned to his text message. Both Marcus and Jonah were wearing black jeans and a black, short-sleeved shirt while Yentl wore a black, long-sleeved blouse and slacks.

The woman, glancing at the front cover of the magazine in her hands that had a picture of Judas on it, faced it towards Yentl and said,

'He is rather hot, don't you think?'

Yentl's expression became very dark as she said, 'All I see is a monster!'

'A monster? But he is so good looking. Why do you say that?'

'Looks can be deceiving.'

'It says here that he is the most eligible bachelor on Earth.' The woman flicked through to the article on Judas and found a picture of him with his parents. She said, 'Even his parents look nice.' She turned the magazine to face Yentl, but Yentl turned her head away and said sternly, 'Believe me, they are no saints, just like their son.'

The woman turned the magazine back to herself and continued looking through the photos.

Yentl's intense stare turned upon the woman as she said, 'That's not his real mother!'

The woman looked up at Yentl with an expression of shock on her face.

Marcus appeared from behind with a tray supporting a coffee mug and a muffin. He said sternly, 'Mum, you promised not to talk about that again to the customers!'

'She started it,' Yentl protested.

'It's okay, I want to hear her story,' the woman said with an expression of great interest.

'My dear, you best sit down,' Yentl said.

'Mum!' Marcus protested again.

'She wants to hear my story, so let your mother indulge herself,' Yentl retorted.

Marcus placed the coffee and the muffin on the table and left with a frustrated look on his face. Jonah turned to face the wall in an attempt to distance himself from the forthcoming conversation and continued to type away on his phone.

Yentl sat down with the woman with an expression of satisfaction on her face as she began, 'His real mother was a prostitute!'

The woman's eyes widened to liken saucers, and her mouth gaped open.

'I didn't find out who she was until weeks later.'

The woman asked, 'So how did you find out about all of this?'

'Well, because I worked for them as a house maid for two years. Anyway, there she was, doubled over out the front of the house about to give birth! We helped her into the house and into a bed. The baby was a breach, you know, bum first. Things didn't look good. I was ordered to find a doctor as the regular GP was on holidays. When I called the local hospital, they wouldn't send an ambulance because a bus load of people had been shot by some terrorist.' Yentl continued as she pointed at the magazine photo of Judas and his parents. 'That woman sent me to go get a doctor and told me not to return without one. I was so young and naive. I couldn't get a doctor no matter how hard I tried. No one would listen. I think they thought I was making it up, but I wasn't. There was such a terrible storm that day, and by the time I got back I was soaked to the core. And that woman ...' Yentl pointed at the picture again as her expression became very wrathful. '... she shouted at me for failing and then fired me! She was such a bitch!' Yentl's tone changed to a more civil nature as she continued, 'I like to watch those missing persons shows on TV. You know the ones? And it was then that I found out who she was.'

The woman opposite her was on the edge of her seat and hadn't touched her coffee or muffin. 'So, who was she?'

'Mary ... Mary something. I can't remember her last name. They said that she was a known prostitute. Probably one of those filthy men she slept with was the father.'

The woman asked, 'So what makes you think that Judas was that baby?'

Yentl sat back in the chair and glared at the woman as she said, 'Sarina can't have children!'

The woman sat back as well and from the expression on her face, it was obvious she didn't see it coming.

Yentl continued, 'That woman had been trying for years to have a baby and eventually she went to the doctor. I overheard the test results—some problem with her ovaries. Then this Mary turns up about to give birth, then she is declared missing a few weeks later, and no word about the baby! Then ...'

The young woman took advantage of the pause to take a sip from her coffee. Yentl placed her hand on the young woman's knee in a gesture to gain her full attention. The young woman was transfixed.

Yentl leaned forward again. 'A few weeks later I see that woman with a new baby! At first, I thought she was minding the baby for someone, but then I saw her with the baby over and over again. So, I put two and two together. Foul play I tell you, foul play!' Yentl said as she prodded the table with her finger. 'Anyway, my mum said I was obsessed and that

I should go and stay with my aunty in New York until I got over it. She didn't believe me either. No one did.'

The woman sat back in her seat and took another sip of her coffee, then said, 'What if they had arranged to adopt a child and Mary was just a coincidence?'

From Yentl's reaction, it appeared that she had heard this question before—her answer seemed rehearsed. 'Her husband John was against adoption and there was no mention of adoption in the house while I was there. Either way, I got my own back in the end. I went back to Israel to visit my family several years ago and seized the moment. I saw their son, told him everything.' She leaned back and her face changing to a puzzled expression. 'What was funny though was that he didn't seem surprised. I think he already knew deep down. He is a strange boy, gave me the creeps. He is too … perfect.'

The woman took a bite of her muffin and a moment later, while covering her mouth with her hand, said, 'Mmmm, that's a nice muffin!'

'Thank you, I bake them fresh each morning.'

After taking another sip of coffee, she said, 'I'm surprised the tabloids haven't got a hold of your story.'

Yentl said, 'Why would they believe me? No one else does. Besides, the tabloids think he's great. The last thing they are interested in right now is bad press.'

'For what it is worth, I believe you.'

A smile grew across Yentl's face and she said, 'Bless you my dear. You have made my day.'

'And you have made mine,' the woman replied before consuming the last crumbs of the muffin. 'Thanks for the very intriguing story and a great brunch.'

'You're welcome my dear. Are you in town long?'

'No unfortunately, I fly back later today. But next time I am in town I will certainly drop by.' The women stood up and said, 'Must go. Thanks again.'

As she left the café, Marcus appeared from the kitchen and waved goodbye. So did Jonah, who seemed to have finally finished his text message. Yentl smiled, satisfied that she had been given the opportunity to tell her story once more.

As soon as the woman was out of the shop, she pulled out her phone and called one of her contacts. 'M, it's Agent Smith. Tell the PM I have found the smoking gun.' She paused to listen to M's reply then said, 'Yes, I will be on the first plane back to London. Bye.'

****

London, UK

Prime Minister Churchill sat before the computer monitor and waited for the others to connect. The first to appear was the Australian Prime Minister.

'Hello Matthew, how are you?' Luke asked.

'G'day Luke. Rather well, thanks. How about yourself?'

'Good, thanks.'

Another window appeared on Luke's screen. It was the German chancellor.

'Hi Johann,' Luke said, shortly followed by Matthew.

'Hi, or should I say, g'day,' Johann said.

Two more windows appeared with the images of the US President Jim Richardson, and the French President Gabrielle Pasteur.

After a flurry of hellos and g'days, Jim said, 'So Luke, you have something for us?'

Luke seemed very pleased with what he was about to say. 'We managed to track down the Salim family's previous maid, Yentl Ustinov. She was employed for two years up until the birth of 'you know who', and she had a very interesting story to tell. According to Yentl, Sarina Salim could not have children, and his real mother was a Mary Frank who disappeared at the same time 'you know who' was born. Yentl claimed that Mary Frank was taken in by Mrs Salim at the point where Mary was about to give birth. Yentl then went on to say that the birth was a breach, and the mother and baby were in trouble. Mrs Salim sent Yentl out to find a doctor, but she was unable to find one. When she returned, Mrs Salim fired her. Mary was never seen again, but Mrs Salim had immediately acquired a new baby. Yentl went on to say that Mrs Salim had not made any arrangements for adoption and came into possession of Mary's baby through foul play!'

There was a moment of silence before Matthew said, 'Well that is good dirt if ever I have heard it.'

Jim asked, 'Can you prove any of this?'

'Not yet,' Luke replied.

Jim added, 'We have good contacts in Israel. I'll have my people look into it.'

'There is more,' Luke said. 'Yentl also claimed that Mary was a known prostitute!'

Gabrielle stated, 'This just gets better and better! Is there more?'

'No, that's all we have so far.'

'I think that will do well enough,' Johann said with a slight smile.

'If we can prove any of this, it could be enough to topple him,' said Gabrielle.

'I agree,' added Johann. 'I can't imagine the Muslim world following someone with such an impure past.'

Matthew said, 'And that would account for some seventy percent of the New World.'

'I think we are onto a winner here,' said Jim. 'But we will need to play our cards very carefully.'

'We should gather what evidence we can then reconvene,' Matthew said.

'Agreed,' said Luke. 'He will be here next week, so I am happy to wait.'

'Yes, may I suggest we see where we are at the same time next month?' Jim proposed.

'Sounds good to me,' Johann stated.

'Oui,' said Gabrielle.

'Is there anything else we want to raise?' Jim asked. There was a unanimous shaking of heads. 'Okay, see you all again in four weeks.'

****

Paul and Stephen arrived at the farmhouse as the weather continued its three-day marathon of rain. It had become a constant drizzle and the gloom was wearing down the morale of the two arrivals. The forecast for the following day was a little brighter with sunny periods, which meant that it was 'all systems go' for the speech at Wembley Stadium.

Stephen drove around to the back of the farmhouse and parked next to the studio hut. The men stepped out of the car, pulled their hooded raincoats over their heads, and headed straight for the front door.

As soon as they were inside, they took off their wet coats and hung them on the coat rack near the front door. Paul and Stephen looked around the room and found it empty.

A familiar voice shouted from the studio room next door, 'We are in here!'

They walked through to the studio and found Peter and Thomas standing around a work bench supporting a large black box. Both were wearing well-worn jeans and T-shirts that looked like they had not been washed in days.

'G'day,' said Thomas. 'Lovely weather!'

'Refreshing,' said Stephen sarcastically.

'Here it is, all ready to go,' Peter announced as he opened the box to reveal the stage light inside.

Paul and Stephen looked at the light, and as far as they could see it looked like a normal stage light.

'It's perfect,' said Stephen.

'Thanks,' said Peter.

'I mean it's *too* perfect,' Stephen stated with a look of concern on his face.

'Sorry?' Thomas added.

Even Paul looked surprised.

'Only brand-new lights look like this and as far as I am aware, we have no new lights to install today,' Stephen added.

Thomas and Peter stared at the light as they fathomed Stephen's observation.

Stephen continued, 'We need to scuff it up, especially around the mounting brackets, and scuff the corners of the case as well.'

Thomas and Peter looked at each other for a moment before Thomas said to Peter, 'Get the rasp, a file and some steel wool.'

Ten minutes later, Stephen looked pleased at the result. 'Now that's more like it!'

'Will it pass?' Paul asked.

'If you put it with the other lights, I couldn't tell the difference.' said Stephen.

'But that could be a problem,' Paul said. 'What if you get it mixed up with the other lights?'

Stephen scratched his head and said, 'You're right.'

'How about a small cross scratched into the case and the light frame?' Peter suggested.

Stephen rubbed his chin as he pondered the idea. 'Yes, that could work. Who is to say that someone marked this light for a particular location? Very few have the same brightness and we often swap the lights around to get the best effect.'

'What if they choose a different light to this because it isn't just right?' Paul asked with concern.

Stephen replied, 'I made sure I am in charge of installing the lights overhead. Also, I plan to place it where there is little chance of it being swapped. Some lighting positions are not so crucial.'

'Okay,' Paul said with some certainty.

'Pass me a sharp knife,' Stephen said to Peter.

Peter handed him a Stanley knife and Stephen scored a small cross on the side of the light, then on the top of the case. 'That should do it.' Thomas folded his arms and with a curious expression on his face, he said, 'I have been meaning to ask—how do you propose to consecrate the stage?'

'During my lunch break,' Stephen said with certainty.

'How? Won't people notice?' Thomas retorted.

'Not if I am under the stage. Remember it is the ground that is consecrated not the structure over it.'

Thomas nodded as he said, 'You're right.'

'But just to be sure, I will perform the casting of the holy water upon the podium itself.'

'Good idea,' Thomas said.

'So, are you still okay with this?' Peter asked with concern. 'You know, for what you are about to do.'

Stephen stared at Peter for a moment, then glanced at the others. It was obvious from the looks on their faces that they were all wanting to ask the same question. Stephen said with conviction, 'I have had a lot of time to internalise this. With the work we have done in ensuring that we can target him directly and not risk someone else's life, I only have to justify in my head that I am killing one. And considering that all who have tried before, have died, then it is obvious to me that we are not making a mistake. The only thing that bothers me is after the event— if we succeed or fail, either way we are all dead.' Stephen, pausing to view the others' reactions, could see that they were all very aware of their impending fate. 'Paul and I have talked about this. He is flying out of the country tomorrow. If I escape the venue alive, I will be heading straight for the airport. You better do the same.'

'We will be flying out tomorrow as well,' Thomas answered. 'We wanted to be around until you have installed the light just in case there is a technical problem. Here is the mobile with the app installed.' Thomas handed Stephen a mobile phone. 'You can reach us on either contact.'

Stephen looked at the only two contacts: John Thomas and Wallaby, and for a moment a smile grew on his face.

'Well, you're all good to go,' Peter announced. He extended his right hand and shook Stephen's hand. 'Good luck.'

'Thank you.'

Thomas did the same and said, 'All the best.'

'Thanks.'

After Stephen placed the light case in the boot, Paul got behind the wheel while Stephen sat in the passenger seat. Peter and Thomas stood at the doorway and ignored the drizzle that relentlessly peppered their faces.

As the car pulled away, both Paul and Stephen gave a brief wave as they disappeared down the driveway. They all had the same pit in their stomachs—a pit forged from the certainty that they would never see each another again.

****

Paul pulled up out the front of a warehouse with a sign across the top of the building that read—*World Stage Productions*.

The main door to the warehouse was open and the rear of a large truck stuck out like a big metal tongue.

Paul looked over at Stephen and said, 'Well, this is it. Good luck my boy. I will be praying for you.'

'Thanks,' Stephen replied with a brief nervous smile.

'I am very proud of you,' Paul said as he looked down over his glasses at his apprentice. 'I certainly made the right choice all those years ago.'

'And you have been a great mentor,' Stephen replied as the pit in his stomach grew to the size of a watermelon.

Initially, Paul put out his hand to shake Stephen's but Stephen just used it to pull him closer for a hug. They sat in the car and embraced for a moment then finished with a serious of pats on the back.

As they pulled away, both drew in a deep breath to prevent the tears from starting.

'If you succeed, you will have saved the world. A saint you will be,' Paul said with a slight smile.

Stephen sighed. 'I doubt that. More like a hunted fugitive, and it is *we* that would have saved the world. We wouldn't have made it this far if it weren't for you.'

Paul just smiled and didn't continue with the conversation. He straightened his back and said, 'Now be off with you. Go be a hero.'

Stephen smiled and began to get out of the car as Paul asked, 'By the way, how do you propose to get the case on the truck?'

Stephen smiled as he said, 'It's all about the timing.' He got out of the car and opened the boot. He stood there for a moment pretending to search for something while he kept an eye on the back of the truck.

Two men dressed like Stephen, in black T-shirts and black jeans, emerged from the truck and headed back into the warehouse. It was then that Stephen made his move. He pulled the big black case and his work backpack from the boot of the car and shut the boot. Stephen walked casually to the back of the truck and up the ramp that extended from the cavernous aperture, to the warehouse forecourt.

Paul's heart began to race as he watched and waited for Stephen to reappear. He pushed the 'Down' button on the window so he could see more clearly into the back of the truck. The drizzle began to pepper Paul as he stared at the truck, but the dull light of the day kept the depths of the truck's interior concealed.

Stephen suddenly emerged, without the black case, and walked down the ramp. When at the bottom, he gave a brief wave to Paul then turned and walked into the warehouse. A moment later, the two men Paul had seen earlier returned with cases in hand just like the one Stephen had carried into the back of the truck.

Paul quickly pressed the 'Up' button on the window and turned to look away from the men. He felt like a spy. Paul hastily drove off and did not dare look back.

****

Twenty-four spotlights were booked for installation at the stadium, and when twenty-five were discovered after the count back before departure, one was removed. The case with the "X" mark was near the bottom of the stack and remained on the truck.

Two hours later, Stephen was in the scaffolding above the stage installing the spotlights. This was often a one-man task, which Stephen usually performed. Today was no different. It was when he got to the case with the "X" mark that his heart began to race. He was extra careful when mounting the light in the position he had predetermined. It went in without incident. Stephen double checked the light position and angle and was satisfied that all was in order. Only half of the podium was in position, but it was enough to align the light with acceptable accuracy. He had nightmares about the light plummeting to the stage floor, shattering into a thousand pieces, and being dragged away by security after the weapon was discovered. But everything was going well—possibly *too* well. 'It was like this was meant to be', Stephen thought. His mind began to race with a myriad of scenarios of why this was so. His mind became so clogged with distraction that while tightening the last mounting bolt, he dropped the spanner, and his heart skipped a beat.

Below, two workers were pushing a wheeled section of the podium across the stage when the spanner clanged off the side of the podium section. Stephen's shocked gaze was met with a round of verbal abuse.

Stephen waved back and offered a flood of apologies. He had to go back down to get the spanner. The shock and embarrassment broke his fixation and after collecting the spanner from the stage floor, Stephen was able to refocus on the job at hand.

It was 2:00 pm when Stephen took his lunch break. He was making good time and had installed most of the overhead spotlights. He had two more hours before the scheduled light testing session, and he was confident that he could meet the deadline.

Stephen climbed down from the overhead scaffold and found the access point that led to under the stage. It was a low, black painted door at the rear of the stage. He glanced around to make sure the coast was clear and for the moment, no one else was about. All the activity was on top of the stage.

Stephen quickly snuck through the door and entered utter darkness. The day before, he had paced out the podium location from the door to under the stage—twenty normal paces straight ahead, then four paces to the left. He turned on the torch app on his mobile phone to see where he was going, then paced out under the stage. When he reached the position that he felt was directly under the podium, he removed his backpack and took out the items for the consecration ceremony: a service book, a bottle of water, and the bible. Stephen was very hungry but he needed to wait till he was back on the stage so he could complete the charade.

Stephen proceeded to perform the consecration. It was a forty-minute ceremony and during the service he blessed the water in his bottle. When it was finally completed, his stomach was rumbling, and his mobile phone was almost out of power. Fortunately, he did not use the phone that Thomas and Peter gave him as it was too important to risk a flat battery.

Stephen made his way back to the door and emerged from the darkness. His supervisor Jake was standing right in front of him.

Jake was a hulk of a man with a large gut and a ginger beard. His black T-shirt gaped over the top of his jeans to cover his great girth. 'Steve, what are you doing under there?' he asked while placing his anvil-sized hands on what would normally be someone's waist.

Stephen shaded his eyes from the glare of daylight as he tried to focus his eyes. 'Gov!' He had to think quick for an excuse, but the retraction of his irises gave him an idea. 'Sorry, just thought I would catch a wink. Didn't sleep well last night.'

Jake stared at him for a moment, his intense gaze scrutinizing Stephen. 'The light test starts at four, you better be ready!'

'Will be, Gov,' Stephen said with certainty, before striding off to the stairs that led back onto the stage.

Jake opened the small, black door and peered into the blackness. All he could see was the faint outlines of the scaffolding supports. After shrugging his shoulders, Jake closed the door and headed off in the direction he was going before Stephen had interrupted his journey.

Stephen headed straight for the podium. The lectern had been installed and one crew member had just finished mounting the microphone stand. Stephen sat cross-legged on the podium, took out his sandwich and water bottle and began to eat. No one seemed to take any notice of Stephen eating on the podium, and no one noticed that he was quietly muttering to himself in between sandwich bites. Not that his mutterings were audible as the noise of the construction around him drowned it out. His muttering was the last prayer in the final stage of the consecration ceremony.

Stephen didn't drink any of his freshly blessed water. Instead, he waited for an opportune moment to wet his hand and shake a small amount of holy water on the stage. Only then did he take a big gulp of water followed by a big 'ahh' and a whispered 'amen'.

As he packed away his lunch gear in his backpack, the crew member that mounted the microphone had returned and said to Stephen, 'This isn't a lunch table, you know!'

Stephen replied, 'Sorry. It was the only spot that was free.' The crew member strode off and climbed back up the scaffolding.

Stephen completed the installation of the last light with minutes to spare. As the lighting engineer went through his routine, Stephen's eyes were transfixed upon the light with "X" marked on it. He positioned himself on the scaffolding walkway on the opposite side of the stage. Stephen instinctively crossed his fingers as he waited for the lighting engineer to press the power button for the bank of downlights.

The down lighting came to life, bathing the stage in a bright warm illumination.

Stephen's heart stopped when he saw the light with the "X" had not come on. He started chanting, 'Come on, come on, come on, come on!' Then it came on.

Stephen expelled a lung full of air as his heart started again. 'Phew!' A beep came from the phone in his pocket. He pulled it out and looked at the screen. There was a message that said, 'Security camera activated. Click to view.' Stephen's heart began to thump in his chest as he tapped the screen. The display changed to a whitewashed-out view of the stage. He could just make out the lectern and a faint outline of the edge of the stage, but that was all. He knew that the light would have to be turned off using the remote to be able to see clearly, but he dared not do that while the light test was underway. He would have to wait till later to test it further, but it was still a good sign. A big smile grew across his face as he pressed the 'Stop Camera' button on the interface.

Stephen sent a text to his contacts John, Thomas and Wallaby stating, 'It's working. So far, so good. Well done!'

****

Paul was watching the evening news on television when the front door to the apartment opened. He stood and stared at Stephen as he entered the lounge room. Paul asked in a nervous tone, 'Well?'

Stephen replied with a straight face, 'It's in, and it works.' A big smile grew across his face.

Paul grabbed Stephen on the shoulders and said, 'Well done, well done. I've been busting to call you, but I dare not just in case.'

'Glad you didn't, security is probably monitoring everything. I did send a brief text to the Aussie boys just to let them know that all was okay, but I made it very ambiguous.'

'All packed and ready to go?' Stephen asked as he craned his neck around to see the large suitcases in Paul's bedroom.

'Yes, just the basics left. I have packed most of your things as well.'

'I wonder how long it will take for them to find us?'

'Who knows? We have covered our tracks well so I think it will be some time,' Paul replied. 'I have ordered our favourite takeaway and I picked up a nice bottle of Scotch whisky for later.'

'Sounds great,' Stephen replied with a melancholy tone.

They ate their fill from the Indian takeaway then sat and chatted while they consumed the bottle of Scotch. The conversation was focused mostly on reminiscing about old times and lost friends. In the end, they both collapsed in their beds and slept well for most of the night—until the alcohol wore off.

They woke up early in the morning and began nursing their hangovers. After a few cups of tea and coffee, and a large breakfast of eggs, bacon and sausages, the throbbing in their heads had eased. They finished packing and Paul offered to drive Stephen down to Wembley Stadium.

The journey was a quiet one with neither speaking a word. Only the radio provided any resistance to the silence.

When they arrived, the stadium was already buzzing with activity and followers were already lining up, some four hours before the speech. Stalls were selling hats and T-shirts brandishing the New World symbol, but most of the crowd already wore the Mark of the beast.

Stephen broke the verbal silence. 'It's incredible. Think of how much has been written about the mark of the beast, and here they all are wearing it proudly.'

'People see only what they want to see. If you told them what it means, they would just argue the contrary,' Paul commented.

They reached the drop off point and Paul stopped the car.

Paul and Stephen turned to each other and shook hands, the handshake turning into a brief hug.

Stephen asked, 'Can you give me a blessing?'

Paul smiled and said, 'Certainly.' They closed their eyes as Paul said a prayer, then they marked themselves with the cross and finished with an 'amen'.

Paul said, 'Godspeed, and may the Lord be with you.'

Stephen replied, 'And also with you.'

'I will be waiting at the local pub, so just let me know when you want me to pick you up.'

'Okay, see you then. Bye.' And with that, he was gone.

Paul watched him walk into the staff entrance point and disappear into the crowd. It was then that Paul realised he may never see his dear friend again.

****

Stephen spent much of the next few hours up on the scaffolding making minor adjustments to the lights he had installed, as directed by the lighting engineer. Thirty minutes before the main event, he was instructed to return to backstage. Instead, he walked past the backstage and continued out of the stadium. He stopped at the staff entrance point and pulled out the phone given to him by Thomas and Peter. He activated the app that controlled the stage light and selected the 'HTTP Internet' option. The spinning doughnut that indicated the page was connecting, performed its monotonous dance. After a minute of spinning, a message appeared. 'Error, unable to connect to host!'

Stephen scratched his head and tried to connect again. A minute later, the same message appeared. Error, unable to connect to host!'

Stephen gasped. 'Bollocks!'

He walked back into the stadium and tried again. Once more, he got the same error message. 'Bollocks!'

Stephen strode up the stairs that led to the backstage and found a point where he could see out over the audience. Thousands of people were on their phones taking photos and uploading them on social media, while others were either texting or Tweeting—the wireless network was overloaded!

'Bollocks!'

Stephen stormed off backstage and began to pace back and forth over the small section of grass between the back of the stage and the stadium entrance.

He tried the wireless connection instead and watched desperately as the words on the screen—'Connecting to security camera, please wait!'—appeared. Seconds seemed like minutes as the words on the screen became burnt into his psyche. Stephen's heart skipped a beat when the display changed to the word, 'Connected.' He could see the washed-out view of the stage and the outline of the podium.

A voice startled him. 'Steve, you are meant to be backstage!' It was one of the lighting crew.

Stephen quickly pressed the power button to make the screen go dark before saying, 'Thought being back here could help improve the chance of making a call, but no luck.'

'Give up if I were you, I did.' He walked off to the stairs to the backstage.

He couldn't risk accessing the weapon while in full view of others, he needed somewhere private. It then came to him—the door to under the stage! He could be close enough to be in range of the wireless transmission and be out of sight at the same time.

Stephen waited a few moments until the coast was clear then darted behind the small, black door and into the blackness beyond.

****

The black stretch limousine casually rolled up to the rear entrance to the stadium. Surrounding it was a cavalcade of police bikes and black cars filled with security staff and Judas's entourage. The first to alight from the cars were the security staff. Several burley men wearing dark sunglasses, black suits and red ties appeared from the cavalcade and began visually surveying the area. After a few moments, they began talking to themselves as the earpiece they wore transmitted to the rest of the team their words, 'All clear.'

The entourage was next to alight, and the media relations staff was immediately met by the stadium officials as they discussed the readiness of the facilities. Once all was confirmed to be in order, a nod was given to the security staff to proceed.

Beyond the sturdy fence that formed the perimeter to the rear entrance, was a crowd of supporters some twenty deep.

As the door to the black stretch limousine was opened by one of the security staff, the crowd burst into life. Jiovani was first to alight, wearing his black kaftan and red sash. It took a moment for the crowd to realise it was not Judas as the surge of noise died down.

Judas emerged next, wearing his white kaftan and red sash. The crowd exploded! Judas casually waved at the crowd before being escorted into the stadium. Judas was led up the stairs to the backstage and into the left wing.

As the entourage and the stage staff fussed over the confirmation that all was ready, no one noticed the sudden concerned expression on Judas's face. Judas felt his strength leave him as a burning sensation emanated from the souls of his feet. Judas knew immediately that he was on holy ground.

He pointed at one of the security staff and curled his finger up a few times to indicate to the large black suited man to approach.

The security agent approached and when he was close enough, Judas whispered something in his ear.

The security agent nodded then said something loud enough for it to be picked up on his earpiece but quiet enough to be drowned out by all the raucousness of the last moments of preparation and the impatient, 80,000 strong audience.

A security agent opened the door to the stretch limousine and immediately Zeus leaped out and sprinted into the stadium.

Jiovani looked at Judas and he could see there was something wrong.

He approached Judas and whispered, 'Is everything okay?' Judas glared at Jiovani then turned away and ignored him.

A moment later, Zeus was at Judas's side. The stage staff and the media relations staff had a quick discussion over the large black dog that had just infiltrated the stage.

Before anyone dared question Judas over the need for his pet to be on stage, Judas stated loud and clear to those murmuring, 'My dog stays, and that is not negotiable!'

Stage staff and the media relations staff fell silent.

Zeus obediently sat in the stage wing but seemed to be in some discomfort as he kept shuffling his paws and occasionally let out a small whimper.

After a flurry of nods and pressing of earpieces into ears, the go ahead was given to start. One of the media relations staff visually scanned Judas's apparel and gave the thumbs up that all was in order.

Judas walked confidently out onto the stage, the roar from the crowd exploding into a deafening sonic bombardment.

****

Stephen sat in silence in the pitch black under the stage. However, his heart was racing so fast that he took an occasional slow deep breath in an attempt to slow it down. His palms were bathed in sweat as was his brow. He began reciting the Lord's Prayer and it helped distract him from his fear. When he finished, the crowd outside erupted—the show had begun.

Stephen tapped the screen of his mobile phone and it came to life. The sudden brightness made his pupils retract and for a moment he had to squint. When his eyes adjusted, he accessed the app for the stage light again and waited while the screen displayed, 'Connecting to security camera, please wait!' Seconds passed like minutes until the dark screen whitened into the view of the stage. He could just make out the shape of the podium and the figure upon it.

Stephen could hear the muffled words of Judas and see his outline moving in conjunction. He had to pick his moment carefully as he had only one chance to get it right. While Judas was mid-sentence, he tapped the 'Off' button for the light. Immediately, he could see the clear image of the back of the Antichrist. Stephen carefully manoeuvred the graticule dot over the back of the Antichrist then cautiously tapped the orange button to reveal the 'Fire' button. He held a trembling finger over the 'Fire' button as he willed himself to press it.

A loud voice shattered Stephen's attention and he almost dropped the phone. 'Steve! We have lost one of the overhead stage lights! Get a replacement and get it swapped out pronto!' It was the voice of the lighting engineer on the walkie talkie that was strapped to his waist.

Stephen removed the walkie talkie from his waist and said, while pressing the 'Talk' button, 'On it!' He turned it off and returned his attention to the view on the phone. The graticule dot had moved away from the back of the Antichrist, so he carefully manoeuvred it over the point that he believed to be the location of the heart. He placed his trembling finger back over the red button and said before pressing it, 'God forgive me!' He then fired the weapon.

****

A flash came from a light above the stage, followed by a small cracking sound. Something impacted with Judas's back and threw him forward into the lectern, his body collapsing to the podium, his back oozing dark red ichor.

For an instance, silence dominated, then the gasps followed, and the inevitable screams.

Jiovani was first to his aid, then the security team. Jiovani kneeled down and cradled Judas in his lap. 'My Lord, my Lord!'

The security team surrounded the two figures on the stage and began scanning the area for the assailant.

Jiovani shouted to the security team, 'Get an ambulance NOW!'

One of the black-suited security men said in a controlled tone, 'It's on its way.'

A weak arm pulled Jiovani closer and with a frail voice Judas said, 'Don't leave me here.'

Jiovani then shouted, 'And for God's sake, get him off this stage!'

A group of stagehands ran onto the stage and carefully carried Judas off. Jiovani continued cradling Judas's head and the security team continued to scan for the assailant as they surrounded the group carrying Judas.

For a moment, Judas opened his eyes and glanced at Zeus as he obediently followed them off the stage. Zeus stopped and began sniffing the stage floor in search of his prey.

As the group carrying Judas left the back of the stage, a team of policemen ran past them and up the stairs onto the back of the stage.

The group was met near the back entrance by two paramedics with a gurney. The group carefully placed Judas on it and the paramedics began their assessment.

The female paramedic asked, 'What happened?'

Jovani replied, 'I think he has been shot in the back.'

The male paramedic carefully turned Judas to his side to assess the wound. 'Looks like a shotgun, and they could have hit his heart.'

After the paramedic tore the kaftan open, he attached sensors to his chest and the other placed a mask over his face.

A portable monitor and defibrillator that was mounted into the gurney came to life and began to beep.

'Blood pressure eighty-five over sixty, and falling,' announced the female paramedic as she read the data on the LCD screen.

'He is going into cardiac arrest,' announced the other. 'Breathing has stopped!' The paramedic attached a tube to his arm and in it was a needle. He jabbed the needle into a vein and secured the tube to his arm.

The female paramedic said, 'Complete cardiac arrest.'

The male paramedic announced, 'Defibrillator eighty percent charge, set epinephrine to one milligram.'

The female paramedic replied after pressing the LCD screen a few times, 'Defibrillator eighty percent, epinephrine one milligram, confirmed.'

'Clear!' shouted the male paramedic.

The paramedics stood back from the gurney as did the audience surrounding them. Jiovani's expression was somewhat deadpan compared to when he was on the stage a little earlier. The rest of the audience comprising Judas's entourage and the security team had eyes like saucers. Judas's body lurched from the gurney, then fell limp.

'No response,' said the female paramedic.

'Again!' said the male paramedic sternly.

This time the female paramedic shouted, 'Clear!' Judas's body lurched again and fell limp.

The male paramedic announced, 'Defibrillator one hundred percent charge.'

His college echoed, 'One hundred percent.' She shouted, 'Clear!' Once again, Judas's body lurched and fell limp.

The female paramedic said, 'No response.'

'Again!' shouted the male paramedic as frustration swelled.

His colleague watched the LCD screen, a bar indicating the charge level of the defibrillator. Seconds passed before she shouted, 'Charged, clear!'

Judas's body lurched once more and again fell limp like a corpse.

The two paramedics stood silently and stared helplessly at the body on the gurney as failure filled their minds.

One of the public relations team members said in a tone of disbelief, 'Is that it? Isn't there anything else you can do?'

The male paramedic ignored the question as he dragged himself back into the proper procedure. 'Time of death.' He looked at his wristwatch and continued, '3:21 pm.'

A shouted protest came from the crowd around them. 'No!' Then the crying started, followed by more announcements of disbelief.

****

Stephen crouched in the dark staring at the mobile screen as he watched the Antichrist fall. Dumbfounded amazement filled his mind as others rushed onto the stage to his victim's aid.

One thought passed through his mind—'I did it!' While staring at the screen, he willed himself to move. 'Run, you fool!'

He stood and used the illumination from the phone screen to light his way back to the small door. When he reached the door, he opened it ever so slowly and quietly to create the smallest of gaps. A beam of light cut through the darkness like butter. Stephen peered through the gap, taking a moment for his pupils to contract. Outside were two of the security team quickly debriefing a team of police officers that had just entered the stadium. He was trapped!

Stephen typed a text message to Paul. 'Trapped! Don't wait for me, I will make my own way to the rendezvous point. Leave now, and good luck!' He pressed 'send' and returned to monitoring the view from the small gap in the hope that an opportunity for escape would develop.

****

Paul sat at a small table in the local pub continually refreshing the *news.com* webpage for the hope to get a near instant update on what was about to unfold. The contents of the coffee mug on the booth table were emptied some time ago and the mug had yet to be removed. The bar tender was busy in a conversation with whom Paul assumed was a regular. The waiting and the not knowing was consuming Paul. If only there was a way to know what was happening.

The television on the wall near the bar was displaying some rerun of a football match and he desperately wanted to channel surf in an attempt to catch a newsflash, but he dared not.

His phone beeped and a message appeared—'Trapped! Don't wait for me, I will make my own way to the rendezvous point. Leave now, and good luck!'

Paul's eyes appeared like saucers on his face as he thought, 'Trapped! How? Leave you behind? Never! Did it work? WHAT'S GOING ON?'

Paul sat frozen to his seat, not knowing what to do. Moments passed before he made a decision and sent a reply text, 'Will not leave you behind. I will be waiting outside as arranged for the next 20 minutes. Good luck and Godspeed.'

Paul stood and headed for the door. As he passed the bar on the way out a news bulletin interrupted the current program. A well-dressed female reporter appeared but the volume was turned down and Paul couldn't hear what she was saying. He stopped and stared at the screen. Beneath the reporter was the moving text string, 'Judas Salim, leader of the New World, shot at Wembley.'

Paul's heart skipped a beat and he quickly rushed out of the pub.

****

Zeus sniffed frantically over the stage seemingly oblivious to the chaos around him. Police and stage staff were darting around searching for the assailant and it wasn't long before their attention fell upon the broken stage light. Zeus ignored them. His demonic senses were picking up the trail of a soul that was tuned in to the reality of the environment. Although his paws stung from the stage floor, he soon zeroed in on the source. He began to bark at a point on the stage floor.

The police officers and stage crew stopped and looked at Zeus. A moment later, one of the stage crew shouted, 'Under the stage!'

As if Zeus could understand what was said, he ran off to the stairs at the back of the stage.

****

Stephen pushed the door open slightly again to see if the coast was clear. His pupils contracted again as they adjusted to the daylight. This time there was no police to be seen. Just when he was about to fully open the door to leave, his phone beeped. Stephen paused to look at the message and it read, 'Will not leave you behind. I will be waiting outside as arranged for the next 20 minutes. Good luck and Godspeed.'

At first Stephen frowned as he was angry that Paul had disobeyed, but then a smile appeared on his face as he realised that he may still make it out alive.

As he pushed the black door open, his vision fell upon a large black dog charging straight for him. The dog's eyes flashed unnaturally red as it bore its arsenal of sharp white teeth.

Stephen's mind flashed to the teachings of *The Secret Book of Saint John*— it was a sentinel!

Stephen slammed the door shut and braced himself up against the plywood door. The impact of the sentinel threw Stephen from the door and made the stage structure shake. Fortunately, the door opened outwards or he would have been sentinel fodder. He stared at the back of the door for a moment. Unless the sentinel grew hands, it was not going to be able to open the door as the external latch was small and cumbersome. But it would not be long before someone did open the door and the sentinel would be upon him. Stephen got up and scurried away to search for another way out.

Zeus barked and growled at the black door while scratching at the latch. Soon he was met by several police officers and one of them pulled Zeus away from the door. Another officer opened the small black door and shone his torch into the blackness. With unnatural strength, Zeus broke free from the police officer's grasp, dashed past the other and charged through the small black door.

Stephen reached the front section of the stage and began scanning for another exit. If only he had paid more attention to the stage construction because now his life depended on it. The light from his phone illuminated only a few feet of blackness. 'Please, please, please. Please Lord, let there be another door!'

Just then Stephen spotted an exit! It was even smaller than the door at the back of the stage but big enough to crawl through. 'Thank you, thank you, thank you!' he muttered, the sense of panic clear in his voice.

Stephen got onto his hands and knees and pushed open the tiny door. Daylight flooded his eyesight as well as the faces of the audience.

He didn't care who saw him now, he had to escape! Stephen crawled through the door and as he stood, something gripped his ankle. The crushing force of the jaw upon his leg made him yell. The unnatural strength of the sentinel dragged him back under the stage and back into the darkness.

The screams from the audience drowned out the screams of the sentinel's victim and the bone-crunching sounds that emanated from the black cavity.

The two police officers pursued Zeus under the stage, but the darkness and the limited range of the torch impaired their pursuit. There were regular scaffolding structures to avoid that turned their pursuit path into a maze. The horrific noise of growls and mauling guided them to the source. In the blackness, the resonance of the perpetration rang sharp and clear in the officer's heads.

Eventually, they arrived at the scene but by then it was too late. When the beam of torch light passed over Zeus, it also passed over the mauled carcass. The two police officers averted their eyes and covered their faces to stop the stench of fresh gore filling their senses.

****

No one noticed the twitch from his right hand, but everyone noticed when Judas gasped. The inhalation was like the first breath of a deep-sea diver—urgent and absolute.

One of the media relations team screamed, many gawked, and some were quick to train their mobile phone cameras upon the miraculous breath.

Judas sat up and opened his eyes. The dark brown of his iris seemed lifeless as if he were more a wax figure than a human. He stood and braced himself against the gurney. The torn kaftan fell away from his upper body, exposing his strong back and chest. Congealed blood stained his back and some fresh red ichor flowed from his wounds. Judas began to strain his insides like a weightlifter would strain as a heavy bar was raised. Judas grunted as several small shiny balls were squeezed out of his back and fell to the lawn with a small thud. The wounds closed, and before the audience's eyes, they completely healed over. Only the blood stains remained.

A concert of gasps echoed around him.

The male paramedic stated, 'That's impossible!'

Then life returned to his eyes and he looked around at the crowd of onlookers. Judas asked with a tone of sarcasm, 'Why are you all staring?' He coughed up a mouth full of blood onto the gurney.

After Judas wiped away the blood from his face onto the sheet on the gurney, Jiovani came to life like an operated puppet and said, 'Behold the Messiah!' He kneeled before Judas, the rest of the audience compelled to follow.

Judas raised his arms and absorbed the worship.

****

The police officers tried to pull the sentinel away from his prey, but it was futile. Zeus would lash out with his strong jaws and sharp teeth, forcing the officers to back away. When the sentinel had his fill, he dashed off back to his master. The officers were left with a near headless body with a chest cavity that was hollow.

****

Judas pulled up the kaftan back over his upper body as Zeus arrived at his side. He bent over and gave Zeus a hearty pat. 'Good boy! Very good boy. Here, let me clean you up.' Judas pulled the bed sheet from the gurney and wiped away the blood and remnants of internal organs from Zeus's face.

Judas looked around at the faces of the kneeling and said, 'Come on, I have a speech to deliver and the audience is waiting!'

11

Brethren's Flight

Paul sat in the car in a 15-minute parking zone outside the stadium, looking at his watch every few seconds. He was a good fifty metres away from the stadium, but he had a clear view of the rear entrance. Twenty minutes had passed and still there was no sign of Stephen. An ambulance had been parked out the front of the stadium the whole time Paul had been observing, but a patient was yet to be brought out. 'Where are you?' Paul thought. Dread began to well up in his heart. The sudden muffled roar of the audience in the stadium startled Paul and he flinched. 'Why was there such a roar? This could not be good.' It was a good minute before the roar of the audience died down. The dread was replaced with despair as he heard the muffled but familiar voice of the Antichrist.

It was then Paul realised they had failed.

He couldn't leave without Stephen. He had the radio on low and when a news broadcast came on, he turned it up. 'In breaking news,' announced the newsreader. 'The leader of the New World, Judas Salim, has been shot by an unknown assassin and was declared dead a short time later. Then, according to the accounts by onlookers, he resurrected himself. Reports are also coming in that the assassin has died during the arrest. The identity of the assassin has yet to be announced.'

Paul turned off the radio as tears began to well up in his eyes. A knock on the car window made Paul jump. He looked up to see an event officer looking down at him.

She said with a loud and clear voice, 'Move on or I will book you!' As Paul wiped away his tears, he nodded and started the engine.

As the car pulled away, the expression on the event officer's face changed from being stern to one of concern when she realised the old man in the car had been crying.

****

The two police officers emerged from under the stage and awaiting them was a group of security staff and fellow police officers. One figure among them stood out and it was clear to the two officers she was not one of them.

The white suit the woman wore looked very out of place compared to the black uniforms of those who surrounded her. She pulled out an ID that neither officer had seen before. To override the speech that bellowed around them, the woman said in a loud voice, 'Agent Smith … MI6. I will be taking over this investigation. If you have any issues with this, you can take it up with the prime minister.'

The officer holding the torch said, 'Fine with me. He is right up the far end near the front, but there isn't much left to identify him.' The officer pointed up at the stage behind him and indicated to the voice that bellowed out over it. 'His dog made sure of that.'

Smith said sternly, 'Get back under there and guard the body. I don't want anyone interfering with the crime scene.'

'Yes ma'am. And you may be wanting this.' The officer handed her a mobile phone. 'It was his.' The two officers then went back under the stage.

Agent Smith tapped on the screen and fortunately it was not locked. She began perusing the text messages and stopped immediately. Looking up at the security team around her, she shouted, 'His accomplice is parked outside!'

The security team began talking into their earpieces as they ran off and out of the stadium.

Agent Smith didn't move. Instead, she pulled out her own phone and opened an app with the symbol of a radar screen. She typed in the phone number that was displayed in the text message and pressed the button marked 'Find'. The word 'Searching' appeared for a moment then the screen changed to an image of a map. In the centre was a red marker that moved over the map. Agent Smith talked into the mic on her sleeve, saying, 'Second target acquired, heading for Heathrow.' She then strode off, determination filling her mind.

At the top of the steps to the back of the stage, Zeus stood at attention, watching, and listening. Everyone seemed to be oblivious to his prior act of bloodthirsty murder. Once the police left the stadium, Zeus left his post and returned to his master's side.

****

Paul drove to the airport as fast as he dared, his mind filled with fear and sorrow. His dear friend Stephen was gone. He could only imagine the horrific circumstances in which the Antichrist would have ended his friend's life. Now Paul was a fugitive, and soon all the world would be hunting him down. He was now well into his seventies and the thought of evading the authorities seemed futile, but he was still determined to follow the plan and disappear. At every set of lights, he checked his phone in the vague hope that Stephen was, by some small miracle, still alive and would text him saying, 'Managed to escape. Fooled them in thinking I am dead. See you soon at the airport.' But no such message came.

He could now see the perimeter fence of Heathrow Airport and would soon be on a plane out of the country. Stephen told him to throw the phone away as he could be tracked, but he didn't care as grief had stolen his common sense.

A black van pulled up next to him and seemed to pause. Paul looked into the passenger window to see who was inside, but it was heavily tinted, and the cabin appeared empty. For a moment he imagined an armed police officer appearing from behind the window telling him to pull over, but the van just sped off ahead and overtook him. At the next roundabout, the van stopped in front of him as it waited for a break in the traffic. In the rear-view mirror, he saw an identical van pull up behind him. 'Surely this could not be a coincidence?' Paul thought as dread swelled within him. When the traffic had passed, the van didn't move! Paul's heart began to thump in his chest and his hands quivered. He looked around to see if he could navigate around the black van but there wasn't enough room.

Suddenly, the back doors of the van burst open. Two armed men wearing black uniforms and black balaclavas appeared, brandishing their semi-automatic weapons.

In a gesture of surrender, Paul slowly raised his hands from the steering wheel.

The driver's door of Paul's car flung open and another soldier dressed in black pulled him from the car and tossed him to the pavement. A moment later, Paul was handcuffed and gagged, had a black hood pulled over his head, and he was tossed into the back of one of the black vans. Paul could see nothing through the black hood as he sat on some hard, metallic bench. But what he could perceive was the van moving quickly through the streets of London. The soldiers that he assumed were in the back of the van with him were silent. Only the occasional noise of someone breathing gave away their presence. After what seemed to be about a fifteen-minute drive, the van came to a stop. Paul listened as the doors to the van were opened. He was pulled from the back of the van and escorted some distance through what he perceived was some sort of building. The journey came to an abrupt stop as Paul was thrust into a hard metal chair. His hood was removed.

Paul looked around at the empty room with black painted brick walls, floor and ceiling. Opposite him was what appeared to be a normal mirror, but he knew it had to be a two-way mirror with some officials scrutinising him from a room on the other side. The metal chair was bolted to the floor, and his arms, handcuffed behind him, were also handcuffed to the chair. The two soldiers that had brought him in, left the room using the door to his right. A single downlight illuminated his bald head and the reflection in his glasses made it difficult to see through them. Paul moved his head around to avoid the reflection so he could see clearly—not that there was anything of interest to observe and it was clear he was now alone.

Moments passed in silence.

The door to the interrogation room opened and a very attractive blonde woman entered wearing a white suit. This Paul did not expect.

The woman circled him before stopping in front of him. She said, 'Do you know why you are here?'

Paul looked her straight in the eye and asked, 'What is an angel like you doing in a place like this?'

Her head tilted slightly, and her bright blue eyes narrowed in admission that she did not expect such a response. 'I could say the same about you Father Paul.' Her retort was completed with a slight smirk, then her expression became stern. 'Answer the question!'

Paul responded calmly, 'It makes sense for me to be here, but not you.'

'Is that an admission?'

'We haven't been introduced. You are?'

She crossed her arms and stared at him saying, 'Agent Smith.'

'So, are you MI5 or MI6?'

'Answer the question!'

'MI6 is my guess.'

'Do you want to know what happened to your accomplice?'

'Accomplice? Accomplice to what?' Paul asked in a sarcastic tone.

'Are you aware that you are to be charged with the attempted assassination of Judas Salim—the New World leader? As this charge falls under the counter-terrorism legislation, you no longer have any rights, and we can detain you for as long as we see fit!'

Paul just stared at her, silent.

Agent Smith pulled out a mobile phone and sent a text. A moment later the phone in Paul's coat pocket beeped. All he could do was look down at the pocket.

'You sent a text to this phone shortly after the assassination attempt. This phone was found on the body of the assassin.' She leaned in close to Paul's face, and with eye-to-eye contact, she said sternly, 'The now dead assassin!'

Paul leaned back and turned his head away.

Agent Smith had hit a raw nerve. 'He was mauled to death by his dog!'

Paul's glare countered Agent Smith's as he said, 'It's not a dog.'

Smith pulled back and stared at him as she said, 'What do you mean it's not a dog?'

'It is a sentinel!'

'A what?'

'It is not of this Earth, and it cannot be killed by any mortal means. And it is the eyes and ears of its master.'

'Do you honestly expect me to believe such nonsense?'

Paul's stare seemed to look right through her as he replied, 'You already do!'

'You seem very sure of yourself Father Paul.'

'I was always very good at summing people up—a useful skill in my former line of work.'

Smith ignored his comment and continued her line of questioning. 'Tell me, why?'

'You know why. Otherwise, you would not have brought me here. It is evident that you want to know what I know.'

'And what do you know?' Smith's tone of questioning lightened.

Paul leaned forward as he said, 'Everything!'

Smith walked around behind Paul before appearing with a chair and sitting down directly in front of him. 'I am all ears!'

'It will not do you any good, such knowledge is a curse if you ask me.'

Smith leaned forward with her elbows on her knees, her head supported by her hands. 'Answer me this—what is he?'

'Why do you ask questions you already know the answers to?'

'Humour me.'

Paul leaned forward so that his stare could drill into her psyche, his expression becoming very dark. 'It is the beast of all beasts, the monster of all monsters. We have dreamed up many a terrifying creature in our books and movies, but they are all pale in comparison. Nothing in the mind of man could fathom such a horror. With just one look, it can tear your soul apart! It is not born of the Holy Spirit like us, it is the spawn of Beelzebub! Do not be fooled by its human form as it only appears to us as so. But through cleansed eyes, the beast can be seen in its true form. It has no compassion, no sense of justice, and it is utterly void of love. It is the destroyer, and its sole purpose is the destruction of our world.' Paul leaned back as he spat out the words, 'It is the Antichrist!'

Agent Smith stared back, silent. Eventually she leaned back in her chair and asked, 'Can he be stopped?'

Paul's expression changed to despair as he said, 'My fellowship has tried a number of times and we have failed.'

'Fellowship?'

'The Brethren. We have been preparing for this for over a thousand years. Unfortunately, it arrived during my watch.'

Agent Smith didn't expect him to open up so easily, and she wasn't going to let this opportunity pass. 'Who else is in the Brethren?' Paul sat back in the chair, his former strong demeanour fading away. 'All dead. I am the last. The beast made short work of my colleagues. Our pontiff was the only one to escape its venom directly.'

'Do you mean Pope John?' Agent Smith asked with an expression of confusion.

Paul frowned as he replied, 'Good heavens, no! I mean dear Pope Julius. Jiovani is the false prophet!'

'The false prophet?'

Paul rolled his eyes, 'Haven't you read The *Book of Revelation?*'

'No,' Agent Smith replied with an air of defiance.

Paul retorted in frustration, 'The False Prophet? The one who aids the beast in his endeavours to destroy the world? It was he who saw to dear Julius's fate.'

Agent Smith folded her arms as she said, 'According to the Vatican, Pope Julius died of natural causes.'

Paul's expression became dark again and he looked over his frameless glasses as he said, 'One of the Brethren, and a dear friend of Julius's, was a witness to the poisoning. There is no doubt that it was the work of the false prophet.'

'Why did you not tell the authorities this?'

'My dear, the Vatican is an authority in its own right. The Italian police have no jurisdiction. So, what would be the point of reporting a murder to the murderer?'

'What if it was your member of the Brethren that performed the alleged murder?'

'Father Michael was simply a parish priest with no possibility of political gain by such a sinister act. However, Jiovani had everything to gain.' Paul glanced at the mirror behind Agent Smith and added, 'He too is dead, another victim of the beast. So, don't waste your time looking him up!'

'As you said, you have tried a number of times to stop him. So, there must be a way.'

'Yes, but it will do you no good.'

'Why?'

'Because my dear, this is all meant to be. You cannot change what God has put in place.'

'But you tried?'

'Yes, because we were meant to try. For some reason our actions, which we are yet to understand, set things in motion that otherwise would not be set.'

'Then why can't we try?'

'Because as far as I know, God does not want you to. Who am I to interfere with God's grand design?'

'Father Paul, you have been very cooperative so far. You do not want to disappoint me now!'

'Or what? Your interrogation experts will beat it out of me? Torture me? My dear, I am an old man, and it is unlikely I would survive such treatment. I am at the end of my time here, and I have completed my life goal as instructed by the Lord. Do with me what you will; I care not!'

Agent Smith stared at Paul for what seemed like an eternity. She then got up and left the room.

Paul just stared at the mirror, wondering who was on the other side.

Agent Smith entered the observation room where two agents sat at a console panel with computer screens and infrared imaging cameras. Before them was the two-way glass mirror that showed the lone suspect handcuffed to a chair. Two men stood behind—one was her superior, the Chief of MI6 David Thompson, the other was Prime Minister Luke Churchill. David was a thick set man whose physique showed he had divorced exercise many years ago. Upon his chubby face was a moustache and a goat's beard to provide some facial definition.

Luke frowned as he asked, 'Is that it?'

Agent Smith placed her hands on her hips and said, 'For now.'

Luke stuck out his index finger and thrust it at the floor as he said, 'We need to know now! Before it's too late.' He turned to David and asked, 'Is she the best we have?'

Agent Smith bent down to one of the men at the console and said, 'Rewind the footage to the question about the Brethren?'

He rewound the footage to the point in question, and replayed it. When it reached the moment when Paul said, 'I am the last', Agent Smith said, 'Pause! Rewind over that last bit.' The technician did so and at the point where Paul said, 'Last', Agent Smith said sharply, 'Pause!' She turned to the prime minister and said, 'Elevated temperature. And he blinked while saying the word 'last'—out of sequence with the typical blink pattern. He is lying. There are others!'

David turned to Luke and said with an air of satisfaction and an ounce of relief, 'Yes she is!'

Luke's tone became less aggressive. 'But we still don't have it.'

'Prime Minister ...' Agent Smith stated, '... If we don't get it out *him*, we know there are others with whom we may succeed.'

'Can't we use a truth serum?' Luke asked.

David replied, 'Sodium pentothal is not reliable, and it is against company policy.'

Luke's eyes widened as he said in a restrained voice through tight teeth, 'The fate of the world hangs on what he knows. Use any means possible, even if it is against company policy!' He stormed off leaving them quietly staring at the exiting prime minister.

David said to Agent Smith, 'Keep working on him and track down the others.'

'Yes Sir,' Smith responded before leaving the observation room.

****

At the end of the speech, Judas returned to the cavalcade with his entourage. Zeus and Jiovani joined Judas in the second limousine while the rest of the entourage filled the remaining two.

As they pulled away to a chorus of cheers, Judas grabbed Zeus by the collar and forced him to make direct eye contact. 'So, let's see what went on while I was preaching to my disciples.' Judas stared into Zeus's eyes for about a minute before letting him go.

Zeus whimpered briefly before returning his attention to outside and the passing scene.

Judas poured himself a glass of fine Scotch from the mini bar and announced, 'So he has an accomplice. They do tend to travel in pairs don't they Zeus?' Zeus didn't react. 'Well, we will have to see to him as well, now won't we?' Judas gave Zeus a brief pat and continued to ignore Jiovani. 'But this time I think we should deploy one of my loyal subjects. It is time to get the main event under way, and what a main event it will be Zeus!' He patted him again, stared out the window and with a slight grin he said, 'The main event to end all main events.'

****

Thomas and Peter sat in the airport lounge waiting to board the aircraft. They faced a nineteen-hour, nonstop flight back to Sydney, Australia which neither of them was looking forward to.

Near the boarding checkpoint, a television on the wall displayed *Sky News*, and both Thomas and Peter's eyes were glued to it. So far, the only reports were about Judas's impending address to his supporters.

Thomas and Peter were silent as neither had it in them to make small talk. Peter's right leg was like a little jackhammer trying to make a dent in the terminal floor as it bounced up and down.

An announcement came over the loudspeakers. 'Ladies and gentlemen, your attention please. Flight QF2 is now ready for boarding. First Class and Business Class passengers, please make your way to the gate. Thank you.'

Thomas and Peter had Business Class tickets but neither wanted to board yet. They waited until all the other passengers had passed through the gate before standing and approaching the desk at the gate entrance. They had their passports scanned and made their way to the gate. It was then that a newsflash appeared on the screen. Both Thomas and Peter stopped and stared.

A well-dressed anchorman appeared and began reading out the autocue. 'News report just in. There has been an assassination attempt on the leader of the New World. Judas Salim, the proclaimed Messiah, has been mortally wounded at the Wembley Stadium rally this afternoon. Salim was pronounced dead at the scene despite lengthy attempts by paramedics to revive him. It was then that the claimed resurrection occurred in front of numerous onlookers. Supporters are now declaring that there is no doubt he is the true Messiah who has returned to save the world. During the attempted arrest, the assassin was fatally wounded. Police have yet to release his identity.'

Thomas and Peter looked at each other, dread and despair clearly visible on their faces. Thomas placed his hand on Peter's shoulder and said calmly, 'Come on, let's go.'

They walked down the tunnel leading to the aircraft, Both silent in word, but neither silent in thought.

****

Agent Smith returned to the interrogation room and sat down in front of Paul. In her hand she held a sheet of paper and on it appeared to be some sort of transcript.

'Are you the last?'

'I already told you.'

She repeated the question but this time with more determination. 'Are you the last?'

'Could I have a glass of water please?' Agent Smith stared intently at Paul.

Paul stared her back down as he replied, 'Yes.'

Agent Smith quickly retorted, 'Don't lie to me!' She placed a sheet of paper on Paul's lap. 'This is a transcript of text messages and emails from your accounts. Who are Wallaby and John Thomas?'

'Just a couple of friends,' Paul replied calmly.

'Read your communications. There is no evidence that they were friends. More like members of the Brethren!'

'They are just friends,' Paul insisted.

'Well, if they are just friends, you won't have any problem giving me their contact details, will you?'

Paul looked down over his glasses as he said, 'It is one thing to detain and accost *me*, but quite another to do so to my friends. They are off limits!'

'Father Paul, we have access to the most advanced search functions. We will find your …,' Agent Smith gestured imaginary quotation marks in the air, '… Friends, with or without you.' She snatched back the paper and briefly looked over the transcript before looking up at Paul and saying, 'Wallaby? Isn't that a small type of kangaroo? A rather fitting nick name for an Australian, don't you think?'

Paul stared back at her for a moment then turned his gaze away to a black wall.

Agent Smith abruptly left the interrogation room. As she entered the observation room, Chief of MI6, David, approached her. 'We could send in the muscle.'

'He answered my question, he just doesn't realise it. We have the comms team working on the two phone numbers. If I am correct, we will need to speak to the Australian Consulate.'

'No need,' David added. 'Approval will come from the top. As soon as you get confirmation, let me know and I will speak to the PM.' He turned and left.

'Yes, Sir,' Agent Smith replied as David walked away.

****

Sydney, Australia

Thomas and Peter walked down the corridor towards the passport checkpoint at Sydney Airport. There were queues of people before the passport checking booths and off to the left were three customs officers scrutinising everyone that passed by.

Thomas said, 'Look straight ahead and smile. We are back home, and we are happy after our trip away.'

'Easier said than done,' Peter replied. 'Right now, I can't tell what I want to do more—run or vomit!'

Thomas laughed as he said, 'That's the spirit. Do you know any good jokes?'

'Jokes? You know I suck at telling jokes,' Peter retorted.

'Okay then, I will tell a joke. Have you heard the one about the Australian, Englishman and Irishman marooned on a deserted island?'

'No,' Peter replied with an air of reluctance. He had heard some of Thomas's jokes before and they were mostly terrible.

'Well, there was a ...' Thomas proceeded to tell the joke and Peter forgot about the customs officers for a moment as they passed by. By the time Thomas had finished the joke, they had reached the queue for passport control without being pulled aside by the customs officers. Peter laughed heartily and for a moment the stress was abated.

As the queue shortened, their stress levels rose again, and Peter's and Thomas's hearts thumped in their chests. Their eyes darted around for any sign of an imminent arrest, but all appeared as normal.

Peter tried to make small talk. 'What are your thoughts on Australia in the next Rugby World Cup?'

Thomas played along and began sharing his opinion. 'We are in for a chance this time. New Zealand is off their game due to injuries and England is in a mess ...'

Before Thomas finished, they were at the passport control booth. A very stern looking woman uttered in a robotic manner, 'Passports and passenger cards please.'

They obediently placed the items on the counter.

The customs officer snatched up the documents and began scrutinising them, from time to time also scrutinising Thomas and Peter. In a very authoritarian way, she said, 'You were in the UK for some time. What was the nature of your visit?' Her dark eyes bore down on Thomas and Peter.

Peter's throat clammed up, but Thomas was able to utter, 'We had some business to attend to.'

The customs officer looked at their passports and back up at Thomas and Peter, then asked, 'So what was this business you attended to?'

Thomas replied, 'We were helping some friends with a charity they run.'

She stared at Thomas with a stern expression and asked, 'What type of charity?'

Thomas's mind went blank. Normally, he would be able to name a dozen charities but right at this moment, none came to mind.

Peter's throat finally opened up and he blurted out, 'Feeding the homeless. They own a kitchen in London.'

The customs officer's eyes darted between Thomas and Peter. Peter's heart began to race while Thomas cleared his throat in a nervous manner. She said, 'A worthy cause. Welcome home gentlemen.' She handed back their passports and passenger cards.

As they walked past the passport booth, Thomas and Peter both let out a sigh of relief.

They collected their bags and queued up for the quarantine inspection. A customs officer followed a beagle as it sniffed the queue of passengers. It sniffed Peter's luggage and he instinctively reached down to pat the dog. The customs officer said sternly, 'No touching the staff, especially when at work!'

Peter retracted his hand and said, 'Sorry.'

They passed through the quarantine inspection without saying a word to each other. When they passed through the exit gate, there was a crowd of people waiting to welcome their friends and family, but no one was there to greet Thomas and Peter.

Peter said to Thomas, 'Maybe they are just watching us to see where we go and who we contact, and then they will arrest us.'

Thomas began scanning the crowd for anyone who appeared to be blending in and not truly waiting for a loved one. A glimpse of hidden cord on an ear would be all that was needed for Thomas to confirm Peter's assumption. His gaze fell upon an old man with a hearing aid, then upon a chauffeur with a Bluetooth earpiece, holding someone's name up on a sign. When his gaze fell upon a woman holding a baby and talking on her mobile phone, Thomas pushed aside his paranoia and began focusing on the next few hours where he would attempt to disappear from society.

They left Sydney Kingsford Smith Airport and stood in the queue for a taxi. It was here that they planned to part.

Thomas spoke first. 'You have everything in place for your disappearance?'

'All in place before I left. Just need to pick up my car and go.'

'Good,' Thomas added.

'And you?' Peter asked.

'Yes. Just need to grab my stuff from home. If we really need to contact each other, we can always use email.'

'Only in an emergency. Stephen warned us that once we acted, email would be a risk.'

'True,' Thomas confirmed.

'Well, I suppose this is goodbye,' Peter announced reluctantly.

'Stay safe,' was all Thomas could come up with. His voice choked a little as he spoke.

The two longtime friends and colleagues hugged briefly and patted each other on the back.

A taxi pulled up next to them and Thomas said, 'You go first.' They separated from the brief embrace.

Peter placed his luggage in the boot of the taxi and got in the front next to the driver. Before closing the door, he said, 'God be with you.'

Thomas replied, 'And also with you.'

Peter closed the door and told the taxi driver which suburb he wanted to go to. As the taxi pulled away, Peter looked back at Thomas through the wing mirror and watched his friend of some twenty years wave goodbye for the last time. A tear welled up in his eye and he quietly wiped it away.

****

London England

Luke waited for all the windows on his computer screen to show the secure feed of the political leaders. Once they all appeared, he said, 'Good morning, or good evening everyone.'

'Morning,' replied Johann and Gabrielle.

'Evening,' replied Matthew.

'Afternoon,' replied Jim.

Luke said, 'No surprises why I called the meeting.'

'So, what is the run-down?' Jim asked.

'It was the work of the Brethren.' Luke responded.

'Are you sure of this?' Gabrielle asked.

'Let's just say it came from a very reliable source,' Luke replied. 'It appears that their objective was always to assassinate him. I can also confirm that they are a society of former Catholic priests with very close ties with the former Pope Julius.'

'Are there any more of them?' Johann probed.

'We believe so.'

'If it gets out that they are connected to the Catholic Church, this could explode into God knows what,' Matthew stated.

'I know, I know,' Luke retorted. 'We are keeping the identity of the assassin under wraps.'

'How could we not have seen this coming?' Johann protested.

Jim replied, 'We had little to go on and this society has covered its tracks very well.'

'We need to make it our top priority to find the rest and diffuse them before they make another attempt,' said Johann.

'We are working on it as we speak,' said Luke.

'Well, if they made an attempt, they must believe there is a way to stop him,' Jim hypothesised.

'I am going to come clean with you all,' Luke announced. 'We have his accomplice in custody!'

'Well done!' Jim said.

'Is he talking?' Gabrielle asked.

'Yes and no. He lied about his remaining colleagues and he won't tell us what he knows about destroying you know who.'

'We must know how; it is our only hope?' Jim protested.

'I have my best people working on it. We will get it out of him,' Luke stated.

'Can we be sure that he is immortal?' Gabrielle asked.

'How about rising from the dead?' Matthew stated more than what was asked.

'What I am asking is if we know for sure it is true. What if this was all staged?' Gabrielle clarified.

Luke replied, 'We have no evidence to contradict what is claimed and the mobile phone footage and eyewitness accounts are somewhat conclusive. Matthew, we believe that two of the Brethren are in Australia.'

Matthew's eyes widened. 'Okay, what makes you believe this?'

'The accomplice had regular communications with two men, and one went by the name of 'Wallaby'. We were able to source a voicemail from one of them and he had an Australian accent. Their mobile phones were last used near Heathrow Airport. They used pay-as-you-go sim cards and paid cash, so we don't have confirmed IDs yet.'

'Do you know what flight they may have been on?' Matthew asked.

'I can do better than that—I have two names!' Luke stated with a big smile. 'Fortunately, out of the two flights to Australia yesterday afternoon, there was only one booking made for two men—Flight QF2—in the names of a Thomas Haigh and a Peter Clarke.'

'Has the flight landed?' Matthew asked with urgency.

'One hour ago. The details only arrived in my hand about ten minutes ago. But you have their names so it should be easy to pick them up,' Luke stated with a smile.

'I will have ASIO on it immediately,' Matthew replied.

'Great,' Luke added.

'If you have no other revelations, then I need to make a few urgent calls,' Matthew stated.

'Let's reconvene next week for an update.' Jim proposed.

'Okay,' the others replied before disconnecting.

****

The fine oak inlays on the walls of 10 Downing Street's boardroom offered minimal reflection from the chandeliers above. Outside, another cold and bleak day was nearing the end as the parliamentary committee finished up the meeting's agenda.

Oliver charged into the boardroom and paused for a timely interruption.

Luke finished his closing direction then turned to Oliver who seemed very anxious. 'Oliver?'

'Prime Minister, Judas Salim has just called an emergency press conference.'

'When?'

'Right now!'

The rest of the committee who were about to leave, abruptly returned to their seats.

Oliver turned on the large, flat screen television at the end of the boardroom and set the channel to *BBC1*. The screen immediately displayed the view of a lectern with several microphones attached to the front. A moment later, Judas appeared in his usual white kaftan with a red sash. The committee was glued to the view on the screen.

Judas's dark eyes bore down upon them with the most intense stare as he announced, 'As you are all aware, an attempt to end my life was made yesterday. But fear not, my immortal soul is not harmed. But this not the first time this has happened. A terrorist group that calls themselves, 'the Brethren', has previously attempted to end my life. This terrorist group was formed and funded by the Catholic Church! Why you may ask? The Catholic Church sees the New World as a threat! Power is what they cling to and they will do anything, including terrorism, to retain it!' Numerous camera flashes from the press bombarded Judas as he stood defiant at the lectern.

'It doesn't stop there. The British Government also supports this terrorist group! My sources have informed me that the British Secret Service is harbouring the assassin's accomplice. They seek to protect the identity of the assassins as they too see the New World as a threat. Several times I have sought counsel with Prime Minister Churchill, and every time he has turned me down. Why I ask, why? The New World is a peaceful nation that has stopped wars, not started them. They have no reason to fear.

I call upon the prime minister to stop this charade and present the terrorist so that he can be brought to justice. Thank you.' Judas abruptly left the lectern amidst a barrage of camera flashes and unanswered questions.

Oliver turned off the television as everyone turned to Luke for a response.

Luke's expression was intense as he said, 'Everyone out except John and Judy.'

Obediently, but with some reluctance, the others left. John Matthers, a fair-haired man in his late forties, was the treasurer and deputy prime minister. Judy Burch was a dark-skinned, slender lady some five years John's junior. Her mixed Indian and Anglo-Saxon blood gave her a very stunning face and model-like body. Her looks, background and sharp wit made her very popular with the voters, and an easy choice for the minister for foreign affairs.

'Well, we are in the shit now!' John proclaimed.

'Luke, is it true about the accomplice?' Judy asked.

Luke stared out the window at the grey, and the sleet that peppered the windowpane. His mind was a battlefield of thoughts. He finally answered, 'Yes, it's true.'

Judy gasped as John uttered, 'We're screwed as well!' John's intense gaze focused on Luke, 'Why didn't you tell us?'

'National security,' Luke replied.

John pointed his finger at himself as he blurted out with fury, 'I am the bloody deputy PM! How top secret does it need to be before I'm kept out of the loop? And what about the foreign affairs minister? Don't you think Judy should be across this?'

Judy stared at Luke with venomous intent.

Luke stood and began slowly pacing along the boardroom. 'If anyone found out about this, it could push us to the brink of war! So, I kept you both out of it.'

'How deep does this go?' Judy asked.

Luke paused his pacing as he replied, 'The US, Germany, France, and Australia are in on it. But only the heads of state and a handful of secret service.'

'God!' John exclaimed. 'We are looking down the barrel of World War III!'

'Don't you think I know that?' Luke retorted.

'Why? I understand the implications of the New World's effect on global stability, but why harbour the assassin?' Judy pressed.

Luke glared at them as he asked, 'What are your true feelings about Judas? What do you really think he is? The Messiah or something else?'

John and Judy looked at each other surprised. John then sat back in his fine leather office chair and looked at the ceiling, while Judy crossed her legs and looked away.

'So, which is it?' Luke pressed.

Judy spoke first. 'I don't know,' she stated as she returned Luke's gaze.

John added, 'You know I am an agnostic, but this guy is something else. What, I don't know.'

'I will tell you what I think, and this is in complete confidentiality. If he were the Messiah, that would make what is in *Revelations* true, but what is transpiring does not line up with the Bible if you accept that he is what he claims to be. However, if you accept that he is the opposite, then *Revelations* is coming true, almost word for word.'

'To be honest,' John said. 'I read *Revelations* many years ago when I was young, and I have to say I barely understood any of it. I even had someone explain it to me and it still didn't make much sense.'

'I have to say, I haven't read it myself,' Judy said.

'I have,' Luke announced as he grasped the back of one of the office chairs for support. 'And it sent chills down my spine. Maybe you should both read it, or at least research it online for the explanation.'

Judy asked, 'So you think he is the Antichrist?'

'So, you do know something of *Revelations*?' Luke retorted.

Judy replied, 'Only what I have heard in passing or from the movies.'

Luke reached over the table and grabbed his tablet computer, then searched for something. A moment later, he put the tablet computer on the table and slid it over to the two opposite him.

One side of the screen was a passage from the Bible: 'Revelation 13:16-18: Let him that hath understanding count the number of the beast: for it is the number of a man; and his number is six hundred threescore and six. And he causeth all, both small and great, rich and poor, free and bond, to receive a mark in their right hand, or in their foreheads'. The other side of the screen was an image of a group of New World soldiers in their new uniforms.

'On the left is an extract from the Bible, on the right is a photo taken by one of our operatives in Israel only yesterday,' Luke described with an air of conviction.

John and Judy studied the text, then the image. Both remained silent.

Luke then added, 'Look at the symbol on their hats.'

They leaned closer and studied the image, then Judy gasped. John said, 'Oh shit!'

Luke continued, 'The emblem for the New World has only just been released, and according to our sources it is supposed to be three nines to symbolise peace, prosperity and dominance. Or something like that. But a nine upside down becomes a six, and when you put them in a circle, you could look at it either way.'

Luke stood firm and crossed his arms as he asked, 'Still unsure?' John and Judy both squirmed in their seats.

John said, 'Either way, we are behind the eight ball. We are harbouring a terrorist and the world knows it!'

Judy's analytical mind kicked into action. 'My question is, how did he find out? Do we have a leak in MI6?'

'If that is the case, we can't keep him under wraps,' John added.

'Yes, we should tell the media we have detained the assassin for questioning, and we will release him to the courts for trial,' Judy continued.

'There is one problem,' Luke announced. 'He may know how to kill the Antichrist. There is a chance we could avoid the Apocalypse!'

'Your argument is compelling, but if we don't act right now then this could be the catalyst for the very thing you are trying to avoid!' said John.

Judy's expression became very stern. 'You've had him for what, a good twenty-four hours, and no luck in getting him to talk. What makes you think he will ever talk? And that is assuming he knows how to kill him, and that it would work, and that he is the Antichrist, and that this is not a big bunch of bullshit that you are risking the future of our country over!'

John concluded, 'Release him to the courts! It is our only choice!'

Luke began to pace the floor of the boardroom, then stopped and stared at the view of the grey cold weather. 'Okay, we will release him!'

****

Sydney, Australia

Thomas turned on the television while he gathered up his belongings. *News 24* only had one story to cover and it was the events in the UK. The news anchor read out the autocue. 'To recap, the British Prime Minister has just announced that the claims by the New World leader are true. The assassin has been detained for questioning by MI6 before being released to the courts for prosecution. The identity of the assassin has still yet to be confirmed, but if the accusations by the New World leader are true, the Catholic Church could become a target for revenge attacks. There has yet to be any response from the Vatican.'

Thomas left the bedroom with two large suitcases in his hands and stopped before the television. 'Father Paul! Oh no,' he gasped.

It was then that the front door to the apartment burst open and a team of armed soldiers stormed in and surrounded Thomas. With numerous automatic weapons pointed at him, Thomas dropped his suitcases and raised his hands. A heartbeat later, he was on the floor, handcuffed and blindfolded.

****

London, UK

Exhaustion having taken hold of Paul, he fell into a deep sleep. Every two hours he was given the opportunity to relieve himself, and twice a day he was fed bread and given water. His protests on the quality of the food fell on deaf ears. It seemed like only moments had passed since he had fallen asleep before he was awoken by a kick on the chair that he was handcuffed to. His glasses flew off his face and slid across the floor to the corner of the room.

Paul attempted to focus as he assessed the faces of the other occupants in the interrogation room. One was the attractive and familiar face of Agent Smith, and the other a man he had never seen before. He was carrying a briefcase. The man placed the case on the floor, opened it and began preparing something out of view.

The expression on Agent Smith's face was very dark. 'Hope you have had a good rest.' Smith didn't wait for a response. 'Your refusal to cooperate has forced my hand. Time has run out. You are about to be sacrificed to the wolves. Let me introduce you to The Doctor. He is skilled in chemical coercion. The Doctor was middle-aged, bald and appeared to be one of dubious moral values.

'This is your last chance to save the world.'

Paul squinted, trying to focus his old eyes on Agent Smith. He straightened himself in the chair as he said, 'It is not I who is to save the world, that is the Lord's role!'

The Doctor looked up at Agent Smith and she gave him the nod. The Doctor stood, syringe in hand. Paul could only guess what it contained but he felt sure it was something to try and make him talk.

The Doctor injected the solution into Paul's arm as Paul winced. The Doctor extracted the needle and replaced the syringe into the briefcase.

They stared at Paul as his eyes slowly glazed over and he became intoxicated. The Doctor pulled open one of Paul's eyelids in an attempt to closely examine Paul's floating gaze. He said to Agent Smith, 'You can begin.' He stepped back from Paul's view.

Agent Smith came up close to Paul's face and said, 'Can you hear me?'

Paul tried to focus on the voice, but his head kept rolling around. All he could manage was a weak nod and a 'Yeah.'

'What is your name?'

'Paaauulll.'

'What is your job?'

Paul let out a brief chuckle as he said, 'To kill the beast.'

'How do you kill the beast?'

'We failed.'

'Paul, how do you kill the beast?'

'We all failed! We did everything the book said and we still failed ... we were meant to, you know?' Paul's eyes fixed upon Agent Smith for a moment before they began floating around again.

'What book?'

'*The Book of Saint John*—the secret book. Sshhh.'

'Where is this secret book?'

'Hmmm?'

'Where is the secret book?'

'Oh, if I told you that, it wouldn't be secret ... we burned ours anyway ... can't have it falling into the wrong hands, now can we?'

'Yours? Are there other copies?'

'Yeah, the others have them, but they are all dead. Such good folk too. What a pity.'

'They are not all dead though, some are still alive.'

'Some.'

'Would they have the secret book?'

'Maybe. It won't help you though ... it didn't help us ... we all died trying!'

'Father Paul, how do you kill the beast?'

Paul's expression firmed and for a moment his gaze solidified, then he shouted, 'YOU CAN'T!' He faded back to toxicity. 'My dear friend Stephen, bless your soul.'

Agent Smith glared at The Doctor. The Doctor replied, 'It is the optimal dose, and as I said it is most effective on the weaker minded. He however, is not.'

Agent Smith paced back and forth then stopped. With her gaze fixed upon Paul, she waved away The Doctor. 'You can go.'

The Doctor picked up his briefcase and left the interrogation room.

'Father Paul, how do you kill the beast?'

Paul's head stayed down as he mumbled, 'You can't. We tried, we died. You can't!' He then fell asleep.

Agent Smith's mobile phone beeped. She pulled it out of her jacket pocket and looked at the text message. It was from a contact titled 'M'. 'Success from Down Under. One of the targets acquired.'

Agent Smith looked down at the sleeping figure before her. 'Well Father Paul, it looks like we have another that may be more helpful. We are done!' Agent Smith then left the room.

****

When Paul regained consciousness, his eyes ached, and his brain throbbed. It was like a bad hangover that afflicted his mind, but he knew it was the after-effects of The Doctor's serum. Two men wearing balaclavas entered the interrogation room and released Paul from the chair. They escorted him to the adjoining bathroom where he was told to shower, shave and put on the clothes laid out for him. The door was locked behind him and Paul did as he was instructed. Once finished, he looked in the mirror at what he was wearing—a black suit and tie. Satisfied, he banged on the door with his fist to let the guards know he was done.

The door opened and immediately, a black hood was thrown over his head and he was handcuffed again.

Paul was led down a corridor and through a doorway, then up a flight of stairs. Another door was opened, which led into a large room that caused their footsteps to echo. A metal door was opened, and Paul was pushed in as a hand pressed his crown down, so he didn't bump his head.

He was guided down onto a familiar metal bench seat as he listened to others enter what Paul perceived as a van.

The van pulled away and it was some time before the hood was removed from his head. Before him sat Agent Smith. Paul studied her face. She looked very young to Paul, possibly still in her twenties. She had photographic features—small straight nose, clear smooth skin, and big, bright, deep blue eyes. He wondered if she had ever wanted to be a model or a movie star when she was a teenager. But despite the beauty, there was a hardness to her physiognomy. Paul could not tell if it was sadness or determination that formed her character. What Paul was certain of was that Agent Smith had not had an easy life.

'What a shame,' Paul announced.

Agent Smith glared at him and responded, 'What is a shame?'

'Your life.'

Agent Smith frowned.

'So much sadness and hardship. And only the same to come. Would have been good to see what you would be like in a happier life.'

'You seem so certain that you are right.'

Paul leaned forward and replied, 'You know I am!'

The van came to a stop, and the two agents seated next to the back door stood and opened it. A rush of noise and light filled the van as did camera flashes and abrupt questions. A few metres away there was a wall of reporters and cameramen held back by a low barricade and several police officers. Further behind was another barrier with an angry mob of New World supporters holding placards with slogans such as, 'The Messiah lives on' and 'Bring back the death penalty'.

Agent Smith unlocked the handcuffs from the bench seat and led Paul out of the van. The camera flashes became blinding and Paul turned his head to protect his eyes. The reporters shouted questions like, 'Do you work for the Catholic Church?' and 'Did the government bank roll your crusade?'.

Paul ignored the interrogation as Agent Smith's earnest guard took them to the front door of The Old Bailey Courthouse. Once inside, the front door was abruptly closed by one of the trailing agents shutting out the commotion outside. Paul was led down a large hallway with a vaulted ceiling and ornate nineteenth century décor, then into one of the adjoining courtrooms. The Old Bailey was in lockdown. No one roamed the halls of justice except for a handful of security guards.

The courtroom housed a sea of finely crafted timber that made Paul feel quite enclosed. He was led to the witness stand that protruded at one side of the room, while Agent Smith and the accompaniment of nameless agents sat on a bench behind.

The courtroom was void of occupants except for a small number of key staff.

After a few moments of silence, the bailiff announced, 'All stand for Right Honourable Judge Jackson.' The agents all stood as a middle-aged woman, dressed in the stereotypical courtly garb, strolled up to the judge's bench and sat down. Her fair-skinned face appeared out of place with the white wig that encompassed it.

Judge Jackson peered down at a document on the bench through her half-moon glasses before fixing her gaze upon Paul. 'Paul Anthony Conway, you have been brought before this court with a charge of terrorism and aiding and abetting in the attempted murder of Judas Salim, the leader of the New World. How do you plea?'

Paul responded to her over glasses stare with his own as he replied, 'I don't recall making any threats to anyone.'

'Mr Conway.' Judge Jackson's tone became very dark. 'You have been accused of the most serious of crimes. This is not the occasion for smart remarks!'

'Your Honour, will I be granted the counsel of a lawyer or has the principle of justice been abandoned in this court?'

'The charge of terrorism forfeits your rights as a citizen of this fine country. However, I am not in agreement with upholding this law in its fullness. I will grant you the right of counsel.'

'Thank you your Honour.'

'Now, back to my original question. How do you plea to the charges presented in this court?'

'Your Honour, to be a terrorist I would need to have terrorised, or attempted to terrorise, the citizens of Britain. This I have not done, and I plead not guilty. To the charge of attempted murder, how can this be when the said victim is immortal and cannot be killed? To this charge, I also plead not guilty!'

'Mr Conway, your alleged accomplice seemed quite certain that the act of murder was very much possible and therefore the charge stands. Make it noted that the defendant has pleaded not guilty. You will have two weeks in which to form your case for your defence. The case will commence the following Monday. This court is adjourned.' Judge Jackson picked up a small wooden hammer and banged the bench.

As the judge stood, the bailiff announced, 'All rise!' But the hearing was so short that many wondered why they bothered to sit down in the first place.

Once the judge left the courtroom, Agent Smith escorted Paul out with the posse of agents in tow. When Agent Smith opened the door to the outside world, a flood of external commotion filled the great hall as they stepped out into the day. They walked steadily towards the awaiting van parked around the corner from the courthouse. Agent Smith led the way, Paul directly behind, and the rest of the agents closely behind Paul.

Shouting could be heard from behind the wall of reporters, before a gap was forced between the reporters and the face of a young man appeared. He hurdled the barrier as a policeman tried to grab him, but he was too swift. He ran to Paul and hugged him as Agent Smith turned to reach for Paul. Two of the trailing agents grabbed at the young man, spinning the couple around; but the man's grip was firm. The young man, of African appearance, shouted, 'Death to the infidels! Long live the Messiah and the New World!' And with that, he pressed a button on a device in his hand and the couple exploded.

Paul's body was torn apart, as was the body of the young man. The two agents that attempted to separate the young man from Paul were hurtled back into the other agents and beyond. Several reporters were tossed away like rag dolls in a melee of blood and bone. Agent Smith was catapulted backwards before being bowled over a police officer and slamming into the side of the van. Her body collapsed to the pavement, limp and bloody.

****

Sydney, Australia

Thomas sat in the cell looking around at the concrete walls and steel door that incarcerated him. Apart from the uncomfortable bed that he sat on, the only other furnishings were a stainless steel toilet and a small wash basin—neither looking clean enough for Thomas to touch, let alone use.

The cell door opened, and two men walked in wearing cheap suits with narrow ties. One man was more heavily set than the other, but both appeared to be in their forties. The heavier set man said, 'Follow me.' Then he turned and walked out of the cell.

Thomas followed, with the other man right behind him. He was led to a small room with a cheap wooden table in the centre, and with two chairs on either side. Thomas was directed to sit on one of the chairs on the far side.

After the two men sat opposite him, the thinner man placed a phone on the table and positioned it so that he could video Thomas. The heavier set man said, 'I am Agent Jones, and this is Agent White. We work for the Australian Security Intelligence Organisation. Do you know why you are being held here?'

'No,' Thomas answered.

'You have been linked with an assassination attempt in London. Can you please tell us your full name?'

'Thomas William Haigh.'

'Did you just return from a three month stay in the UK? London in particular?'

'I did.'

'Did you travel with another?'

'Yes,' Thomas answered tentatively.

'What was his name, and do you know of his current whereabouts?'

'Peter Clarke, and I don't know where he is.'

'What was the nature of your business in the UK?'

Thomas became nervous as lying was not one of his strengths, but he had rehearsed his answer many times. 'We were assisting some friends with a charity.'

Agent Jones pulled out two photos and placed them on the table in front of Thomas. 'Do you recognise either of these men?'

Thomas looked at the photos, immediately recognising Paul and Stephen. He didn't know if he should admit if he knew them or not, but in the heat of the moment, he decided to lie. 'No.'

Agent Jones pulled out his phone and played an audio file on it. 'G'day Paul. We will be there around 10:00 am. See you then.' He pressed the 'Stop' button and asked in a deadpan tone, 'Is this your voice Mr Haigh?'

Thomas's heart began to race. 'Sounds a bit like me but no it isn't.'

'Mr Haigh, you are lying. We ran this voice across yours on your own message bank and received a 99.4 percent match. In a court of law, such a percentage can be used as a positive match!'

Thomas could only say, 'Oh.'

'Are you going to tell the truth Mr Haigh?'

Thomas's throat closed and all he could do was clear it.

'Mr Haigh, will you please identify these two men?' he said as he pointed at the photos.

'I want to call my lawyer!' Thomas protested.

Agent Jones's tone became very serious. 'You have been accused of attempted assassination, which falls under the counter-terrorism legislation. Under that law, you no longer have any rights. That includes a lawyer!'

Thomas's heart sounded like the hooves of a racehorse in full gallop. He did not know what to say. Peter would know what to say, but he was not here. Thomas was alone. He gave in. 'This is Paul, and this is Stephen. I don't know their last names.'

Agent Jones sat back in his chair with a pleased expression on his face. 'It seems odd to me that you went all the way to England and spent some months with people you don't know the last names of.'

'Yes, I suppose it is,' was all that Thomas could come up with.

'What was the name of the charity?'

'Ah, I don't recall the name.'

'What did the charity do?'

'Feeding the homeless.'

'Where did you go to feed the homeless?'

'Not sure exactly.' Thomas's replies felt weak, even to him.

'Mr Haigh, you are lying again, aren't you?'

Thomas could only stare at Agent Jones as nothing that could come out of his mouth was going to get him out of this.

'You assisted them, didn't you? You are a part of a terrorist cell, aren't you?'

Thomas's hands began to shake, and he suddenly felt very cold. 'We are not terrorists!'

'Then what are you Mr Haigh?' Agent Jones and Agent White sat forward in anticipation.

Thomas's demeanour changed to one of strength as he announced, 'Archangels! We are here to save the world!'

Agent White asked, 'Save the world from what?'

Thomas leaned forward and said quietly and with great conviction, 'The Antichrist!'

The agents sat back in their chairs and looked at each other, their expressions clearly showed that they did not expect this revelation. Agent White's phone beeped to indicate a text had been sent. He pressed the 'Pause' button on the video and reviewed the message. His eyes widened, and he showed Agent Jones. Agent Jones raised his eyebrows then turned back to Thomas. Agent White returned the phone to the table and restarted the video.

'You are a very wealthy man Mr Haigh,' Agent Jones stated. 'You have over seven million to be precise. The tax office confirmed that this was declared as inherited from someone. Would you like to explain who that someone was?'

'You would not understand,' Thomas retorted.

Agent White said, 'May I suggest that this was blood money, for a would-be assassin!'

Thomas's expression hardened in disgust. 'This was no blood money!'

'Then, what it is it?' Agent White persisted.

'Survival money,' Thomas blurted out.

'To survive what?' Agent Jones asked.

Thomas leaned forward, his stare becoming intense. 'The Antichrist has many supernatural powers at his disposal, and he has the power to manipulate the wicked. We needed to disappear for fear of discovery by his minions. That costs money.'

'So, where did the money come from?' Agent Jones continued.

Thomas straightened his back as his confidence returned from telling the truth. 'From the papacy!'

'The Pope?' Agent Jones frowned.

'Popes.'

'Which Popes?' Agent Smith pressed.

'All of them,' Thomas replied with great honour.

'I don't understand. What do you mean, all of them?' asked Agent Jones.

Thomas sat back feeling far more comfortable as the great weight of secrecy was lifted from him. 'Since before records began, the papacy has been saving up for when the beast would come to destroy the world. As it is written in *The Secret Book of Saint John*, the anointed must rally and thwart the beast before he comes to power. They must be prepared and gather resources across the ages.' Thomas paused then continued, 'And so the papacy did as instructed.'

Agent Smith's eyes narrowed as he asked, 'What is *The Secret Book of Saint John?*'

'It is one of the few writings held from the public. Written by Saint John the Apostle when he wrote *Revelations*. It was deemed unsuitable for the public—and for good measure I believe.'

'So, the Catholic Church is behind this?' Agent Jones stated.

'No, the church knows nothing of us. It's the head cardinals that are corrupt, especially former Pope John.'

'So, are you plotting against the Pope as well?!' Smith exclaimed more than questioned.

'No! We are not killers or assassins of any kind. The beast is not human, and it is only the beast that we seek to destroy.'

'Well, you failed Mr Haigh,' Agent Jones stated with an air of satisfaction. 'If you had succeeded, you would have brought on the Third World War. Millions would have died.'

Thomas said with great conviction, 'Maybe, but as he still lives in the world, the beast will start a war that will destroy billions! And the whole world with it.' Thomas sat back as he felt he was done here.

Agent Jones said, 'Thomas Haigh, you are under arrest for terrorism and attempted assassination. And both of your British partners in crime are now dead.' Agent Jones paused to savour Thomas's reaction. Thomas's eyes widened. 'Yes, Paul was killed by way of a suicide attack outside the Royal Courts of Justice in London a few hours ago.'

Agent Smith stopped the video recording and the two agents stood. Agent Jones said, 'Back to the cell for you.'

****

London, UK

David Thompson walked down the corridor of the hospital towards the ward that had two police officers standing guard. Behind David was the steel-faced Prime Minister Luke Churchill. The police officers stood aside and let the officials enter the ward. There was only one bed in the ward and around it was several complex monitor machines with numerous readouts displaying live data. From the machines came several tubes and wires that all ended at the frail figure on the bed. Behind the bed stood a nurse who was tending to one of the machines. Her Jamaican heritage was in stark contrast to the bland white of the hospital ward décor, and her bright smile, clearly for the famous guests, added some warmth to their mood. She said, 'Well look here, you have some very special visitors here to see you.'

'How is she doing?' Luke asked.

They all looked down at the battered figure on the bed. Agent Smith's face was swollen around her left eye, which was as black as her nurse's skin. Her typical well-groomed, blonde hair was an unraveled mess and still had some streaks of blood in it. Behind the oxygen mask were some cuts to her face, and her right arm was in plaster.

'She is very lucky to be alive,' The nurse said with a hint of a Jamaican accent. 'She has concussion, two broken ribs, a broken arm, a dislocated hip and fingers, a ruptured spleen, and a collapsed lung. We have placed her in an induced coma while the swelling on the brain subsides. The paramedic said it was the body of a policeman that slowed the impact with the van that saved her life. I was told the policeman didn't make it.'

'Will *she* make it?' Luke asked.

The nurse placed her hand on Agent Smith's bandaged right hand as she said, 'She's a fighter. We think she will pull through. But we are not out of the woods yet, are we pet?' she finished off with a soft, kind smile.

'Her father served in the agency as well,' David announced. 'An analyst and a fine one at that.'

Luke glanced around and said, 'Where is her family?'

'Remember the terrorist attack on London back in 2005?'

'Yes, many casualties. Awful.'

'She was about seven then. She was with her mum and dad, and her little brother, on the Liverpool train. The suicide bomber was only a few feet away when he blew himself up. Unfortunately, her family had a front row seat, and she was the only one to survive. Barely a scratch on her they said. Very much a miracle.'

'God!' Luke gasped.

The nurse just stared at Agent Smith with a sad expression.

'I was apprehensive when I saw her application to join the agency. An experience like that can really mess you up. But her determination was irrepressible, so I gave her a chance to prove herself and I wasn't disappointed.'

'Keep me posted on her condition, I want to know if she wakes.'

'Certainly, Prime Minister.'

12

Checkmate

The morning light beamed through between the tiny gaps in the silk curtains and onto the luxurious marble bedroom floor. The butler entered the bedroom and walked over to the curtains to open them. He carefully slid the curtains across so as not to disturb the sleeping figure in the super king-sized bed in the centre of the vast bedroom. Once the curtains had been opened, light bathed the room and highlighted the solid gold fixtures. The figure in the bed stirred, then raised his head slightly.

'Good morning my Lord. Did you sleep well?'

Judas stretched his arms and sat up. 'Yes, thank you.' He did not utter anything about the events that unfolded during his slumber as the torturing of the souls within was not morning conversation.

The butler walked back out of the bedroom and returned pushing a silver trolley laden with breakfast items and a tablet computer. He stopped at the bedside and lifted the lid of the large silver serving platter. Beneath was a picture-perfect meal, steaming away casually. 'Your breakfast today my Lord—freshly smoked herring with poached eggs on a bed of tomato and vegetable sauce.' The butler picked up the tablet computer and presented it to Judas. Judas accepted the tablet and began perusing the device.

'Will there be anything else my Lord?'

'No, thank you.'

With that the butler left the bedroom.

From the far end of the room Zeus got up from his own woolen bed and approached Judas. He sat beside the vast bed awaiting his breakfast, but that would not come until Judas had finished his.

'So, what is happening in the world Zeus? Let's see.'

After tapping the screen a few times, he began to scroll down through the news bulletins. He paused then tapped a briefing. 'Well, what do we have here?' Judas began reading out loud. 'A Lebanese national has suicide bombed the only remaining assassin of the New World Messiah, Judas Salim. Although the attempt on the leader's life failed, the accused Paul Conway was about to go on trial for the Messiah's attempted murder.' Judas dropped the tablet to his lap as he continued, 'Well, well, well, how about that? Looks like the people of the New World are ready to fight for me. Admittedly, with a little coercion from my good self. But before we go off and start World War III, let's just make sure they are truly ready. Tonight is the night for my dear parents to be brutally murdered! You have a job to do my boy,' Judas finished with a big grin.

Zeus let out a small whimper.

'I know you don't want to Zeus, but it is for the greater good. Besides, the Western world and their out-of-date religions will need to be blamed. And of course, we will have to go to war over that, won't we?' Judas let out a small chuckle as he wallowed in his own success.

****

Sarina and John sat at the dinner table, the evening news on the television on the adjacent kitchen wall. The aroma of the falafels on their dinner plates filled the kitchen and their nostrils. John looked much older since his retirement as he struggled with the notion of no longer working. His raven black hair was now as grey as Sarina's, though looking a little thinner. John's thick moustache was almost as grey as his hair and the lines around his dark brown eyes were permanently defined. Sarina however was pleased with her husband's retirement as she now had company through the days that were once lonely.

Sarina placed her hand on John's arm as she said, 'Look, it's Judas on the television again.'

John glanced up at the footage of the recent speech in London and said, 'Would be good if he had some time for his family!'

Sarina scowled, 'He is the Messiah! He has the world to save.'

'When did he last bother to even call us? What, a year ago? He should make time!'

'John!' Sarina retorted. 'I told you before I won't have you talking about him like that!'

John returned to his dinner and ate quietly while his mind fumed.

The sound of paws on the roof made the two look up.

Sarina said, 'What is that? Sounds like a cat on our roof?'

John swallowed then replied, 'Sounds very heavy for a cat. I'll have a look.' He stood and went upstairs.

When John reached the first floor, he looked around and remained as quiet as he could while listening intently. Although it had been a while since he had retired, the habit of wearing a suit had not yet left him. Most days he would be well dressed but a tie was now a rarity, and tonight he had accepted the open collar casual style. Sarina often encouraged the semi-formal look by telling John how handsome he was.

He heard muffled movement from above. Something was definitely on the roof. John walked around to the stairs that led to the roof garden. He climbed each step slowly and listened intently. When he reached the top of the stairs, he unlocked the roof door and slowly opened it.

It was a clear night, and the moon was full in the sky. Between the moonlight and the ambient glow of Jerusalem's city lights, the roof garden was well illuminated. However, much of the rich colours of the plants were lost in the limited light, but the ornate bench seats were still clearly visible.

John stepped out onto the roof and looked around; his eyes fixed upon a large dark shape in the corner. John said, 'Zeus, is that you? What are you doing here?' He looked around and said, 'Judas?'

As John looked away from Zeus, he heard running paws and a slight growl. Before he could turn back towards the impending impact, John was knocked to the roof floor by Zeus's large frame. Zeus's massive jaws clamped onto John's throat, depriving him of air and voice. The best John could do was thrash about and emit a slight gurgling sound.

Sarina heard the distinct thud of a body hitting the roof. She gasped as she stood from the dinner table, then shouted. 'John, are you alright?'

There was no response. Sarina dashed up the stairs as fast as her arthritic knees could carry her. When she reached the roof garden door, Sarina could see it was left ajar. From the roof garden came the sounds of a beast, feeding on something. Sarina tentatively pushed the door open to witness the gory prostrate figure of John. The large, bloodied head of Zeus lifted from the corpse's torso to fix his gaze upon Sarina. Zeus's eyes were like bright red orbs—lifeless and chilling.

Sarina screamed!

With unnatural vigour, Zeus launched at Sarina. He cut off her shriek with his great jaws as his bulk threw her body back down the stairs. Moments later, the sentinel had a second corpse to feed upon.

****

Judas sat on the deck chair near the pool, listening to Vivaldi on his portable music station. Jiovani was next to him, running through some stately issues with his Messiah.

Judas's attention flicked between Jiovani, the music and the lowball glass of Scotch in his hand.

Out of the darkness at the far side of the estate grounds came a bloodied monstrosity. Zeus trotted up to Judas and sat obediently by his side. Jiovani's eyes widened as a chill shot down his spine. The Antichrist looked over at its sentinel. 'How was dinner?' Zeus whimpered.

'You look a mess! Jiovani, go clean up Zeus. He has been a very good boy, haven't you?'

'Yes, my Lord,' Jiovani responded as he stood and led Zeus away to the pool shower area. Part way around the pool, Zeus stopped, groaned and vomited up a section of small intestine. Jiovani turned his head away as the stench of half-digested human filled his senses. He reciprocated by vomiting as well.

The Antichrist turned his head away from the disgusting display as he protested, 'You two are pathetic!' Judas stood and commanded as he walked back to the villa. 'Clean yourselves up … and that mess. I am going to bed!'

****

The armoured limousine pulled up in the underground car park right in front of the elevator door. Judas had arrived early at the new presidential palace built near the centre of Jerusalem. Since the assassination attempt, four security agents were waiting to escort him to the secure chambers of the palace. Despite his reluctance to accept it, Judas was never without protection. The parliament insisted that their Messiah always be protected, but Judas protested saying it was a sign of weakness and vulnerability to his enemies.

As the limousine door was opened, the security team visually scanned the car park for any risks. Once satisfied, they let Judas alight and walk to the elevator. Judas wore his business uniform of a white suit and a blood red tie.

His chief advisor was waiting for him at the lift. 'Good morning my Lord,' she said. Louisa Ghattas was in her early forties but looked more like she was in her early thirties. She had worked hard to get to where she was now and kept herself fit in order to keep up with the gruelling pace set by Judas. Louisa wore her usual black business suit with a short skirt and red scarf, and she kept her long black hair tied back in a ponytail that helped tighten the skin on her face; or at least she believed so.

'Morning,' Judas replied. 'What do you have for me today?'

Louisa hugged her tablet computer as she followed Judas into the lift. The four security agents entered last, making the lift quite crowded. 'Good news! Argentina has applied to join the New World.'

'Great!' Judas responded.

The security agents appeared more robotic than human and seemed ignorant of their conversation.

The lift doors opened on the ground floor, the security team exiting first to check that all was safe for Judas. One of the team gave a nod and Judas and Louisa walked off in the direction of the business wing.

Judas continued, 'Make all the necessary arrangements and set up a meeting with the Argentinian president.'

'Yes, my Lord.'

When they arrived at the business wing, two posted security guards opened the double doors to the media office. Inside were two rows of desks with people seated before their computers, busily typing and tapping their touch screen monitors. Between the rows of desks was a walkway that Judas and Louisa proceeded down. The security team remained at the door with the posted guards.

As they arrived at the golden gilded doors at far end of the media office, the doors opened inwards to reveal the main office of the New World Leader.

Judas and Louisa strode in and the two security guards that opened the doors for them closed the doors behind them, shutting Louisa and Judas inside.

The office was circular with ornate gold leaf inlays in King Louis style walls. The ceiling and floor were of the finest quality white alabaster, and the floor was adorned in the equally fine silk cashmere rugs.

A set of leather lounges filled part of the expansive office, but the centre piece was the desk. Made of Moroccan Thuya Burl wood, the desk, some five metres wide, dominated the room. Behind the tall leather office chair was the flag of the New World with the familiar three sixes in the middle of the sun.

Judas sat at his desk and logged into the built-in computer in the desk. A large section of the desktop was a touch screen that was slightly angled towards Judas.

Louisa said, 'You have two meetings today, one with the Italian Prime Minister and one with the Russian president.'

'Any news on Russia's stance on joining us?'

'Not yet, my Lord. But we are confident that they will come around.'

The office doors burst open and one of the security guards stormed in. 'My Lord, I bear terrible news!'

'What is it?' Judas demanded.

'You're parents!'

****

Judas marched down the hallway of the city morgue with his entourage and security team. The door to the last room on the right was left open and was guarded by two police officers. Judas approached and walked straight into the room, ignoring the police guard. The security team remained outside and only Louisa and two other members of his office team felt they should follow.

Judas was met by the police commissioner, Abid Mahmood, and the head of his security team, James Frank.

Abid, a man in his late fifties, of slender build and with receding grey hair, said, 'My Lord, please accept my deepest condolences. Your parents were the finest of society and will be sorely missed.'

The expression on Judas's face was cold, dark and intense. His black gaze was fixed upon the two covered figures on their stainless steel autopsy tables. 'What happened?'

James, who was in his early fifties and looked fitter than many people twenty years his junior, replied, 'They were attacked on the roof of their house. We don't know what it was, but whatever it was, it was large. It could have been some sort of rabid dog.'

'How could it have got onto the roof?'

'We don't know. It would have had to leap from an adjacent roof, which would have been some feat. Must have left the same way it arrived as there was no trace of the animal elsewhere.'

Judas's stare fell upon James. 'Was anyone else attacked?'

'No, Sir.'

Judas's masquerade of fury swelled. 'Are you telling me that a rabid dog miraculously leaped up onto the roof of my parents' house, killed them both, then leaped off the roof, without a trace?'

Judas's deadly stare made James's neck hair stand on end. James had never sensed true fear before but right now, fear filled his brain. 'Yes Sir. Sorry, no Sir.'

'Then, what are you trying to tell me?' Judas shouted in fury.

James glanced at Abid before proceeding. 'This could have been a professional hit, my Lord. And by someone who wanted to make a point, thus the mauling. Maybe because their attempt on you failed, your parents were the next easy target. We did find some scratch marks on the balcony rails that could have been made by a grappling hook.'

Judas came face to face with James with an expression of pure disdain. 'Why was there no detail on my parents' house? Or did you not think that was important?'

James turned away from the venomous stare and muttered, 'My deepest apologies, my Lord.'

Through gritted teeth, Judas expelled, 'GET OUT OF MY SIGHT!'

James made a hasty exit and left Judas to stare at the covered corpses. The onlookers were too terrified to utter a word. Even Louisa was silent as no one had ever seen their Lord lose his cool.

Judas finally uttered with restraint, 'I have run a peaceful country, we have not even raised a finger at the old world. Still, they accost me. Well, no more. No more will we sit back and take this. Greed of the old church must be extinguished along with the countries that support it. Louisa, gather my generals, we are going to war!'

****

Judas entered the boardroom wearing his white kaftan and red sash. His expression was one of intense determination. At the long table sat twenty uniformed men with numerous stars upon their shoulders, and on the front of their caps, the New World symbol of the three sixes inside the sun. Each man represented one of the former countries, now factions of the New World. The palace boardroom was decorated similarly to Judas's office, with fine marble and cashmere rugs, but the occupiers took little notice of the fine décor.

Judas arrived at the lone empty chair at the far end of the room, but he did not sit down. Instead, he leaned on the back of the chair and stared into the faces of his generals. 'Gentlemen, are you men of peace or men of war?'

They looked at each other for a moment before unanimously replying, 'War!'

'Well, you are about to execute your true calling. Gentlemen, we are going to war!'

The generals nodded and smiled.

'The old church has played their last card. No more will I tolerate its greed and deceit. Nor will I tolerate any of its factions or the governments that support it.'

Judas was met with more nods of approval.

'We are closing our borders and our air spaces. As you know our country has embraced newfound wealth and prosperity, and the religions of the past are all but dissolved, and with them the shackles they represented. To protect our country from almost certain attack from the old regime, we are going to put in place our trump card. I want twenty of your best soldiers from each of you—ones that will obey an order without question and carry out that order implicitly. General Khan, begin research into portable nuclear weapons, ones that can be carried in a backpack.'

The general that represented what used to be Pakistan, nodded. 'We have been experimenting with the concept for a while and have a working prototype. I will proceed with finalising the development.'

'Gentlemen, the first sign of military response from the old world, we are going to strike without hesitation and tear out their hearts. We will obliterate every major city! The devastation will leave the old world in tatters. Then to conquer the old world will be as easy as a walk in the park.'

General Khan cleared his throat before nervously saying, 'They will surely respond with a nuclear strike that will lay waste to our own cities.'

Judas glared into the brown eyes of the middle-aged General Khan. 'I have already considered this. Twenty-four hours prior to the strike, we will evacuate our cities. Satellite towns will be prepared to take the influx of refugees. Our special postmen will already be in place, waiting for the order to execute. When their spy satellites tell them there are no clear targets to strike against, they will falter. That is when we invade. We will neutralise all their military installations, and any remaining signs of leadership. Any remaining military strength will be focused on saving their homeland rather than attacking ours. Gentlemen, before this year has ended, we will rule the world!'

The generals thought for a moment before realising the perfection of the plan. As no one could see a flaw, they responded with a round of applause. Judas stood back from his dominant stance over the chair and his generals and raised his arms to bathe in the glorification.

****

Washington DC, USA

President Richardson sat at his desk going through the bill for a new legislation. The morning sunlight filtered through the windows behind as the vapour from a fresh cup of coffee danced slowly and provocatively.

The president's personal assistant Lucy abruptly entered the office. 'Mr President, the Director of the CIA needs to see you urgently.'

'Sure, send him in,' Jim replied.

Nancy nodded to someone behind the door and stepped aside.

Marcus Whitehead entered the office wearing a stern expression. Nancy left the office and closed the door behind her. Marcus was in his early fifties, of thin build and had a full head of greying hair. His good looks made him very popular with the ladies and an affair with a former secretary had almost cost him his marriage of fifteen years.

'What's up Marcus?'

'Mr President, our surveillance on the New World borders has shown increased activity. We believe they could be closing them!'

'There has not been any communication to that effect, and there has been no comms from our embassies.'

'This is footage on Cyprus from the former Turkish border. Marcus placed his tablet computer on the desk before Jim and pressed play. It displayed a satellite view of a border crossing that looked familiar. A couple of armed guards were standing at their posts at a pillbox with the barriers dropped to prevent any unauthorised access. Before the border crossing, there was a queue of vehicles waiting to cross the border, but none were passing through. The first few vehicles turned back and let the next in line come to a halt at the border. Then those few vehicles turned around as well. 'Watch the truck that has just entered the picture on the New World side.' A large truck pulled up near the border gate and several soldiers got off the back. They proceeded to unload metal barriers and barbed wire rolls.

Jim studied the footage for a while then looked away and stared out at the view over the White House gardens. 'Alert our consulates for possible evacuation from the New World territories.' He turned back to Marcus and asked, 'But why? Why now?'

Marcus stopped the footage and played another video. 'This was aired last night.'

The video was of a young attractive woman dressed in a suit and skirt, holding a microphone. On the bottom corner of the video was the Al Jazeera logo. The reporter began her monologue, occasionally pulling away her long black hair from her face, thanks to a light breeze. 'Last night the parents of the Messiah were brutally mauled to death on the roof of their Jerusalem home by what is believed to be a large animal. The authorities have no explanation how the animal could have got on the roof of their home, and inside sources suspect that this could have been a cold and brutal assassination. We have yet to hear from the Messiah, but it has been reported that he is intensely distraught, with the words 'fire and brimstone' being used to describe his disposition.'

Jim sat back in his chair and thought for a moment. Then, with a tone of intense conviction, he said, 'Please tell me we had nothing to do with this.'

'God no!' Marcus replied.

'We need to put our military on alert—this could be big.'

The door to the Oval Office opened again and Nancy poked her head in. 'Mr President, you might want to turn on the news!' She proceeded to stare at Jim with a look that clearly said, 'NOW!'

Jim grabbed the remote on his desk and turned on the large, flat screen television on the wall. The screen came to life and was already on the *CNN* news channel. As Nancy closed the door behind her, the image of a news anchorwoman appeared with the words 'Breaking News' displayed below. The anchorwoman commenced reading the autocue with a concerned tone. 'To recap, we have a live feed from Jerusalem where the proclaimed Messiah of the New World will address the nation.' She briefly raised a hand to her right ear as the hidden earpiece conveyed the voice of the program producer. The anchorwoman nodded and said, 'We will now cross live to Jerusalem.'

The image changed to a view of an empty lectern, with the sounds of scuffles as unseen reporters settled themselves ready to report on whatever the breaking news would be. A moment later, Judas appeared at the lectern wearing his white kaftan and red sash, a very stern expression on his face. He paused for a moment while the last of the reporters settled themselves, then he began. 'Thank you all for coming at such short notice. For too long the old world and their old religions have attacked me and attempted to assassinate me. That I can tolerate, that I can forgive. But yesterday, the line was crossed. Yesterday, my parents were assassinated. They fear us because we are new and strong, and until now that fear has been unfounded. Now, their final desperate act has invoked my wrath. Not the wrath of a man, but the wrath of your Messiah. In response, I have closed the borders to the New World and our airspace to foreign aircraft. All old religions within our borders will be abolished as the pure religion of the New World begins. Every man, woman and child will bear the symbol of the New World and with that comes the benefits of safety, prosperity and wealth. Those who do not bear the mark will be cast out! This is my pledge to the old world—if you raise so much as a finger to us, I will unleash the leviathan and crush your old world out of existence. You have been warned. Thank you.' Judas left as abruptly as he arrived, a barrage of questions upon his back.

Jim turned the television off. 'Well, we now have an answer! Marcus, see what you can do about assisting evacuation of our embassies and citizens from the New World.'

'Will do,' Marcus replied.

Jim, rather than using the intercom, shouted, 'Nancy!'

As her head was already inside the office from behind the door, Nancy said, 'No need to shout.'

'Sorry. Get the Joint Chiefs of Staff and arrange a cabinet meeting for this morning.'

'Yes, Mr President,' Nancy responded before disappearing.

Jim said, 'In the meantime, I need to make an important conference call.'

****

Jim waited for the images of the political leaders to appear on the computer screen. Once they all had come into view, James said, 'Hello all. No surprise why I called this meeting.'

There was a succession of greetings before James continued, 'First I just wanted to ask if any of you were responsible for the assassination of Judas's parents.'

James's question was met with a chorus of 'NO!'.

'What about the Brethren, could they have really done this?'

Australian Prime Minister Matthew Turner replied, 'It doesn't sound like something they would do. Their target has always been you know who.'

'I agree,' Luke Churchill added.

'Still, I think we should not cross them off the list,' Jim continued.

'According to our intel, the last remaining member is at large here in Australia, and we believe he is still within our borders,' Matthew stated.

'There may be others that they were not aware of. Or maybe another faction?' Jim proposed.

French President Gabrielle Pasteur said, 'What if it was you know who that did it?'

There was a pregnant pause before German Chancellor Johann Schiffer broke the silence. 'If he is who we think he is, then why not him?'

Jim said, 'Well yes, that is a good possibility.'

Luke said, 'He wants this war, don't forget that. It is all he has ever wanted in my opinion. It is his reason for existence.'

Matthew added, 'And a clever way to create a reason for starting a war if you ask me.'

'We must diffuse this. Must!' Jim demanded.

'I'll have the priest questioned again, see if there is anything else we can get out of him,' said Matthew.

'Matthew, if you don't mind, I would like to send down one of ours to assist with the questioning. Since we have had some success already questioning the Brethren, our combined efforts could come up trumps,' Luke requested.

'Sure, no problem,' Matthew replied.

'In the meantime, may I suggest we don't do anything to give you know who the excuse to start World War III?' Jim stated.

'If we assume he was responsible, he could create the next incident to give himself the excuse.' Luke theorised.

'True,' Matthew confirmed. 'We need to be ready for all-out war.'

'Possibly nuclear war at that,' Jim added. 'We have already commenced the evacuation of our consulates and citizens from the New World. And I will be meeting with the Joint Chiefs later today.'

'Yes, we are also in the process of getting our people out,' said Gabrielle.

Johann said, 'We are deploying our troops to the borders. Do you think we should prepare for invasion, or a nuclear strike, or both?'

'Nuclear strike would be my bet. They have access to advanced weapon technology as well as the missiles to deploy them,' said Jim.

'They are not long-range missiles though so only the immediate bordering countries would be at risk,' said Gabrielle.

'They have a navy, ships and submarines,' Luke stated. 'They could deploy from all of our doorsteps!'

'We need to call an emergency UN meeting,' said Johann.

'Yes, I received a missed call from the UN president about five minutes ago,' said Luke.

'Well, there is not much else we can do right now apart from keep our heads down and keep safe,' said Jim. 'I have to go.'

'Same here,' added Johann.

'Good luck all and keep us in the loop if you find out anything that can diffuse this mess,' said Luke.

'Will do,' replied Matthew.

'Bye,' they all replied.

****

London, UK

Prime Minister Churchill strode down the hospital hallway with his security team in tow. Recent events had raised the risk of assassination and wherever Luke went, so did his security.

As Luke arrived at the guarded room, one of the two police officers opened the door for him. Luke entered and his security team attempted to follow but Luke put up his hand and said, 'No, you stay out here.'

'Prime Minister,' one of the team protested. 'We must not leave your side!'

'I will be fine. Stay here. And that is an order!' With that Luke entered the room.

Inside, David Thompson stood at the far side of the bed. It appeared that Luke had interrupted a conversation.

On the bed was Agent Smith, and she was conscious. She looked bright and in good spirits. Her hair had been washed and blow dried with no sign of dried blood. Her swollen black eye had regressed to a just a dark shade underneath. Agent Smith smiled at the prime minister.

'We'll it's good to see you bright and well,' Luke stated.

'Thank you,' Agent Smith said with a slight flushing of her cheeks.

'You had us all very worried,' Luke continued. 'How do you feel?'

'I have felt better, but not too bad considering. My ribs still hurt when I move.'

'The nurse said that she is coming along well. The induced coma did the trick,' David injected.

'Do you remember much?' Luke asked.

Agent Smith looked up at the ceiling as she tried to access her thoughts. 'I remember the courtroom but after that it is all a blank.'

Luke asked cautiously, 'Now think carefully, did he say anything to you on the way to the courthouse before he died?'

Agent Smith searched her thoughts for a while and said, 'He talked about me. Said that my life was sad and that it will only get worse.'

'Life of the party from the sounds of it ... not!' Luke added with a smile.

Agent Smith let out a brief laugh before wincing from the pain in her ribs.

'Sorry,' Luke apologised.

'That's okay,' Agent Smith replied as she recomposed herself. 'Don't think I will be watching any comedy shows for a while.'

'When you are up to it, how would you like to fly Down Under and see what else you can get out that other priest? Our counterparts in Australia have done well to get some more out of him, but I would like our best to see if there is anything else we can extract. Then you can go and have a nice holiday break, maybe see some of the sights. How does that sound?'

'Sounds good,' Agent Smith said with a smile.

'Great. Now you rest up and get well. That is an order!'

'Yes, Sir.'

Luke looked over at David and nodded. 'M,' he said then left.

****

Saudi Arabia

The stealthy Learjet landed gracefully on the runway of the military base in Saudi Arabia while the sunset bathed the scene in the remaining reddened light. Once taxied, the aircraft stopped before a large hangar. The hangar doors were wide apart and inside stood a platoon of soldiers obediently waiting for their next order.

The cabin door opened and immediately two security officers emerged, surveying the surrounds for potential threats. They made the call that the area was clear, and Judas emerged from the aircraft in his black suit and red tie. He strode up to the group of twenty generals standing beside the platoon and paused for them all to solute. There was a snap as synchronised arms, four hundred strong, saluted their commander-in-chief.

When their arms returned to their sides, Judas ordered in a large commanding voice, 'At ease.' The platoon and the generals all stood at ease with their feet shoulder width apart and their arms neatly folded behind their backs. 'You are probably wondering what your mission is. Well, you have all waited long enough. You are our secret weapon against the tyranny of the old world and their greedy out-of-touch religions. As you know, they have attempted to take my life and failed, and out of frustration they took the lives of my parents. I will no longer stand for this injustice. Their fear of us, and their greed and jealousy, will ensure that they will strike and soon, but we will be ready. Our borders are closed and our airspace with it. Our troops are at the ready. And you are the key to the success of our forthcoming campaign. Your mission is to deliver one of these to each of the major cities of the old world.'

General Khan walked over to a table where an unassuming backpack was carefully placed. He picked up the heavy backpack and brought it to Judas.

Judas took it and paraded the backpack before the platoon. Its weight seemed light to Judas. 'You will place one of these at the top of the tallest building in the city that you are assigned. Each has a thermal nuclear weapon with a one hundred kiloton yield. Such a yield in such a small package was not possible until a few years ago, thanks to the great team of researchers under General Khan. The high location will extend the range of the weapon, and it must be placed in such a location that it will not be discovered until detonation. So, choose your locations wisely. The bombs are safe to handle and are well shielded. Each has a simple timer that can be set for up to a twenty-four-hour delay. This will give you time to leave the city and await your next orders. They are heavy though, comparable to a full field pack, but I am sure you are very accustomed to carrying around such a weight. Many of you will remain in the country that you have been designated to provide intelligence, while others will return to the submarines that will deploy you. You will also be given a satellite phone each as normal forms of communication will be lost. Any questions?'

Judas paused for a moment to allow the men time to speak up, but all were steely. 'If you accept this mission, take a step forward.'

Immediately, four hundred elite soldiers took a synchronised step towards Judas. Judas smiled. 'Congratulations men, you are about to make history!'

****

Somewhere in the Atlantic Ocean

In the dark of a moonless night, a periscope appeared from beneath the waves and performed a three-hundred-and-sixty-degree survey of the surrounding cold black ocean. With the area clear of vessels, the submarine surfaced. Moments later, the hatch atop the conning tower opened and eight soldiers exited the submarine like ants from a nest. They scaled down the conning tower and congregated on the hull. A hatch was opened, and a rubber dinghy was removed and inflated. Six of the soldiers, dressed in stealthy black garb, prepared to enter the dinghy once it was dropped into the ocean. All wore infrared googles to enable them to see in the total darkness. Six heavy duffle bags containing supplies and the apocalyptic ordinance that the special force would deploy, were placed into the centre of the dinghy. Some duffle bags contained two backpacks as some of the soldiers had more than one city in which to deploy the ordinance. One of the six started the small outboard motor and they sped away towards the New Hampshire coastline. This was the first of eight teams to be deployed upon the USA mainland.

On the other side of the Atlantic Ocean, another special force was deployed off the Cornish coast of England, as well as the off the coast of France. For the next two weeks, identical operations were performed across the globe—without detection.

13

Dawn of the Apocalypse

Kashmir, India

The northern border between Pakistan and India has always been a potential flashpoint for war since the creation of the two countries after World War II. And that division had strengthened since Pakistan joined the New World alliance. Compared to its neighbour, Pakistan had struggled financially up until recently as India had had great success with its support for computer and Internet services across the globe. Now, with the wealth of the New World flooding in, Pakistan had changed dramatically. Poverty was on the decline as factories were being built all over the country to service industry requirements of the New World. Beggars were no longer seen, poorly maintained motorcycles and rickety old bicycles were a thing of the past, and houses were being rebuilt to proper building standards. Electric cars and new bikes were everywhere, and people were at last not struggling to make a living.

On the other side of the border however, what was once considered a better economy and a better way of life, had deteriorated into much poorer living standards. Jealousy had swapped sides at the border, and too often old differences were raised in the streets of India.

Pakistan was on top for once, and the citizens relished in the fact. Taunting across the border at their old foe was commonplace for the former Pakistan, now New World border guards. Daily, a loudspeaker was raised above the six-meter-high concrete wall, to convey the day's insults. The Indian guards retaliated by reopening old wounds via their own loudspeaker, but their taunts were old. The New World Pakistan's, on the other hand, were current and had greater potency.

Citizens from the west were pouring out over the border to India as this border had been designated as one of the few places where refugees could exit. Many were consulate staff, some were businessmen who certainly faced redundancy, and some were intelligence agents assisting the successful passage of their countrymen. As the days passed, the New World border guards became more aggressive; their verbal taunting of the refugees now further backed with shoe throwing. This new physical attack fired up the Indian border guards, and the New World guards knew it—and relished it.

The refugee count had quickly reduced to a trickle, and as there were so few, each received the full brunt of the border guard's abuse. This daily act had become a hot topic for the locals, some even joining in on the taunts and shoe throwing to the point of smearing the shoe in faeces before casting the shoe at the victim. But others were appalled and boycotted the event.

Among the day's refugee count was the German Ambassador for Iran and his family. To ensure their safe departure, Secret Service agent Hans Schoffel accompanied them. Rolf's wife, Emilia, was holding their newborn baby—the reason for their delay in fleeing the New World. The small group was huddled together in the line of refugees permitted to cross the border, one group at a time. Once their passports were checked, they needed to run the gauntlet in no man's land. The first fifty metres was the most dangerous as this was still in the New World territory, and on the wrong side of the border wall. The shoes they threw at the refugees were tied to a string so they could easily be pulled back behind the wall and reused for the next victim. None of the assailants would risk standing in the line of fire of the Indian snipers just in case a marksman could not resist the temptation.

It was time for the Ambassador's group to run the gauntlet. The border guard that stamped their passports said upon finishing, 'Goodbye infidels and good riddance!'

As the gate rose to let them pass, Hans said to Rolf, 'You stay on the left and I will stay on the right, and together we can shield your wife and baby.'

Rolf nodded and they double hugged his wife and child, before walking quickly down the gauntlet.

The shoes began to fly along with the taunts. The smell of an unflushed toilet wafted from some of the shoes, one such shoe hitting

Rolf on the side of the head. He shook his head to regain his focus as they gained speed across no man's land, but in doing so he exposed his wife to the fray.

It was then that a hard healed shoe struck Emilia on the side of her face. The shock made her lose her footing and she fell to the ground, dropping her infant. Rolf and Hans tried to keep Emilia from falling but with the added complication of a newborn in arms, they failed to do so. They all fell to the ground under a barrage of filthy shoes and verbal abuse.

On a nearby rooftop on the Indian side of the border was Rama Patel, lying prostrate in the standard military sniper position. Rama had watched, day after day, week after week, the innocent being abused. Through his sniper scope, all was too clear. Men, women, the old, and the young were subjected to the intolerable—no detail was withheld from his right eye. At the end of each shift, he would return home and sit in silence as his wife wondered what he had seen that day, his face a vision of conflict and restrained anger. Many family conversations turned to the ill feelings against the neighbouring country and the treatment of the refugees, and his relatives would look at him to invoke a response. But all they ever got in return was a distant stare. Rage filled his mind— an unbridled rage to accost the bullies from the other side of the border.

Today, the witnessing of a baby being defiled pushed Rama's steely resolve beyond breaking point. He scanned the break in the wall for a target to unleash the conflict within. Normally, his scope could only see barbed wire or the occasional hand flash out from behind the safety of the wall. Rarely did an opportunity present itself to take down an assailant, but today that rare opportunity was gifted to him. A teenage boy foolishly extended himself beyond the safety of the wall and for a split second his head was an offering.

Drummed into Rama was the order, 'Do not fire unless fired upon!' Normally, the words played over and over in his head, but today his rage was much louder, and Rama acted upon the rare offering.

Crack went the rifle. The boy collapsed over the barbed wire fence that lined the street, blood oozing from his fatal head wound.

Rama's heart raced but his mind was numb. Then fire fight started. At first, the bullets struck inanimate objects inert, but as the guards manoeuvred to get a clear shot at a target, they exposed themselves. Steadily, the death toll rose on both sides of the border. Rama, drunk with rage, began firing at any target that presented itself. Finally, he could release the torment that enraged him and for the first time in weeks, he smile a smile that turned out to be the last expression he wore. A sniper bullet from over the border found its target. Rama's head jerked back from his prostrate position on the roof as his brains exploded from the back of his head. The torment had finally ended.

The small, vulnerable group in the midst of the fire fight stood and began walking towards safety. They did not run, they walked. Cradled in Emilia's arms was the limp infant. Hans utilised his training to keep a clear head during the melee and kept saying to his just as terrified companions, 'Keep walking, don't stop!' The journey across no man's land took less than a minute, but for the refugees it felt like hours. Occasionally, Hans would glance up at the guards returning fire and watch some of them fall, but he kept on his journey trying his best to be oblivious. The New World guards were too preoccupied with those firing at them to focus on the small, huddled group as it made its way across the border.

Then a voice shouted, 'Here, over here!' A man appeared from behind a building, gesturing towards them. They blindly followed. The group was directed to behind the building and brought inside. A small medical team was waiting for them in the room as the sounds of gunfire continued outside.

The man that had brought them inside said in an urgent tone, 'Place your baby on the table and our medical team will have a look.'

Emilia nodded, tears flowing down her pale cheeks. The stainless steel table was surrounded by medical equipment. The infant looked so tiny on the cold, flat metal platform as the medical team examined her.

The doctor placed a mask over the infant's face and began squeezing a bag on the end. He asked, 'What is your baby's name?'

'Angelica,' Emilia replied through her tears.

The doctor firmly pressed her tiny chest a few times then returned to squeezing the bag. 'Come on Angelica, your mum is waiting for a hug!' He pressed her chest a few more times and was rewarded with a healthy cry. 'Good girl, good girl!'

Both Rolf and Emilia cried tears of joy as the doctor stepped back and let them cover their baby with loving kisses.

Hans stepped away, pleased he had succeeded in his mission. But the pleasure was short-lived as his attention turned to gunfire outside. He may have saved the lives of his assignment but at what cost? Could this be the spark that starts the war to end all wars?

****

London, UK

The digital radio came on, the clock display showing 6:00 am. Luke Churchill stirred and threw an arm out to turn off the alarm.

His wife Lindley stirred and mumbled something that sounded like 'Is it morning already?' then went back to sleep.

Luke replied with a groan, 'Yes.' He got out of bed and headed for the shower. When dressed, he left the bedroom and went to the lounge room and turned on the television. He had the volume down low so as not to disturb Lindley. Luke wandered into the kitchen and turned on the kettle, filled a glass of water and took his vitamins. He walked back into the lounge, his attention immediately going to the live news program. He watched as the television displayed footage of the shootout at the Indian border. Luke dropped his glass of water on the floor and dashed for the door that led to outside the private living quarters of 10 Downing Street. He took a few steps towards the end of the hall where a stairway led to the other floors. He stopped in his tracks as emerging from the stairway, was Oliver. He stopped as well as the two stared at each other, faces filled with horror. Oliver said, 'You saw the news?'

'Yes,' Luke replied.

They both uttered simultaneously, 'Bollocks!'

Luke said with great urgency, 'Get Thompson and Whursley in my office, NOW!'

****

Luke paced back and forth in front of David Thompson of MI6 and the Minister of Defence Charles Whursley. 'What do we know gentlemen?'

David and Charles sat on the vintage leather lounge before their prime minister. Luke's tall stature, coupled with his ferocious demeanour, made him a formidable presence.

David spoke first. 'We have been monitoring the borders and have not seen any unusual activity outside of the casting out of all noncitizens. They have commenced evacuating their consulates though.'

Charles added, 'Their armed forces have been very active, but we are yet to see anything to suggest a military offensive. What does concern me is that most of their subs have been off the radar for weeks?'

'Missile strike from the sea?' Luke proposed.

'Potentially,' replied Charles.

'How do we defend against such a strike?' asked Luke.

'We can deploy our destroyers and subs to sweep our waters to intercept and neutralise, and we have our new anti-missile laser guns on some of our fighters, but there are no guarantees. We will need to get the population trained to take cover in building basements and the Tube. Just like back in World War II.'

'David, do we have any intelligence that sheds some light on their intentions?'

'Nothing solid. But what is interesting is the construction activity around their cities. From what we can make out, they are building many temporary structures. They could be pre-empting an evacuation.'

Luke rubbed his chin and ran his fingers through his thick dark hair. 'They are expecting us to attack their cities, and therefore, them ours! If they use a nuclear strike, what would be the best defensive measure?'

'Surely they wouldn't, that would be global suicide!' Charles retorted.

Luke glared at the two men seated before him. 'A nuclear attack is almost certain.'

'Prime Minister,' said Charles. 'A nuclear strike on our small country would render much of it uninhabitable. The blast is one thing, but the fallout is the real danger.'

'Well then, we need to stop that strike—at all costs! Gentlemen, let there be no mistake, we are on the brink of World War III,' Luke declared. 'What about the Messiah, can we take him out with a precision strike?'

David replied, 'He has been difficult to track over recent weeks, but we think he is back in Israel.'

'You think? You will have to do better than that!' Luke bared down upon David and jabbed a finger at the ground as he said with great conviction, 'I want to know exactly where he is every minute of every hour of every day from now on. That is your prime directive! And at the first sign of a missile strike on us, I want his location. No matter where that may be. I want it nuked immediately! Do I make myself clear?!'

'Yes sir!' Charles replied. 'But Sir, we don't have to use a nuke, we could use a surgical strike with a conventional weapon?'

Luke's eyes widened as he retorted, 'If you haven't been paying attention Charles, he is goddamn immortal! I want his body subjected to the heat from the centre of the sun. I want every molecule broken down to atoms! Understand?! Then let's see how immortal he really is!' Luke stepped back and said in no uncertain terms, 'From here on in, we are at war!'

****

Washington DC, USA

'Mr President!' Nancy knocked on the door to the private quarters of the White House. 'Mr President!'

There was a shout from the other side of the door. 'Come in, we are decent!'

Nancy opened the door to find Jim and his wife Stacy sitting on the lounge. Jim was going through some paperwork while Stacy was looking over a briefing for one of her charities. From the hi-fi system, the Frank Sinatra song, 'Something Stupid' was playing, the music filling the room with a calming ambience.

'Mr President, sorry to disturb you at this late hour but it has happened!'

'It?' replied Jim with a confused expression.

'A fire fight broke out at the Indian border!'

Jim and Stacy looked at each other as realisation set in. Jim turned back to Nancy, 'Get the joint chiefs immediately! And notify the cabinet!'

'Yes, Mr President,' Nancy replied and dashed out the door.

****

As Jim entered the Cabinet Room at the White House, it was filled with military generals and admirals trying to find a vacant seat. Jim headed to the middle of the long table and sat at the seat set aside for him. Beside Jim sat the Director of the CIA Marcus, whose expression was as stern as Jim's.

Jim waited a moment as everyone settled before beginning. 'Gentlemen, the incident at the Indian border could be the reason for Judas Salim to strike. This could well be a nuclear offensive and a strike could be imminent. How do we defend against this and how do we strike back?'

Admiral Johnson, a middle-aged African American sitting opposite Jim said, 'We have our aircraft carriers at the ready, they are deployed at strategic positions across the globe. Our nuclear subs have been searching for theirs, but we have had little luck. Contacts have been few and far between. Right now, we only know roughly where some of them are. What is interesting is that they are widespread across the globe.'

'Nuclear strike from their subs?' Jim asked.

General Walker, the commander-in-chief of the army who was seated two seats away from Admiral Johnson said, 'That is the most likely scenario. Their long-range missiles are not advanced enough to be a solid threat. However, they do have the previous generation of cruise missiles. They are not as advanced as ours but are still an effective weapon. Our laser batteries on our ships and strike aircraft will be very effective against ICBM strikes, but they will not be as effective against their cruise missiles. It is one of the main reasons why we have not continued investment in our long-range strike program. If they do deploy a cruise missile strike, we will need our forces in place at the strike locations to have any chance of neutralising the attack.'

Jim asked, 'So do we have sufficient defence on our home soil?'

Admiral Johnson replied, 'General Walker and I agree that we are well placed to defend our home.'

'Do we have spare capacity to assist in the defence of some our allies and to mount an offensive?'

Admiral Johnson replied, 'We have an aircraft carrier in the Mediterranean and another in the Gulf.'

General Walker added, 'And we have bolstered troops in Germany, the UK, India, and Australia.'

'So, gentlemen, are we ready for a war?' Marcus asked.

'Yes,' replied Johnson, Walker and several other generals.

Jim asked. 'Are we ready to control the inevitable panic by the public? What if they succeed in a land-based offensive? Can we repel them on our own soil?'

General Walker replied, 'We have all of our bases on standby. Bases near our cities are at the ready to be deployed to maintain law and order.'

Jim looked around at the confident faces and felt some ease. 'Well then, let's just pray that this is all just a false alarm. That is all.'

The military leaders began to leave as Marcus leaned over to Jim and said, 'I strongly suggest you and your family board Air Force One and run things from a secure location.' Jim responded, 'Such as?'

'Area 51,' Marcus replied.

Jim looked back at Marcus. 'Area 51?'

'It is our most secure location and has facilities that are nuke proof.'

'Jim thought about it for a moment and replied, 'Okay, make the arrangements.'

****

Jerusalem, Israel

Judas turned off the television after watching the evening news report on the battle at the Indian border. Zeus was at his side and Jiovani sat opposite him on the lounge at his private residence near Jerusalem. They had finished dinner and the remains were left upon the large oak dining table for the butler to clear up after they had retired. Jiovani wore his black kaftan and Judas was garbed in his black suit, but the red tie, having been removed, laid strewn over the coffee table.

Jiovani asked, 'My Lord, does this constitute as the straw that breaks the camel's back?'

Judas gently shook his near empty glass of fine whisky as he replied, 'I am a god of my word.' He picked up his tablet computer and turned on the Skype app.

Moments later, the tired face of Louisa appeared. The corners of her mouth were stained red from the unseen glass of wine next to her.

'Yes, my Lord?'

'Apologies for such a late call but I have an important task for you,' Judas said casually.

'Certainly, you know I am always available,' she said with a slight smile.

'Thank you. Could you please pass the following message on to my generals?'

'Yes, my Lord.'

'Apocalypse!'

Louisa looked puzzled. 'Just that my Lord?'

'Yes, they will understand,' Judas said with a smile.

'Yes, my Lord. I will do it right now.' With that the image of her on the screen went blank.

'There we go,' Judas said as he placed the tablet back on the coffee table. 'Wouldn't want to disappoint my subjects.'

Jiovani's face looked grim. Despite much of his free will having been stripped from his soul, the Antichrist still left a little behind. Jiovani felt it was deliberate to torment what was left of him, and torment filled him. 'Just like that, you have started World War III?'

'Yes. Just like that,' Judas said with a smile as he sipped the remaining contents of his glass. 'Now Jiovani, you have been a faithful subject. However, I'm afraid that your usefulness has come to an end. But do not despair, Zeus here could use a companion. Goodbye!' The eyes of the Antichrist flashed red as he took full control over Jiovani.

Jiovani's expression deadened, then he stood and walked over to the kitchen and stood statuesque.

Zeus let out a brief whimper as the Antichrist walked over to Jiovani. He pulled out a large knife from the knife stand, taking a moment to gloat. Pleasure filled his expression as the Antichrist drove the knife into Jovani's heart.

Jovani collapsed to the floor, a pool of blood oozing from his dying body.

The Antichrist made a small cut in the palm of his hand and let a few drops fall into the open, weeping wound. The wound began to fizz as if acid had been dropped on it, then the wound began to heal over. Once the flow of life had been stopped, the agonising transformation began. Like a scene from a horror film, Jiovani's body mutated into an animal. When the transformation was complete, a Doberman like Zeus lay on the floor covered in loose human garb. The dog stood on shaky legs at first as it gained its balance. The kaftan fell away, and it looked up at the Antichrist and whimpered.

Judas gave him a quick pat. 'There you go, all ready to serve! Now, what are we going to call you then? Hmmm, how about Thor? Do you like that?' Judas gave the dog another brief pat as it panted. 'Thor it is then.' As Judas turned to walked away, he said, 'Clean up the mess you left and put your old clothes in the bin. There's a good boy!'

Thor began licking up the blood, occasionally gagging during the consumption as Zeus watched on with a sympathetic expression.

****

New York City, USA

The plain expression on the face of the physically fit man helped to disguise the intense thoughts that filled his mind. The weight of his heavy backpack seemed inert as it bore down upon his strong shoulders.

He entered the express lift that took all passengers to the observation deck on level 100 of the One World Trade Center building in New York. The lift filled up with tourists behind the man carrying the heavy backpack, the last in being the lift operator who stood at the lift control panel. The lift operator was in his seventies and enjoyed his one minute of having a captive audience. As the lift doors closed, he said, 'Welcome aboard everyone. This is an express lift to the observation deck of one of the tallest buildings in the western world. The One World Trade Center is the world's third tallest building. It is 1,800 feet high and is 104 stories. It was built on the foundations of the former World Trade Center site that was destroyed during the 9/11 terrorist attack in 2001. Unlike the predecessor, the One World Trade Center is now well equipped to withstand a direct hit by a commercial aircraft. If you haven't visited the 9/11 memorial yet, it is at the base of the building. The weather is perfect today for a breathtaking view of The Big Apple.' He then said to the young Asian woman standing next to him, 'That's what we locals like to call New York City' and finished off with a cheeky smile.

The young Asian tourist smiled and giggled briefly.

The lift slowed down and came to a stop as the floor indicator displayed, 'Level 100 Observation Deck'.

'Here we are at the best view in town!' said the lift operator.

The lift doors opened, and the passengers alighted leaving room for the man with the heavy backpack to alight as well. As the man passed by the lift operator, the lift operator asked, 'Back packing around our fine city?'

The man stopped and gave the lift operator a blank look, giving the lift operator a start. The man smiled and replied in a rough voice and indiscriminate accent, 'Camera gear. I'm into photography.'

The smile and calm reply put the lift operator at ease again. 'Well, you came to the right place. You will get some great shots today. Have a great day Sir.'

The man walked off in the direction of the nearest window as the lift operator shook his head in response to the cold demeanour of the man. The lift doors closed.

The soldier studied the New York skyline for a while before turning away and heading for the men's toilets. As he entered, he went straight for the last cubical and found it unoccupied. The soldier entered and closed the door behind him. He took the backpack off, pulled out a screwdriver and proceeded to remove the wall panel that concealed the toilet cistern. This was his second visit to this toilet. Two weeks ago, he was here looking for a suitable place to plant the bomb and had discovered that the cubical on the end was ideal. He carefully removed the panel that exposed the cistern. Above the cistern was an opening to a larger cavity with plenty of space for the contents of his backpack. The soldier removed a large, heavy electronic device from the bag, about the size of a slim briefcase, and carefully placed it into the cavity above the cistern. At the base of the device was an LCD screen with some buttons beneath it. He pressed one of the buttons and the LCD screen came to life. The screen displayed the time value '24:00:00'. He checked the time on his watch and as he pressed the other buttons, the value changed to '22:49:00'.

The instructions given to the soldier the day before via the satellite phone were, 'Post the package tomorrow and set the delivery time for the following morning—9:00 am on Monday 6 June.'

The soldier pressed the 'Set' button and the LCD screen briefly displayed the word 'Armed' before returning to the time display that steadily counted down from the set time. He replaced the wall panel, screwed it back into position, and checked that it was correctly secured. Once satisfied that all was in order, he left the cubical and the toilet and headed for the snack bar. He purchased a few cans of Coke and a few packets of confectionery and put them in his backpack. When he returned to the lift, his backpack looked just a full as it did before, and the lift operator assumed it still contained camera equipment.

'Did you get any good shots? You weren't there very long?' the lift operator asked.

The man smiled briefly as he said, 'Long enough. Great view by the way.'

'As I said, it's the best view in town,' he replied as the doors closed.

Meanwhile at Canary Wharf in London, the Eiffel Tower in Paris, the Sydney Tower Eye in Sydney, and at six hundred other tall buildings in cities across the world, special forces soldiers were strategically placing their destructive packages and setting the time so that all would detonate in synchronicity.

****

London, UK

Agent Smith watched the footage of the fire fight at the New World India border on her tablet computer as she waited to board the aircraft. She knew this could be the catalyst for all-out war between the old and the New World, and the urgency to get to Australia and find out the secret to stopping the Antichrist, was paramount. For the past few weeks, she had been in a rehabilitation clinic, only having been discharged a few days ago. The only physical reminders of the incident were a surgical scar on her abdomen where the doctor repaired her spleen, and a small scar beside her left eye. Apart from that, she had found that sudden loud noises made her flinch more than they used to. Firearms training at MI6 was very difficult as she would flinch too much when the pistol was fired and consistently miss the target. Fortunately, she wasn't required to pass the firearms test to continue her role at MI6. Her sleeping had improved, and the nightmares were now less frequent. However, there was still the odd night where she would wake up and scream as she relived the moment the heat from the bomb stung her flesh, and the slow motion view of hurtling towards the police van and seeing the police officer's face as she impacted with his body. And sometimes, a nightmare from long ago would arise, blending in with her new nightmare—those being the worst of all.

A general announcement broke her concentration. 'British Airways flight BA0015 nonstop to Sydney, Australia now boarding.'

Agent Smith put the tablet computer in her handbag and went through the checkpoint before boarding the aircraft. As she walked down the tunnel to the aircraft, she took a moment to admire the Boeing 818 as it stood upon the apron. With the ability to take six hundred passengers and to fly nonstop, halfway around the world, made it the aircraft of choice for airlines for long haul flights. Agent Smith turned away to walk the final stretch of tunnel to the aircraft and a thought passed through her mind—would she get to Australia before World War III broke out?

****

Prime Minister Luke Churchill and his wife had relocated from 10 Downing Street in London to the country residence of Chequers in Buckinghamshire. The rural location gave him some peace of mind that if there was an all-out attack on the country's major cities, his wife would be reasonably safe. Luke had the special computer running the secure webcam software in the study, and he waited for the familiar political faces to appear in their allotted windows.

Jim Richardson was the first to appear, then Matthew Turner and Gabrielle Pasture, and finally Johann Schiffer.

Jim spoke first. 'Hello everyone.' A concert of hellos was returned.

Luke said, 'Well, the stage is set. Not much else to do but wait and see if he does make the first move.'

Johann said, 'We have shored up our borders and have our antimissile batteries on the ready. If they launch an attack, we are ready.'

Gabrielle added, 'Oui, we are also at the ready.'

Matthew said, 'The temptation to evacuate our cities is great but who knows how long it could be before they strike, if at all. But think of all the lives we could save?'

Jim responded, 'Yes, if only we had some solid intelligence on their true intentions then we could act, but we have little to go on. And if we did, think of the panic and lives that could be lost in the rush to evacuate the cities, and the disruption it would cause to the country.
I think the action that we have deployed is the most sensible, and we have faith in our militaries that they can protect us.'

Matthew said, 'We just need to hunker down and be ready for whatever comes—and pray that we survive.'

Luke said, 'By the way, our agent is on her way down to you Matthew, to see if she can get some more intel on you know who.'

'Yes, ASIO have informed me of her trip Down Under. We will welcome her input.'

'Well, I have nothing else to report, so I wish you all the best,' said Jim.

'And you too,' replied Luke and Matthew.

Johann and Gabrielle said, 'Bye and best wishes.'

As the windows went blank, Luke looked out the window at the cold landscape and wondered if any of them would survive the forthcoming conflict.

****

Somewhere in the Atlantic Ocean

The Argentinian submarine cruised through the depths of the Atlantic Ocean, searching for the communications cable linking the USA to Europe. The sensitive sonar pulsed then listened for the echo as it examined the details on the sea floor. The sonar operator announced, 'Target acquired, one hundred meters dead ahead.'

The captain who was standing in the centre of the bridge, ordered, 'Prime torpedo bay two.'

A moment later, another officer seated near the captain said, 'Torpedo bay two primed.'

The captain looked at the analog clock on the wall of submarine and said, 'Hold this position.' They all watched the minute hand as it closed on the hour of 9:00 am on Monday 6 June. When the minute hand merged with the hour marker, the captain ordered, 'Fire torpedo two!'

From the bow of the submarine came a flurry of bubbles and a long metal torpedo. The torpedo darted out across the ocean bottom to the inert target ahead. When it struck, an almighty burst tore the cable in two.

The sonar operator announced, 'Direct hit!'

The captain ordered, 'Launch the comms buoy and send the message—comms highway one disconnected.'

Four other New World submarines also completed their mission and successfully dismembered the world's communications. Apart from limited satellite bandwidth, there was now no other means by which the world could communicate.

****

New York City, USA

The Korean tourist entered the last toilet cubical on the end and proceeded to drop his trousers to do his business. As he sat down, his watch reached the hour of 9:00 am. He heard a beeping sound coming from the wall behind him. He turned around and listened, wondering where it was coming from. He put his ear to the wall and could hear the beeping sound clearly as it changed to a continuous tone. He pulled his head away from the wall and said, 'Maybe the plumber left his phone behind in the wall.' He shook his head in disbelief.

The continuous tone stopped, and the fusion reaction commenced. From the top of One World Trade Center, the nuclear fireball expanded at almost the speed of light, engulfing much of Manhattan. In an instant, millions of souls were vaporised, never to conceive another thought again. From the cloud came the shock wave of destruction that obliterated all in its path, stretching out over the Hudson River, the bay and beyond. Behind the shock wave came the lethal radioactive cloud and whatever the shock wave failed to annihilate, the cloud would irradiate and leave to experience a slow and agonising death.

Worldwide

The burst from the Canary Wharf in London engulfed all of Westminster and the Whitechapel areas. This was then followed by the shock wave that flattened Greater London. The radioactive cloud irradiated all within the M25 motorway ring then was casually blown north by the prevailing winds.

The blast from the Eiffel Tower wiped out most of Paris, razing all buildings to the ground. The radioactive cloud then drifted over the country, killing farmers and their livestock.

The blast from the Sydney Tower Eye disintegrated the entire CBD, inner suburbs, and North Sydney. The radioactive cloud then drifted north-east, irradiated the northern beaches, and was blown out to sea.

This story was repeated across all the major cities of the old world. The punishment for the failure of the Russian president to meet with Judas before the New World closed its borders, was the destruction of Moscow, Saint Petersburg, and several other major cities.

China also was not immune as Hong Kong, Beijing and Shanghai were wiped out. Across the globe, some six hundred cities were destroyed along with the surrounding areas and with that, one billion souls.

****

Buckinghamshire, UK

The tremor woke Luke Churchill from his already disturbed slumber. For a moment, he wondered if it was a small earthquake, then another thought exploded in his mind. Luke got out of bed and went to the window. He pulled the blockout curtain across, his pupils contracting from the unnatural ambient light. All went dark. A storm-like wind buffeted the trees around Chequers. With the wind came the grey snowflakes that settled across the country landscape. Luke knew instantly that London was gone and who knew how much else of his country.

Lindley raised her head and asked, 'What is that noise, is it a storm?'

Luke replied in a sobering tone, 'No, it is the start of World War III.'

Lindley could only stare at Luke as he strode over to the bedroom door and opened it. He stood in the corridor to see Oliver and several other ministry staff running towards him.

Luke said in a loud and commanding tone, 'Get me Charles, I want some payback!'

****

Area 51, Nevada, USA

As per the requests from his wife Stacy, Jim Richardson patiently moved the sofa around in the private quarters of the secret underground facility of Area 51.

'Just a bit more to the left,' said Stacy.

'How's that?' Jim replied.

'That's better.' Stacy sat down on the sofa and said, 'Do we really have to stay here, of all places?'

'It is the safest place there is.'

'Why can't we stay at Camp David? It is beautiful there this time of year. I feel like a prisoner in this hole in the ground.'

'It's just for a little while sweetie. As soon as it is safe, we will move to Camp David.'

Jim noticed a tear rolling down Stacy's cheek. 'Stacy!' He sat down next to her and gave her a hug. 'It won't be for long. We will be out of here before you know it.'

There was a knock on the door and Stacy quickly wiped away the tears and composed herself. Lucy didn't wait for a reply and opened the door. 'Mr President. Sorry Mrs President. But we have a situation!'

The look on Lucy's face was enough to convince Jim. 'I'll be right there.'

Moments later, Jim entered the war room headquarters of Area 51 where several military heads were seated around a large oval table. Jim sat at the empty chair on the end and asked, 'What do you have for me gentlemen? '

Marcus spoke first. 'Mr President, we have been hit by multiple nuclear strikes on all of our major cities.'

Jim stared at Marcus for what seemed an age before gathering the will to utter a single strained word. 'How?'

'We believe they were all hand delivered and detonated via small specialist ground forces. Very difficult to detect.' Marcus turned to one of the generals and said, 'Put it on screen.'

A large, flat screen television on the wall came to life, displaying a video of the remains of several major cities across the United States.

The veins in Jim's temples expanded as his face became red with rage. He stood from his chair, grabbed Marcus by the tie, and punched him across the jaw. Marcus was sent tumbling to the floor as his chair went skating across the room. Jim shouted, 'Our country has just been destroyed, millions of lives have been lost, and you deliver this to me as if it were NOTHING!'

Marcus wiped the blood from his lip and began composing himself as he stood.

Jim turned his rage upon the generals. 'You lot were supposed to protect us! Look at it, all of you! This is all your fault! Why the hell didn't any of you think of this type of attack? Well?'

The generals all sat quietly, not knowing what to say. General Walker and Admiral Johnson just bowed their heads in disgrace. Jim turned his back on them as he composed himself. After a long pause, Jim turned back towards Marcus and asked, 'Are you okay?'

Marcus, rubbing his jaw, replied quietly, 'Yes Sir, that was a good right hook by the way. Those days spent in the boxing ring when you were young haven't gone to waste.'

Jim turned back to the war room of generals and said, 'Nuke that son of a bitch, nuke them all!'

****

Choosing to stay in their capital cities rather than flee, Matthew Turner, Gabrielle Pasteur and Johann Schiffer lost their lives in the nuclear apocalypse.

****

Sydney, Australia

Thomas had just finished his cup of coffee when the cell door opened. Agent Jones entered and stated, 'Come on Mr Haigh, question time again.'

Thomas looked up at Agent Jones and noticed the light from the small, high window reflecting in his eyes; but the light escalated in intensity at a parabolic rate. Agent Jones barely had time to avert his eyes before the thermal nuclear blast vaporised him, the cell and Thomas.

****

Near Sydney, Australia

The Boeing 818 shook violently then fell into a nosedive as it made its approach to Sydney Airport. The pilot grabbed the controls and turned off autopilot, but all the flight controls lost power and went dead.
Without power, the fly-by-wire modern aircraft was out of control. The pilot and copilot fought with the electronic systems to get them back online, but they were unresponsive. Agent Smith stared out the window of the plummeting aircraft as she watched the giant mushroom cloud rise

from the ashes of Sydney in the setting sunlight. Agent Smith thought, 'I'm too late!'

****

Peter gathered firewood from around his campsite on the remote ridge of the Blue Mountains, west of Sydney. The beautiful, rugged landscape and the peaceful sounds of the wildlife gave Peter a sense of separation from the turmoil of the world around him. The large store of money and his camping skills enabled him to remain hidden from the authorities. Only the occasional bushwalker was lucky to come across Peter, and they thought nothing of someone wanting to spend a few days camping in the spectacular landscape.

A bright flash in the distance made Peter raise his gaze from the woodened bushland. He dropped the firewood he was collecting and ran to the top of the rocky escarpment that overlooked the valley and the city in the distance. His heart sank as he witnessed the giant mushroom cloud rise from the city he once called home. Peter fell to his knees and said, 'The Apocalypse!'

Epilogue: From the Ashes of Hell

Buckinghamshire, UK

The military green, camouflage painted lorry pulled up outside Chequers, and a ramp was lowered from the back of the trailer. Two soldiers exited in military green camouflage radiation suits and abruptly made their way to the main entrance of the grand building. A short time later, three figures emerged from Chequers, one adorned in a white radiation suit. They quickly made their way to the ramp at the back of the trailer and disappeared within. The ramp retracted, sealing the occupants inside.

Luke pulled off the radiation mask as he was greeted by David Thompson. 'Prime Minister, we have the green light.'

Luke looked around at the mobile command centre and took in the several soldiers at their monitor stations. He looked at the large monitor on the wall that displayed a satellite image of a building. 'Are you certain he is there?' Luke inquired.

'Yes, our eyes have been on him for the past week. He is at his private residence in the Jerusalem hills. Since a few hours ago, we have been solely reliant on our satellite communications as they have cut all the cross-continental communication cables. Fortunately, we installed enough bandwidth on our military satellites for such a scenario. Our sub is off the Israeli coast and has a cruise missile ready to launch. As requested, it has a nuclear warhead. It is a low yield warhead with a destruction diameter of five hundred metres. His residence will be completely vaporised along with all within.'

'How accurate is the cruise missile? President Richardson and I agreed to not destroy Jerusalem, so I don't want the damn thing going off target and blowing up the city.'

'The cruise missile can navigate roads and streets if it has to, and it has a GPS accuracy of half a metre.'

Luke stared at the satellite view of the building as his heart began to race. 'I now have some idea of how my great, great, grandfather Winston felt.' He looked back at David and said with conviction, 'Launch the bird!'

David nodded to a soldier seated near him who had his attention focused on the two commanders-in-chief awaiting the order. The soldier said into his headset. 'We are a go, repeat, we are a go!'

Over the loudspeaker came the voice of the submarine captain. 'Bird is away, repeat, bird is away.'

The view of the building quickly changed to a view from the nose of the missile as it darted across the sea. The ocean vista soon disappeared as it crossed over land, homes and buildings that darted by below. The missile followed a roadway up into the hills, then turned at a road intersection at a seemingly impossible rate. It turned another corner and headed over a small country road for a short distance, then zeroed in on the private residence of Judas Salim. The view on the monitor went white before cutting over to the satellite image. It too was a blank image for a moment, then it changed to a slightly angled, aerial view of a large mushroom cloud.

The soldier next to David said, 'Direct hit confirmed. Target neutralised.'

David responded, 'Well done men. Pass on my congratulations to the captain and his crew.'

Luke asked, 'Can we get a close-up of the where the building was? I want to be sure.'

'Yes, Sir,' replied the soldier.

The view zoomed into the previous location of the building, now awash with fire. The fires soon died down and only embers remained.

According to the basic laws of physics, matter cannot be destroyed. It will change state based upon the amount of energy used to change its state. Beneath the ashes, matter had changed state to a plasma, then as it cooled, it changed state to a gas. As it cooled further, it changed to a liquid. The liquid seeped up though the ashes and began reforming the original state of the matter. The matter finally formed the monstrosity of a red, scaly, horned creature that was the Antichrist! The Antichrist looked up into the sky and smiled, exposing a sinister needlepointed grin, then began to laugh. Nearby, two other groups of matter began to rise from the ashes. They reformed into the two sentinels. Like phoenixes from the ashes, the three immortal monsters stood abreast, defiant of the greatest weapon mankind could wield.

As Luke, David and the soldiers watched the metamorphosis of the Antichrist back into his original form, Luke announced, 'God help us all!'

For the exciting conclusion to the *Apocalypse* series, look for Apocalypse - The Holocaust. Coming soon.

CPSIA information can be obtained
at www.ICGtesting.com
Printed in the USA
LVHW110200290323
742928LV00004B/66

9 780645 099201